TOWARD
THE
LIGHT

TOWARD THE LIGHT

A THRILLER

BONNAR SPRING

OCEANVIEW PUBLISHING
SARASOTA, FLORIDA

ISBN 978-1-60809-408-0

Published in the United States of America by Oceanview Publishing

Sarasota, Florida

www.oceanviewpub.com

10 9 8 7 6 5 4 3 2

PRINTED IN THE UNITED STATES OF AMERICA

For Bill, always.

ACKNOWLEDGMENTS

The journey of *Toward the Light* has taken so many amazing twists and turns it's hard to remember them all!

First, no thanks are possible—although a million and one are due—to a man whose name I never knew who, at a party years ago, posed some offhand questions that animated the entire gathering of wine-fueled guests. He wondered how far we would go if we had the power to destroy someone evil, what consequences we'd be willing to accept, how we saw the results of our actions. The questions stayed with me, prompting other discussions over time, although it took many years to germinate the seed.

Many thanks to . . .

early readers Shannon Schuren and Christine Finlayson who helped shape the story into a coherent whole,

fellow Seacoast Writers Amy Ray and Jed Power who pored over later versions and returned them with my most egregious excesses x-ed out,

my agent, Lisa Abellera at Kimberley Cameron & Associates, who's also a tenacious and talented editor,

and Bob and Pat Gussin and the great staff at Oceanview
for their efficiency, enthusiasm, and professionalism.

Guatemala City is real—and a really interesting place that rewards
those who stick around long enough to look below the gritty surface
and absorb its rhythm. Because this is a work of fiction, however, I
hope those of you who know and love Guate will forgive me for painting the city with artistic license to suit the narrative.

CHAPTER ONE

On a breezy autumn afternoon, Maria Luz Concepcion returned to Guatemala to kill a man. As the airplane banked, its descent through thick clouds brought the first view of her country in almost twenty years. Corrugated mountains, a trackless sea of green and brown. The plane drifted lower. Misty rectangles on hillsides resolved into a patchwork of fields and houses. A serpentine line became a road. A silver flash, a lake.

Once at the gate, Luz joined the rolling wave of deplaning passengers. They all shuffled up the jetway and along an interminable corridor to Luz's first hurdle—Immigration. The tide carried her toward black swinging doors at the far end that swallowed each arrival in turn. Then the doors flapped for her, and she emerged—not in the dark maw of some carnivorous beast but in a bright, echoing room.

As she waited her turn, Luz studied the gatekeepers who stood between her and Martin Benavides: The bald guy with thick Coke-bottle glasses who barely looked at the supplicants but spent tedious minutes flipping each page of every passport. The bulldog-faced woman with the pen stuck in her hair and the crisp khaki uniform. The younger man who asked so many questions.

They held the key to her future, these civil servants in their cages of glass and metal, destined to spend their days in noise and harsh light, vigilant against the undotted *i*, the uncrossed *t*. Against criminals, the indigent. Against young women planning murder.

The talkative younger man beckoned. Luz's stomach rose to her throat. She pasted on a smile when she approached his kiosk. He stuck out a hand for her passport, a first-rate fake that gave her name as Luz Aranda. Once she relinquished it, Luz smoothed her shirt over her hips with damp palms and stood before him, fingers intertwined, mimicking as best she could the decorum of a Catholic schoolgirl at early-morning Mass.

The agent flipped to the photo page. He squinted at her.

Luz no longer believed in God, but the habit of prayer lingered. Bargaining, really. *Dios, por favor. If you'll get me through Immigration, I'll . . .* What in heaven's name could she promise? *Let me go home, so I can kill Martin Benavides.* No, keep it simple. *Let me in, and I won't ever bother you again.*

Luz released her hands and wiggled her bloodless fingers, willing her expression into nonchalance as the man compared her face to the photo. Too late—and unnecessary—he'd already looked down and was riffling through the pages to stamp her entry. Ink-stained hands with fingernails bitten to the quick, a bald spot at the top of his head, photo of a chubby woman holding a snaggle-toothed child tucked in the corner of the glass partition. Not a dragon guarding the gates after all.

Luz beamed when he handed back the passport. She'd taken one more small step toward Martin Benavides' death when the man said, in soft Spanish that reminded Luz of her father, "*Señorita*, you have been away for a long time."

A long time, yes. Luz pressed her palm against her open mouth as her mother's hand had silenced her screams of terror that last night in Guatemala while they fled blindly in the dark. Pinpoints of lights threaded through the trees and distant gunfire came closer. They ran on.

But that was a long time ago, and this . . . this pencil-pusher was *not* going to block her path. She summoned the spirit of her mother to her side, not the pale and wasted woman in the drab New Hampshire apartment who'd lost all hope, but the beautiful fighter from her childhood. Luz had promised her mother to return.

So she straightened and found her voice, although she hesitated over the fluid cadences of her native language, which she'd seldom used in the months since her mother's death. "I—I had a good job working as a nanny in Florida," Luz lied, "but I missed being home." The second part, at least, was true.

"Ah, that is a good reason for your beautiful smile. *Bienvenida, señorita.* Welcome home."

Luz claimed the bulging suitcase containing all she had left in the world. Customs inspectors waved through the throngs of tourists with their dollars or euros to spend on hotels and nice restaurants, on embroidered skirts and handbags, carved masks, tour guides to Mayan ruins, boat rides around Lake Atitlan. But for those with Guatemalan passports, the line dragged as inspectors upended suitcases and poked through the contents to exact the proper duty for every single item purchased abroad.

Luz had receipts for new shoes and a small radio, and she had double- and triple-checked her paperwork for the all-important black jar lying, swaddled in layers of clothes, in the center of her suitcase. Unlike Immigration, however, even the worst stickler at Customs could only gouge her for a few extra quetzales. In any event, it was an efficient woman who totaled the receipts on a handheld calculator and presented Luz with a modest bill.

Taxi drivers swarmed when she walked outside, but she waved them off. Richard had told her to turn left outside the terminal, walk past the taxi stand and a multistory parking garage to a covered bus stop at the intersection with the main road. Then take the number 83 bus into the city. She was to sit in an empty row on the right side of the bus, near the middle, placing her suitcase so it blocked access to the adjoining seat. After a few stops, a man would get on and ask, in gringo-accented Spanish, if he could sit. He would carry a folded *Prensa Libre*, the inaccurately named morning newspaper that was no free press at all but the propaganda arm of the Benavides, which Martin had started a decade earlier when he was still president of the country. The man would leave the newspaper when he got off. In it, Luz would find an envelope containing specifics about the coming days, details about how she would get close enough to kill the man who'd murdered her father.

Beyond the tumult of competing taxi drivers, the sidewalk narrowed. Few arriving passengers slipped through the gauntlet of taxis to take the inexpensive city bus into town. Ahead of Luz, a small boy wrestled with a stroller while his mother, baby on her hip and suitcase in her other hand, tried to help him steer. The group wobbled inches from traffic streaming into the airport. The woman turned as Luz approached. She raised her hand and began a hesitant smile that evaporated when the woman glanced at Luz's heavy suitcase. She dropped her hand, smoothed her child's hair, and swung around. With the pause in their progress, the little boy let go of the stroller. One arm wrapped around his mother's leg; the other scratched his cheek. The stroller slid toward the curb.

Three steps and Luz was beside them. She shot out a hand to steady the stroller. "Can I help?"

A line of sweat beaded the woman's upper lip. The baby, red-faced and crying, pulled at her hair. A bundled-up child of indeterminate sex lolled in the stroller. "But you have your hands full already," she said.

Luz stifled a chuckle. The boy couldn't be more than three; the child in the stroller looked too young to walk; a baby in arms. "Not nearly as full as yours, *señora*."

"That is very kind of you." The woman considered her straggling brood. "Perhaps you could carry Tomas?" She grimaced as she untangled a chubby hand from her hair and held out the crying baby.

"Of course," said Luz, regretting her impulsiveness. But the baby, warm and smelling of sour milk, curled against Luz's chest. Tiny fingers clutched the front of her shirt and, with a tremulous shudder, Tomas closed his eyes. Perhaps his reaction was a testimonial to her day-care experience; more likely, the child was simply too spooked to complain.

"I'm Teresa. My children," she said, with a sweep of her chin encompassing infant, little boy, and swaddled child in the stroller. "We've been visiting my parents." Teresa chattered, self-absorbed, talking over her shoulder about her extended family.

A bus rolled up shortly after the little caravan reached the bus stop. It was a school bus, in shape and size exactly like the ones Luz had ridden to high school in New Hampshire. There the resemblance ended. This one was painted tomato red. Exuberant drawings of parrots and monkeys decorated white rectangles on the side. Garlands of pink plastic flowers wound around the luggage rack.

Teresa shooed the older boy ahead and then clambered on board, kicking the stroller up one step at a time. Luz followed, baby Tomas in her arms. The boy took the window seat behind the bus driver. Teresa jammed the stroller next to him and then sat across the aisle.

Teresa scooted over, an invitation. Luz couldn't walk to a seat in the middle holding Teresa's baby. One simple instruction and she'd already screwed up. The baby's soft hair tickled her cheek as her arm tightened around the tiny sleeping bundle. Time to give him back.

When Richard broached the possibility of Luz's participation in his operation, he first spent a long time systematically making his case against the Benavides: their control of the major pipeline funneling cocaine from the fields of Peru via Colombian labs to North American markets; their negotiations with an organized crime distribution ring in the U.S. that would vastly increase the efficiency with which coke found its way to street corners all over the country; the importance of crippling the cartel before that happened.

Gradually, the noose of his logic tightened, and Luz got a tantalizing glimmer of the question he would pose. By the time Richard suggested *she* might be the person who could get close enough to kill Martin Benavides, Luz had said, simply, yes—but Richard couldn't know the lightness in her limbs as though she had sprouted angel wings and was turning cartwheels in heaven. Dancing for joy at the prospect of killing. She had no business pretending to be a good person.

Luz loosened unresisting fingers from her shirt and planted a feather-light kiss on the baby's head. Tomas arched his back, stared open-mouthed into Luz's forfeit soul, and reached for his mother, who opened her arms to claim him. Luz continued up the aisle alone.

She'd never taken this route from the airport into town. When Luz was little, the closest she got to an airplane was her father pretending to be one as he ran up mountain tracks with her on his back, both of them with their arms outstretched and careening side to side. Laughing. And when she and her mother were evacuated, it was from a postage-stamp mountain clearing. Both of them spattered with her father's blood but alone and mute in their shock, they'd clung together on the floor of the helicopter, its back gaping open, and watched their dizzying ascent as the pilot swerved to avoid incoming flack. Until their life in Guatemala disappeared and only darkness remained.

These sights and smells signaled home, though. Baskets of bananas, oranges, melons. Overripe and redolent in the humid air. Instant saliva created pressure at the back of her throat, a remembered taste of mango. Acrid charcoal smoke mixing with diesel exhaust. Roasting meat. Corn and peppers.

Vendors on every corner—fruit, of course, and other food, but also bootleg DVDs, knockoff watches, lottery tickets—each stand shaded with a tattered tarp lashed to streetlamps and store awnings. Dozens of tinny radios competing for attention. Balconies hung with laundry. Signs along the roads for the small shops: *lavandería, joyería, carnicería, mechánico.*

A man sprinted from the *farmacia* on the corner and hopped on. He paid the fare, pushed sunglasses to the top of his head. When he walked up the narrow aisle, however, his dark copper hair brushed the low school-bus ceiling, and the sunglasses slid back. Although he retrieved them with an athletic backhand catch before they hit the dirty floor, a blush spread over his pale cheeks. Hunching his shoulders in a vain attempt to make himself shorter, the man looked briefly at her. His jaw set in a determined frown told Luz he had a job to do. He wasn't a slumming American tourist taking the cheap bus into the city. This had to be her contact.

"*Con permiso?*" he asked when he got to her.

Luz checked for the newspaper—yes, tucked under his arm. Without speaking, she began to shift the heavy leather suitcase closer to her feet. It caught against a broken fitting on the seat in front of her. As Luz attempted to maneuver it, the man pushed from his side. The bus lurched away from the curb, the bag shifted, and the tall man toppled into the seat next to Luz. His nose squashed against her temple. She smelled spicy aftershave.

"Sorry," he said, ears scarlet, freckles standing out on his cheeks.

In Luz's fantasies about her arrival, this contact was always a military man, taciturn. With a crew cut. A gun in a shoulder holster. A scar on his cheek. But this guy, with his freckles and the totally non-piratical gold hoop in his ear, was hardly older than she and looked like a strong wind would blow him all the way to the ocean. Luz smiled.

Whoever these friends of Richard were, she didn't care. They'd provided her plane ticket from Boston to Miami. The hotel in Miami where she'd memorized her new identity and practiced assembling the bomb. Luz had always considered her identity a fluid concept. This latest incarnation hadn't seemed more of a stretch than re-creating herself from a daughter of the revolution to, say, the daughter of a broken revolutionary, or from a lonely immigrant child to a smart-alecky teen.

The bomb, though—for Luz, who had trouble programming her damn cellphone, that was a challenge. Speed and precision, her instructor said, were the keys. Luz could do speed *or* precision, not both. Hurrying fingers never got Tab X precisely into Slot Y. And when she worked for accuracy, the timer always blared with a shrill, adrenalin-heightening jolt.

Luz spent a couple of long, nerve-wracked weeks before muscle memory took over. Once she passed their quizzes, she received her onward plane ticket, some cash, and keys to an apartment here in town. Now, this stranger would hand over the last details of her mission.

She didn't know how many were involved. Richard, whom she'd known all her life, her American life anyhow. With his bushy eyebrows and hair the reddish-orange of *jocotes de marañón*, with his stàccato bursts of incomprehensible words, Luz had initially regarded Richard as a potentially scary woodland animal—not tooth-and-claw dangerous, but the sort of creature who might jump out at you in the dark. Countless hours spent trekking in the mountains with her father, however, had instilled in Luz an appreciation for watchful patience. Richard's brusque ways got things done in this strange place, yet he was gentle with her bewildered mother. Gradually, Luz stopped seeing Richard as an alien species, recognizing—even at the age of twelve—that *she* was the alien here.

Curiosity blossomed, and she adopted Richard as her totemic guide to this strange new world. Tracking animals, knowing which plants were good to eat, telling directions by stars and sun—those lessons from her father were precious but of relatively little use in downtown Portsmouth. It was Richard who showed her how to use a blender, chopsticks, the remote control. How to drive a car.

She learned Richard's moods, then his language. She sought his advice, took him to parent-teacher meetings when she could. Got him to chaperone an unforgettable eighth-grade field trip to Canobie Lake where, on the bus ride to and fro, he dazzled the preteen boys with magic tricks—instantly elevating her status to *okay to sit with in the cafeteria.*

In addition to Richard, there was his associate John—"call me John," with a wink to suggest his lack of concern at so transparent a pseudonym—whom Richard had taken her to meet in a State Department conference room. The guys in Miami, both the one who patiently explained the bomb and the one who brought her documents, were definitely military. Or ex-military.

John had used the phrase "off the books" to describe the multi-departmental drug task force he was recruiting to bring down the Benavides. Luz figured he meant something more like "unauthorized and totally illegal." Even if they were acting unofficially, Luz would look the other way with pleasure. They'd given her what she wanted; now she would return the favor.

How had this young man gotten mixed up in Guatemalan politics, though? Luz imagined tapping his arm and asking why *he* wanted Martin Benavides dead. She didn't realize she'd laughed out loud until he turned, startled.

Calm, inquisitive cat's eyes—green and gold—explored the false, every-day face she showed the world. Pale lashes. Small furrows, even paler than the rest of his face, at the outside corners of his eyes where he smiled or squinted in the tropical sun.

Dropping her head in retreat from his scrutiny, Luz caught sight of his hands, long and narrow like the rest of his body, one index finger tracing a lazy figure-eight on the newspaper. The warmth was as real as if he were stroking her arm.

She swallowed. That life was finished. Preparing to kill—even when it was simple justice, an eye for an eye—exiled her from the rest of humanity. The lesson of Teresa and the baby fresh in her mind, Luz shifted closer to the window and fixed her eyes on the passing scenery.

The bus chugged along, picking up and dropping off passengers. When they veered onto a busy avenue, the man settled the tight rectangle of newspaper on the seat between them. He stood, hand grasping the metal bar above the seat, and a soft current of air passed between them, separating them further. The phrase "good luck" popped into Luz's head, that all-purpose encouragement to an airplane seatmate running for his next flight, to a young adult off for a job interview, to a fifth-grader at the start of a spelling bee. To her, an aspiring assassin? The man didn't speak, however. He released his hand and pushed his way toward the front of the bus, leaving Luz alone.

The clouds, which had earlier been billowy white meringues in a dazzling blue sky, had darkened. Now thick storm clouds massed over the western mountains. Through the dusty, half-opened bus window, Luz watched them drop toward the city, coiled thick and dirty, like the forward line of an advancing army. A single gray shadow broke off from the rest and covered the sun. A crack of lightning. The smell of ozone in the air. The street vendors scrambled to lay sheets of plastic over their wares. Women with shopping bags took shelter in doorways, as if they could escape the coming storm.

Luz knew she couldn't escape. She slid the newspaper into her bag.

CHAPTER TWO

A cloud blew across the sun as Evan stepped from the bus. In the sudden change of light, the shabby city buildings glowed with haphazard splashes of paint—melon, lime, maize. Then a sudden drum roll of thunder rattled windows. All around him, people with café-au-lait faces and bright clothes paused and raised their eyes to the sky. Evan saw the scene as a mural extending larger than life along the walls of some grand public building, a mural he would paint one day—the vibrant and diverse people of Guatemala. His secret ambition that, as yet, existed only as a series of sketches.

His old painting teacher's voice echoed like the refrain of a favorite song: *To find the big picture, first you must go small.* So Evan singled out a young Indian hunkering on the sidewalk, an infant cradled in a woven cloth sling on her back. She wore a flowered *huipil* over a long lavender- and red-striped skirt, and she fanned a charcoal brazier on which sat a half-dozen ears of tiny mountain corn. The rest of her body motionless. Her eyes toward heaven, waiting for rain.

With a belch of sooty exhaust, the bus pulled away from the curb. The girl pressed her hand to the smudged glass and swiveled to keep her pensive gaze on him as the bus carried her onward to . . . whatever she came for. Evan walked a block to an intersecting *calle* and hailed a cab. No sense getting wet in the thunderstorm that was surely going to drench them all.

Richard had said to call as soon as he could, so Evan paused only to grab a cold beer before picking up the phone. The connection opened on the first ring.

"Clement," announced the familiar rasp at the other end.

"Hi, Richard. It's Evan. I'm home."

"You sat next to the girl?"

"Yep, no problem." Evan pulled off his shoes. He spread his toes and massaged the soles of his feet on the rough homespun rug.

"That's great. Let's hear the rest of it."

Evan pulled a sketch pad from the bookcase. "She sat so I could see her from the drugstore. I took the seat next to her. Left the paper. End of story."

"Did she say anything?"

"No, was she supposed to?" Evan sketched while he spoke, quick strokes of charcoal: the street scene, dark clouds, sparks from the brazier, the corn-roaster's face tilted to the sky.

"No, no—I only wondered how she seemed to you."

Evan penciled in embroidery detail on the woman's *huipil*. "Seemed?" he asked, not sure what Richard wanted to know. Evan did occasional errands for Richard, delivering keys or envelopes, like this job had been, often plump with cash. When it came to their business transactions, Richard, otherwise genial and outgoing, seldom asked more than if the job was complete. "She wore dark slacks and a red shirt," said Evan, always more at home with the visual. He replayed the minutes on the bus—the quick glance when she checked for the identifying newspaper, careful not to acknowledge any familiarity, her distress when he bumped into her, her obvious embarrassment when he jumped at her laugh. How she'd stared out the window then, her hands—brown on the backs, ivory on the underside—at rest on her lap. Not nervous, self-contained. "She didn't say anything, but she laughed once. Must've thought of something funny."

"So you would say she didn't appear overwhelmed?"

"Yes, Richard—I mean, no, not overwhelmed. Tired. Cautious." Evan visualized the scene. "She sat quietly, like she was one of those market women who can squat for hours at a time." He took the pencil he'd set aside. Evan sketched hands, one on top of the other, palms up, fingers cupped.

"Good, good." Richard should've hung up then, but he didn't say goodbye. The silence lengthened. Thousands of miles away, Richard cleared his throat. "It's just that Luz is—" Then, abruptly, Richard barked, "Okay, bye," and was gone.

Evan let the last of the beer slide down his throat. He moved to the back window of his house where the light filtered in, too green and soft to be good for painting, but with spectacular, long views over his neighbors' gardens to the distant volcanoes.

Luz. The woman on the bus was called Luz. Evan thumbed through his sketches. He'd intended to draw the woman fanning the charcoal fire, but they were *her* hands, Luz's hands. Her wide-set eyes with straight brows. Her nose, strong and uncompromising, but with a voluptuous flair at the nostrils. The slope of her neck, her forehead. Her dark hair, heavy like rope, except where it curled around her ear. Luz. Richard had never let slip a name before, never volunteered anything.

Luz. She was the empty space in the center of his masterpiece, the missing image. Evan needed to paint her.

CHAPTER THREE

Luz handed her letter through the bars of the gate to a man in military khaki. He left her standing there while he withdrew to the adjacent guardhouse, where he read the letter and then picked up a phone. As he spoke, he smiled, letting his eyes wander over her body.

Luz retreated behind a stone pillar. The letter, an appointment for a job interview, had come tucked in the newspaper along with directions to the Benavides' compound and a small, padded manila envelope with a separate last-minute request from Richard.

This morning, she followed the unnecessarily detailed directions. It was quite simple—bus from a corner two blocks from her apartment to the center of the city, change at *Avenida de las Americas* to go south to the fancy *colonias* where the rich people lived.

Rich people. In Portsmouth, they lived—well, they didn't actually live *in* Portsmouth but in Rye and Kennebunkport and Newcastle-by-the-Sea—in multi-gabled white houses with mullioned windows, deep front porches, and lawns, precisely cut in diamond patterns, sloping to the ocean. Houses shuttered nine months out of the year.

But these Guatemalans were in an entirely different category of *rich*. As her bus rumbled southward, the colorful tapestry of Guatemalan street life subsided. The catchy percussion of street performers, gone.

The calls of pushcart vendors hawking their fruits or vegetables or sweets or fresh bread, silenced. Graffiti, whitewashed.

Houses became grander: two-stories, three stories, four. Fountains, statues, topiary, uniformed doormen. Hummers and BMWs glided along the streets, helicopters idled on rooftops. A giraffe peered over a wall, munching low-hanging tree leaves.

Luz's destination was a compound that extended an entire city block. A security barrier of retractable steel posts blocked the driveway entrance. Beefy men in black uniforms patrolled the perimeter; two stood watch in a tower at the corner, each carrying a long gun. Everything except a small section of the uppermost floor was hidden behind a towering wall, painted anonymous white, the top embedded with shards of glass and coils of razor wire. Martin Benavides had come a long way since he was a soldier of the revolution like her father—sleeping in a tent in the mountains, skinning iguanas, cooking over a fire, bathing in cold streams. She was going to kill him with a smile on her face.

"*Señorita.*"

Luz jumped. The guard had returned.

"Everything appears to be satisfactory," he said, speaking directly to her breasts.

He opened the gate just enough for Luz to pass and motioned her in. As she squeezed through, he stood so close she could see the enlarged pores on his neck and the sparse black bristles on his chin. Overpowering cologne with the scent of cheap laundry detergent blasted Luz when he reached across her body to check that the gate had relatched. When his damp fingers clutched her elbow, however, Luz yanked her arm away.

The man narrowed his eyes. A smile played around the corners of his mouth. "Wait there," he said, motioning to the guardhouse. "Someone will come to collect you."

The place was, at most, ten feet on a side. One wall was covered with video monitors, another with filing cabinets stacked floor to ceiling. A wooden bench opposite the filing cabinets was dusty and littered with old newspapers. The door and a small window took up the side facing the gate. Luz stayed next to the door to avoid being penned in. But the guard, who remained outside only long enough for a throat-clearing gargle and spit into the bushes, shooed her inside and slammed the door behind them. He slouched on a stool in front of the window, feet hooked around the rungs. His splayed-out knees bumped Luz's leg. She moved closer to the bench, but there was a sticky spot in the middle next to an overturned cup.

Luz had dressed carefully this morning in her blue silk suit. With its long skirt and conservative lines, it would suffice for the most important job interview of her life. Besides, her mother had taken her to buy it, one of the last times she'd been strong enough to leave the house. The dress was way too subdued for her taste, but it caught her mother's eye and unspoken between them was the understanding she needed something suitable for her mother's funeral. Luz hugged her mother and agreed it was lovely.

She remained standing and maneuvered toward the far wall. "I guess you don't get many visitors coming here," Luz said to the second guard, an older man who never moved his gaze from monitors displaying the barbwired perimeter of the estate.

"This is the service entrance," he said. "If you get the job, you will come and go this way but with a coded name tag you'll swipe in a reader outside the gate. You'll still have to wait for us to match you to the photo on file and free the lock. But it's routine at that point, and you won't need an escort."

Luz countered her mounting claustrophobia by reciting memorized facts about her imaginary life in Miami: two children in her care, a girl and a boy, eight and ten. Father traveled a lot, wife often joined him. Light duties except when the parents were away. It fit admirably with what she might be expected to do with this job.

At the security gate, the guards authorized deliveries. A plumber was escorted in. Several people placed their badges in the reader. The screen inside showed a face shot, which the guard matched to the live person standing a few feet away. The clock on the wall crept toward eleven thirty. Her skirt clung to her legs, and small beads of sweat trickled down the nape of her neck and gathered at her temples. Luz hoped she hadn't sweated enough to stain the fabric under her arms.

She'd spent the night tossing and turning, unable to quell the pressure to perform her best and get the damn job. It was only that strain, Luz told herself, not the beginning of another downward spiral, but sounds echoed, and cloudy, blurred shapes peopled her world as if her head was wrapped in layers of gauze. Thank goodness she'd explored the kitchen this morning. Whoever had set up her apartment—the man from the bus, perhaps—had left coffee beans in one of the bright red canisters on her white tile kitchen counter and a bag of sugar in another. So she'd made a pot and drunk it, dark and sweet. The cobwebs receded, but by the time she'd finished and dressed, she was quivering with fatigue and nausea.

The door flew open. A woman with the air of an exotic tropical bird swooped in on the highest heels Luz had ever seen. As she glided to a stop in front of Luz, her billowing emerald scarf settled over a scarlet dress. A quetzal, Luz thought.

"I am Alicia Muñoz," the woman said. "Come with me." Luz's extended hand hung in the air in an unmet handshake when Alicia made a sudden about-face. "Señor de la Vega has been waiting," she called over her shoulder.

I've been waiting, too.

Seventeen years since Martin Benavides murdered my father. Seventeen years of watching my mother's spirit shrivel and die, of being the awkward, brown-skinned outsider.

Luz struggled to keep up as Alicia darted along a covered portico that ran the length of the mansion. She stopped at a small door about halfway along the arcade and keyed a code. Once inside, they walked on industrial carpet past nondescript beige walls. Alicia knocked on a door at the far end of the hall before cracking it open an inch. "I have the nanny."

A short, round man with a trim mustache and beard came to the door. He waved Luz in with a courtly gesture. "*Pase adelante, señorita.*"

Appear as tall as possible when facing danger—a proverb from her father's infinite store of folk wisdom—sprang to mind as Luz reached the threshold. So, shoulders thrust back and chin high, and an inner smile of gratitude to her father for the many ways he shared his world with her, Luz stepped into the lion's den. Alicia walked on.

"I am Raul de la Vega. I have served Martin Benavides since his time leading the revolution. I was his personal secretary while he was president. Now I handle the staffing for his household." De la Vega settled into an ornate chair, losing only a few inches in the process. He lifted a thin folder from his immaculate desk and, balancing it on his belly, opened and read from it. He enunciated the bald facts of her made-up position in Miami. Luz, right hand covering the trembling left, waited for his questions: *What, exactly, were your daily responsibilities? What challenges and problems did you face? How did you handle them? Most rewarding part of the job? Least? Biggest accomplishment?*

Unless he threw her a curveball, Luz knew she was well prepared. Richard, at their last meeting, had played de la Vega's role. In the living area of her Miami hotel room, curtains closed against the blazing afternoon sun, Richard had posed question after question. He'd played it avuncular—*So, my dear* . . . He'd played it borderline hostile—*What makes you think you can* . . . He'd adopted a fake German accent—*Vat vould ve haf to pay you fur zhis vork*—which had her giggling uncontrollably.

Finally, Richard slapped the pages together and applauded slowly. "Señorita Aranda," he said, as he walked into the kitchenette, "I don't know about you, but I sure as hell could use a cold beer right now." She was ready.

De la Vega set the folder down. "So, Luz Aranda, you have been away from home for a long time," he said, echoing the sentiments of the airport immigration man, "but we are delighted to have you join our family. I have checked your references, of course. Your former employers have nothing but praise."

After all her preparation, after the waiting and the ogling, after Alicia Muñoz's rudeness, it wasn't an interview at all. Luz had the job. She'd had it all along. A sense of buoyancy—light-headedness, really—replaced the morning's nausea. Dizzy with the suddenness, with relief and incredulity. How Richard made this happen could remain a glorious mystery as far as she was concerned. It didn't matter. She was *in*.

By the time Señor de la Vega concluded his pleasantries, he was on the phone to arrange her ID. One more giant step. Each obstacle in her path she overcame, each door that opened, brought with it increasing quiet in Luz's head, as though she was moving in stages away from the cacophony of crowded rooms into a more private space. In one sense, of course, it was the hollow quiet of doors closing, leaving her increasingly isolated. But Luz preferred to imagine the wind at her back, wafting her onward.

Then de la Vega said, "Let's go to the children's wing."

No.

She squeezed the front of the chair cushion. Her practice sessions always ended with a walk on the beach or a beer with Richard. With her sole focus on getting the job, Luz had postponed acknowledging the inevitable consequence: *getting* it meant close daily contact with the Benavides. She diverted her gasp of discomfort into a bright day care–cheery grin. "Tell me about the children."

"Only one child. Cesar requires a nanny in the afternoon from 1:00 p. m., when his tutor leaves, until bedtime. His sister was recently sent to a private school in Spain." The man paused, and with the first sense of the steel behind his florid manner, said, "The family does not wish that information to become general knowledge, Señorita Aranda." He slid down from his perch. "Come with me. We'll go see Cesar."

There's nothing to worry about. He was a kid. *Nothing to worry about.* He'd never lived in the mountains, never fought. He hadn't killed her father. But his grandfather had. *Querido Dios, don't let there be enough family resemblance to see a killer in the boy's face.*

De la Vega led Luz to an elevator at the end of the hall. "This is the only access to the living quarters," he said. When the door slid open, Raul pushed the button for the third floor followed by a four-digit code. Only then did the doors close and the elevator begin its ascent.

The elevator opened onto a windowless corridor with six closed doors. Diffuse lighting illuminated deep-pile rose carpet and pale-blue walls. Small carved tables at intervals held fresh flowers. De la Vega knocked on the last door on the left. A bent man in musty black and wearing a priest's collar opened the door and leaned heavily on the knob.

"Father Espinosa, good day to you. I've brought the afternoon nanny to meet Cesar."

The priest enclosed Luz's hand in his misshapen arthritic fingers. Behind him, a small boy with dark curly hair sat curled like a question mark, his head bent over a hard-bound book. He stood, skinny—all elbows and wrists and knees. Cesar Benavides.

The boy nodded at the introductions, his face a mask, eyes not quite focusing on Luz, even when he shook her hand.

Finally, de la Vega put one hand on Luz's shoulder and the other on Cesar's. He smiled like a proud father. "Well, that's that. Back to work for me," he said.

Father Espinosa called Cesar to his desk to go over a reading assignment. Luz remained in the background, silent, gauging her reaction. Indifference mixed with relief. Cesar was simply a little boy. A lonely child—one look at the setup here, two minutes in his presence, made that clear. Indifference would make it easier for her. Luz would take care of him, but she'd keep her emotional distance. It wouldn't do to actually care *for* him.

When the door closed behind Father Espinosa, Cesar whirled to face Luz. "Are you my father's new girlfriend?"

The unexpected question made Luz laugh. "Of course not! Why on earth would you think that?"

"Because the last one was, and the one before her, too. He didn't tell me, but I'm almost nine, you know." Shoulders hunched high and tight, lower lip curled, and hands squeezed into fists at his side—a bantam-belligerent pose she might've snickered at in other circumstances. "And besides, I'm not blind. He was always touching her when he thought I wasn't looking. Once I was supposed to be in the bathtub, but I couldn't get my shoelace undone. I came back in my bedroom, and they were kissing." His voice cracked on the last word, and his valiant stance melted. Cesar wheeled away.

"*Asqueroso!*" exclaimed Luz. Gross! The long-forgotten Spanish word came out of nowhere, surprising Luz at least as much as Cesar.

That earned her a small smile and a step back. An unclenching of fists. "Are you *sure* you're not?" asked the boy.

"I'm not. *Te lo juro.* I've never even met your father." Luz reflected on the incongruous reactions to her presence—the lascivious gaze of the gatekeeper, Alicia's insolence, de la Vega's bonhomie. If they all assumed she was Roberto Benavides' girlfriend, that could make life really complicated—or else she could use it to her advantage. She needed time to think.

"The others lied all the time." Cesar shrugged as if to say the subject was closed. "I like football. Do you want to see some of my stuff?"

The boy turned without waiting for her answer, so Luz followed the grandson of Martin Benavides into his bedroom.

CHAPTER FOUR

The latch clicked, and the gate squealed open. Luz pulled it closed behind her. It was the end of her first full day back in Guatemala. The end of her first workday, and the beginning of the end for Martin Benavides.

Street noise diminished here in the compound. Crickets chirped; a night bird called. Luz stood on an asphalt pad, parking space for a panel truck, a small sedan, and several motor scooters. Beyond, two buildings faced each other, surrounded by masses of flowering bushes—hibiscus, bougainvillea, plumeria, heliconia, bird-of-paradise, and many Luz didn't recognize. There were twelve apartments altogether, three up and three down in each building. In the semidarkness, Luz trudged along the cobbled path to apartment 3. Ground floor, left side. She unlocked the door and dropped her bag.

Her apartment was tiny but not much smaller than the utilitarian cubicle where she'd spent her teenage years, the one Richard's resettlement people had arranged for her and her mother in the U.S. Here, a living room extended along the left side of a rectangle. To the right of the front door was a miniature kitchen and, beyond it, a little bedroom and bath. Watercolors of local scenes hung on the walls. A colorful homespun spread covered the bed.

Since she hadn't had the energy to unpack more than essentials the night before, Luz lugged her suitcase into the bedroom and heaved it onto the bed. Zero floor space, although her apartment's position at the end of the building allowed for a bedroom window. She walked toward it, bumping her shin on the corner of the low bureau. Beyond the cotton print curtain, the window—stoutly barred as befitted a ground-floor opening—overlooked a lush tangle of hibiscus bushes. It was raining again. Fat drops splattered onto the windowpane, a good night to be snug and dry at home. *Home.*

She began to unpack. Her clothes didn't come close to filling the dresser, nor her toiletries and medicines the bathroom cabinet. On the table by the living room couch, she placed her favorite photos—one of her impossibly young parents, long before they became her parents, smiling, not at the camera, but only for one another. In another picture, Luz was seven years old. Her father had grown a thick mustache, and her mother's hair was tied back in a long braid. Although Luz now squeezed between them, so close all their cheeks squashed together, her parents still smiled over her head with their private look. They cherished her; Luz knew that. She also knew their love for her flowed seamlessly from their love for one another.

Luz wandered into the kitchen and opened the refrigerator. She stared into the empty space, suddenly ravenous but too tired to explore the neighborhood in hopes of finding an open store. Since there was nothing in the canisters on the counter except coffee and sugar—not what she needed at bedtime—Luz inspected the upper cabinets. In one, she found acceptable emergency rations: a stack of microwavable flavored noodle bricks, the kind with a sell-by date sometime in the twenty-fourth century and enough sodium to send you casket-shopping. Not that she was picky. Luz made a packet and devoured it curled up on the living room sofa.

From the bedroom, there came a slight rattle, then a scratchy tap-tap and a squeal of metal. Luz eased around, wishing she were not sitting beside the one bright light in an otherwise shadowy apartment. There was a raspy clunk, like a bureau drawer opening. Someone was in her bedroom. Only inky black showed through the half-closed bedroom door. Luz crawled behind the sofa. Although she was out of sight from the bedroom, light still shone on her—and now she was exposed to the rear windows. Hiding in her kitchen wouldn't offer any refuge. She'd have to chance running out the front door.

Wait—there were iron bars on the bedroom window. Luz hadn't made sure they were solid, but no one could've gotten past them without a lot more noise than she'd heard. *Outside then.* The tapping must be at the window, a burglar trying to get in. She should stand up, walk into the bedroom, and turn on the light. Show him the place was occupied. Simple enough in theory, but her clenched shoulder muscles knit even tighter at the thought of moving toward the unseen intruder.

Elbows on the cold tile, Luz cradled her head in her hands. Here she was, planning to assassinate the former president of Guatemala, and she was crawling on the floor like a baby. She began to laugh. Since she wasn't going to let a bomb worry her, she might as well get this over with.

Luz rose and, keeping away from the pool of light cast by her table lamp, tiptoed across the room to her bedroom door. She peeked in. Ambient light filtering in from the living room confirmed the room was empty. The tapping appeared to come from the window. And what she'd identified as squealing metal was also outside. Crossing the room in four quick strides, she thrust aside the curtain. A squawk, a flurry of motion. A large black bird sheltering from the passing thunderstorms flapped its wings and disappeared into the night.

Luz sank onto her mattress, laughing—a bit hysterically—as she shook with waves of released panic. When her breathing calmed, she

clambered to her feet and cleared the bed of her remaining posses-
sions. Finally, she placed the little black jar containing her mother's
ashes on the living room bookshelf. The prayer that came this time
was not bargaining. Of course, it wasn't really praying either. Luz
rested her fingertips on the urn and squeezed her eyes shut.

Her mother, so slight by then that she scarcely dented the mattress
or pillow and too weak to rise, had motioned Luz nearer when she
awakened that last morning. Luz got up from the chair where she'd
passed the long night and lay beside her. Her mother's cold hands had
pressed hers, squeezing with all the force her ravaged body could mus-
ter. She whispered, "Take me home when I die."

"Almost home now, Mama," Luz spoke out loud.

*   *   *

Two envelopes Evan delivered to Luz had been sealed; however, he'd
written a third item himself. Richard had phoned two days before
Evan's rendezvous with her on the bus. "I've got one more thing for
you to do tomorrow," he'd said.

"No can do," said Evan. "I have a meeting with a potential buyer
here at the studio and then Margo's *bon-voyage* party. Maybe later in
the week." It was worth a try. The stipend Richard paid him was not a
princely sum to the United States government; it did, however, repre-
sent an exceedingly comfortable cushion that allowed Evan to paint
full-time.

"Tomorrow."

Not this time. Richard, Evan had long-ago decided, was good at
what he did precisely because he channeled that military, can-do style.
Translation: *Do it when I say, the way I say. No buts. And don't ask
why.* Whether it was executing a precise three-point turn on a busy
city street or cooking paella, Richard always had an excellent reason
for whatever *it* was.

Without waiting for Evan to cave, Richard said, "Don't worry. They won't start the party without you." Then he gave Evan two addresses in the city and told him to scout out the bus schedule from the first to the second. "And don't just fucking Google the damn thing—I can do that myself from the States. Confirm the bus numbers, check their frequency. Then make the trip yourself, late morning. Figure out how long it takes. And write detailed instructions to include in the packet for the contact."

That micromanaging call had been the first crack in Richard's normal equanimity, an even earlier indication of his concern than when he'd blurted out Luz's name. In the years Evan had been doing this part-time courier gig in Guatemala, he could remember only a handful of times Richard had similarly insisted on Evan's nailing down every conceivable detail. One night over bad Chinese food and one too many Mai Tais, Evan had worked up the courage to ask why—as in the handoff he'd just completed in the lobby of the Radisson in the *Zona Viva*—Richard didn't trust him to do the job right.

"Oh, it's not you." Richard had tossed back a last huge gulp of his drink and slammed his glass on the table. "It's these fucking amateurs."

Now Richard was being nitpicky about Luz. Inference: *She* was an amateur. A young Guatemalan woman, she was probably someone who knew someone or could go somewhere or hide in plain sight in a way Richard's usual cohort of middle-aged men could not.

An amateur who was still somewhere in the city?

Evan had filled reams of paper with her image. The sweep of her hair as it fell onto her shoulders, the slight space between her front teeth when she smiled, the small diamond-shaped birthmark on her chin. And her hands—clenched tight as she tugged her suitcase, lying quietly in her lap, fingers spread against the dusty bus window in a silent goodbye—he'd drawn them so often he imagined himself like one of those Northern Renaissance masters, Rembrandt or Dürer, whose notebooks abounded with sketches of hands, cheeks, ears, eyebrows, breasts, lips.

Evan hit the wall after two sleepless nights, two days of unproductive speculation. He couldn't complete a decent painting with isolated images from those few minutes on the bus. There were too many gaps. He needed to see how the sun would fall on the planes of her cheekbones, the curve of her neck when it wasn't covered by her hair. He needed to see her walking, see how her hips flared. He needed to see Luz again.

From Richard's call about the buses, Evan guessed Point A was where she was staying and her arrival at Point B must be time-sensitive. On the other hand, Richard had been cagey about the precise addresses; he'd given Evan only street-corner intersections.

The next morning, Evan double-knotted his running shoes and, instead of taking his usual route, jogged to Point A, a corner in a quiet middle-class neighborhood not too far from his house. The day he'd done the buses, Evan hadn't paid much attention.

Now, he ran up and down the adjacent streets. It was more upscale than where he lived but lacked the loud camaraderie of his own block, the pushcart vendors selling *helados*—or balloons or fried chicken—or gatherings of the underemployed in their faded shirts and straw hats drinking midmorning beers while they played cards on their front steps.

Here, there were only gates and trees and more gates. He passed a group of teenagers laden with backpacks, all in the matching navy blazers of *Colegio San Bernardo*.

"*Hola, muchachos,*" he said on impulse. "I'm looking for a, um, friend who lives around here."

Beyond her first name, a thumbnail description, and the date she arrived, however, Evan had little information. So he pulled out his pocket notebook and sketched her. The boys whistled appreciatively.

Evan assumed they were admiring his drafting skills, but then one spoke sotto voce to another, a comment that translated roughly as, "Boy, this guy's got it bad!"

Another, with patchy hair sprouting above his upper lip, said, "There's no one like her around here, *señor*." He turned to his companions. "*Vámonos.* We'll be late." They walked on, laughing and shoving each other. Evan replaced his sketchbook in his pocket.

He made another circuit of the neighborhood. While a few people he asked about Luz, like the boys, thought him a forlorn lover, Evan soon realized that others considered him a stalker—and they wouldn't admit seeing her even if she *was* here.

Still, the following day, Evan developed an urge to visit a friend who, not coincidentally, lived a few miles from Point B. Evan kept a blue Ford Fairlane—one of the Made-in-Argentina Fairlanes that migrated into Central America during the '80s, an old wreck his mechanic kept in working order with duct tape and baling wire.

Luz's destination was Guatemala City's ritziest neighborhood—massive walled mansions, most with their own private security guards. Zero foot traffic. Mainly bulletproofed and chauffeur-driven SUVs. A few tradesmen's vans. His beat-up Ford stood out, and wandering around was out of the question. Five minutes on the corner and guards were already pointing. Evan started his car and aimlessly circled a few blocks. Nothing to see here, either.

CHAPTER FIVE

The morning after Luz's interview, she took the jolting bus ride again. In the States, she'd thought nothing of traipsing all around town with her work ID dangling from a lanyard, but de la Vega had lectured her about rampant drug-fueled street crime—which Luz considered rich, since the Benavides were the likely source of the drugs in question. He warned Luz to leave the badge in her purse. Also, not to carry credit cards or her passport or more money than she needed for the day or wear jewelry or a fancy watch. He was as much of an old fussbudget as Richard had been when she took a job in Boston.

That's when Richard had bought Luz her first cellphone, programming it with his numbers—home, cell, work, emergency switchboard—AAA, and several for local law enforcement. Luz couldn't help noticing his offhand but regular calls—like ten minutes after she walked in the door. *No, nothing special,* he'd say. *I just wondered how your day was.* And they'd chat, sometimes for half an hour or more, about nothing special while she puttered around the kitchen.

Luz got off the bus. The prison-blank walls of the Benavides compound loomed. Inside, her job: a single polite and toilet-trained charge, lunch and dinner served, no cleaning or playground duty. And his grandfather. Outside, a squadron of armed men and a security checkpoint.

They'd had another day to investigate her. Although Luz doubted one more day of research would crack the cover Richard had so meticulously arranged, still she must pass through the gauntlet of guards. There was only one way to do it, thought Luz, and that was with aplomb—a word Richard had long-ago explained as "grace under pressure"—and then illustrated with one of her discarded princess dolls, consigned to a box in the bottom of her closet. He took the doll's arm and rotated it into a decorous, sideways twist. The fact that the princess was naked and covered with crayon marks where Luz had once tried to draw on a ball gown made Richard's demonstration unforgettable.

So Luz sauntered up to the guardhouse, scanned her ID in the reader, and flourished her best princess-wave at the sentry. The gate clicked open.

In a week's time, play-acting had become unnecessary.

Also, by then, when Luz opened Cesar's door, she saw *him*, a cub shedding his baby fat, clumsy from a growth spurt that had lengthened his limbs. As soon as she arrived, Cesar would slam shut whatever book or paper he was supposed to be studying and run to Luz, eager to get her approval for their lunch order. It didn't hurt that Luz—like Cesar—had a soft spot for *hamburguesas y papas fritas* and didn't have the previous nanny's problem of insisting on a green vegetable.

Her attempts to familiarize herself with the layout of the mansion met with failure. She had codes for the staff door and for the floor where Cesar lived, but asking de la Vega for the other codes brought a peremptory throat-clearing and quick, negative headshake.

Toward the end of her first week at the Benavides', Luz spied Alicia Muñoz at the far end of the spartan downstairs hallway. Hoping to avoid a repeat of the woman's snippiness at their first encounter, she slowed to give Alicia time to move on.

Gone was the flamboyant quetzal. This morning Alicia, in a tight-fitting sheath of brown, gold, and black, resembled a *terciopelo*, the gorgeous—but deadly—pit viper of the Central American highlands. The first time Luz spotted one, she reached out to stroke the shiny black diamonds on its brown skin. Her father rushed in faster than she'd ever seen him move and scooped her away before the snake could strike.

Alicia's toothy smile, Cheshire Cat–like, was at odds with her jutting chin. Luz sensed an ambush. "Where're you from?" Alicia asked, without preamble.

"Santa Clarita." Luz pressed the call button. *Get me away from her.*

"Where's that?" As Alicia continued to smile, her lips drew tight like a *terciopelo* readying to strike.

"It's near Puerto Barrios." Luz and Richard had argued about Luz's fictitious background. He insisted she not divulge she'd lived in the mountains. That, he said, would scream "rebel sympathizer." He wanted her to be an expat city girl—Guatemala City born-and-raised—but Luz convinced him she knew nothing of the city and could get tripped up too easily. They compromised: She was from a small coastal town, far from the mountains and also far enough from the city that no one would know much about it.

"But you've been living in the U.S.?" The question came too sharply to be conversational and with a distinct furrow of Alicia's brow. *Not casual chitchat.*

Luz could have been back in the girls' locker room changing before tenth-grade gym class, her bony body and brown skin on display to every curvaceous milk-and-honey upperclassman. Of course, they mainly ignored her, preferring to talk among themselves. When they didn't, it was fake camaraderie. "Luz, who ya going to prom with?" She'd swallow, ashamed to admit no one had asked her, knowing a lie would make the rounds of the school in five minutes. So she'd shrug or turn away. Someone would mutter "loser"—their favorite play on her name—and everyone would laugh.

At Luz's nod of agreement, Alicia pressed, "How did you hear about this job? The former nanny didn't give notice. She simply called in last week to say she'd taken a new position."

Luz smiled, grateful once again for Richard's persistent coaching. "But she'd told her cousin weeks ago she was unhappy being so far from her family in Santiago Atitlan. When she found a position there, she grabbed it, and her cousin told me." At Alicia's uplifted eyebrow, Luz added, "Her cousin lives in my neighborhood, my old neighborhood in Miami, and she knew I was looking for a change."

The cousin story was a total Richard fabrication. "I'm not asking, Luz—I'm *telling* you this part," he'd said.

It was one of the first things they'd thrashed out the day Richard met her at Miami International and drove her to the hotel. Once he showed her around the suite, he took a couple of bottles of water from the fridge and sat her down at the little dinette table. Then he pulled out his list—Richard always had a list. This one was longer than usual and didn't cover the old stuff: once it had been report cards, summer camp, driving lessons. More recently, he'd scheduled her mother's chemotherapy and made sure Luz paid the bills on time.

"They can and they *will* check. We have people in Miami to vouch for you." He leaned back in his chair and smiled his super-pleased-with-himself grin. "Also, we have someone else inside at the Benavides', someone who can smooth your way, but who we have, let's say, other plans for."

Luz opened her mouth, but before she could ask who it was, Richard waggled his index finger so hard his bushy eyebrows, now faded from auburn to a distinguished silver, also vibrated. "Don't ask," he said. "To protect *both* of you, I don't want you to know anything else about what's going on, nothing a new girl wouldn't know."

The elevator doors swooshed open. Alicia stepped inside. Isolated with Alicia in that tiny box? *Uh-unh.* Luz would rather drape a *terciopelo* around her neck and dance the tango. But Alicia hip-checked the door when it began to close. "You going to work or not?"

Yeah, just like gym class. And Luz, seeing nothing else she could do, stepped into the elevator. Although she claimed the opposite corner from Alicia, the other woman immediately crowded into her space and shot out rapid-fire questions. "What was the name of the cousin who told you about the job?—You lived in Miami?—For how long?—Who'd you work for?"

Luz stumbled over dates and the name of the fictitious cousin. Heat built up. She rubbed her forehead, her cheeks. This was the interrogation Luz had anticipated at her interview with de la Vega, not a week later stuck in an elevator with Alicia.

"Why are you asking me all this? Don't you work for Señor de la Vega?" Luz asked.

"Me? Heavens, no." Alicia compressed her lips and muzzled laughter bubbled up from the back of her throat. "I'm Señor Benavides' personal assistant. I'm in charge of his calendar and all his scheduling."

In charge of fetching visitors and announcing them to the real *senior staff,* Luz concluded. Clearly, Alicia—like those other taller, whiter girls who once taunted her—was one of those people Luz had spent a lifetime muttering at under her breath. Still, it wouldn't do to alienate this woman in her first week on the job—a woman whose barely disguised hostility had morphed into faux-friendliness.

"The older Señor Benavides or . . . ?" Luz asked, unsure how the staff distinguished between the two adult men of the household—her target, Martin, and his son Roberto, Cesar's father.

"Señor Martin." Alicia stretched her neck and favored Luz with a predatory smile, the pecking order—big boss's assistant condescending to child care worker—clearly established. Not much of an attempt at Miss Congeniality.

The elevator dinged to announce their arrival on the residence floor. When the doors opened, Alicia hurried away, her high heels working small divots into the thick carpet. In a flash, Martin Benavides' personal assistant had rounded the corner and disappeared.

Shortly thereafter, Luz met Delores. Unlike Alicia, Delores professed delight at making Luz's acquaintance. She was also short and dark-haired, like Luz, though considerably rounder. Delores had managed to turn the housekeepers' uniform into an art form: An aqua T-shirt peeked out from under the prim white shirt, and colorful woven belts circled the ample waist of her black skirt. She wore a headscarf of dancing hippopotamuses over tight, coiled braids, and her cheeks bulged like those of a mischievous kewpie doll. She ruffled Cesar's hair and produced a small bag of cookies, which she slid under a pile of papers with a sideways grin at Luz, all the while emptying wastebaskets and wiping the woodwork. Delores was the housekeeper in the family wing.

"That means," she said, with a swipe of dust rag at Cesar's desk that turned into a caress of his cheek, "whatever this boy messes up, I make neat and clean again. And I make sure he gets a little love from time to time."

"Do you clean the entire house?" Luz asked as she followed Delores around the living room.

"Oh, no." Also unlike Alicia, Delores dispensed with the honorifics. Martin and his wife, Dominga, were the "old folks," and Delores wasn't allowed into their wing of the house. When she progressed to mopping the bathroom, she looked around to ascertain Cesar was out of earshot before continuing, "Ever since Paulina left, the old man has become a recluse."

Luz ventured into the bathroom behind Delores and held up a finger—wait. "Paulina?" she whispered.

Delores inclined her head toward the room where Cesar sat. "His sister," she said, barely audible.

The girl who was sent to Spain. De la Vega's cryptic warning at her interview had left Luz dying to ask about her. "What happened?" mouthed Luz.

"A problem. I don't know what." Delores gazed into her open hands as though she held a crystal ball. "And, believe me, I asked. One morning everything's fine. Then, all of a sudden, Señor Roberto's yelling at his father, and the old man's screaming back. People are crying, and I'm packing Paulina's clothes, and the car takes her to the airport, to some fancy school in Europe." Delores crossed herself. "The old man was very fond of Paulina. Now he never goes out. And almost no one is allowed in."

"What about her father?"

Luz meant to ask how Cesar and Paulina's father was coping with the absence of his daughter, but Delores answered a different question, or at least one not directly relevant. "Señor Roberto, he's the only one who goes anywhere. He travels all the time now."

"You clean for him, too?"

Delores' hands swept a large circle. "Oh, yes—sweep, dust, mop— his entire suite." She jangled the key ring hanging from the broad cloth loop around her skirt. "Señor Roberto is in Miami—" Delores hesitated, took a step back, bumping into the tub.

Oh, shit. She must be aware of the nanny-girlfriend connection. Too bad. Delores, with her ready supply of gossip, was the person who held—literally—the key Luz needed.

Delores leaned on her mop and regarded Luz with a speculative smile. "You might be coming from Miami, but I don't think you have anything to do with Señor Roberto's business there."

"Me? Business?" The words burst out with total confusion before Luz could censor herself.

Delores' eyes crinkled, and her smile widened. "No, I didn't think so." She hoisted her mop and moved past Luz into Cesar's bedroom.

Luz had—naively—assumed she'd stay in Portsmouth while she transitioned to her new identity. That was logistically unworkable, Richard told her, because of the other people involved. So then she figured he'd take her to D.C. with him. But no—it had to be Miami. It had to be the fancy residence hotel on North Beach where the other female guests spent their days at the spa and their evenings decorating the arms of well-dressed older men.

It was beginning to sound like Richard's team was actively promoting this nonexistent connection between her and Cesar's father. A headache blossomed in her temple.

The second envelope in the newspaper swap had described an extra task Richard wanted her to complete. This last-minute addition to their plan, he said, was an insurance policy that he now believed necessary to absolutely ensure Roberto Benavides' political ruin after the death of his father. He'd underlined *absolutely* twice. She was to gain access to Roberto Benavides' study and substitute the thumb drive in the envelope for an identical one in his briefcase.

Luz sank onto the couch as Delores called out "*hasta mañana*" and left her alone in the spotless apartment with Cesar and her thoughts. *Gain access to Roberto's quarters.* Richard's little by-the-way errand suddenly struck her as being a lot more complicated.

CHAPTER SIX

Then there was Cesar. He'd said he liked football, but that was the understatement of the century. Cesar *lived* for football. The first afternoon, as soon as he accepted Luz's denial of involvement with his father, he dragged her into his room and showed off posters of Álvaro Hurtarte, caught mid-stride with the black-and-white ball, and Carlos Figueroa, fists clenched aloft in triumph. He diagrammed plays when he should have been graphing his math assignment. He did everything except go outside and kick the ball around.

Outside of football, Cesar had few interests. He preferred television—football, if possible, even videos of long-ago games—to engaging her, which suited Luz fine. She was determined to be perfunctory with him. She helped with homework, they ate, watched television, and she made sure he was clean and ready for bed on time.

Yet sometimes when Cesar tilted his head, squinting and chewing on a pencil, Luz saw her friend Hector sitting cross-legged on the ground under the camouflaged tarpaulin that served as a makeshift school where her mother taught the children who had been rendered homeless by the latest attacks. And dried their eyes, found them clothes that fit and grown-ups to watch over them.

Hector, like Cesar, was all arms and legs and elbows. Sharp angles. He was a year younger than Luz—and lucky, everyone said, because

he arrived at the camp with a backpack of belongings and both parents, unlike the children whose families had been slaughtered, so
many of whom were found wandering alone in the forest.

Hector also loved football. Although not one of the oldest, his
enthusiasm and intensity soon molded the ragtag group of children
into a sort of after-school football club. They met in the clearing
behind the school tarp. Hector began by showing them different
ways to flick the ball with their feet. Soon they were doing carioca
drills, practicing passes, and kicking goals. When they played games,
it was never girls against boys or big kids versus little kids. They
played together. They played to forget the war around them and to
be, simply, kids.

Hector, if he hadn't perished that night in the forest, was probably
dead by now.

Whenever Luz caught herself floundering, one foot in the dark
past, like that, she'd jump up and organize a drill of her own. *"Vente,"*
she'd say to Cesar. *"Vamos a explorar."*

And off they'd go exploring. Paulina's room, locked. Cesar scuffed
the door with his foot, almost a kick. "Paulina used to let me play with
her puppy." Three guest rooms where cousins who were coming for
Christmas would stay. "Victor's okay," Cesar said, "but Rosa whines if
we don't do everything her way, and Benny cheats all the time."

Down one floor was Cesar's father's suite, locked and empty.
Roberto Benavides had not yet returned from Miami. *"Papá* says
maybe I can go back to school with my friends next year."

From an assortment of these outbursts, Luz pieced together the recent upheaval: After whatever led to Paulina's being shipped off to
Spain—and Cesar was as much in the dark about specifics as
Delores—Cesar was pulled out of his school and confined to the
house with Father Espinosa engaged as a tutor. Once, a boy from
school had come to visit. The way Cesar told the story, it sounded as

though, despite the thrill of a helicopter ride, the presence of armed guards at such close quarters had intimidated the child, and he never came back.

As they wandered, their footfalls fell inaudible on thick carpet; subdued lighting blurred their shadows. Occasionally, Luz caught a whiff of furniture polish. Otherwise, it was sterile air-conditioning, all hints of the vibrant Guatemalan life flowing in other city neighborhoods filtered out. And in the week she'd spent with him, the poor kid hadn't seen a soul who wasn't paid to be there: the tutor, the nanny, the maid.

They reached the hall where Alicia had disappeared after their confrontation in the elevator. "Is that where your grandfather lives?" Luz guessed, pointing.

Cesar nodded, then turned his back on the hall and busied himself running his fingers along the nubbly wall covering.

As Luz stared down the passage, a bubble of tension rose from her gut. Martin Benavides was *right there*. Using Cesar—Luz mentally rephrased—having Cesar smooth her path into his grandfather's wing of the house was the obvious way forward. She'd ensure Cesar was safely away the day of the bombing, but the boy was her ticket to becoming an inconspicuous regular.

A deep inhale for strength, long exhale for calmness. Luz asked, "Can we go visit him?"

Cesar hung his head. "*Papi* doesn't feel good. He said I was a big boy, and I had to learn to wait."

Wait. Cesar infused the word with a frustration Luz shared. Richard might consider her impatience unprofessional, but it's not like she had any experience in his clandestine world. She did not sign up for this in order to play babysitter. Luz smiled to herself. Actually, of course, she *had*, but her mind condensed the day-care part to a few brief interactions—meet kid/locate grandfather/ka-POW.

She hadn't bargained on the downtime, the delays, the *waiting*. Obviously, she had to take care of the Roberto flash drive stuff before the shit hit the fan, but her real job required paving the way to Martin's lair. Luz thought for a minute, trying to come up with an innocent way to ask about the information she needed. "Can't we go down the hall and knock on his door, ask if he's feeling better?"

Another desultory headshake. "You have to call, and then they send somebody to let you in. One of his stupid guards."

Call ahead, let you in. Luz filed the information. Her gut settled. She'd have to make it happen.

As Father Espinosa prepared to leave the next afternoon, he indicated a stack of papers on the desk. "Cesar has fallen behind in mathematics," he said.

The boy puffed into his tough-guy stance but didn't speak.

"These exercises must be done," said the priest as he exited, "by tomorrow morning."

Cesar deflated instantly when they were left alone. His head sank, bony arms twining around his chest, possibly the only hug he'd get all day.

"It's not fair," Cesar cried. "I do everything I'm supposed to do, but it takes me a really long time." The boy ran across the room and sank onto his perch by the window.

Luz riffled through the assignments the priest had flagged. "That's a lot of work." She pursed her lips.

Cesar hunched at his window seat, his head cradled in his arms like an abandoned puppy at the pound. And she saw herself, the little girl who hadn't yet learned English, crouching at the window of their brand-new apartment in Portsmouth to spy on kids playing in the park across the street. Day after silent day, Luz watched those children with whom she had no way of communicating play the game she knew so well. One day, as she walked home from school, an errant ball came her way. And she kicked it, hard and true. From then on, she was part of the neighborhood.

Cesar had stopped snuffling and was eyeing her through a shock of dark curly hair. He might be manipulating her, but it didn't matter. Her resolve to remain distant crumbled. Luz knew what she wanted to do and to hell with the stuffy priest. "*Bueno*, Cesar," she said. "I'll make a deal with you."

By three o'clock, with Luz's encouragement and a bowl of ice cream smuggled from the kitchen by a sympathetic Delores, Cesar had finished half his work—his part of the deal—and they were outside on a makeshift soccer field. Cesar brought his ball. Luz enlisted a couple of the younger gardeners to provide stakes to mark boundaries. Taking the ball from Cesar, she kicked it to test the goal they'd fashioned from green rubber netting.

Cesar was incredulous. "*You* play football?"

"I used to play," said Luz. With a not-quite-prayer to the memory of her friend Hector and their games in the small forest clearing, Luz added, "When I was in school."

"Really?"

"Really. I *said* I wouldn't lie to you." Luz offered what she hoped was a reassuring grin. *I haven't actually lied yet*. Her very presence was, of course, one enormous falsehood, even if it wasn't the cushy-job-for-the-girlfriend fiction some people assumed.

Soon, she would finagle access to his grandparents' tightly restricted private space and kill them.

"Obliterate them," Richard had said the last afternoon in Miami as he checked once more that she'd mastered the bomb assembly. "Blast a hole in the roof, make it loud, rattle the windows for miles, send a message." Richard began pacing. He could never sit still when he talked about the bomb she was going to unleash.

That explosion was going to turn Cesar's life upside down. Since only Martin and his wife were to be eliminated, he'd still have his father. Unlike her mother, Roberto probably had millions stashed in numbered bank accounts. They could take off for Switzerland. Or perhaps Roberto would fight to resurrect his family's business in Colombia. Or Miami. Cesar would become a refugee like her, grow up far away, learn another language, play with children again. Perhaps.

It couldn't be helped, Luz thought. Besides, Cesar would have *his* father. And if she could survive, so would he.

For more than an hour, Luz drilled Cesar on dribbling technique, standing on the sidelines as much as possible, making the boy do ninety percent of the running. Even so, muscle fatigue left her wobbly, and she signaled for a break. As Luz lolled on the grass, a man came to lean against a fat white pillar at the edge of the porch. He was a little too tan, his hair a little too brilliantly black. His teeth too white, his smile too wide. An extra undone button left little of his torso to the imagination.

Cesar stopped dribbling and followed her gaze. "*Papá!*" He shot across the lawn.

The man held out his arms, and Cesar leapt into them. He clutched Cesar tight and turned round and round in a dancing bear hug. Roberto Benavides, Cesar's absentee father and Luz's second Benavides, was back—and there, next to him, lay his briefcase containing a thumb drive with enough incriminating material to prevent him from continuing the Benavides' stranglehold on Guatemalan politics. All Luz had to do was get it.

She moistened her lips, then scrubbed them dry on her sleeve before stepping across the lawn. The briefcase never left her sight. As soon as she completed Richard's task, she could proceed with her real mission.

Cesar, back on the ground, grabbed his father by the hand. "*Papá, Papá.*" Cesar yanked him along like a toy train.

The man, to his credit, stumbled along with good grace. Luz
stopped when she reached the edge of the polished terra-cotta tile
porch. The briefcase sat a few feet behind Roberto, unattended. If
only he wanted to stay outside and kick the ball around with his son
and asked Luz to take his briefcase inside.

"*Papá*, this is Luz."

Roberto extended his hand, smooth and warm, with nails polished
to a high gloss, and held hers a shade too long. "A pleasure to meet
you, *señorita*. Roberto Benavides, at your service."

"My pleasure as well, Señor Benavides."

"Call me Bobby. All my friends do."

Bobby stayed to dinner. His briefcase stayed in his quarters. They
ate *bistec, arroz,* and *ensalada* at the little table in Cesar's sitting room,
Cesar chomping the crunchy greens without a squawk. Luz studied
the pictures of Bobby scattered about Cesar's room. They had been
touched up to eliminate the spider's web of fine lines crisscrossing his
cheeks and the red veins distending a once-aquiline nose.

The last time Luz had seen Martin, he'd been a few years older than
Bobby was now. By then Martin had been wounded twice that she
knew about—and probably more often. He cultivated the aura of a
field commander who'd lead every charge and be in the thick of the
action, exhorting his men to follow. Luz couldn't detect any of
Martin's toughness in Bobby, with his playboy wardrobe and
oily-smooth moves.

A cheerful Cesar monopolized the conversation; Bobby listened.
Cesar bubbled over with enthusiasm about incidents Luz had thought
insignificant, but the afternoon's drill was the highlight.

"How'd my boy do?" Bobby asked when he could get a word in.

"It was our first practice," said Luz, "and I'm not in good enough
shape to run the field with him. It would be much better if he had
other kids to play with."

"His cousins are coming after Christmas. They can play all day if they like." Turning directly to Luz, Bobby added, "I'm sure Raul de la Vega explained the security here. It's too dangerous for Cesar to be out in public right now. He stays in the compound at all times. In and out by helicopter only, absolutely no ground transportation. On that, if only on that, do my father and I agree."

The edge to his voice at the words "my father" reminded Luz of Delores' tidbit about the men arguing when Paulina was sent to Spain. She *still* hadn't found out what had happened.

CHAPTER SEVEN

Nine o'clock bonged on the church bells. Evan, arriving far too early, had stopped in a café near the market and nursed one coffee after another. Trucks and vans jockeyed for position to unload their wares in the narrow street. As horns honked, barrel-chested men scurried about, carrying on their backs gunny sacks and woven straw baskets overflowing with produce from the country. Evan paid for his coffees and drifted toward the outermost ring of market stalls.

Richard had phoned again, this time waking Evan from a sound sleep at dawn. "Up and at 'em, sleepyhead."

A heartfelt grumble at Richard's cavalier assumption that the pittance he paid Evan granted him 24/7 access was about to erupt, but it evaporated the second Richard continued. "It's the girl from the bus last week—would you recognize her again?"

The girl from the bus? Evan sat straight up in bed. *The girl from the bus?* It had been eleven days, not a week, not that he was counting. And, of course, he'd *recognize* her. Good Lord, he'd *memorized* her. Drawn nothing but her—watercolor portraits in a range of lighting conditions, pen-and-ink drawings of her hands in repose on her lap, a charcoal profile he was particularly fond of that captured her aloof intelligence.

"We need a source on the ground," Richard was saying as Evan struggled to pay attention, "someone she's already met who can contact her regularly."

Luz, the girl whose name Richard had let slip, was still in town.

"So, here's the deal: She goes to the old downtown market every morning around nine, making the rounds, chatting with the old ladies. Bump into her this morning." Richard detailed her route through the market. "Remember, I want you to keep this low-key. Let people there see you together. Buy a few things for yourself. Be amiable. Tell her you'll show up regularly in the mornings, and she should hand you the material she's collecting for me—it'll fit in her shopping bag," Richard hurriedly added. "When you get it, call me immediately. There are some timing issues."

Evan fingered a row of cheap silver necklaces. *Be amiable.* I can definitely do amiable, he thought. Maybe even charming. He plucked at the sparkling necklaces on display as though he were picking out a melody on a guitar and watched the arriving throngs of shoppers. By ones and twos, in larger chattering groups, they paraded toward the market entrance. Evan tried to scan each face, but they came in dizzying waves of color and form—infinite variations on bright shopping bags, high slanting foreheads, and shiny dark hair, most costumed in striped fabric with floral embroidery. To Evan, it was like being in a live-action *Where's Waldo* book, looking for the one exact match in a sea of look-alikes. He'd wait a few more minutes, but if Evan missed Luz here, he'd have to wade into the dim interior of the market to search for her in the crush of shoppers in the narrow aisles. What had sounded reasonable on the phone now seemed hopeless.

Then Luz appeared, half a block away, on the shady side of the street, swinging her plastic shopping bag in time to the salsa from a passing boom box. She stopped to greet a flower seller with his great sprays of gladiolus. She exchanged *buenos días*es with the old melon ladies. Too feeble to walk, the women were carted here each morning, along with a truckful of fruit, and left alone all day in the hot sun. Luz bought a melon, then rooted in her bag and set a couple of bottles of water in front of them. The one with a tiny topknot of wispy white hair said something and patted Luz's hand.

Next, Luz paused to admire a collection of birds in tiny bamboo cages mounted in a huge framework on the back of a grizzled barefoot Indian. She told the bird-seller she needed to get on with her shopping and said *adiós*. She came closer. Crisp white blouse, moisture on her cheek, a red hair ribbon. Closer still. A glint of gold, an ornate ring on her finger. Evan strolled toward her. Before he drew near, however, she skipped across the street. All he could do was turn and look after her as she walked away.

"*Señorita!*" A dozen faces—youthful, brown-skinned, expectant—turned. Luz walked on. "Luz! Wait a minute! Luz, is that you?"

She stopped, and her head swiveled round. Her eyebrows drew together, and she glanced around as if looking for someone she recognized.

"Hi, it's me, Evan. From the airport?" That should jog her memory.

She didn't run, but that was the only good news. He stuck out his hand. She put hers on her hips and squinted up at him. "Hello," he tried again, "remember me?"

Luz rotated her head in a tension-relieving arc. Then, with a sigh, she folded her arms in front of her chest. "I don't believe we've been properly introduced," she said finally.

"That's right. But we have a mutual friend. Richard Clement. I'm Evan McManus. I live here in Guatemala City." He moved his hand toward her, slowly. This time she took it, her fingers cool and dry.

"I'm Luz Aranda," she said, "and I live here, too."

"Richard asked me this morning if I'd seen you around."

"*Richard* did?"

Shit, I should have called him "Mr. Clement." This was business, after all. "Yes, he telephoned and happened to mention you shopped here."

Luz narrowed her eyes and tiny pearl-white teeth nibbled her lower lip. "He *happened to mention* that?"

Evan ducked his head and rubbed his forehead. *Richard would fire my ass if he heard me making such a mess of this introduction.* He cleared his throat. "What Richard said was, 'Meet her at the market this morning and talk.' So here I am."

"Ah." Luz puckered her face, as if weighing the odds he was telling the truth.

A donkey cart piled high with cartons of Coca-Cola pulled up on the sidewalk behind them. The bent old driver tossed the reins to a little girl sitting next to him on the wooden bench and jumped down to rebalance his cargo—and immediately got into a shouting match with the owner of the *tienda* whose outside displays he now blocked. Evan took Luz's rigid elbow and steered her to a quieter spot under the awning of a clothing store that hadn't yet opened for business.

Luz shrugged off his hand and stared at the sightless mannequins in the window. "*Bueno,*" she said. "Come on. I need to get a few things."

Evan hustled into step next to her before she could change her mind. The silent muse of his fantasy was even more striking than he remembered—her flawless skin glowing rosy under the cocoa surface, the perfect color balance between her hair, hair ribbon, and pristine white blouse. The very real and no-longer-silent woman walking beside him turned out to be a study in contrasts, too. Amateur she might be, but Luz was not intimidated. She wielded her words like a sharp knife—but with ironic detachment instead of malice.

"So, Evan McManus, what is it *you* want to talk about this morning?" Luz zinged the *you* with a head-toss, leaving no doubt who they

were really talking about, so Evan squelched *his* important question—
will you come to my studio so I can paint you?

Business first.

"Richard wants an inconspicuous way to touch base with you,"
Evan said quietly. "I got elected go-between. He wants a hang-out,
be-friends thing. So no one would think twice if they noticed you
handing me a small package—which is what you're supposed to do
with something you're getting for him."

Luz paused beside the doorway leading into the covered market.
Her eyebrows arched into twin half-moons. "Why didn't he contact
me himself?"

Thank goodness he didn't. Still, Luz had probably been brought in—
because she was Guatemalan? A woman?—for a job none of the regular personnel could do. Evan thought of one complication resulting
from that, so he asked, "Does Richard need to be careful about any
direct links between the two of you?"

"No freakin' clue."

The clipped New England accent and American slang so out of
place gave Evan the odd sensation of talking to an actor slipping momentarily out of character.

Luz abruptly swiveled on her heels and waded into the tumult of
the covered market. In the outermost ring, dozens of flower sellers
competed for attention: *"Mira, señores, señoras. Rosas hermosas y fra-
gantes. Los mejores precios. Mira."*

Luz didn't look back at him until she arrived at the meat and seafood vendors. Then she slowed and tapped her foot with an exaggerated display of impatience. This was starting to feel like a classic First
Date from Hell. He was going to have to try harder.

When he reached Luz, however, she said, "So we chat. I guess I
should ask how you come to be here."

"Here, like at the market or—"

She cut him off with a slicing backhand. "I know why you're *here*." Luz rotated an upturned palm to encompass the radiating lines of stalls where you could buy anything from a lemon to a cellphone, diapers to roofing nails.

Evan ran his fingers through his hair. *Focus.* He'd been gauging the proportions of Luz's shoulders in relation to her waist and hips, too distracted from the flow of conversation.

"Why are you here?" Luz repeated her question extra-loud and with the slow cadence Evan associated with boorish American tourists to Guatemala who assume *anyone* can understand English if you e-nun-ci-ate.

I *could* tell her why I get to be Richard's errand boy, Evan thought. Richard had never forbidden him to divulge personal information; it had just never come up before. But that could remain a last resort to keep her talking. So Evan said, "Well, I've lived in Guatemala for six years. I came on vacation, to paint, and stayed because of the light."

"The light," she said, as though *light* was not in her vocabulary, or was, at least, a novel concept. Then, for the first time, Luz looked right at him and smiled. "The light was what I missed most in the States, the way sunshine takes on a physical presence here. How it washes over the lakes and rivers, the mountains, the sky—and molds everything into this huge solid *presence*. It isn't anything like that in New Hampshire."

Evan came to an abrupt stop. The woman behind him stepped on his heel. He deflected her apology and waved her on her way, reeling in icy clarity, like the shock of an unexpected dunking in a cold mountain stream that dislodges and rearranges a host of unexamined assumptions. The last time Evan had trotted out that line had been at one of the mixers for Margo's new staff and the attractive young nurse—or lab tech or doctor, whatever—had smiled warmly at him and said, "Oh, a *painter*. How cool." Sometimes, "lucky you" was the response, said variously with jealousy or admiration.

But Luz—she got it.

"The 'staying for the light' thing?" blurted Evan. "It's, like, the short version for a quick introduction, at a bar, a party. No one's ever understood what I meant before." Her reply had opened the door wide, inviting Evan to enter. He whirled to face Luz. "Can I paint you?" he asked.

"Oh, I don't think so."

She hadn't hesitated. He pressed, "You said 'think.'"

"Well, then. I do *not* want you to paint me." Luz sidestepped around him and began walking up the aisle before she finished speaking.

Evan took two hurried paces and stopped in front of her. *Change her mind*—while being amiable and charming—had driven away all rational thought. "No, I meant you said you didn't think so, but you didn't take any time to consider it."

"In that case . . ." Luz scrunched her face into a cartoon version of deep concentration and tapped her index finger on her chin a half-dozen times. Then, opening her eyes wide and flashing a broad, insincere grin, she said, "Nope, don't think so."

"It's really important."

"Ask me later." Luz laughed. "Later." She started walking again. "You're not *only* here to paint," she added over her shoulder, not making it a question. "You're doing whatever for Uncle Sam—taking care of me and who knows what else."

Evan's face crinkled. Luz had just given him the perfect setup for his big disclosure. *That* should buy him more time to persuade her. "Actually, I'm doing it for Uncle Richard." He waited, watching her expression while she processed his words.

She rewarded him with a wide-eyed "*Uncle* Richard?"

"Yeah, he's my uncle. When I settled here, he asked me to keep an eye out for people passing through that he would send my way."

"People passing through."

Every time she repeated his words, he heard them as though they'd been translated from a foreign language.

But Luz had moved on, and again Evan had to play catch-up.

CHAPTER EIGHT

Luz set off at a brisk pace, frantically assessing whether to follow her normal routine, a path that would take her right past Juana's stall. It had taken Luz almost two weeks of patient conversation with the market ladies to establish that Juana was the right person, and Luz had the note for Juana in her pocket, folded with the money she would use to buy her oranges.

The man had screwed up everything.

First, instead of sending her off solo, as she'd expected—*and* counted on—Richard wanted to stay in touch. Even worse, he must be having her watched. Otherwise he wouldn't have known to direct Evan to the market. The stupid flash drive thing—that had to be the package Evan mentioned—was turning into a huge hassle. And, *Madre de Dios*, Richard's intermediary was none other than his nephew, a direct pipeline. Luz needed to be on her own. Richard would not approve of the other things she had to do.

Her first impulse was to abort and try later. The next day was Saturday, though, and another seller took Juana's place on the weekend. Luz guessed that was when Juana traveled home to see family, returning with fresh fruit. And information.

I can't wait another whole week. I'll have to get creative.

She *could* detour to the tourist market on the far side of the building where endless stalls of local crafts—brightly painted wooden masks, straw hats and baskets, ceramic angels, woven fabric, leather bags—might engross Evan long enough for her to slip away.

No, she couldn't count on him being that easy to lose, and she didn't want him getting suspicious. Better to get it over with. So Luz veered into the covered market at her usual entrance by the flower stalls, not to buy, but to be soothed by the harmony of their fragrance and rainbow hues.

They crossed into the food section. Slabs of meat dripping blood hung from overhead hooks, glistening fish on ice, live chickens in cages. Evan stayed a few paces behind her. Thank goodness he'd stopped trying to be her new best friend. Then once, when she turned back to check on him, he had disappeared. If she hurried, she'd have time to dash across two aisles to complete her mission with Juana.

No, darn it. Evan was only twenty feet away and coming toward her, his height making him an easy target in the four-foot-six to five-foot-six crowd. A wide smile lit his face, and his long arms were hidden behind his back. Luz, who'd already half-turned to continue bustling through the narrow aisles, paused. Something was up.

When Evan reached her, he whisked a bouquet of zinnias from behind his back. "For you," he said, with a bobbing half-bow. "I saw you looking at them as we passed."

Of course she'd been admiring the zinnias. Whenever money wasn't too tight, her mother often treated herself to a bunch, for the welcome burst of color in their otherwise drab apartment. Richard and Luz had both brought zinnias to the funeral.

Luz buried her nose in the flowers, equal parts touched and terrified by his perspicacity. Equally unwilling to let Evan see her tears. "Thanks. They're beautiful," she said when she could make her voice calm. But, Luz wondered, *what else will I inadvertently reveal?*

As they continued on their way with Evan strolling at her side, they progressed to small talk—favorite foods, Spanish words for the more exotic items on display. When Luz bought eggs, she asked where she might get a good price on sugar. The woman directed her down the corridor to a large stall with a yellow awning and a row of barrels out front.

"You don't have the sugar lady on your radar?" asked Evan.

"I haven't had to buy any before—in fact, I shouldn't even have to now. Whoever set up my apartment filled a big canister with sugar, but ants got into it. I tried to get rid of them, but they kept coming. I finally dumped it this morning. I'm going to start over. And this time, I'll keep it in the freezer."

Luz bought sugar. Around the corner, bread of all shapes and sizes. She bought a few *empanadas de leche* and some savory tarts. They entered the vegetable zone—tomatoes, garlic, onions, cucumbers, carrots, squashes, a thousand kinds of peppers, all stacked or piled in crates, baskets, and bowls. She chatted with the vendors, mainly older women wearing *huipiles,* intricately embroidered blouses, who scolded her about her eating habits and teased her about her skinny American friend. Evan parried their comments about his weight with ease, deftly mixing in Mayan words and addressing them properly as *ustedes*, rather than *vosotros*, which is taught in American schools. He must've faked his gringo accent on the bus the day she arrived. If he— if *Richard's nephew*—could do that, who knew what else he was faking, what else he was observing as they walked along.

Luz led them down another aisle. This time, fruit—mango, pineapple, papaya, oranges, bananas surrounded them. They neared the corner where Juana sat. Completing a few transactions had given Luz the glimmer of an idea.

"Señorita Luz," called Juana. She wore the traditional, boldly colored *traje* of women from the highlands, and her head was crowned with a bright purple *cinta*. "*Cómo está?*"

"*Bien, gracias, Juana.*" While she exchanged pleasantries with the old lady, Luz fleshed out her plan. "Juana's oranges come from her family's farm," she told Evan. "They're so sweet and juicy." Closing her hand around the prepared bundle of quetzal notes in her pocket, she said to Juana, "*Doce, por favor.*" Luz scooped a few oranges in her hand and, turning to Evan, held them up. "*Maravillosas, verdad?*"

At the same time, she let the change purse slip from her fingers. When it hit the cement floor, coins spilled and rolled in all directions. While Evan bent to retrieve her money, Luz handed over payment for the oranges, along with her note, before kneeling to help.

*   *   *

"How about coffee?" Evan asked as they left the market.

Luz stopped right in the middle of the sidewalk and turned to face him. A stream of exiting shoppers flowed around them. "Listen, Evan, I'm not sure of the rules. Maybe there aren't any, but are we supposed to know each other more than neighbors running into each other occasionally?"

Surely, Richard's instructions—casual meetings at the market—could be stretched to include coffee. While the flowers had smoothed Luz's prickles, she'd continued to parry his attempts to discuss drawing her. Maybe if they had a chance to relax, sip some coffee, he'd find the right words to persuade her.

"I think a coffee now and then would be fine," he said. "And perhaps you'd let me get out my sketch pad?" He tacked on what he hoped was a no-pressure grin. "Whaddaya say, Luz?"

"Coffee, yes. Sketch pad, no."

The smile dancing around the corners of her mouth curved her lips. Challenging, inviting. Confusing—like he'd stumbled into an amusement park funhouse where mirrors multiplied and magnified those rounded lips, slightly parted.

Kiss her. The thought walloped Evan squarely between the shoulder blades, shoving him forward. He staggered, his breath caught in his throat, and he masked the shiver of desire by shuffling his feet, as though he'd tripped. *Bad idea.* Anything more than café and market meetings and he'd be walking a tightrope of careful half-truths. He shook away the impulse; those tiny images of Luz and her red lips distorting his vision dissipated like popping bubbles. When they had all vanished, Evan matched her smile with one of his own. "Come on," he said. "There's a café down the street." As Luz fell into step next to him, he asked, "How long will you be in town?"

"Oh, I'll be gone before Christmas," she said.

Almost a month. He could get the painting done by then, channeling his sexual tension onto the canvas. Then she'd be gone, his life could go on undisturbed—and he'd have the centerpiece for his mural. He ought to observe Luz in different lighting conditions, though. "How about getting together tomorrow evening?"

"Sorry," she said, not sounding the least bit apologetic. "I work evenings."

She has a job. She comes to the market in the morning. Evan's smile widened. *She's staying until Christmas. I can make this happen.*

Back off now; no need to press. "Oh, where do you work?" Evan asked.

"I don't suppose it hurts to tell you." Luz laughed. "I'm the nanny for Martin Benavides' grandson, Cesar."

"The Benavides?" Evan hoped he didn't give away how startled he was at Richard sending Luz into that nest of vipers. He knew the stories. Hell, everyone in Guatemala did—how the old man had betrayed each of his allies in turn, displaying their bullet-ridden bodies as a warning to others. How he'd parlayed political power into a personal fortune and used both to forge distribution alliances with South American drug cartels. Making him ever richer and more powerful. Sure, his supporters pointed to how the family plowed money back into the country—roads, bridges, dams, schools—but it was dirty money, distributed tit-for-tat with complicit local strongmen.

"Yeah, Richard couldn't have found a better job for me," she said.

A better job for what? Evan had never allowed himself to think about the people who crossed his path because of his errands for Richard, preferring to keep a comfortable distance from their world. Until now. Until Luz. "Isn't that dangerous?" he asked.

"The closest I get to danger is being hit in the head with a soccer ball." She laughed again.

But Evan could've sworn she flinched—a momentary hiccup, like an engine stalling out—before she recovered and laughed. Despite his limited exposure to the covert world of U.S. intelligence, Evan knew you didn't insert an agent into such a tightly guarded situation merely to play babysitter. "Richard didn't say anything about the Benavides when he was here last month."

"Richard was here?"

"Yeah, he stayed with me for a week at the end of October. Oh—" Memories from his uncle's visit coalesced: Richard arranging an account with *Empresa Eléctrica*, ordering furniture over the phone. "I bet he set up your apartment then."

"I wondered if you'd done that," said Luz, with a soft smile.

That tingle of excitement again. This time, desire mingled with his concerns, and Evan let the awareness linger. "No, I don't know where you live. I'd love to stop by, though."

*　*　*

After dodging their way across the crowded street, they grabbed a table in the shade of a striped awning. She really should have turned down Evan's invitation, but having accomplished the mission with Juana, heady exhilaration tempted Luz to play hooky. She had time to kill before work, and after weeks of isolation and play-acting in a stressful role, she was having fun.

It was more than merely the chance to let down her guard. Luz had spent the better part of two decades resenting the loss of her native tongue and culture, but it had taken only a short time back in Guatemala to realize those two decades had changed her forever. At the Benavides', in the market, with neighbors, Luz was constantly reaching into the dim recesses of her past to recall grown-up words and phrasing to substitute for the child's Spanish vocabulary she possessed, forever fearful of making a mistake that would brand her a foreigner, or worse, an impostor.

But with Evan—speaking English, the language of her adolescent put-downs, her adult flirtations—the words tripped effortlessly from her tongue. Her evasions and lies were crisp; her repartee, witty. This morning, she was smarter, funnier. Sexier.

They ordered coffees, and then there was that awkward moment when they started speaking at the same time—like the promising, but uncoordinated, stumbling of a first date. They both stopped and motioned the other to continue. Luz laughed. The weight of her masquerade slipped away. Goose bumps raised on her skin, as if a cool breeze had brushed her.

"Ladies first." Evan zipped an index finger across his mouth.

"Is Richard really your uncle?" She needed to clear *that* up immediately.

"Yeah," said Evan. "He's my mother's brother. My dad died when I was in high school, so Richard looked after us. He traveled for work a lot and couldn't always be there, but he didn't miss much—holidays, science fairs, school plays, baseball games. We did some great camping trips in the summer."

The waiter brought their coffees then and bustled around, refilling the saucer of sugar cubes and emptying the ashtray. While Luz stirred the lump of sugar into her coffee, she surreptitiously studied Evan. Now that she looked for it, the resemblance between him and Richard was unmistakable—both men tall and fair, slender with broad shoulders. Evan's face was narrower and sprinkled with freckles, however, his eyebrows tamer, and his hair a more subdued color than Richard's startling bright-penny copper that had spooked Luz when they first met. It was weird, seeing a younger Richard in this man she hardly knew. And it was galling that he'd actually gone camping with Richard, while Richard had only *arranged* summer camp for her.

Stop it, Luz. They're family. Richard was paid *to watch over you— and he went far beyond what was strictly necessary.*

"I've known Richard since I was a kid," she said, in apology for her uncharitable thoughts. "He was the man the State Department assigned to relocate my mother and me. Part of his job was to check in on us regularly, but even after he retired from State, he visited several times a year. He always came around my birthday. I'd get all dressed up, and we'd go off to a fancy restaurant."

Luz wasn't going to share what had happened at her last birthday lunch. Richard had taken her to their favorite place, an elegant bistro overlooking Portsmouth Harbor. It was raining, and the harbor appeared misty and monochromatic, like an old photograph. Over gourmet hamburgers in the almost empty restaurant, he had woven his Benavides web and snared her in it. If Evan believed she was just another one of the "people passing through," then Richard hadn't told him what she was doing in Guatemala.

* * *

Evan took a cab home, his thoughts darting like mating dragonflies. Despite her reluctance to model, Luz agreed to rendezvous at the market. He figured he could eventually persuade her to sit for a portrait. If not, second best would be to spend time with her, memorizing lines and shades to re-create on canvas later.

Meanwhile, it was all good. He loved the incongruity between her Guatemalan exterior and her idiomatic English with those flat New England vowels. Her odd twists of conversation, as though she saw beneath some surface he was barely aware existed.

But then she'd said something Evan *knew* was false. She was lying. Or she didn't know the truth. He'd never questioned Richard about an assignment—and for all he knew Richard would tell him to butt out—but he had to at least try to find out.

Evan ran up his steps two at a time. He punched in Richard's number but got a secretary: Mr. Clement was away. Did Mr. McManus have a message for him?

"No," Evan said. "I need to ask him a question."

Would Mr. McManus care to leave the question with her? She would be happy to relay to Mr. Clement when he checked in.

"When will that be?"

The secretary was insincerely sorry, but she couldn't say.

Mr. McManus said no thank you, but please tell him I called.

Evan dropped the phone and stood staring out the back window. He'd have to wait.

CHAPTER NINE

The extra time at the market, flirting with Evan, a missed bus. Luz arrived late for work. Delores, still the only smiling face Luz regularly encountered, saw her running down the hall and, with silent complicity, broke a cardinal rule by keying in the code and then holding open the elevator for her.

"*Gracias,*" Luz panted.

Upstairs, she jogged to the end of the hall and opened the door to Cesar's suite. Singing in the bedroom? It wasn't like punctilious Father Espinosa to stay even one minute late—and singing, too. But before Luz processed the dissonance, she burst into the room, and all the dread she'd kept at bay—and the atmosphere of danger she'd denied to Evan—rocked her like an earthquake. She tripped over the claw-foot of Cesar's bureau. The man whose face she would never forget sat in the big yellow armchair with Cesar on his lap. He was older, yes, and a receding hairline exposed more of his domed forehead, but the hawk-like nose and wide-set eyes, eyes Luz had once believed could see into the shadows, were unmistakable. Even reclining with slippers on his feet, his barrel chest and muscular arms looked strong enough to crush Cesar.

The singing stopped. He frowned at her. Martin Benavides would recognize *her*, too. She'd never reach the door in time, never get as far as the gate. Luz couldn't even turn her head. She was beyond foolish to believe she was strong enough to stand up to him. Her vision blurred as she relived the night of her father's death, the last time she'd seen Martin Benavides: far-off staccato blasts, screams, incandescent flashes, her mother's hand yanking her to safety.

No. Not now. This was *her* time to prevail. To kill. She had to regain her composure. Luz put a hand on the bureau to steady herself. "I didn't know—"

"Of course not," interrupted Martin Benavides, with a dismissive sweep of his hand. A flick of his wrist; a machete flashed in firelight. Luz shivered once more. "I sent the good Father home early today. My heart has been heavy, and nothing soothes me more than spending time with Cesar."

Martin Benavides wrapped his arm around his grandson, and his hand—the hand that had murdered her father—squeezed the child to his chest. "Eh, Cesar," he said. "We had fun this morning."

"Yes, *Papi*." The boy wiggled happily and called to Luz, "Would you play the piano for us? We can sing *Papi*'s favorite songs."

Sing? Play? Luz's hands were shaking badly.

Martin stood and tipped Cesar to his feet, keeping one of the boy's small hands tucked into his large paw. "Do you know '*Y en Eso Llegó Fidel*'?" he asked Luz.

"Of . . . of course." She couldn't look at him. *I will do this for my father*, Luz told herself, as she dropped onto the piano bench and began, at first hesitantly, to play the revolutionary favorite about Fidel Castro wresting control of Cuba from those who, according to the lyrics, lived in luxurious houses and didn't care if the people suffered.

Luz let Martin and Cesar belt out the words. She only got through the interminable verses by silently reviling Martin. *Murderer. Liar.* Two-faced hypocrite who traded an honest workingman's life for one of those fancy houses, whose traffic in illegal drugs inflamed the

suffering of thousands. They sang about land reform and income dis-
parity, about young people making their voices heard. *Exploiter.*
Tyrant. Crook.

Panic subsided; anger took wing.

After they exhausted Martin's repertoire of protest songs, they
sang hymns, children's counting songs. Cesar asked for "*Submarino
Amarillo*," which prompted a segue into the Beatles repertoire. They
sang until Martin said his throat was too dry. Then they played checkers and Monopoly, Martin's hands moving the little markers as precisely as he wielded a machete. A game.

Martin's mouth, the same Martin who had shouted in the forest
"No prisoners!" called out "You won!" and insisted on a treat from
the kitchen in honor of Cesar's coup. The cook sent up blood-red watermelon and the three of them sat, sticky juice dripping down their
arms, spitting seeds out the window.

*　*　*

Later, Luz blamed what happened that night on coming face-to-face
with the man who'd fueled the nightmares that still woke her, crying
in sweaty confusion. Cesar's need for a soothing routine kept her
going through the familiar motions until his night nurse relieved her
at bedtime, but as Luz returned home, fragments of memory, disorga-
nized and unwelcome, overtook the present.

She stopped for an uncharacteristic bottle of rum. Her father had
never drunk rum, although most of the other men did. They'd gather
around a fire in the evening, with a bottle and cigarettes, and clean
their rifles. Luz hung outside the circle and listened to their stories
about the resistance and about the people they loved, the people they
fought for. Those men died in the mountains.

Luz cried for them as her key fumbled in the lock.

Turning on only a small table lamp, Luz squeezed oranges into the rum and sat in the dark as she had done the night of her mother's death. Next to her, the silver frames of her family photographs glinted. Luz picked up the one in the middle. Although she couldn't recall who had taken it, she remembered precisely when. They'd gone into a town. Luz and her father walked around the plaza, and he bought her a small cup of strawberry ice cream for a treat. When her mother rejoined them, she was excited, her cheeks flushed. Apparently, that was enough of a signal for her father to wrap his arms around her and kiss her. Later, over another treat—*caldo de pollo* at a small restaurant— they told Luz she was going to be a big sister. She was too young, that morning, to understand any more than her parents' joy.

Not long after, however, Luz returned to their tent to find her mother moaning, the blanket around her bloodied. She'd rushed out to find help. The women who came called for her father. Gradually, Luz understood the baby growing inside her mother hadn't managed to live. In fact, her mother had almost died from the loss of blood.

"At least I have you," her mother said after the other women had taken care of everything. She picked up Luz's hand and squeezed it, but she was looking at her husband. Although it was the cancer that finally stopped her heart, her mother had died of heartache, of loneliness.

And so Luz cried for her mother.

Of her entire family, only she survived. In the last months of her life, Luz's mother had sprinkled many rambling reminiscences with "and when we all meet in heaven," but Luz didn't expect to be reunited with anyone. Heaven didn't figure into the sort of world where men murdered children with impunity—worse, they murdered them, achieved victory, and lived long and prosperous lives. Whether her parents were at peace, Luz didn't know. She could only say for sure that their struggles had come to an end.

Not hers. Tomorrow, she had to go to work.

And so, finally, she cried for herself.

Luz had just gotten out of the shower, her cheeks still splotchy from tears even though she had scalded herself until the water ran tepid, when Evan called.

"Hi, remember me?" he said, unmistakable eagerness mixed with a touch of self-deprecating humor sparkled in his soft voice. "I was going to go out for a beer and hoped I might persuade you to come along."

Tonight, Luz didn't care what Evan knew or who he knew or what his agenda was. She needed not to be alone with her memories. Tonight, there would be nightmares, ghosts would arise, and she didn't want to sleep alone. By tomorrow, when the sun shone once more, she would have the demons under control.

She said, "It's late. Come over here instead. You said you wanted to see my place."

* * *

Evan woke to cool morning air. Motion under the covers as Luz inched away from him. He reached out a hand and caught her wrist. "Mmmm."

"No, Evan. I've got to get up." She squirmed out of his grasp. "You, too." Luz flicked on the bathroom light, turned on the faucet, bent over the sink—a da Vinci nude in chiaroscuro, brushing her teeth.

Luz had taken his hand in hers last night to draw him inside her door in a way that *could* have been casual friendliness. She led him to the sofa and sat next to him, not relinquishing his hand.

"Beer?" she asked, but she lifted her face toward him, voice faint and eyes half-closed.

Gone was the aloof Luz from the bus, the prickly Luz from the market. Gravity, the inexorable pull of a dying star, curved his body toward her. If unchecked, momentum would soon overtake all reason and caution. He had only to say yes to the beer, and she'd release him.

Luz increased the pressure on his hand.

Nobody has that much self-control. "Nah," he said. "I'm good."

Her free hand, feather-light, reached across his body and traced a line down his cheek, neck, across his chest. Her thumb grazed his nipple. Evan pulled her toward him. Luz's hand slid under his shirt. And Evan was lost.

He couldn't remember how they'd gotten to her bedroom. Evan stood and pulled on his pants, discarded by the nightstand. He found his shirt in a ball behind a couch cushion.

Such a tiny place, but the simple, modern furniture and bright native fabrics suited her. Of course, Richard set it up for her—Richard who'd known her since she was a girl, Richard who no doubt had arranged a space he thought Luz would like. Richard who'd placed her in the fortress-like residence of one of the most-feared families in Guatemala where she was going to *get something* for him.

God, this could go wrong so many different ways. I should never have come over. Should've asked for that beer and kept my mind on painting.

It didn't feel like the huge mistake it could become, though. Being with Luz felt natural; inevitable, even. Fantastic. *He* felt fantastic. Besides, she didn't have to be at work for hours, and he certainly didn't need to hurry home. The bathroom door stood open. Luz, in silhouette now, behind the shower curtain. Luz reaching to lift her hair, bending to let warm water stream over her. Her body slick, naked. Evan hesitated two steps into the bathroom. Better not screw up by expecting morning-after sex. He'd prove he wasn't just some horny guy—he'd make breakfast instead.

Evan could reach everything in the kitchen by standing in the middle. In the refrigerator he found eggs, cheese, and an onion. He'd make an omelet, fry a few slices of ham. Coffee? The bright red canisters on the counter were empty. The freezer—yes, there was coffee and sugar, safe from pests. Evan rummaged through the drawers until he found knives. He had just set down the cutting board when Luz walked in wearing shorts and a T-shirt, a towel wrapped around her hair.

"What are you doing?"

"Making breakfast. You *do* eat breakfast, don't you?"

"I told you it was time for you to go." A deep furrow he'd never seen before creased her brow.

"You didn't give me a chance to answer." Evan was winging it. His Mr. Nice Guy persona was probably best. "I thought you might let me whip up breakfast for us. You must be starving."

"Evan, listen—"

"No, I won't. Go dry your hair while I chop vegetables."

As Luz neared the counter to survey his preparations, Evan laid his arm on her shoulder. She sighed but didn't pull away, so he looped his other arm around her waist. Luz gave another little sigh, more of a hum this time, and leaned into him. Evan tugged at the fold holding the towel in place. It fell, and her hair spilled out. He ran his fingers through the ringlets, then twisted them into a knot, inching closer all the while.

Her tongue licked the triangle at the base of his neck. Evan shuddered as heat built between their bodies.

They made the omelet together, later, and called it brunch. Luz withdrew again while they were eating. She was gearing up for her day, Evan thought. For whatever she was involved with at the Benavides'.

* * *

When Evan finally left, Luz showered again and hurriedly dressed for work. He was sweet, and his passion had released long-stifled desires—as though, at the point of asphyxia, a cool breeze had revived

her. But this morning had not been in her plans, and Luz cursed herself for again indulging in careless emotions. Now, she was going to
have the devil of a time getting rid of him. On the other hand, he was
young and strong and, well, *sweet*, and it had been a while.

This morning, her head was clear and her trembling muscles strong.
She could face the Benavides this morning.

CHAPTER TEN

Evan had sketched in a rough outline after returning from the market the day before. Now, after a night and a morning with Luz, her scent of cinnamon and lemon on his skin, he stood in front of the canvas and redrew a few lines. Erased them and tried again. Luz's face, particularly her nose, still wasn't right.

Evan backed away from the canvas and squinted at it from his ratty green upholstered chair. He tried a different angle, moving to his little table along the rear wall where, systematically cracking his knuckles, he contemplated the charcoal sketch.

It looked nothing like Luz. *What was wrong?*

He tried the yoga exercise a long-ago girlfriend had taught him. Closing his eyes, he began a systematic relaxation of his body—shoulders and arms, neck, chest, lips, cheeks, mouth, tongue, jaw. Usually that was sufficient, but today the image of Luz burned a hole through his eyelids. And when he persisted with the centering exercise and tried to relax his hands, he found he was absently finger-drumming.

Restless hands and eyes—not a good place to begin painting. He needed distance from the inadequate charcoal figure in his living room as well as from the vivid memories of Luz in bed. Evan traded his felt slippers for sneakers and tucked his house key into a pocket.

He walked outside and jogged past the card-players who'd set up a table in front of the convenience store on the corner.

His house, a sort of Guatemalan-style condo, comprised the first floor of one residence in a long row of jewel-toned townhouses. It was an older neighborhood, recently discovered by artists and other expats, who were gradually crowding out Guatemalan families. Although "crowding" was not the right word: The expats—singles, couples, the odd threesome—replaced families who lived three generations together, and often ran a small business out of the front room as well. Evan's section, painted a buttery yellow with aqua trim, sat between that of an elderly British couple—rose with white accents—and a bicycle shop—largely unpainted, with scabrous patches of flaking stucco.

Past the women doing laundry at the outdoor tubs in the little square. Past the little girls jumping rope in the dusty schoolyard to the shouts of their counting rhyme—*A la una, anda la mula. A las dos, tira la coz. A las tres, tira otra vez* ... and on and on until the jumping girl missed. Past the cemetery, a quiet neighbor. Evan turned right into a maze of tiny cobbled streets that straggled up the hill and ran on the narrow, paved sidewalk shaded by elms. He tried to quicken his pace, but it was as though he had ten-pound weights attached to his ankles. Gradually, his scattered thoughts dropped away. He slowed mentally. By the end of the first mile, Evan was latching onto splashes of color—cinnabar in the shadows of the earthen walls, lemon ochre for the brilliant autumn leaves, the sky a wash of lazurite ... *colors*.

The oppressive weight melted. Nothing was wrong with the painting he'd started. The problem was that it existed only in black and white, while the living Luz was a feast of color. Pozzuoli red for her lips, raw umber for the highlights of her skin, and for the underside of curves, one of the earth tones—perhaps hematite or a burnt umber.

Yes, the painting would be fine, but he was going to have to compartmentalize like crazy to visualize Luz solely in terms of pigment.

He'd counted on the thrill of their nascent attraction to concentrate every last bit of creativity into her portrait. Sex with Luz—with Richard's agent, for crissakes—could so easily get complicated. Not, Evan thought, as a long slow smile curved his lips, not that he'd resisted.

Evan slowed to a walk and headed home. Now he had a month to get her out of his system and finish the damn portrait.

On his return, Evan showered quickly, then picked up a clean palette. He arranged the colors he wanted and brushed in the background. The light failed about the same time he ran out of energy.

Sounds of laughter from across the street. His neighbors with the big-screen TV were lugging it out to the front steps, and another family set up their outdoor cooker, an oil drum sliced in half on a rickety stand. Already a crowd had gathered to watch tonight's football game. They'd cheer together, boo, second-guess the refs, passing around roasted chicken and bottles, children running around, babies sleeping.

Evan nuked a plate of leftover lasagna and ate it standing at the counter, his gaze swinging from clock to door. He washed the single plate and fork. At nine, when he thought Luz would be home, he called.

One ring. *He could be cool, just ask about her day—Hi, how was work?*

She picked up the phone, her breathing shallow and rapid, her voice high. *"Aló?"*

Two syllables. They vibrated through his body, knocking out his levelheaded plan. "I want to see you," he said.

"Come. I'm waiting." She closed the connection.

Evan shoved on his sneakers and loped through the quiet streets. He buzzed at her gate. With an immediate answering clack, the automatic lock disengaged. Luz had her front door open. When he got close, she stepped into his arms and buried her face in his shirt. As much as he'd like to imagine her fierceness was pure desire, red blotches marred her cheeks, and she quivered like a candle flame.

There'd been a desperate intensity to her unexpected passion the night before. Now tears and trembling. Luz—the amateur—tangled up in some godawful mess of Richard's. Whatever the complications, whatever the consequences to him, Evan resolved to ease her distress. So he folded his long arms around Luz and stroked her hair, letting her take the comfort she needed from his embrace.

When she calmed, Evan lifted her in a bear hug and half-carried her inside. He slammed the door shut with a well-placed kick, shutting out the darkness. They stood in a cone of golden light from a small lamp next to her couch. Luz began to unbutton his shirt and slid her fingers over his sweat-slicked skin. Her mouth found his, and she kissed him as though only the bond of their lips kept her from falling into the abyss.

Finally, they slept, sprawled on the sheets in Luz's tiny bedroom, the fan cycling lazily overhead.

*   *   *

It was the next afternoon, Sunday, Luz's day off. Evan, hoping to see her in soft, natural daylight for a change—and to escape the temptations of her bedroom, for crying out loud—had invited Luz on a picnic to the Botanical Gardens. They'd taken the self-guided tour of the gardens, wandered briefly into the museum, and now they lay in the shade of a massive *caoba*, an ancient mahogany encircled with vines.

Luz lay on her back with her chin tilted toward the sky. "What's the earliest thing you remember?" she asked, another in the string of offbeat questions she'd been tossing at him all day. Waiting for his answer, Luz rolled onto her side and tickled his cheek with a blade of grass.

"That's a funny story," said Evan. "For years, I thought I remembered my birthday party when I turned one year old. Everyone told me you don't start having memories until you're two or three, but I swore I remembered it all: the little jumper-seat I sat in, the red and blue spinning things on it. I wore a striped shirt and the cake was chocolate with white frosting with one big fat red candle in the middle.

"One day when I was a teenager, though, I found some old pictures in the bottom drawer of a big chest in our dining room. And *one* of the pictures," Evan said, rolling toward Luz and laying his hand on her hip, "was a photograph of that birthday party—my striped shirt, the cake and candle. Exactly as I remembered it. I must've seen the picture when I was little. I should have known—because in my memory, I could *see myself*, see my face like I was looking at myself. I was already painting a lot, and that nudged me to start exploring questions of how we see and what we see."

Luz inched nearer. "So is there a *real* first memory somewhere?"

Evan wrapped his arm around and caressed her back. "I think it's holding my father's hand as I walked on a stone wall at the base in North Carolina. We moved there when I was three, so that fits. I don't see myself, but I see my father, see him holding my hand."

"Where's your dad now?"

Luz was close enough to kiss, but instead, Evan found himself wanting to prolong this peaceful interlude in the grass. "He died in a car accident. I was fourteen."

"Oh, right. I remember you said he died when you were young—something we have in common, our fathers dying as we were becoming adults."

"What happened to your father?"

"A soldier hacked off his arm with a machete, and he bled to death."

CHAPTER ELEVEN

Luz had tried hard all day to deflect the personal questions Evan lobbed at her. He kept circling around why she came to Guatemala, what she was doing here, her job with the Benavides, her relationship with Richard. Perhaps it was genuine curiosity, but after a crash course with Richard and his cronies and two weeks in the secretive world of Martin Benavides, she had developed a healthy mistrust for face value.

Now, one fucking second of distraction—and she'd blurted out her most personal, life-defining moment. Evan's head had jerked back; a tiny nervous smile hovered at the corners of his mouth.

Luz sat up and held out her palms like twin stop signs. "I'm so sorry. I shouldn't—it's still—can we *please* talk about something else? I'd rather hear more about how you got started painting."

Evan eased himself to seated, keeping a barrier of grassy space between them. Possibly, the change of subject came as a welcome relief to him, too, for he began speaking quickly. What an idiot she was to get lulled into such ridiculous vulnerability. No matter how good-looking or how artlessly sincere he seemed, she should not have allowed him behind her defenses.

When she tuned back in, Evan was saying "and once I began to lighten the dark shadows, my palette became clearer and cleaner. My paintings began to sell, too. The light, that's what it's all about."

"You're a funny man," said Luz, seizing the new topic. "So this morning, when you were kissing the Luz in bed with you, you were thinking about *la luz*, the light, instead."

"But, no, you misunderstand," said Evan. He turned to look directly at her and ran his thumb along her jawline, tilting her head so she appeared to be nodding no and then yes, then no again. "You *are* '*la luz*' for me—inspiration, model, guide."

Deep inside, Luz experienced a sensation of unraveling. Teardrops scalded her eyelids, not the angry and alone and sorrowful tears that had devoured her the previous nights. These tears welled up from the spring of hope. An insubstantial, wispy wraith released from imprisonment as though by some magic incantation, reached from her center, hands outstretched, supplicating: *Save me.*

"In that case, when are you going to show me what you're working on?"

* * *

Oh. A little too late, Evan tuned into the flow of Luz's parries: get too close, and she'd fend you off with one of those *non sequitors* she'd peppered him with all morning.

"It's complicated," he said finally.

"You don't want me to see? What, you think I'll look at your paintings and decide you stink?"

Best to let Luz think that was the reason, since she'd thought of it herself. His home was off limits.

* * *

Luz didn't want Evan anywhere near the Benavides', so most nights she met him at a funky neighborhood bar near her bus stop. The bar was open to the street—a rough plank railing, chest-high, formed the outer limit and payment was strictly in advance. Evan would rest his beer on the railing, one eye on the local toughs playing pool, but Luz could tell he was really watching for her. He'd drain his beer and join her as she walked by. They'd rush to her house and shed their clothes.

Martin Benavides had only visited Cesar twice. His first visit, when they sang songs, had been bad enough, but then he came back the next afternoon and joined them outdoors to watch Cesar play soccer. Luz—the only other player, of course—had been made to run the field while he looked on, genial and shouting hearty encouragement.

Running up and down, until she was panting.

Running.

Running for her life in the dark, shouts and screams all around. Running holding her mother's hand, both their hands slick with blood that dried before the U.S. soldiers loaded them into the helicopter, so their hands remained glued together as their old life receded and then shrank to a cartoon pinhole of nothingness in the space of a few seconds.

If Evan hadn't called again that night, she would have gone crazy.

But Martin's disruptions had not been repeated. More nights—and mornings—of wildly inventive sex had cleared the cobwebs from her head. The tremor in her left hand diminished. Her legs carried her effortlessly. It was only sex, but as an antidote to the stresses of her days, nights with Evan were just what the doctor ordered.

*   *   *

Evening, night, breakfast, market, paint. Repeat.

At first, evenings were simple. As they hurried to Luz's, they talked about their day—at least, *he* did. Luz shared nothing about the Benavides except the occasional cute-kid Cesar story. One evening,

Evan was telling her about an artist friend who'd invited him to work on a mural in *Cuatro Grados Norte*.

"What's that?" Luz asked.

"You don't know?"

"C'mon, Evan. You know I've never lived in the city before."

"I keep forgetting." He stretched his arm alongside hers, pale against chocolate. "It's too weird that *I'm* the old Guatemala hand."

Luz pulled her arm back and rolled her eyes the way she did when he teased her.

Evan grabbed her hand. "No, listen—it's a cool place, the Brooklyn of Guatemala City, lots of street art, shops, cafés, galleries. Let's go."

"Now?" But Luz looked more intrigued about the excursion than scandalized he'd suggest an outing when her bed was so close.

"Sure, it's the late-night place to be." Evan tugged Luz so they were walking in the opposite direction. "C'mon."

At first, Evan played tour guide. They strolled through the well-lit pedestrian area in the heart of *Zona Cuatro*, in and out of galleries. Then, an eerie flute melody rising above a syncopated marimba beat caught their attention.

Luz pressed a finger to her lips. "Shhh," she said. "That's . . . that's . . ." She stretched out her other hand as though she would grasp the fragment of mislaid memory. Then, giving her head a decisive toss, she took Evan's arm and unerringly followed the music to an out-of-the-way corner where they found a family of Kaqchikel Maya street musicians. Evan thought he could've disappeared for all Luz, swaying to the beat, noticed him. After a long while, she sidled up behind him and dug her hands deep into his pants pockets—tantalizingly—but only to retrieve coins to toss into the straw hat set out for tips.

Another evening, they took a cab downtown and mingled with the elegantly dressed high-rollers as they descended from their limos and sauntered into the nightclubs and casinos. When Luz tired of the glitz, they walked along the wide median parkway of the *Avenida La Reforma*, and made out under the *Torre del Reformador*, a small copy of the Eiffel Tower.

They spent Luz's day off in a crowd of local families wandering around *La Aurora* Zoo, Luz mugging for silly photos with the lions and tigers and bears. Later, they lingered over sushi, playing footsie while they sat shoeless on low cushions at a Japanese place across from the park.

Mornings were for the market. Luz seldom needed to buy much. It seemed she went as much to socialize as to buy food. Although she occasionally brushed him off, Evan became adept at inventing errands of his own—he needed bread, light bulbs, a new pair of sneakers—so he could tag along.

And the painting was exhilarating.

*   *   *

Guate, as Evan called it, was a much more varied and interesting city than Luz imagined. Her neighborhood could be any place in the world where people had locked gates instead of front lawns, and the Benavides' compound could be on the freaking moon for all it had to do with Guatemala. For weeks, she'd done nothing but shuttle between the two.

The city itself, however, sprawled like a drunkard taking a siesta. Exploring with Evan whetted her appetite, but Luz needed to experience it on her own, as a Guatemalan, rather than on the arm of a skinny Anglo. She began leaving for work early and taking buses to other parts of the city. The *Zona Viva* with its upscale malls. *La Linea*, the red-light district, with train tracks running between tiny houses. The University campus.

She also returned alone to *Cuatro Grados Norte*. Evan had compared it to Brooklyn, a place she'd never been, but to Luz it seemed like an edgier, more boisterous Portsmouth. Daytime brought out jugglers on stilts weaving through the pedestrians and an eclectic variety of street performers. One exhilarating morning, Luz joined a group dancing an impromptu *samba* line around a six-piece jazz band, just like she belonged here. Energized, she gave up her seat on the bus to a bent old woman carrying a mammoth sack of exquisite embroidery. She greeted the guards at the Benavides' mansion with a mock salute and a cheerful *buenos tardes*.

Her buoyancy lasted until she arrived at Cesar's room. He sat cross-legged on his sitting-room rug in a damp puddle of dejection. "My father got home last night."

Okay. Bobby was back. He'd sent word, once, twice, that he was "tied up in meetings" and would stop by later. If he had time. And then he was gone again. Cesar had brandished an expensive new remote-control race car and the subdued expression of a crestfallen child.

"So why the long face?" asked Luz.

"He isn't up yet."

"And?"

"And he doesn't answer the door when I knock. And Delores won't use her key to let me in."

Luz looked around. Delores had gotten an early start. She stood, bucket and mop in hand, in the door to Cesar's bedroom shaking her head *no*, mouthing *no*, shifting her elbows and hips side to side in a whole-body *no, no, no.*

Luz got the idea. "You'd better let him sleep this morning. He's been traveling. I bet he's tired."

"But I want to see him. Why can't we go now?"

Why indeed? There was no good answer, only prurient speculation, so Luz went for distraction. "While we wait for your father to get up, how about starting today with football practice—unless you want to finish your lessons first."

Cesar jumped up. "Could we practice throw-ins again?"

Luz pretended to consider. "Sure, but you have to change into shorts and a T-shirt."

"What's going on?" Luz asked, the second the two women were alone.

"Whew." Delores wiped mock perspiration from her brow. "That was close. Cesar wouldn't let it go. I don't know how he knew Señor Roberto had returned. He's been pestering me ever since I arrived, and when I bent over to scrub the bathtub, he grabbed my key ring. It's a miracle he didn't get it today like he sometimes does."

Luz lost her remaining bounce and crashed to earth as she drilled Cesar on the correct form for inbounding the ball. Sex. Blue skies. Even her clear head and dancing feet. It was only a reprieve, the calm before the storm. Bobby was back. The briefcase was back. Delores' keys were vulnerable. Cesar occasionally stole them and snooped. And—miracle of miracles—as Martin Benavides had said *adios* the afternoon he'd watched their football practice, he himself had given Luz a marvelous idea that should get her into his lair. She'd been too upset to jump on it then, but she'd begun making casual suggestions. The bomb would go off on time.

CHAPTER TWELVE

The mattress shifted. Luz muttered in Spanish, something Evan didn't quite catch. He stroked her smooth back while she sat on the side of the bed, invisible in the moonless night. "You okay?" he whispered.

Luz moaned and arched her back. Then she stood quickly, and her feet slapped on tile as she ran into the bathroom, retching. The noises stopped, but when the bathroom door finally opened, she padded out into the living room and turned on the small table lamp. Her elongated shadow writhed on the walls.

Evan followed Luz into the living room. She sat slumped sideways on the sofa, forehead resting on a fat cushion, arms wrapped around the swell of her breasts. "What's wrong?" he asked. While she had occasional bouts of what appeared to be vertigo, Luz had never vomited before.

Instead of answering, Luz rushed past him, back to the bathroom. This time, she returned to bed instead of joining Evan on the sofa.

When he entered the bedroom, she said, "Go away. It's my stomach—everything's going to come up, and I don't want you to watch me puking."

Montezuma's Revenge, thought Evan. *Delhi Belly*. "It must've been those *chuchitos* we bought last night," he said. "You had more of them than I did. It's almost funny—you, the native, getting sick on the local bacteria."

Luz rolled over and glowered. "Yeah, well, as everyone keeps reminding me, I've been gone for a long time. And it is *not* funny." She turned away from him and buried herself under the covers.

* * *

Luz had seen the sign dozens of times by now. In ornate gilt letters on the second floor of the building across the street from her bus stop: Dr. Hector Guzman, Internist. Her stomach, completely empty, roiled at the sickly-sweet smell of ripe pineapples at the fruit stand on the corner. All her high spirits, all the energy from the best weeks she'd had in months, gone.

After the sky had lightened, Luz showered and dressed. With Bobby back and with her plan to get Martin to invite her into his space, she had to go to work. She couldn't decide if she should take her pills. Nothing was staying down. And while what she'd told Evan probably was correct—she'd eaten something that violently disagreed with her—it could be more serious, perhaps a reaction to her meds. She thought about calling her doctor in New Hampshire, but he couldn't diagnose her long-distance. Luz curled up on the sofa and bargained with God again. Perhaps it was a real prayer. *Ay, Dios, what can I do? I have to go to work.*

And perhaps God answered, for only then did Luz remember Dr. Guzman's sign. A revolving door led into the lobby. Huge wooden ceiling fans rotating high overhead illuminated dust motes pulsing to the rhythm of the blades. The elevator, an open metal cage, had an "out of order" sign taped across the door, the paper yellow and fly-specked with age. Luz almost reconsidered. In fact, she walked back onto the street, right next to the fruit vendor. Her stomach gave another nasty lurch, and she retreated into the building.

Wide stone steps curved around a central atrium. On the next level, old-fashioned heavy doors with pebbled glass insets: *Abogado, Contador, Dentista,* and there on the left was Dr. Guzman's office. A woman with gray hair pulled into a knot on the top of her head and stuck through with a pencil said, "Can I help you?"

"Is it possible to see Dr. Guzman without an appointment? I've got . . ." Luz couldn't remember the Spanish word for what ailed her so she settled for "I'm vomiting and have diarrhea."

"Certainly. One moment, please."

Luz sank into one of the heavy dark armchairs. Wooden bookcases with glass fronts held pottery shards and loose-leaf notebooks. There'd been a few attempts to modernize—magazines scattered on a coffee table, a water bubbler in the corner, a leggy dieffenbachia thriving in the window. And they either had radio piped in or a tape mix playing. "Tequila Sunrise" was followed by Elton John's "Your Song." And like so many other times in the past few months, Luz became suspended on a thread between the present and past. In New Hampshire, her mother had developed a secret crush on the flamboyant singer.

So many times, she'd walked into their apartment to music abruptly silenced—"Circle of Life," "Daniel," "Tiny Dancer." And "Candle in the Wind," the one that put her mother into a tailspin. Luz never asked her mother about it, and she doubted there'd be a time later when she'd get the chance to ask. Luz figured death meant oblivion. No more wondering about things for which there was no answer, like why her once-revolutionary mother now found so much pleasure in saccharine pop music or what Evan thought about when he looked at her, the way he narrowed his eyes and seemed to see right into her, as he had the morning he delivered the newspaper on the bus, and like that Sunday afternoon they'd gone to the Botanical Garden when he'd waltzed right through the barricades she once thought inviolable. Luz had been much more careful about divulging information since then.

A man with a halo of fine white hair opened the inner door. "*Señorita*, come in."

The massive desk occupied a parallelogram of sunlight. Boxes, books, more books. Three leather club chairs around a low table. Dr. Guzman took Luz's elbow and ushered her to one of the chairs.

"This way, please, where it's less messy. I'm closing my practice at the end of the year, and I've sent most of my patients to other physicians. So." He slapped his hands on his thighs. "What can I do for you today?"

"I've been throwing up since about two this morning. Even a sip of water comes right up again, yellow and bitter. My stomach is empty now, but I still feel queasy."

"Diarrhea?"

Luz nodded.

"Did you eat anything unusual yesterday?" he asked.

"I bought *chuchitos* on my way home from work."

"Mmmm, delicious." Dr. Guzman nodded appreciatively. "So that's not something you normally do?"

"Oh, no, but at the time they smelled too heavenly to pass up. I've been living in the U.S.," added Luz.

"Ah, *los Estados Unidos*. Our son is living in Iowa." The old man pronounced it as though the letters were Spanish—*Ee-oh-gua*. After rolling out the syllables with a flourish, he continued proudly, "In a small town where he has a general practice much like mine. My wife and I will be traveling there next month for an extended stay. Anticipating that visit is the only thing keeping me from despair while I dismantle my life's work." He sketched a wide arc with his arms. "For now, however, let's concentrate on getting you well again."

"Something you should know before prescribing anything," Luz began, opening her purse. "I brought the medicines I'm taking." She rattled each pill bottle as she pulled it out of her bag. "Riluzole. Baclofen. Gabapentin."

Dr. Guzman slumped lower in his chair when Luz brought out her stash of pills, as though the gravity of her situation weighed him down.

"I see you understand what the problem is," murmured Luz.

He leaned closer and patted her knee. "Oh, my dear girl."

* * *

Dr. Guzman prescribed ciprofloxacin, which got Luz through the afternoon, shaky and pale, and not up for playing games.

"Should I take my other medicines?" Luz had asked the doctor.

"The riluzole will upset your stomach, and I worry about its potential side effects while you're recuperating. Stay off it for now. The others, too—unless you begin to have problems with muscle spasms. Let's make an appointment for you to see me again in a week, next Wednesday. Any questions in the interim, call me. Also, I prescribe chicken soup tonight. If you buy soup at the market, make sure to boil it for at least ten minutes when you get home, but," he added with his brilliant smile, "it would be ever so much nicer if you have a friend who can cook for you."

So Luz called Evan after work to ask if he could make chicken soup.

"It's your lucky day," he said.

"What, you actually have the ingredients on hand?"

"Nah, but I have an entire cupboard of cans—chicken noodle, creamy chicken, chicken with vegetables, with orzo, with stars, with rice. You name it, I can heat it up for you."

Although she gave up after a couple of bites, it stayed down. And in the morning, she ate a piece of toast before shooing Evan out the door.

Her strength came back slowly. Afraid to screw things up by proceeding too fast while she was weak, Luz concentrated on her job and bided her time. Thursday passed, with no measurable progress, and Friday as well.

CHAPTER THIRTEEN

"Luz?" Evan pushed aside the hair on her neck and whispered in her ear. "You awake?" He pressed his morning erection against the cleft of her buttocks. It responded instantly to her heat, but Luz swiveled her head as though avoiding a whining mosquito and wiggled out of contact.

"Not this morning," she said, pivoting her feet to the floor. "I promised to bring Cesar some cookies. That's going to take me every second until it's time to leave for work."

"Cookies, wow. Sounds like you've made a complete recovery."

"You said that last night—the recovery part," said Luz with a half-grin, impatience clearly overriding affection. She pushed him away and shuffled into the bathroom. Closing the door, she said, "Time to go."

Their time together had awakened Evan's memories of skydiving. Skydivers, they say, know why the birds sing. Skydiving isn't falling; it's the thrill of flying, all the while knowing you really don't have wings.

Evenings with Luz began with banter spiced with innuendo—the plane's anticipatory liftoff. One touch, another—the rush of wind. They'd kiss—and for unmarked time he'd soar, oblivious to all save the rhythm of their bodies, until the catch of a parachute and the gentle let-down. Then back on earth again, with Luz dismissing him and his world snapping back into place. Another day of waiting to fly again. Those exhilarating leaps into the void had become familiar. Familiar, but always breathtaking and exhilarating. Like Luz.

Evan reached his front door and let himself in. A dusty hush awaited him, as it had every morning for the past few weeks. Today, with thick dark clouds promising more rain, the gloom prodded him into action. He circled the living room, raising shades and cracking open windows for fresh air. Evan wandered into the kitchen. He rinsed his empty beer bottles in the sink. Then he tackled the cluttered kitchen table, sweeping last week's newspapers into the trash, sorting through the accumulated mail, wiping away a fine layer of dust.

Finally, Margo's sagging Peace Lily was the only thing left on the table. Evan took the neglected plant to the sink and set it under a drizzle of water. Immediately, two spoon-shaped white blooms detached and lay like ghostly corpses on the potting soil. Three blooms remained. One bowed its head lower and lower until it doubled over; then it, too, fell into the dirt. For the next minute, there was only the muted drip, drip from the faucet.

Shit, he'd promised to talk to the damn thing. Yet another black mark against him. "I'm sorry," he said. "You deserve better."

The remaining blooms trembled in the air currents from Evan's words. He leaned closer, holding his breath to avoid disturbing the delicate plant. Two knobs at the tips of stems indicated new growth, and the leaves still retained some of their former gloss. There was hope, then. "From now on, I'll treat you right," he murmured.

Luz was leaving Guatemala around Christmastime, she'd said. When she went away, his life would revert to the predictability of rising from his own bed, stretching, opening curtains to see the cloud-covered volcanoes, breakfast at the table by the back window. A prickling of anxiety. The lies—sins of omission, really, because Luz had never asked—were mounting. Evan set the lily gently in its saucer on the table.

Luz's brush-off this morning still rankled. Evan's hands twitched. He rubbed his bristly cheeks. A shower, a shave, and a change of pace. He would start a new project to take his mind off Luz.

*   *   *

Saturday again, two weeks since Luz had handed over the original note. Hoping for a speedy reply, she'd stopped at Juana's stall every day except the one morning she'd been too sick. Nothing so far except dozens of sweet, juicy oranges. Luz always pocketed her change without counting it to keep Evan from seeing any note Juana might stash among the quetzales. Perhaps Juana would need to speak to her, though, so Luz had begun distracting Evan while she bought oranges. *Forgot the bread. Could you get it? Watch out for the mess on the floor.*

Then yesterday, Juana had gone out of her way to mention she wasn't going to the country for the weekend. Would Luz be coming to the market as usual on Saturday? This morning, positive Juana would be bringing news, she had shooed Evan away early. But Juana had nothing for her except a dozen oranges.

Luz crammed the superfluous fruit into her shopping bag, a momentary fantasy of flinging them back at Juana and demanding—no, that wouldn't help. She still had time. She'd made precious little headway on her tasks for Richard. Despite dropping heavy hints, no one had—so far—invited her into Martin's apartment.

Access to Bobby's briefcase remained elusive, too. His return the previous week, when he'd disappointed Cesar, hadn't even lasted the day. Luz and Cesar were still out on the soccer field when Bobby, in a black silk suit, briefcase in hand, had stopped by for five minutes. The helicopter was being refueled, he said. He'd be back soon. Cesar had clung to him until finally Bobby snapped at Luz to *deal with the child, for crissakes.* He walked away adjusting his suit jacket. *Bastard.* The next time Bobby was home, Luz promised herself, she'd find a way to swap the thumb drives. She'd take care of him. For good.

Still, no news translated into nothing needing to be done now. It was only nine thirty, and Luz was experiencing a sensory high as her nausea subsided. She never should have rushed Evan out so quickly. *Evan.* Silky tingling became a ball of heat that spread throughout her body.

*   *   *

An hour later, the doorbell rang. Evan wiped his hands on a rag and padded to the front window. Luz stood on the top step, a covered plate in her hand. He pressed a clenched fist to his solar plexus. If only he'd gone for a run instead of painting. Gone out to lunch.

Luz rang the bell again. She spotted him by the curtain and uncovered her plate with a flourish, revealing a mound of cookies. Evan couldn't leave her standing on the steps—and he could never explain her presence—but his vow to confine their relationship to her house evaporated faster than his earlier resolve not to get involved with her in the first place. He fumbled at the lock with shaking hands.

Luz scooted across the threshold and brushed her cool cheek against his. She must've settled the plate on a table for the next thing Evan knew she'd taken both his cheeks in her hands and slowly rubbed them. Then, going up on tiptoes and leaning into him for balance, she slid her hands around to knead the tight muscles at the base of his neck.

In the entire universe, there was nothing except Luz's body and his body and rhythmic pulsing. "How'd you know where I lived?" he managed.

"The telephone book?" Luz made it a question. "Last name comma first name or initial, address? For a solitary McManus in a sea of Martinezes, it was a cinch." She dug her fingers into the center of his trapezius and held them there. His muscle resisted, quivered, and finally submitted.

"I missed you after you left," she murmured, "and then it didn't take me as long as I thought to put the cookies together. I brought you some." Luz finished with a toss of her head that brought with it the scent of her shampoo and body heat. Then she danced away from him and walked into the room.

"Ah, you're working." She stopped in front of his new project, a sketch of the Botanical Gardens which, after so little effort, didn't resemble much of anything. Luz twirled, completed a three-sixty on her toes. "I expected more, you know, *stuff*. Paintings. Art stacked on the floor. Drawings thumb-tacked to the walls."

The paintings. Perhaps this wouldn't be a complete disaster after all if he could amuse her for a while, show Luz his old work. "Then this is what you're looking for." Evan yanked a tarp off a neat stack of canvases along the side wall. Then he placed the tarp, with what he hoped looked like careless nonchalance, atop the canvas of Luz that stood in the corner facing the wall. Banished.

Evan was as nervous as a diver on the high board for the first time while she riffled through the pile, afraid she'd dismiss his art as completely as she'd dismissed him this morning or turn to him with a forced smile designed to mask her disdain.

"I like this one a lot."

He'd done that painting last year in the hills above Chichicastenango, a romantic weekend getaway.

"This is what you meant about the light, isn't it, Evan? What a beautiful spot!"

Lunch on a rooftop terrace, leisurely drive through the countryside. Sunset, luminous tendrils of mist rising from a wooded valley, turned gold by slanting rays of sun. Perfect.

"Yes," Luz was saying, "you're awfully good." She replaced the paintings she'd moved aside and drifted toward him, her face flushed with giddiness and desire. It was the thrill of attaining this forbidden goal, he thought. She'd known damn well he hadn't wanted her to come over. Perhaps the same recklessness also propelled her toward the thing with Richard.

He felt pretty reckless, too, having so effortlessly breached the line he thought could separate Luz from that other part of his life. She came nearer, stalking catlike, and all at once spilled onto his lap. Evan pulled her close. Finding her mouth, he kissed her hard as his hands lifted her skirt and traveled up the inside of her thighs.

Evan tried to paint again after Luz left for work. After an hour of slapping paint on the canvas and swiping it around, starting over, he admitted defeat. He found some chicken curry in the freezer. When he slammed his plate on the kitchen table, the last blooms of the Peace Lily dropped.

It had been a huge mistake to let Luz come in—worse, to make love to her here. Worst of all, though, he now knew she belonged here. Evan's old reality had dissipated like the evening mist from the canvas Luz admired. That evening, the mist had turned from gold to gray, to deep charcoal. A flight of noisy birds, swooping among the tree branches, distracted him. When he'd looked again, the mist was gone.

Now only his static, painted facsimile remained.

It would be the same with the portrait of Luz. He'd drawn her leaning forward, her head turned slightly, mouth open, the red ribbon she often used to tie back her hair floating past her cheek—a pose creating the illusion of movement. But soon Luz, too, would be gone, leaving

Evan to wonder what she would say if only those open lips in the painting could move, leaving him only the memory of her beauty and vibrancy.

Thank goodness Luz showed no lingering malaise from her brush with dysentery. It *was* funny she'd succumbed to some intestinal bug that hadn't bothered him. At least it had come and gone quickly. And although it *could* be related to her occasional dizzy spells, he hadn't noticed any episodes recently. There was that pill she was supposed to take twice a day—he'd snooped in her bathroom cabinet, of course.

Evan turned on his computer. He Googled riluzole.

Fifteen minutes later, Evan closed the browser and stared across the room. Luz's presence lingered, less in the fragrance he now associated with her, but more as a parade of indelible marks, visible only to him, as clear as fluorescent paint in a black light. Today she'd left her mark on every surface she'd touched. Evan saw his paintings through her eyes, his old green chair, the tiny shower stall, the dusty tile floor, even his threadbare felt slippers.

The lines across his face grew tight as internal pressure built. A wordless cry arose, and with it, a hollowness that he'd likely meant nothing more to her than a friendly fuck, someone insignificant to her real life. She should have trusted him.

Trust *him*. And she should do that because he'd been so honest about himself—yeah, right. She'd as likely believe in the tooth fairy. And it was clear Luz didn't believe in much.

When the phone rang, he picked it up absently. *"Aló?"*

"Hey, Evan. It's been a while. What's up?"

Shit. "Hi. Where've you been, Richard?"

"Out of town. On business. My secretary said it wasn't urgent." There was a hint of reprimand.

"It's Luz. I had a question." Suddenly, there were too many questions. He would start with the one at the root of it all.

"What is it?" The edge in Richard's tone disappeared. He sounded curious.

"I met her at the market." *True as far as it went.* "She told me a little about when she and her mother arrived in the U.S. She thinks you're with the State Department. Resettlement."

"You didn't tell her different, did you?"

"Give me a little credit, Uncle Richard." Heavy sarcasm on the seldom-used *uncle.* "If your job calls for her not to know, I can respect that. It startled me, though, and I wanted to check in with you. I wonder what else I should know. Or what else I need to keep quiet about."

Evan waited out the throat-clearing that was his uncle's way of buying time.

"Background," Richard began. "Luz's father was Emilio Concepcion. Concepcion's her real last name. Emilio, like Martin Benavides, was an early opponent of the junta. A lawyer by trade, not a military leader. Very charismatic. He was a major reason the insurgents had such popular support."

Richard explained how Emilio's group briefly joined forces with Martin Benavides, but they clashed over strategy and policy. And in the '90s, when the Benavides' forces became ascendant, Emilio led the opposition to them.

Richard cleared his throat again. "*Deep* background. U.S. military interest in the outcome of the civil war meant we had observers on the ground. I was monitoring the Benavides' radio transmissions from nearby the day Emilio died."

When he realized what was happening, Richard said, he called in a chopper to evacuate as many women and children as possible, including Luz and her mother. The State Department *did* take care of their resettlement, but because the CIA had questions about the extent of Josefina's—Luz's mother's—continuing involvement, Richard was tapped to become their liaison.

"As it turned out, we were wrong. Josefina came to the U.S. and put that part of her life behind her. Losing Emilio was a blow she never recovered from. Neither Luz nor Josefina was ever aware I'd had anything at all to do with the fighting in Guatemala." Richard pounded each word home. "This stays between us."

Richard rolled on with heavy affability that relegated Evan's acquiescence to a foregone conclusion. "And how is the lovely Margo?"

Evan looked around—and saw only those abiding images of Luz. Not Margo reading by the window or deftly shuffling pots and pans in the kitchen or brushing her hair by the bedroom window. Not Margo at all. Like a magician's razzle-dazzle to keep attention focused elsewhere, he'd been pretending the object was to avoid Richard's ire at muddling his courier work with extracurricular fooling around— when he was only fooling himself that being with Luz amounted to a little vacation fling.

Your chickens, his grandfather had been fond of saying, will always come home to roost. And here they were: The complications, the consequences he'd tried hard to finesse. The lies.

Shit. Evan swallowed and said, "Margo's fine. She's been in Honduras for the past month, a medical conference and then training the new public health nurses hired by her NGO."

"Will she be home by the time I come down to conclude this little mission?"

The bottom fell out of Evan's stomach. "You're coming? When?"

"That depends entirely on Luz. When she's ready, she'll give you a package, and I'll bring the rest of what she needs—and, Evan, that transfer is the only reason for you two to have any contact."

Whoa. That last frosty crack sounded like Richard suspected something. Evan was in too deep to survive a pointed interrogation, so he'd better forget about asking the rest of his questions. Admitting Luz had told him about the Benavides would open a huge can of worms, and he definitely shouldn't know about the pills Luz took.

"Oh." Evan's gasp was little more than a loud inhale into the too-lengthy silence.

"*Is* there something else, Evan?"

"No." He had to get off the phone before his uncle had a chance to pry. Evan had just put two and two together: Luz, whom he now believed to be seriously ill, was taking—stealing?—something from the head of Guatemala's largest drug cartel. That was already horrible, but *afterward* Richard was bringing something to her. Luz would be going back in.

After the men said their goodbyes, Evan, chin cradled in his palms, stared out the window until the light faded and the sky turned inky black.

CHAPTER FOURTEEN

The man wore jeans and a Houston Astros warm-up jacket. A machete scar disfigured his left hand and wrist. When Luz headed home after work, he got on the bus behind her, with a crowd of others. He got off at her stop, only the two of them, stepping down at the last second as the bus rumbled away from the curb. It was out of sight now, brake lights disappearing in the distance.

Although her *colonia* was a moderately safe neighborhood, her antennae vibrated an alarm. It was nine o'clock, pitch black, streetlights too widely spaced to brighten the gloom. Everyone was inside behind their locked gates, watching TV, talking and drinking. If anyone heard her shout, they'd probably turn up the TV. No one would venture out.

She had to shake him off, but to get to a commercial area with people around, she'd have to zig and zag through a grid of streets that offered no shelter, not even parked cars to hide behind or under. No, Luz had to go to the one place where she had a key. If she got to her gate, she could unlock it, run in, and slam it shut behind her. All this went through her head in the few seconds it took her to orient herself. It could be a coincidence, that the man lived out here, too. Luz knew she was fooling herself. In the time she had hesitated, so had the man. He was waiting for her to move.

As she turned to walk home, Luz rummaged in her purse for the ring of keys; it could double as a weapon if necessary. Her footsteps sounded like gunshots on the pavement. The man must've been wearing sneakers—his feet were quiet, like the mountain lion, not giving away his location until he pounced.

Mountain lion. *Mountain?* What if this was the contact she'd been waiting for?

They shouldn't come for me like this. Everything's in my apartment.

With a second backward glance, Luz broke into a run. Now, the man jogged faster, his shoes slapping the pavement. From a long-ago fragment of her father's wisdom, she understood he could have overtaken her. He was cruising, keeping pace.

Luz had almost reached her gate. In a few seconds, she'd put on a burst of speed, gain enough distance to lock him outside. Then she'd run in and grab it. *Ready. Set.*

Now. Luz streaked for the finish line.

A dark van, invisible in the shadows of overhanging branches, flashed its lights directly ahead of her. Luz tripped. The man caught up to her and pinned her arms behind her back.

"No, no! I need to get something inside first. Let me go. I'll be right back." She jabbed a key into his midsection and twisted it. He screamed and loosened his grip. She lunged for the gate.

The van glided forward. Its lights grew brighter, bathing them in a harsh glow. The man with the machete scar pulled her away. She grabbed a wrought-iron bar on the gate with her free hand and wrestled the key into the lock with the other.

Luz sensed movement from both sides. Large dark figures entered her peripheral vision. One smashed his fist on her outstretched arm. Stunned, she lost her hold on the iron bar. The other man tackled her. They both landed on the sidewalk, Luz on the bottom. Uneven concrete dug into her back when she tried to kick the man off.

"Wait," Luz cried. "I'm supposed to bring something."

A cloth jammed into her mouth choked her as she sobbed. They fitted a hood over her head, none too gently, tied her hands and feet, and tossed her into the back of the van. Luz landed on a lumpy pile of sacks between rows of boxes.

The driver reversed away from her gate, and the van lurched as they bumped off the sidewalk. Seconds became minutes. Time measured by stopping and turning. The man she'd gouged gave an exaggerated account of his injuries—unless, thought Luz, she'd struck a much luckier blow than she supposed.

Lying alone in the dark, Luz took stock. They hadn't stolen her keys to ransack her apartment. Not a robbery. Probably not a rape, either. And Juana *had* asked if Luz would be at the market as usual. Not to give Luz a message, though. She'd bet anything Juana had pointed her out, and the men had followed her all day. *Damn.* She'd never imagined they'd handle it like this.

Luz had little trouble spitting out the rag the men had stuffed in her mouth, a foul greasy thing like you'd use to wipe a dipstick. But her calls to turn around were met with laughter, so finally she wiggled and twisted until she created a relatively smooth cubbyhole among the boxes.

She was stuck. She'd have to do some fast talking when she arrived.

Minutes became hours. The air became cooler. They must be heading into the mountains. Then a quick series of turns, level land, a slower pace, and a half-dozen brief pauses; they were in a small town. The roads deteriorated after that. There were times Luz imagined they weren't on a road at all, but a rutted cart track.

The van whined and groaned. The driver cursed and downshifted. They climbed sharply, braked even more sharply. The driver smoked in the cab while he directed his sleepy underlings to reposition make-shift roadblocks. The men left her alone and were careful not to disclose anything about their location. From that, Luz took heart. It was a fuck-up, but she could survive.

CHAPTER FIFTEEN

Luz drifted off into troubled sleep. She woke to a heated discussion among her captors. Turn left or right? There were two votes for *izquierda,* but the driver pulled rank and turned right instead. The van jolted onward, inch by inch. The subordinates' irritated grumblings intensified to profanity when the path apparently petered out into an impassible track. Reversing the van required something like a thirty-two-point turn, an eternity of increasingly testy course corrections.

They crept back to the crossroads and, after more bickering, onward. Luz was now wide awake and anxious for their arrival. She also had to pee, the pressure in her bladder an agony, aggravated every time she squirmed to change position. With her hands bound behind her and legs lashed at the ankles, she couldn't lie for long without pressing awkwardly on one limb or another, reducing the blood flow until she became numb. Then Luz would shift as best she could, and the slow burn of pins and needles intensified as circulation resumed.

The debilitating sensations mimicked what had begun happening over the summer. When Richard, who'd visited regularly as her mother's condition deteriorated, arrived for the funeral, Luz blamed her dizziness and awkwardness on the stress. Between then and two months later, when Richard came up with some papers for her to sign, her symptoms worsened to the point she had trouble standing in the mornings, and she'd missed so much work her supervisor at the day-care center had warned there was talk of letting her go.

The second Richard saw her, he insisted she see a doctor. The doctor he found ran an impressive battery of tests—and, she suspected, sent Richard a large portion of the bill she could never have paid on her own. Process of elimination, the doctor said. And he'd eliminated one thing after another. Until her appointment shortly after Labor Day. When he called to arrange the consultation, Luz had even experienced a surge of hope that now she could get proper treatment and the weakness and trembling would go away. Luz knew it was bad news the minute she stepped into the office. The nurse's bright chatter and unwillingness to meet her eyes told her almost all she needed to know. The doctor only added details.

Afterward, she stood on the sidewalk. It was still Wednesday afternoon; the sun shone; a school bus passed, kids shouting. Luz walked across the street to the bus stop and thought about dying.

Well, she would die soon enough, but not now. She still had things to do.

The van slowed around a curve. The driver beeped the horn and hit the brakes hard.

"*Aquí estamos*," said one of the men. They had arrived.

A high-pitched squeal announced the opening of the van's back door. Air rushed in, immediately identifiable as cool early morning mountain air. The scent of wood fires mixed with mountain laurel. The dirt would be black, moist. Stick a piece of bark in and a tree would grow before morning, her father always said.

Callused hands yanked her ankles and pulled her out, hiking her skirt around her waist.

"*No me chingas*," Luz yelled. If the men hadn't brought her to the camp of the *Frente Popular de Liberación*, a little foul language was the least of her problems.

A voice Luz might've recognized—although it had been so long ago—called out for them to undo her hands so she could settle her clothing. This they did.

Taciturn men, ripe with body odor and cigarette smoke, pushed past her to remove supplies from the van. In a few minutes the men moved off, mission complete. Her head still shrouded, Luz stood alone next to the van. Footsteps approached, deliberate tread crunching on dry leaves. Luz strained to see through the hood's rough weave.

All at once—a hand at her throat. Reaching under her sweater. Rough, cool. Undid the top two buttons of her blouse and pulled the left sleeve down.

"Satisfied?" asked Luz. She gagged as the rope pulled tight around her neck. Hands worked the knot. The man swore vividly a few times before releasing the rope. He yanked off the hood, and there stood Antonio Torres. He was a man now, bearded and muscular, not the wide-eyed, wiry boy who—seventeen years earlier—had saved Luz's life. The black rifle looped across his shoulder seemed part of his body, like he'd grown an extra appendage.

"The second I heard you swearing at my men like a bratty eleven-year-old, I knew." His laugh rumbled like a freight train. "But I checked for your chicken pox scars anyway. Aunt Juana might have been conned—it wouldn't be the first time someone has tried to trick us."

"Toño," she said, "I have to pee. Desperately."

The man had bent to sever the ropes around her feet. Now he stood and swatted her behind. "Over there," he said.

Luz gave her cousin a fleeting hug and ran behind the shed.

"Why in the name of God did you ask to come here?" he said when Luz returned.

"It's awfully important, but your stupid, incompetent, overeager, macho . . ." Having run out of adjectives, Luz continued. "Those idiots abducted me on the street before I could get it. My mother, she—"

At the change in her voice, the man she called Toño came forward and covered her hands with his. "What happened, Lulu?"

"Mama died."

A pool of liquid gathered at the inside corners of Toño's eyes, overflowed, and etched a zigzag trail through the stubble on his face. At the sight of his tears, Luz broke down. And Antonio Torres, outlaw commander of the *Frente Popular de Liberación*, pulled her close. He rocked Luz back and forth, like her grandmother used to. When her tears slowed, he pulled out a handkerchief and patted her cheeks dry before passing the cloth across his face. He studied the damp cloth for a moment, then folded it precisely into a tiny square and stowed it once again in his pocket.

Luz hugged him. "It's so good to see you again, Toño."

"And you, too, little Lulu, my favorite cousin all grown up. But how is it you managed to return? You're not using your real name and—we followed you—you work for that bastard Benavides. So have you gone over to the dark side? Am I going to have to kill you?"

Toño's voice was light enough to defuse his threat, but his expression serious. Luz had to give him as much of an explanation as possible, without revealing the extent of her involvement. He clasped her hand and led her across the small clearing to a group of sawed-off logs around a campfire. Beyond, under tree-cover, were several Jeeps under a netting of brush and camouflage tents into which men were stacking the new supplies.

"Let's sit here." Toño parked himself on a stump with a clear view of the only track into the encampment and patted the log next to it. After Luz sat, he stared at her in silence long enough to make her uneasy. "You're so very much like your mother," he finally said.

Tears filled her eyes again, for Toño was remembering Josefina from the old days when she was their group's unofficial logistics manager—

dedicated and smart, intensely practical, a wizard at procuring blankets and enough food for everyone.

"She must have missed your father so very much."

"Oh, yes." Luz told Toño a bit about their life in the States and about her mother's decline—refusing to learn English, gradually confining herself to their apartment, getting sick.

"Do you remember that story your father told?" Toño asked. "The one about the bird?"

"Of course."

"He never came right out and said it was about him and your mother, but I think everyone knew it was."

Her father began the story the old-fashioned way: *Había una vez.*

It went something like this: Once upon a time, way back at the beginning of the world, God created a bird. It wasn't a bird like we have today; this bird had no wings. When it looked at the sky, the bird knew it belonged in the clouds, but it couldn't reach them. God, recognizing his mistake, made the bird a wing. In the language of the old days, this wing was called "man." The bird joyfully flapped its wing and lifted up—but could only fly in bobbling circles. So God called the bird back and gave it a second wing to balance the first. This wing, he called "woman," and the bird rose up to the clouds and soared away.

Although the words in the main part of the tale varied with each telling, her father always finished ritually, like a priest giving benediction, "As a bird needs two wings to fly, so do people fly highest and straightest with two wings of equal strength."

Luz spoke through the lump in her throat. "Mama knew. Papa would call her *mi otra ala.*"

Toño bent to light a cigarette from the fire and, Luz thought, to wipe his eyes again. "Your return worried us," he said, straightening. "How did you know to make contact through Tia Juana?"

"The Aunt Juana part is easy. When Mama knew she wouldn't get well, she told me about the old-lady market network. She gave me three names, Juana and her sisters, but she also said I should try anyone selling oranges from La Esperanza. To wear her rings and see if I got a reaction."

"Juana noticed." Toño blew out a long plume of smoke. "It was brilliant of your mother to remember that after staying out of touch so long."

Luz tugged his arm. "Toño, you have to understand. Mama never adjusted to life in the U.S. She longed to come back here, but we knew it was too risky. Then she got sick." Luz squeezed her eyes tight-shut against another wave of tears. "Mama made me promise—it was her only request, Toño—not to bury her under a mountain of cold dirt, where snow would lie on top of her. She told me to have her cremated, and when it was safe, to bring her ashes back. She wanted to return to the waterfall."

"To your father." Toño nodded, took another long drag on his cigarette. "She must have known we would bury him there."

"Yes, married for life at the waterfall and buried there together. It was only the belief they would be together again that sustained her. Sometimes the talk of heaven drove me crazy," said Luz with a shrug, "but in the end, that hope was all she had."

Toño exhaled heavily. With the wince of someone expecting bad news, he asked, "And the ashes?"

"In my apartment." Luz jabbed his belly. "Your men abducted me on the street before I could get the urn. I *told* them to wait."

Toño made a stop sign with his hand. "They were following my orders—"

"I need to come back to bring them."

"Oh, Lulu, you ask too much. These trips are dangerous. And the waterfall is far from this camp. Ten hours' march, at least. Longer still, believe it or not, if we go mainly by road."

"Can you get word to me through your aunt? Please?" The corners of his mouth quirked up. He was softening. "Please, Toño. We could do it another weekend, but it'll have to be soon."

He exhaled a massive lungful of smoke. "How soon?"

Yes! Luz resisted going for high fives and considered the variables. In the lead-up to Martin's assassination, Toño, as a major—if currently outlawed—player in Guatemalan politics, would soon be moving toward Guatemala City.

"Before Christmas?" With her lack of progress into Martin's apartment or Bobby's briefcase, the bombing couldn't happen before then.

"Not a chance." Toño swiveled his head decisively. "It'll have to wait for spring. We're moving camp next week, Lulu. We'll take advantage of the coming dry season to consolidate our positions in Alta Verapaz."

What? That was the wrong direction. "You're not heading south, closer to the city?"

Toño snorted. "So we can run right into government patrols and get slaughtered?"

A log crashed, dislodging several others; flames sparked higher. Luz gazed into the now-raging fire. The *Frente Popular* had already been tipped off about the assassination. Toño's plans didn't make sense.

"You understand, don't you," Richard had said, "that getting rid of the Benavides is a win-win. In addition to putting a monkey wrench in their cocaine network, it will remove the biggest stumbling block to true multi-party democracy in Guatemala. We've made sure the *Frente Popular* is prepared to walk into the power vacuum."

When Richard took Luz to meet John, he had been explicit: "With Martin dead and his son disgraced, the FPL's leaders will have an excellent shot at leading the government."

Perhaps she'd been out of the loop too long. "Aren't you thinking in terms of getting ready?"

"Ready for what?"

"Returning to the capital."

Toño leaned back against the tree and roared with laughter. "No hurry, Lulu, no hurry," he said when his guffaws subsided. "We have many months to go—a year, more—until we'll have the strength to mount a definitive assault. Meanwhile we're circling here in the north, you see. We'll wait until we have the strength to control the major highways, cut off the large cities. Only when—"

Toño stopped. Luz guessed he was reacting to her obvious confusion at his sensible, long-term strategy to wrest power from the oligarchy in the city.

"I'm not really telling you too much, Lulu," he said. "It's on the news, what our plans are. The army is simply spread too thin to be able to do anything about it. Oh, they try—and the villagers pay a heavy price. But they're with us. The small towns, the small shopkeepers, they're with us, too. The teachers. Some of the priests—not all."

"I'm confused, Toño," Luz blurted. "People say you're the commander of the *Frente*?"

"I am."

His words were resolute, but the way Toño rolled his wrist back and forth—it was like her father equivocating *maybe, maybe not*. So Luz asked, "Just you? Or are there others who might challenge you?"

Toño sat forward on the tree stump, and his eyes narrowed. He took a last long drag on his cigarette and tossed the butt into the fire. "I control the largest group of fighters, but there are two others. We agreed to cooperate to bring down the corrupt government." He slapped his hands to his lap. "After that, who knows, but for now, it is in all our interests to work together."

Luz said slowly, "As you noticed, I've come back to work for the Benavides. I'm providing information about their household to the U.S. government."

Until five minutes earlier, positive Toño was already aware of the plot, Luz's biggest worry had been soft-pedaling the extent of her involvement in the assassination. Toño had once risked his life to save hers. If she disclosed her role, he'd try to stop her. Luz still had to safeguard that information, but now . . . now Toño had to know more.

"A man from the State Department, someone I've known for years, recently approached me about returning to help them. They needed a Guatemalan they trusted, someone who could work unobtrusively in the residence." Luz looked down at her sensible sneakers, which were windshield-wipering the black dirt. She brushed away a beetle climbing up her leg. It was time to spit it out. "Toño, they plan to assassinate Martin Benavides and discredit his son with the goal of shifting the balance of power toward the FPL in next year's election."

"I know nothing about this."

CHAPTER SIXTEEN

Saturday evening, after he got Richard off the phone, Evan tried—and failed—to come to terms with what he had learned and what he now suspected. His thoughts became disjointed, unglued. Evan retreated to the world of images, mute and immutable: Luz, always Luz, in the thousand ways he'd seen her. The light faded, and his kitchen grew chilly. An insistent car horn eventually pulled him away from his inner slideshow.

Get a grip, Evan. He shut all the windows he'd opened that morning. He closed the curtains. He took the stupid Peace Lily—he'd always thought the flowers smelled like cat pee—into the bedroom and slammed the door. He retrieved Luz's portrait from the stack in the corner. Then, from his ratty green armchair, Evan held a one-sided conversation with his creation: *What do you want?* he asked the canvas.

Silence.

What can I do?

Luz remained mute.

Faced with unrelenting silence, Evan finally decided to show up unannounced. He'd tell Luz he knew she was sick, that he hated how Richard was taking advantage of her. He'd beg her to reconsider the danger. He'd promise to take care of her. Forever. They'd leave

Guatemala and get her the best medical care. No—he'd *stay with her* in Guatemala. He'd buy a house in the mountains, not too far from town, so she could have anything, everything. Whatever she wanted.

It was getting late, so Evan hurried over. No one answered his buzz at the gate. *She must be in the shower.* At nine thirty, he buzzed again. *Working late?* Ten o'clock. Evan pictured Luz lying in bed, too weak to respond. He gave up at midnight but called periodically through the night.

On Sunday, he buzzed each of her neighbors in turn. Several came out to talk to him. None admitted seeing Luz recently. None let him in.

By Monday morning, Evan had hardly slept. He rang Luz's bell one more time and was about to go home to call Richard and ask what he should do, a call that would inevitably reveal he knew far more about Luz than he should, when he spied her coming round the corner. She wore the same embroidered shirt she'd had on Saturday morning at his house, her cheeks rosy and her hair in a loose knot. She looked like someone who'd been riding horses or flying a kite, not like she'd been lying in her apartment all weekend, too ill to answer the phone.

He ran toward her. "Where've you been?" he called as they approached her gate from opposite directions.

Luz jumped when he spoke.

"Sorry," Evan said. "I didn't mean to startle you, but I've been calling all weekend. And when I didn't see you at the market earlier, I worried something was wrong." Evan linked his arm through hers, but Luz pulled away.

"I was busy," she said.

"But I asked your neighbors and they said—"

Luz whipped around, hands on hips, elbows wide. Her face drained of color, leaving only red spots high on each cheekbone. "You *what?*— for crissakes, Evan." From radiant to deeply distressed in the space of seconds. "*Ay, Dios mío*, what did you say? Did you talk to anyone else?"

"No one had seen you all weekend," he continued, "so I was afraid you were sick again."

"I can't—" she began. Then, passing her palm over her mouth, Luz shook her head and resumed marching toward the gate. Without turning around, she said, "Go home."

"But—"

"Don't follow me," she muttered as she walked away. Then louder, "I don't want to have anything more to do with you."

Whatever the misunderstanding, he had to clear it up. Evan sprinted ahead of Luz and stood blocking her gate. He imagined cupping her chin in his hand. He'd make her look at him, make her see she didn't have to do Richard's dirty work.

Luz backed away so fast she bumped into the high stucco wall and a flurry of scarlet bougainvillea blossoms from an overhanging branch rained down on her.

Evan reached toward her once more. "What's wrong?"

Luz batted his hand away, looking like she would bolt again. "Why are you interfering? Leave me alone."

"I can't, Luz. I know you're sick. I know—"

"You know absolutely nothing about me. Nothing. Do you understand?"

That wasn't true. He pitched his voice low and gentle, as if calming a skittish colt. "I know you're doing something dangerous for Richard. I know he's taking advantage of you. I know you have ALS, Luz."

Luz raised her head then. She wasn't looking at him exactly; she was seeing a different place and time. The silence lengthened between them, a long vibrating tunnel of words selected and then discarded.

"Have you ever really hated someone?" Luz's voice wasn't even heated. She could have been asking if he wanted a beer. Without waiting for an answer—which, in Evan's case, would've been *no*—she continued, "You spend your life hating. You're taught the person you hate is *El Diablo* himself. You remember his face, red and shiny, in fire-light, light you now imagine as hellfire. Then this golden opportunity lands in your lap." Luz almost smiled. "What if you got the chance to avenge the cruelest injustice ever done to you and your family?"

Since he didn't have an answer to that, Evan proffered his first objection. "Richard doesn't seem to care about the danger you're being exposed to. I do."

"Oh, Richard knows *exactly* what I'm doing. I'm going to blow Martin Benavides straight to hell."

"A bomb?" *Oh, no. That was worse than any of his jumbled conjectures.*

Luz ran her fingers across her mouth, a retroactive zipping of her lips.

"My God, Luz, their compound is a fortress. How can you smuggle a bomb in? And how the hell are you going to get out?"

"I'm not coming out."

Evan's ears started ringing. The scarlet of the bougainvillea momentarily blazed so bright he had to shut his eyes against its intensity; then it faded to sepia. He pulled his collar away from his neck, but breathing didn't come any easier. "What are you saying?"

"The bomb that kills Martin will take me, too." A brief pause. "It's my gift to everyone who didn't survive."

"You can't—"

She was in his face before he finished, hurling words instead of punches. "Oh, yes, I can and I will. I'm dying anyhow. Now, a year from now, what's the difference?"

I could be the difference. "But we—"

"Listen to me," she shouted. "In a year, I'll be bedridden, on a ventilator. I can't cope with that. This is what I want to do."

What I want to do.

What Luz wanted . . . not the clichéd romantic fantasy he'd created in consultation with her imperfect image, also his creation. If that was what *Luz* wanted, what did *he* want? *Protect her*, said a vehement voice in his head.

Help her! Quietly, a sigh on the wind. Then louder: *Help her.*

"Don't come over here again, Evan. I'll keep going to the market in the morning, but stay away from me unless you have a message, and in return, I promise to let you know when I'm ready to move."

There had to be more he could say or do. "At least let me come in."

"No, I've got to get ready for work." She shot him a look, hard and cold as a diamond, but one in which Evan imagined a trace of underlying fracture.

"Have you been gone then?" Evan meant to stay casual, a lame attempt to eliminate the elephant of her revelation that jostled between them. It came out sounding banal, he knew, but right now banal was all he could process.

"I spent the weekend with another man."

He recalled her tangled hair, her bright eyes and flying feet as she ran around the corner. Luz held out a hand as if she would grasp his. Evan, more confused than he'd been a second before, reached out. Luz used his outstretched arm to push him, hard. Evan took two tripping steps backward and stumbled over the curb. She was at the gate and inside before he recovered.

CHAPTER SEVENTEEN

Luz slammed her front door and shot the bolt. She stormed into her bedroom. *Damn. Damn.* She stubbed her big toe on the bureau as she rounded it, too fast and too angry.

Damn.

She'd returned to Guatemala City via a faster route than her outward-bound journey with the soldiers. After waking her in the gray light of early morning, Toño kissed her goodbye. Then he'd given instructions to her drivers, a well-dressed young couple, and blindfolded her. They took the rickety van to a settlement about an hour from the camp. There, the man had maneuvered into a garage or shed, and they'd switched to a small sedan. The woman guided her into the rear seat, had Luz lie down, and tucked blankets around her. And left her to her thoughts.

On the way to the mountains, as the hours had slipped away and Luz had become increasingly confident the men were taking her to see Toño, she'd worried about how to explain her absence to Evan. And if he notified Richard, she was screwed. This was a private matter; Richard would go ballistic if he found out she'd lied about contacting the guerrillas.

She'd have to invent a story neither man would question. Luz's first idea was to tell Evan she'd been pressed into working overtime at the

Benavides'. Maybe they'd taken her somewhere without phones. *En sus sueños.* She hadn't concocted a more sensible fiction before Toño's ignorance of the U.S. plot against the Benavides had derailed everything else.

Toño had grilled Luz for hours. The only lies she told him were about the endgame—and there, instead of admitting she'd detonate the bomb, Luz pleaded ignorance. He asked who set up the project, what Luz knew about them, and how she funneled information to the conspirators. When she described her connection with Evan, Toño had been blunt. "He's a security problem. Get rid of him."

Inventing another man as the reason for her absence was the only thing she could think of to drive Evan away. It had the added benefit of being difficult to disprove and something Evan wouldn't necessarily tell Richard. But that lie, which she'd accepted as necessary at the mountain camp, had been much harder to speak than she imagined.

As they got closer to the city, the car slowed. Horns honked. A blaring loudspeaker, probably mounted on a pickup truck, broadcast its message of responsibility and safe sex while it crept along. Long pauses that must've been traffic lights. Then the woman removed Luz's blindfold. They were on a busy street two blocks from her house. The man pulled to the curb and told her to get out. She was anticipating a hot shower and another cup of coffee when Evan jumped out at her.

At least he hadn't talked to Richard.

The push had started as an apology of sorts—it's not you, it's me—a stupid impulse she instantly regretted as hope and desire blazed afresh for Evan.

Damn.

* * *

Sunny, dry air had streamed over the mountains during the weekend. The rainy season, people said, had finally run its course. Winter had arrived, a transition from stormy to sunny. Just in time for Christmas.

Change accelerated at the Benavides'. Luz arrived at work to find tiny white fairy lights wound around the iron bars in the gates. Fake candles illuminated the glass-shard-topped security wall. In the yard, an elaborate *nacimiento*—Mary and Joseph with baby Jesus, surrounded by shepherds, sheep, angels, donkeys, goats, oxen, magi, camels, boxes wrapped with red paper and garlands of gold ribbon. Aromatic pine garlands festooned the house, and it was surrounded by tubs of poincianas. Ten days until Christmas.

All of which left Cesar, in the vivid words of a former coworker at the Portsmouth day-care center, bouncing off the walls. Still frazzled from her weekend abduction, from Toño's unanswered questions, and from encountering Evan before she was ready, Luz held a book in front of her nose, oblivious to the unintelligible squiggles, and let Cesar's manic waves wash over her.

If only I could see Richard again. Talk to him. Hear his voice—that, mainly. Funny to think that's what she longed for: Richard, sitting on the brown sofa by the lamp hung with little ivory tassels while he patiently answered her questions, her mother bustling in and out as she prepared dinner.

Richard was never the huggable sort of Honorary Uncle. More like a kind schoolteacher, one who was always willing to stay late and explain what you'd been confused about in class.

One unexpected torment of getting sick was not being able to talk to him about it—not so much the getting-sick part, but about her decision. That sunny September afternoon after the doctor had failed to sugarcoat the grim diagnosis, Luz went home to her sweltering apartment. After hours staring at nothing, a strange honking outside roused her. When she opened the window, a huge flock of geese flapped by, their V extending farther than her eyes could see.

Flying south. Too early. Watch the animals around you, her father always said, and you'll find the clues you need to live in harmony with your environment. The geese were getting out ahead of the coming bad weather.

And that's when she decided.

After Richard's first call, when Luz pretended to be in too much of a rush to chat, she'd let the rest go to voicemail. But she returned home a few days later to find Richard pacing outside. He followed her into the apartment, pointed her into a chair, and sat down on the old brown sofa. "What's going on?"

Delaying tactics on the phone were one thing; lying to his face was impossible. So Luz told him. Just the facts, what the doctor said. Richard rallied, though his pallor told a different story. He moved quickly into problem-solving mode—second opinions and home health aides and medical trials.

When her lack of interest in his suggestions became obvious, his left foot began tapping on the wooden floorboards. "Tell me the rest of it," Richard said.

"It was the geese." Luz pointed out the window, fluttered her fingers to mimic wings beating. "Heat like this in September—it doesn't fool them. Geese always know when it's time to go. I thought I should pay attention."

"Go?" Richard turned into a statue. "What are you saying?"

"Why wait until there's ice on the ponds and rain has turned to pellets of sleet? Why not go when you can still feel the warmth of summer?" Luz shrugged. "I want to leave on my own terms, leave before it's too late."

He argued with her into the night, but for the first time since she'd known him, Richard didn't have an argument to steer her onto his preferred path.

It was chilly a few weeks later when they met for her birthday lunch, and rain blew sideways as they walked from his car into the restaurant. After the hostess seated them, Richard took her hand in his. "It's going to be winter soon," he said. They both knew what he meant. "I brought some things." He laid a stack of glossy brochures on the table by Luz's plate—long-term-care facilities.

The losses had already begun. She'd quit her job to save the embarrassment of being fired. No longer feeling it was safe to drive, she'd sold her car.

"Richard, don't." Luz swept the papers aside. "We both know that's not what I want."

Richard nodded—rather it was the down stroke of a nod. His chin remained tucked. "Okay." He raised his head and spread his fingers on the white tablecloth as though it were the keyboard of a piano. "Okay, Luz, in that case, I want to tell you about something going on at work you might be interested in."

If she could only ask him, Richard would make everything clear. Once Luz denied an interest in contacting the guerrillas, any alliance Richard had formed with one of the other commanders would've been beyond her need to know. If she asked, though, he'd tell her how the *Frente* fit into their plans. But Luz was in Guatemala, sent off without a panic button. There was Evan, of course. He could relay a message. *I don't want to send a message. I just want to talk to Richard.*

But it was Cesar, jiggling her arm, who wanted to talk to *her*, so Luz laid down her book, and they constructed an obstacle course for his remote-control car.

Then Delores poked her head in to say that the return of dry weather meant she could start pre-holiday house cleaning. Today, she wanted to take up the rugs and beat them on the roof. She'd enlisted the help of two burly guards standing behind her in the hall.

Forty-eight hours earlier, Luz's tasks were stalled, out of reach. Now that she craved more time, perversely, solutions began dropping like fruit ripe for harvest. Delores played drill sergeant, assigning one man to lift the furniture while she and the other man knelt and rolled up the rugs. They completed the living room and moved to Cesar's bedroom. In the back corner of the bedroom, an old oak bookcase proved too heavy for a single guard to shift, so he called his partner over to join him.

"*Uno!*" called one man. Delores hunched over the rug.

"*Dos!*" She took hold of the leading edge.

"*Tres!*" They lifted the bookcase, and Delores yanked on the rug. It came loose with such momentum that she tumbled backward and landed on her behind, wailing. Her hair came unpinned. Her key ring skipped across the floor. Her stubby legs, encased in magenta tights, splayed. Cesar laughed at the spectacle. The men dashed over to hoist Delores to her feet. Luz kicked the key ring under the bed. The men lifted the rugs onto their shoulders and followed Delores out.

Luz's pulse raced as her thoughts shifted into high gear. She didn't need much time, but she had to distract Cesar—and cajoling would take too long. A treat, then. She had a couple of DVDs she'd been saving for an emergency. This qualified.

Luz settled him in front of the TV. She returned to the bedroom, closed the door, and had just assembled her material when the phone rang—Delores asking about her keys already? Tears of frustration welled as she ran into the living room to answer it. *So close.*

But it was only Father Espinosa who wanted to give Luz detailed instructions on how Cesar was to complete a history assignment. Cesar, still antsy, drifted over and listened to Luz's side of the conversation. He soon wandered away—back to his video, she assumed—

but when Luz got off the phone and turned around, Cesar wasn't in front of the TV. Instead, she found him in his bedroom, rolling her clay into little balls.

"Look, Luz, it's a caterpillar. And I can make a snake, too—watch. This stuff is cool. Where'd you get it? D'you have some more?"

Once the clay was removed from its sealed package, it dried to a rock-hard lump in ten minutes. Luz took a step forward, ready to pluck the clay from his hand. Less than ten minutes now. If it came to an argument with Cesar, she would lose one way or the other. Luz stilled her hand. She could probably come up with a Plan B to create her mold, but would she be able to do so while she still had the blasted key?

"*Ay, querido,*" she said to the boy. "*Es muy hermosa.*" Her mind whirring, Luz took the bright pink snake from Cesar's hand, assessing as she appeared to admire it. He hadn't taken *that* much clay. She could make the duplicate key with less than the full amount.

Luz eased Cesar toward the living room. "This is very special clay, Cesar. I thought we could use it for—we could use it for surprises for each other."

Yes, that was the right tack. Christmas, surprises, secrets. Cesar beamed.

"The problem is, this clay gets hard really fast, so let's turn off the video and set your homework timer. *Bueno.* Now you have exactly seven minutes."

Cesar, intrigued, looked from Luz to the clock and back again. He hid the lump behind his back.

To forestall time-consuming questions, Luz said, "I'm going into the bedroom *right now* so I can't see the surprise you're making for me. And *I'll* make something for *you.*" She walked away while she spoke, finishing on the upbeat "isn't this fun!" note popular with parents.

Luz closed the bedroom door and leaned against it. Her breath, in the hush of Cesar's room, sounded as harsh as a rusty saw on an iron bar. She held her hands to her face. They were cold and trembling and her cheeks burning hot, but she had no time to waste.

She opened the empty metal tin of hard candies she always carried with her and pressed polymer clay into both halves. One side remained slightly concave. Luz needed more clay to create an accurate impression. Since there wasn't any more, she had to find something to take up space in the mold. She could tear off a section of cardboard from a paperback cover, but Cesar would be punished for defacing a book if Father Espinosa noticed. For the second time in as many minutes, Luz pulled back her hand. Then she laughed out loud. All she had at stake right now, and she worried Cesar might lose TV privileges! The changes she would unleash on Cesar's life would dwarf anything the child had ever experienced—Where would he go? With whom? Would he grow up an exile like her? Would he be safe? Her questions ricocheted around his uncertain future. *Stop. No time.*

Some debris on the bookcase caught her eye—a small piece of cardboard covered with a jagged line of hard plastic where batteries for his new remote-control car had been ripped out. Luz grabbed it and tore off the plastic layer. She pried out the concave lump of clay. Placing a folded section of cardboard in the tin, she replaced the clay and pressed it firmly against the cardboard. *Yes.* Enough.

She smoothed the clay. Then she detached the key with the blue tag, the key to Bobby's suite. Her hands working with precise muscle memory from endless practice in Miami, Luz dusted the clay with graphite from a cavity inside her mechanical pencil to keep the clay from sticking together so Luz could retrieve the key after the two halves hardened. She removed the clear plastic cover of her tiny eyebrow brush, which formed a funnel-shaped collar. Luz slid it around the key's handle and laid the key on the clay, orienting its point to a tiny yellow dot, barely visible on the outside. Then she snapped the two halves together, exactly as they'd shown her.

Luz had not dared glance at the clock while sweating over her task. Now she looked. A whimper of release escaped her lips. It would solidify in a minute or less. She swallowed and exhaled. Slipping the tin into her pocket, Luz cracked open the door to the living room.

"Don't come in," Cesar yelled. He was still manipulating his clay, so she had to wait.

"Time's almost up."

Luz counted to one hundred. She bent her paperclip to a fishhook and opened the tin. Tapped the edge of the clay. Solid. Careful not to mar the imprint, she slipped her fishhook into the funnel, which had kept the key's center hole from clogging with clay, and lifted the key out. She dusted off as much as she could of the graphite. Then Luz threaded the key back on Delores' loop and tossed it under the bed.

Opening the door to the living room, she called out, "Ready or not, here I come!"

Delores stood next to Cesar, her head bent toward the boy, as he showed her the treasure cupped in his hand.

CHAPTER EIGHTEEN

As Evan slunk home from his encounter with Luz, he passed a young Guatemalan man walking proudly with his two sons. Sons, because of the unmistakable family resemblance. Proud, because of the conspicuous pleasure as the trio swaggered, three abreast, along the sidewalk, the boys skipping at their father's side. The man greeted passersby with a proprietary nod instead of relinquishing contact with his boys.

Family. That story Evan had told Luz about his first memory—holding his father's hand while they walked—had been one of only a handful of memories of him and his father alone together. And he'd only told her the first part: They'd met some men from the base, and his father had told him to run along home. *Run home.* Evan had no idea where they were, and besides, he wasn't allowed to cross streets by himself. Whether he'd found his way home alone or cried and embarrassed his father—how that long-ago afternoon had ended was lost in the fog.

Evan grew up thinking his bisected life normal: When his father left, Evan's toys lay strewn throughout the house for days at a time; bedtime became flexible. Sometimes he and his mother had popcorn for dinner, sitting together on the rug while they watched movies on their old VCR.

When his father was home, the house filled with soldiers. Richard, his mother's brother and his father's comrade-in-arms, often showed up. His mother usually cooked a huge pot of something savory before the men arrived, then retreated to her room. Now that he was grown, Evan understood she'd been steering clear of them.

It was more complicated for Evan. When he joined his father and the other soldiers, they sat too straight. They apologized for swearing, asked diligently about school, about sports, about stupid shit. Evan caught the looks that occasionally passed between the men—glances that said, *When's this kid's bedtime?*

Evan became invisible so he could pretend to be hanging out with them. Sitting in a dark hallway or outside the windows on a summer night, he listened to their uncensored stories of heroism and disaster. Evan—always more at home in the visual world—*saw* their experiences: firefights and rescue missions, sand, torrential downpours, explosions.

Inevitably, in the course of eavesdropping, he heard stories not suitable for children. Comrades mangled when their tank detonated an IED, slaughter in the jungle, execution-style killings. Evan began having nightmares. He stopped sneaking around. His father's world was not Evan's. He, too, began to stay in his room when the men arrived.

Evan grew taller and filled out. He turned thirteen, fourteen. His father deployed to Germany to train demolition teams. His jeep flipped over on an icy road, and he died there.

His mother accepted the flag at his funeral. She accepted the condolences of his friends. Then she put the flag in the bottom drawer of her bureau and applied to graduate school. The men—the single or divorced ones—came by, offering to cut the grass or take Evan to a ball game, but she discouraged their attention, until only her brother Richard came around.

Richard took Evan under his wing in a way his father never had. He'd left the Army by then. Although his new government job as a civilian analyst at the CIA involved a lot of travel, he was no longer stuck overseas for lengthy postings. Richard treated Evan as an intelligent equal, took him around to colleges, took time to explain the importance of his work. Later, Richard introduced Evan to Evan's own small role in the big machine protecting American interests throughout the world.

Richard. Evan could not fathom how Richard squared his beliefs about spreading democracy, about a strong and just America, with discarding Luz.

And Luz. His unspoken grand romantic declaration now seemed as childish as a kiss and a Band-Aid to make it all better. From his first sight of her on the bus, Luz had ignited a spark in him. Yes, it began simply as selfish interest, but he'd known since Saturday that wasn't all. He'd sensed her incandescent passion before he understood she was living the rest of her life in a hurry because she had so little time left. All the vibrancy, all the warmth. *And all the lovers.* Yes, that hurt, but Luz had made no promises to him. An empty chasm opened in his chest at the thought of her bright flash of light blowing out. Blowing up.

It wasn't right, what Richard was asking her to do.

And since it wasn't right, Evan had to divine some miraculous way to thread a microscopic needle—protect Luz without betraying his uncle.

Evan trudged home. When he opened his front door, he realized his day had only just begun to go downhill.

* * *

No mystery men lay in wait outside Luz's gate. The street was empty of friend or foe. Her tiny apartment echoed with the absence of sound from the empty nights that remained. Luz hung her jacket in the closet; she put away the single bowl and spoon she'd used for break-fast. With a fleeting glance at the telephone that would not ring to-night, she set a pan of water to boil.

Luz took out the little tin with the clay impression of the key and, using a jeweler's screwdriver, she removed two almost invisible screws around the yellow mark and lifted off a small section of the edge, ex-posing the conical depression in the clay. Then she clamped the tin, funnel-shaped hole on top, to a sturdy bookend to hold it upright.

Into the saucepan of hot water, she set a coffee cup containing a St. Christopher medal that always sat innocuously in her velvet-lined jewelry box. The medallion had been fashioned from gallium, a metal—solid at normal room temperatures—which liquefies at ninety-five degrees. The shiny silver disk dissolved into an amorphous blob oscillating at the bottom of the cup. Luz lifted the cup from its water bath and poured a tiny amount of liquid metal into the opening of her clay mold. She tapped it to remove air bubbles. More gallium. Another tap. Luz was on automatic pilot now. Again and again, until it was full. The man who'd demonstrated this in Miami had made her practice the process dozens of times until she could accurately gauge the amount of metal required.

When she was done, Luz moved the setup to her refrigerator, where it sat next to the oranges and eggs. Half an hour later, she opened the mold and threaded the makeshift key onto her key ring.

Luz smiled as she recalled her shock at seeing Delores inspect Cesar's Christmas surprise, fearful Delores would be suspicious about the unusual material or about the missing keys. But no—Delores, having discovered her loss, was merely retracing her steps. Luz joined in the game of searching and coached Cesar on places to look, so he "found" them.

And as a bonus, Delores revealed she was off to air out Bobby's quarters since he was expected home in a day or two. Soon, Luz could swap out the flash drives. Then she'd melt the damn key. No evidence would remain.

* * *

Luz considered not going to the market the next morning, but even the slightest chance of news from Toño propelled her there. She wasn't sure what to do about Evan, though. Her successful duplication of the key was a milestone to report, but the "Bobby" assignment held secondary importance. Discrediting him was all to the good, but her main job was the death of Martin Benavides. Besides, she only had the key, not the locked-away thumb drive.

Notifying Evan could wait. So Luz took a different route to the market. Evan sat at his usual table in the café, facing the direction she'd normally appear. She'd almost made good her dash into the covered market when a police siren screeched. Evan, looking around for the source of commotion, spotted her. He stood and waved when she passed. Luz lowered her head and raced away. It wasn't the business part that distressed her, but the personal stuff. Luz had treated sex with Evan casually, and she assumed he felt the same, but something had happened Saturday at Evan's house. He wasn't feeling casual anymore.

And increasingly—kicking the ball around with Cesar, absently folding and refolding laundry, picking at dinner—Luz flashed back to Evan's hands, hot and insistent as they slid between her thighs, his low moans of excitement, their explosive release.

It had become so good so quickly. Luz had already begun steeling herself to the idea of forging more emotional distance. She had to keep Evan from succumbing to the illusion of a real, developing relationship.

Then came her weekend in the mountains. Damn Toño—of course he was right about Evan being a security risk. He'd already gotten too curious. Richard wouldn't have told Evan she had ALS. There was no reason to divulge that, and Richard operated strictly on need-to-know. Evan had dug up that secret on his own.

And she'd been so off-balance by what he learned that she'd thrown the whole bomb thing at him, making things a thousand times worse. For that, she had no one to blame but herself.

So much for the easy let-down. Judging by Evan's pale face and slumped shoulders, it was too late. Luz hurried into the market. Juana greeted her with warmth, perhaps even with a twinkle that tacitly acknowledged her role in conveying Luz to Toño, but she had no news.

A peremptory knock at Cesar's door a few hours later heralded her next advance.

"*Pase*," called Luz, looking up from the book the boy was reading to her.

In walked Alicia, in day-glo lime, reflections from her jangly ankle bracelet making rainbow prisms on the wall. Behind Alicia appeared one of the rifle-toting black-uniformed men of Martin Benavides' personal militia. The men, reputed to have been culled from the ranks of the Army as a reward for loyalty and—it was whispered—for ruthless extermination of any Benavides enemies, hung around the compound when they weren't needed to safeguard drug shipments in transit.

Luz's stomach dropped to the soles of her shoes. *Guilty. Run.*

CHAPTER NINETEEN

The soldier accompanying Alicia stopped at the door and stood, arms crossed, blocking her escape.

"Your presence is requested elsewhere," Alicia said. Something overlaid Alicia's normal expression of snooty superiority. A gleam in her eyes suggested excitement—no, it was more vulpine. Or perhaps Luz was merely projecting her own anxiety.

"W-what is it?" Time slowed as though Luz might have eternity to examine the bluebottle fly buzzing at the screen, the pale green walls with the watercolors of local birds, simply framed in pine, the rag rug, the plush sofa where she and Cesar sat, a beam of slanting golden sun lighting a path across the floor.

She'd tell them about Toño immediately. How grateful she now was for the blindfold. About six hours from the city, an hour up a steep track from a small town smelling of roasting coffee beans and *chicle*, that was all she knew. Surely, they couldn't locate him with those paltry directions.

"Come on." Alicia snapped her fingers, a gesture that could have been directed at Luz—or just as easily been a signal for the guard to grab her and drag her away.

As though her terror was contagious, Cesar curled closer on the couch. "I don't want you to go." He entwined his fingers in hers.

"I shouldn't leave Cesar."

"Unfortunately for all of us, I'm supposed to stay with him," said Alicia with ill-disguised peevishness. "*La Señora* wishes to talk to you. This man will escort you."

Dominga. Luz swallowed hard. Not torture and the firing squad after all. Perhaps her hints had finally borne fruit.

Luz laid her free hand on Cesar's clenched fingers. "*Está bien, mijo.* I'll be right back."

She joined the man at the door. They walked in silence, footfalls extinguished by the thick carpet, down the wide corridor, past the elevator Luz normally rode, toward the center of the building and the heavy door—bulletproof, Delores had once told her—that barred the way to Martin's lair.

The guard, blocking sight lines with his body, punched in a code. The door sprang loose with a hiss, and they went through. Wordlessly, the guard motioned Luz into an elevator at the far end of the central wing. Another code. He pressed "up." They exited on the roof, facing a helipad. Keeping a muscular hand pincer-like on her elbow, he led Luz to a pergola covered with leafy vines. In the center, an old lady in black lay atop an inclined hospital bed. Grossly fat, with ankles puffing out over her old-fashioned black lace-up shoes. She fanned herself with an elaborate folding fan.

Although it was cool on the rooftop, the woman was sweating profusely. She lifted her hand and, with a fluttering wave, dismissed the guard. He retreated to the wall by the elevator.

"Be seated." Her voice was a reedy whisper, feathery light on the breeze.

Luz sat.

"You know who I am."

"Of course." Luz bobbed her head, an attempt at a seated curtsy. "I'm honored to meet you, Señora Benavides." And *that*, thought Luz, was two lies in one sentence. It was no honor, only necessity, to be back in the presence of this old woman, a woman Luz had met a few times when she was a little girl.

Dominga placed her fan on a side table, her chins and upper arms wobbling with the effort. Then she steepled her sausage-like fingers and raised her hands to massage her upper lip. Dominga looked out at Luz over her hands and said, "I understand you enjoy reading out loud."

Yes! As Martin left the soccer field the day he'd attended their practice, he said—he grumbled—that his wife had become too weak to hold a book in her hands for long, and she'd recruited him to read to her every afternoon. Immediately, Luz understood this was a task he disliked. And one she could easily take over. She'd begun dropping hints.

"Yes, indeed, *Señora*," Luz said. "Of course, I read to Cesar, but at his age, I'm encouraging him to read for himself."

"There's a book on the table. Do you know it?"

Luz picked it up. *Men of Maize,* by Miguel Angel Asturias. A meandering allegorical novel based on traditional Maya legends, it was a story of unbearable loss and dramatic, magical rebirth. It had been a favorite of her mother.

"No." Luz refused to make even the slightest mental connection between reading to this beached whale and to her emaciated mother as she lay dying.

Dominga nodded. "You may begin."

Half an hour later, the old lady's eyes fluttered closed. Luz let her voice grow softer. She spaced her words. Slower and slower.

Dominga's eyes snapped open. "Return tomorrow. I'll arrange for someone to watch Cesar."

Luz cruised through the rest of her shift on autopilot, giving Cesar extra time in front of the television and serving his dinner at the earliest possible moment. The second he finished his *hilachas*, a beef and tomato stew that was the only "mixed-up" food Cesar tolerated, she hauled him off to the bathtub. Tantalizing visions of *torrejas*, the custard-filled sweet that was the Central American equivalent of sugar plums, must've been dancing through his head, as Cesar had been alternately giddy and dreamy that long, long afternoon as Luz considered how to proceed.

Point: Toño did not know about the bomb.

Luz owed her life to Toño. Her cousin had not saved himself with the other evacuees that night but had remained a soldier in the mountains. Now he was the leader of a popular resistance. Or, Luz reminded herself, *a* leader of *the* resistance. Toppling the Benavides' behind-the-scenes control of the political institutions and crippling their drug-trafficking network could propel the rebels into positions of real power for the first time in a generation. Their chance of success would skyrocket if they were on hand to direct the narrative—and to prevent those loyal to the Benavides from regrouping. But Toño did not know about the bomb.

After their long talk in the mountains, Toño decided to send an emissary to the other two insurgent leaders. At the same time, he gave instructions to the young couple who drove Luz back to Guatemala City. Apparently, they had highly placed contacts both in the Benavides-controlled government and among official and unofficial U.S. government sources.

Point: Toño estimated at least a week before all the questions would be answered to his satisfaction. Until she heard from him, she would do nothing.

Point: *But.* In the two days since her return from the mountains, Luz had assembled the most important missing pieces. She had a key. Bobby would be home the next day. Soon she could steal the information Richard needed to neutralize him.

And Dominga had invited her to read. Luz would have access to their private suite every afternoon. Although she hadn't seen Martin today, he seldom left the apartment, and Dominga had called for him when Luz was leaving. She had the perfect setup to detonate the bomb.

Even if Toño was unaware of the plan, it didn't change her desire to obliterate Martin. The murderer of her father—and of so many others—deserved to die. Since her thus far futile mission to bury her mother's ashes had had the inadvertent result of alerting Toño to the upcoming opportunity, Luz would give him as much time as possible to get organized.

Richard needed at least a week to get the explosives to her. With the endgame firmly established and now in Dominga's pudgy hands, she'd better get that part of the puzzle in motion.

So, mission on. Luz wouldn't wait for morning. She'd stop by Evan's after work to give him the message for Richard.

CHAPTER TWENTY

The woman who answered the door was almost as tall as Evan. She had long hair the color of cinnamon twisted into an intricate braid and piled on her head. Before Luz could speak, the woman said in excellent Spanish, *"No necesito nada, gracias."*

Luz, her work clothes covered by a cheap vinyl poncho and carrying her straw shopping basket, had been mistaken for an itinerant vendor by this stranger who'd responded to the doorbell. Lights were on in Evan's studio, and a jazzy piano piece played in the background. The woman held a beer in one hand, a magazine in the other. Jeans and an oversized sweatshirt. No shoes.

Confusion and doubt warred in Luz's head with the job she had to do. Her toes jiggled inside her shoes, itching to run away. She moved one step down, and the woman loomed even taller in the doorway.

"I need to see Evan for a minute," Luz said finally—in English.

The language change startled the woman. Luz got the quick once-over, what kids in New Hampshire called the hairy eyeball.

"What do you want?"

"To see Evan. It's important." Luz thrust out her chin and stood as tall as she could.

"Wait here."

She closed the door on Luz. In the last second before it shut, Luz recognized the sound of running water, the squealing pipes in Evan's shower. The woman's voice echoed on the other side of the door. "Evan? Honey?"

Honey? Evan, you bastard. You cheating bastard! And I felt awful about lying to you, when I only pretended *to have another man!*

Luz swallowed the hot taste of some emotion she didn't want to feel. She stuffed it deep down, buried it with the rest in her cemetery of losses. Her stomach hurt from the strain, and she was so angry her eyes overflowed to create a world blurry with tears.

The presence of the woman explained a lot, though. Luz revisited her memories of Saturday morning when she'd arrived unexpectedly. Evan's obvious desire seemed mixed with . . . oh, respect or at least an unwillingness to pin her to the wall and unzip his pants. *That* was when it crossed her mind that Evan was getting too emotionally involved. He'd shown her his paintings. They'd talked. About art, about his neighbors, about running. She made the first move, tumbling onto Evan's lap in that big armchair. They'd kissed. Again. And again. Evan's hands moved under her shirt. He unhooked her bra and cupped her shoulders, pressing her breasts hard against him. Then his fingers traced the length of her spine. Lower, lower, until Luz gasped with pleasure. There'd been an awkward pause, both of them panting.

The front door squeaking open returned Luz to her present problem. Evan stood in the doorway. His quick intake of breath was almost a hiccup. With a shaving cut on his chin and his hair plastered to his scalp, he, too, was a stranger.

Luz looked over his right shoulder, not meeting his eye. Wary of being overheard, she pitched her voice low. "I have a message for Richard. I—"

"Luz, let me explain." He stood silhouetted by the soft lights in his living room.

"Don't interrupt. This is important. Tell Richard it's time to get started." Luz turned and ran down the street. The oblong of light from Evan's living room cast her shadow in front of her as she raced away. *In a few weeks, none of this will matter. I'll be dead.*

A second shadow joined hers. Luz glanced back. Evan had sprinted down the steps. She couldn't talk to him now. Talk, argue, listen to his lies, whatever—she couldn't face it. God only knew what she'd say, and he'd see her tears and think she was upset, when she was just too furious.

Luz had only about a fifty-foot head start. She bolted into a small alleyway beyond the line of attached houses. Evan's feet slapped on the sidewalk. If he'd seen her turn, he'd spot her, so Luz pressed farther into the alley and ducked behind a short wall that concealed a line of trash cans. Evan clattered past. Luz remained motionless, hugging herself against the unexpected pain radiating from her chest.

Evan would guess he'd missed her once he came to the end of the street—and he'd turn back. Unfortunately, the alley where she hid dead-ended in a brick wall, so waiting for him to throw in the towel was her only option. A light drizzle spattered on the cobblestones, and Luz pulled the collar of her poncho tighter on her neck. She knelt trembling in the dark.

Her thoughts circled back to Saturday morning, how Evan had wrapped his arms tight around her after they kissed in his chair. He'd lifted her up as he stood. *Now, to the bedroom . . .* but they'd shed their clothes in the bathroom instead and screwed in Evan's shower, a cascade of hot water bathing them as Evan hoisted her high, and her legs circled him.

She'd misread the change she'd imagined on Saturday. Evan wasn't in pain because he'd fallen for her. No, Luz was a short-term lay who—as far as he knew—was just passing through. He simply felt guilty for cheating on his girlfriend. And he wouldn't fuck Luz in their bed. Evan had been spending whole nights with her, so the woman hadn't been conveniently off shopping or at work that morning. The tall woman with the braid had been away. Now she was back.

Evan's footsteps echoed once more. Luz peered from the shadows when he passed, barefoot and shirtless in the rain, walking toward his house. Silence. As soon as the coast was clear, she would slip away, go home and get dry. Sleep. Try to forget. Luz peeked out from the side of the building.

Evan stood in the center of the street, the glow of the nearest streetlight illuminating rain-slicked skin. He still blocked her retreat. Seeing him there provided a laser focus for pent-up rage to erupt. *Liar. Cheat. Loser.* Her sniffles retreated. She could damn well wait him out. The girlfriend was bound to call to him soon—and he would have some explaining to do. Luz doubted he was as good a liar as she was.

Evan faced away from her, his words indistinguishable. Tracing a circle, he wheeled in her direction. "Luz, if you can hear me, please come out," he called. "I have to talk to you." He did it a few more times, turning and speaking to shuttered windows and locked doors, to a cat slinking along. He stuck it out longer than she expected, calling her name, saying he needed to talk. The woman came out once. Luz didn't see her at first, but Evan stopped his slow-motion circling. She came into view and put her arms on his shoulders like they were dancing. Her lips moved. Then she left.

Rain picked up, dinging on the hard stones and slate roofs and metal trash cans. The continuous jangling muted his calls. Luz was drenched. Anger faded and tears started again. Evan stretched his long arms, lacing his hands behind his neck. He swiveled his head once more, then walked away.

*   *   *

Margo sat in the green chair by the easel. She'd gotten another beer. When Evan came back inside, she set it down with a thump that sloshed sudsy liquid onto his little lacquered table and said, "Time to talk to *me?*"

"She's one of Richard's people," he said quickly.

Margo lifted an elegant eyebrow and cocked her head. "And that explains exactly what?"

"And I wanted to paint her."

Margo turned to look out the window. *"Paint* her?" Leaving little doubt as to the verb she thought Evan meant.

"Richard needed me to stay in touch with her, and then I realized she'd be a perfect model for a new project." True as far as it went, but it felt like a lie because what mattered was impossible to sort out. The black-and-white of the truth on the outside had little to do with the knot inside. Even if he was nothing to Luz, she was a woman with a bleak future mired in a wicked predicament. She didn't need him as a lover right now. Luz needed a friend—more than that, an ally. She was being disposed of. Richard's arrogance, his complicity, in considering this a solution to Luz's illness, shocked Evan.

"So I begin to understand your distinct lack of enthusiasm at my return. How long have you been *painting* her? Ever since I left?"

Evan hung his head. "Close enough," he said to the floor. "But I'm not—" No, he was not going to explain why his relationship with Luz was over. Because it wasn't. Not really. The honesty of sharing Luz's private tragedy with Margo seemed more like a betrayal than any lie he'd tell, so Evan finished, "I never meant to hurt you."

"Of course not." Margo tossed her head hard enough for a section of her hair to swing loose. She jammed it behind her ear. "You never mean to. It just happens. Like *we* just happened. Yeah, it was a thrill, snatching the extremely popular and talented Evan McManus, Mr. Eligible Expat Bachelor, from under the noses of those women in their garden party dresses and fuck-me heels. But you know what? That was the high point. You're great with the grand romantic overture, Evan, but lousy on the follow-through. When was the last time we had a *real* conversation, one that wasn't actually foreplay? Mainly, when I'm trying to, you know, *communicate* with you, you're looking off in the distance."

Margo lifted her beer and took a long swallow. "You save all your emotions for your art. Painting her, that's rich!"

Evan swallowed hard. His cheeks burned. Damn Margo. He'd always loved her Emperor-has-no-clothes skewering of others' foibles. Now that she'd turned it on him, he saw his plan to care for the dying Luz through Margo's eyes: wishful thinking. His hope to rescue her from Richard's plot another pipe dream.

"These days, even when you're here, you're somewhere else in your head. And—" Margo hiccupped.

Evan mentally upped the number of beers she'd consumed. She teetered to her feet and lurched toward him.

"And," Margo repeated. But then she stopped halfway across the room. She gnawed on her lip, indecisive. Then her hands flew to her hips, and she glowered at Evan.

"And let me tell you one other thing as long as you're standing there, pretending to pay attention, imagining you're earning points for taking it like a man—your fucking duty, your obligation to the woman scorned. Let me tell *you*. Your irreproachable Uncle Richard is involved in some really sketchy stuff. And if your little friend is a friend of his—she's up to no good, too."

Margo came close enough for Evan to see her quivering with fury. Her hands came off her hips and curled into fists, which she held close to her side like a boxer ready to jab. "Do you remember the last time Richard was here? That night we were talking about civilian casualties in rural areas? And I said our medical staff was stretched too thin, and I hoped something was *finally* being done to reduce civilian bloodshed because I'd heard General Osambela had been called back to Guatemala City for talks. And Richard was, like, 'Osambela, who's he?' My God, Evan." Margo's hands clapped her cheeks. "If he hadn't said it right then—that very second—the next words out of my mouth would've been, 'Did he say anything to you about the talks?' Because I'd seen them having drinks together at the bar in the Sheraton the night before, laughing and talking—your Uncle Red-White-and-Blue and the Army commander directing the forces against the guerrilla opposition."

Margo's expression was half outrage, half pity, one hundred percent disgust. "He's playing a deep game—and you, you're just playing. I don't even know which one of you is the bigger manipulator. My two cents," she tossed over her shoulder as she walked away. "You can sleep on the couch tonight."

The bedroom door slammed shut.

"I don't have a couch," Evan said to the door.

CHAPTER TWENTY-ONE

Luz sat exhausted and alone with her coffee. She'd been drenched by the time she got home from Evan's but so tired she could only wrap a towel around her sopping hair and crawl under the covers. She lay half-awake, unable to block the stream of images that flashed against her eyelids—Toño laughing in the mountains, Cesar laughing as he outran her on their soccer field, Evan by streetlight, Martin cuddling Cesar while they sang, the tall woman calling Evan "honey," Dominga on her high hospital bed, Evan in her bed . . . She woke to a stiff neck, snarled hair, and deep lethargy.

Luz pressed the steaming coffee cup to her cheek. A distant sun, too far away to warm her. *Why bother.* It had been like this after her mother died, after she'd completed the flurry of tasks that death in the civilized world entailed. Exactly like those weeks after she got sick and before Richard offered her the opportunity to shine—however briefly—and go out in a blaze of glory.

What once sounded simple had become complicated. The images that defeated sleep rolled again: Evan outside her gate, bereft; Toño, questioning and suspicious; Cesar hunched in his window seat, alone. The clock on her wall ticked; its rhythm counted down each passing minute of the total allotted to her.

Perhaps it was the same for everyone. For her father, who accepted death, but surely hadn't anticipated its arrival that quiet evening while they sat outside their tent finishing dinner. Her mother knew, too, but she was buoyed by belief, sure she was going to meet her beloved in a better place.

Luz believed in oblivion. You had one small period of time to live, then—poof. Her *poof* would remove the possibility for her to do any more. But she *should* be feeling happier about ending the reign of drugs and corruption that was the legacy of the Benavides.

Ya basta. She'd given Evan the heads-up. The rest was in his hands. In Richard's. And in Toño's.

That left the problem of her mother's ashes. Once again, she considered skipping the market, but if Juana had information about going to the waterfall, Luz wanted to know. She'd have to avoid Evan today. She was moving too slowly, physically and mentally, to spar with him should he turn up. Which, she feared, he would. He'd wanted *something* last night. To explain about his girlfriend? Perhaps he merely had a message from Richard to deliver.

The hell with him. All of them.

As she tidied the kitchen, Luz spotted a white card she'd stuck on the refrigerator. *Shit.* This morning was the follow-up appointment with the doctor she'd seen after her attack of dysentery.

Her first thought was to cancel. Or simply not go. She took the card and slapped it against her other hand. Another image percolated to the surface: Dr. Guzman patting her knee when he learned she had ALS. His spontaneous kindness had almost toppled her unsteady emotional equilibrium.

Luz bit her lip. Rather than disappoint the lonely old man, she'd go see Dr. Guzman and listen to his stories of patients past and dreams for an uncertain future. Better to spend her time that way than to stay here brooding. Plus, if she hurried, Luz could check in with Juana beforehand.

She arrived at the market much earlier than usual, with Evan nowhere to be seen. Juana, however, handed over nothing but oranges. Luz opened her mouth and almost protested. *No news?* It was Wednesday already. And while Toño hadn't committed to arranging a speedy return visit for Luz, he'd promised to try. He knew her Sundays-off schedule, but of course, he didn't know this would be one of her last Sundays.

Perhaps she ought to compose a brief note for the next day begging Juana to make the arrangements a priority as she would be—what? —leaving town soon. Or she could simply bring the ashes to the market with her. *Oh.* Like a balloon untethered, her spirits floated higher. *Of course.* If Luz didn't get news by Friday, she'd write instructions, wrap the urn, and present it to Juana, saying it was a gift. Luz wouldn't be at the waterfall, but she'd *said* goodbye. Let Toño and the older men who remembered her parents take care of it.

With the sense of one more item crossed off her to-do list, Luz took a bus uptown. The once-elegant building housing Dr. Guzman's office smelled like an old lady, faintly flowery with undertones of furniture polish. The air had the same hush as on her first visit. Dust motes still pirouetted in the slipstream of the heavy wooden paddles of the ceiling fan. Luz had the sense things seldom changed in this space, that should she come back in one year, or ten, she'd find the same yellowing sign taped to the elevator, the same fluffy drifts of dirt at the corners of the steps.

Of course, Dr. Guzman wouldn't be there. Luz shook her head as she mounted the marble steps. Iowa. Snow and rolling farmland. Cows and American football. And his family, she conceded.

This consultation didn't matter. He'd tell her to stay off her ALS medications or to start taking them again. Either way—well, she probably wouldn't bother. In the days since her intestinal disturbance had cleared up, Luz had felt stronger than she had in a while. It was some kind of remission, she guessed, although her U.S. doctor had not been optimistic she'd experience anything like that.

But Dr. Guzman surprised Luz. As before, he took her arm to escort her into his examining room, seated her in the same leather chair. "I've been doing some research this week." He stopped and, sounding embarrassed, added quickly, "I have too much time on my hands. As my practice has shrunk and all my patients have dispersed, I find I miss the puzzle each one presented. You see, my strength as a doctor of internal medicine was as a diagnostician." The doctor leaned forward intently. "If you will permit me, I would like to do a complete work-up this morning. There are one or two things about how you describe your symptoms and their onset that have me curious."

Luz hesitated. Not wanting to sound impolite, she restrained her impulse to tell him it didn't matter.

Dr. Guzman must've read her reluctance as a money worry. She'd asked him to send a bill for her first visit since she didn't have health insurance and hadn't brought enough cash to cover the cost. "I wouldn't charge you for this," he said, picking up a pen with the zeal of a smoker reaching for his first cigarette of the morning. "It would be a welcome diversion." His bleak look around the office took in the dismantling of his professional life.

So I'm to be your distraction, as you are mine.

"Really," he added, and Luz read the unspoken entreaty in the tension at the corners of his mouth, "it would please me to go over a few things with you."

An old man with too much time. "Of course," she said. "But what—"

"Let me start with some questions and then examine you. Based on what I learn, I'll write a request for lab work." Dr. Guzman picked up a legal pad covered with tidy handwriting.

Covered. Luz settled back in the chair. If those were his questions, she'd be here until time for work.

* * *

Evan almost didn't answer the phone. Before it interrupted him, he'd been sitting on a hard cane chair at the kitchen table with his sketch pad in front of him. At first, his pencil had drawn only doodles. Then one of the swirls had reminded him of Luz's ear and hairline, and he'd begun sketching in more detail.

Mid-stroke, Margo's gripe zapped him as distinctly as if she were still in the house. *You leave all your emotions on the canvas.*

Maybe that's what he was doing. But what *should* I do, Evan temporized. Breakfast was over; time to get to work.

Good try, Evan. But actually, you're ignoring that your girlfriend left you because you screwed another woman, and your uncle is orchestrating a scheme that will cause the other woman's death. And then there's that other woman herself.

Luz. Evan crossed the room and removed the Botanical Gardens sketch from the easel, where he'd hurriedly placed it to hide Luz's portrait the afternoon Margo returned. He paced back and forth, side to side, squinting at it. He needed to soften the lines under her eyes. The jaw still wasn't right.

Evan slammed the sketch back onto the easel. *Damn.* He was doing it again, letting his thoughts ricochet to avoid looking at the real problem. He stomped back to the kitchen table and flipped his sketchbook closed.

Okay. Identify the problem: Margo didn't approve of Richard. No, that wasn't accurate. Margo had cited a specific instance in which she claimed he lied, and she used that lie to suggest a pattern of dishonesty.

Evan accepted that Margo had seen Richard with the general, but the meeting probably came with an innocent explanation, like the lie Richard had told Luz about his job. Richard, after all, lived in a world of secrecy. Margo didn't know her indictment of Richard's honesty coincided with Evan's own misgivings. Not about his honesty, but about his methods. There was a quote Richard occasionally spouted—something about applauding "extremism in the defense of liberty." So if Richard was charged with the disruption of the Benavides drug cartel, *of course* he would concoct a rationale for assassinating its leader.

It was his next step that shocked Evan. Sending Luz on a suicide mission, no matter what the state of her health, violated everything Evan believed in. If this was the sort of extremism Richard accepted, he had crossed over the line.

The real problem was Luz. In the background—churning beneath his pencil strokes, behind the nice linear progression he was constructing to indict his uncle's methods, beyond his own distress—ran an undercurrent of disordered ideas, none of which seemed sufficient to persuade Luz to abandon this whole indecent scheme. He had to figure something out. And soon.

Evan's phone rang. Conscious of once again choosing distraction over introspection, he crossed the room and grabbed the receiver, punching the wall hard as he did.

"*Aló?*" he barked.

"Evan, my boy!" came across a line that crackled and popped.

Evan frowned at the wall, where the charcoal dusting his hand had left a faint outline of his clenched fist. He placed his fist precisely on the charcoal shadow and beat a fierce rat-a-tat-tat before saying, "Hi, Richard. What's new?"

"Oh, this and that, this and that." The call sounded like it came from the end of a long tunnel, but Richard's buoyancy came through crystal clear.

"You're in a pretty good mood," said Evan, not bothering to cam-ouflage his acerbity.

"Yep, it's shaping up to be a good day for the good guys."

O-*kay*. Clearly Richard thought congratulations were in order, but the effort was too great. Evan didn't care why it was such a good day. And if *he* was having such a bad day, that must make *him* one of the bad guys.

"Where are you, Richard?" he asked instead. "It's a lousy connection."

"Can't do anything about that, so we'll keep it short. Tell me what's happening in the big city."

"Not much." Here was his chance to pin Richard down. But he had to ask—and get the answers he needed—as a trusted business associ-ate, not some wet-behind-the-ears kid.

"The weather's cleared," Evan said, buying time.

"You're getting to the market daily?" Richard asked.

So he was calling about Luz. Evan contemplated her unfinished portrait on his easel. Maybe he wouldn't complete it; it could stay for-ever sketchy and imperfect, like his understanding of her.

"Evan?"

"Sorry. Yeah, I go."

"What has she reported?"

Evan brushed away the smudge of charcoal on the wall. He glanced back at Luz's portrait. "Hey, Richard, I want to ask you something."

"Shoot."

CHAPTER TWENTY-TWO

Raul de la Vega called while Cesar was in the tub. "You need to stay overnight. The blasted night nurse called in sick, and the regular replacement is out of town."

"Tonight?" Luz had just reached seventeen minutes in her countdown to escape. "Overnight?" Dr. Guzman's questions had indeed occupied her all morning. So many picky points, dredging up memories of those days in early summer when—still rocked by her mother's death—Luz's occasional problems with balance escalated to frequent falls and debilitating muscle cramps.

"You want to keep your job, you stay. I'll have a housekeeper bring clean sheets for the bed in the alcove off Cesar's room."

She wasn't going to get out of this. Besides, she didn't *need* to go home. That morning, in addition to asking a million questions, Dr. Guzman had given her a complete physical. Afterward, he recommended she stay off her meds for another week unless her muscle tremors resumed, so *that* wasn't an issue. She kept a little toothbrush in her purse; she could shower here. And it solved the problem of a potential Evan ambush. She'd varied her routines to avoid him but, in the deserted late-night streets of her neighborhood, straight home was the only smart option. Let Evan think what he liked when she didn't return. Asshole.

When Luz told him she was staying overnight, Cesar rushed around assembling his idea of necessary supplies for an impromptu sleepover: an extra pillow for the little bed, a fuzzy blanket, one of the soft toys that lay hidden under his pillow—never acknowledged, since Cesar was too old for baby stuff. He also brought out a small clock to put on his bedside table, explaining that he liked to look at the numbers if he woke up, but the regular nurse had banished the clock. Its glowing green lights annoyed her.

Guilt, an itch that sent Luz's arm twitching toward Cesar. She'd battled him so often over his bedtime routine—but not tonight. He was clean and in his pajamas in record time, sitting on his bed, dark hair curling over his forehead, cocker spaniel–style.

"How many stories can I have?"

Guilt, now irresistible, a fiery prickling that cried out for relief. This time, her arm encircled the boy's shoulders, and he snuggled next to her. So instead of reading from the too-familiar books in Cesar's little library, Luz told him tales she remembered from her childhood—*Los Tres Sueños, Los Puercos del Rey, El Compadre Malo, Los Niños Perdidos.* The last was a Central American version of Hansel and Gretel, a tale of abandoned children finding their way home. It was the one Luz had always requested first.

Cesar resisted sleep in the way of young children: *Can I have some water? Tell me another story.* After she'd exhausted her entire repertoire, Luz lay down next to Cesar and yawned. She pretended to have trouble keeping her eyes open and responded only in a soothing monotone, *mmm, uhhh.* His chatter subsided. His breathing deepened.

Cesar slept, and Luz rolled slowly off the bed. In the adjacent alcove, she took off her sweater and, noticing the wrinkled Band-Aid the young lab tech had slapped on her arm after taking blood, she removed it as well. She untucked her thin cotton shirt, unfastened her bra, loosened the catch on her pants, and curled up under the covers.

It was warm in the house, and quiet, except for Cesar's light snuffle. There were none of the night sounds Luz was accustomed to: the off-balance squeaking of her refrigerator, the rustle of the silly bird who'd adopted her bedroom window sill as a shelter, the slow drip of the hot-water faucet in the bathroom.

Luz and a lonely little boy. Lonely Luz. She stopped herself. No, she was *not* going to end the day as it had started, with a pity party.

Putting Cesar to bed had reminded Luz of her first years in the U.S. The upheaval had turned her from a tomboy into a fearful child. After a day at school, she came home—not to endless giggling phone conversations or trips to the mall with her boisterous classmates—but to hot chocolate prepared the Guatemalan way, with chocolate shaved from big disks added to boiling water, and to nursery tales she'd outgrown years earlier.

So tonight, Luz had lain there, with her hand light on Cesar's chest, and played her mother's role—telling the old stories, speaking Spanish, soothing a solitary child whose needs she could never meet.

A noise in the bedroom woke her. Another creak. Movement. Concerned Cesar was trying to get to the bathroom in the dark, Luz jumped up.

A figure stood by Cesar's bed. She gasped. It turned at the sound.

Martin Benavides put a finger to his lips and mouthed *shhhh*. He crossed the room in a few quick paces.

"Where's the nurse?"

"She was unable to come tonight, sir, so I stayed in her place."

His body was closer to her than it had been to her father the night Martin betrayed him, the night, dark and still like this one, when his machete swung—once, twice, and left her father to bleed to death. The night Luz's mother lost her *otra ala*, her other wing, and forever lost the ability to soar. The night Luz lost her father, the patient and kind man who always made time to nourish her curiosity.

She could smell his cologne, his musty old man smell, hair cream. She hated Martin Benavides. He was so close she could reach around his neck and squeeze. And squeeze.

With an abrupt yearning more intense than she'd ever had for a lover, Luz needed him to see his death in her eyes. If she set off the bomb the way Richard wanted, Martin would die without seeing death approach, never knowing that she, Luz, would finally exact retribution.

"Go back to bed." His words were peremptory but the tone mild. "I often come here at night when I can't sleep. Watching Cesar helps me see the future more clearly."

He waved his hand in dismissal.

Luz ducked her head and retreated. She sat on the little bed, tingling with this new raw emotion. Personal vengeance. Not an anonymous blast but an angel of reckoning.

She would make it happen.

Martin Benavides, I am Maria Luz Concepcion, daughter of Emilio Concepcion. His eyes would widen. He'd sense danger. She'd say, *I watched you murder my father. I saw his blood soak the ground. I still hear his screams in my sleep.* Then she'd have a gun, if she could get one, or perhaps it would be the bomb after all. But before the blast, he would beg her for mercy. He would beg and plead and cry, and she would obliterate him.

Luz watched Martin through a gap in the skimpy curtain. He stood beside Cesar's bed, head sunk low and shoulders hunched, an old man. She could kill him tonight, now—but, no, not in front of Cesar. And she'd promised Toño to wait until he knew more.

Martin sat on the edge of his grandson's bed, mumbling words too faint to discern. Then he sagged. Placing one hand on Cesar's chest, much as Luz had done earlier, he rubbed the other across his forehead and cheeks. Oddly, Luz found her earlier explosion of hatred, her desire to face him in death, had prepared her to see Martin as a person, not the mythic ogre of her upbringing. A drug trafficker. Cesar's grandfather. A man who traded his ideals for easy money. The only person in Cesar's family who showed him simple affection. A double-crossing murderer.

A rustle of bedclothes and a creak. Martin stood. He smoothed his grandson's blanket and shuffled out of the room.

Long after he left, Luz lay awake in the dark.

CHAPTER TWENTY-THREE

After his testy telephone exchange with Richard, Evan had returned to the kitchen table and grabbed a piece of charcoal. Doodling again, but—the hell with Margo and anybody else who objected—that's how he worked out his problems. At first, he drew only angry slashes; then a slip of his hand created a sloping blur. As Evan sketched, his subconscious began to hum. He tidied the slashes into logs piled askew; the blur became a plume of smoke. He added flames, a path, a distant hill.

Evan's idea took shape along with his drawing. If he couldn't persuade Luz to abandon Richard's odious scheme, then he was going to do his dead-level best to get her to consider an alternative. So Evan drove to Luz's house early the next morning, hoping to catch her leaving for the market. Instead, she came rushing home around mid-morning. The boyfriend again.

And here *he* was, outside her gate once more. Luz might think he was stalking her, but it couldn't be helped; he needed to talk to her. "It's not what you think."

Luz's head snapped back as though his words had lashed her cheek. She stared into space, her head still bent at an angle. She looked distracted. Not angry. And not like a woman satisfied. A songbird filled the space between them with melody. *Something* was different this morning. Evan waited. This difference held possibility. Perhaps she would listen to his proposition.

Finally, Luz said, "Nothing is."

"Huh?"

Luz massaged the back of her neck. She said in a low monotone, "Nothing is what I think."

Again, Evan waited. Tiny gold balls in her ears glistened as her head swiveled slowly side to side, her mouth slack. When nothing more was forthcoming, he said, "I'm not going to tell Richard anything yet, Luz. You have to talk to me first."

Her head tipped to one side. She *could* be trying to process his words, but Evan sensed her thoughts were far away. He tried once more. "When you came to my house Tuesday night—" No, that wasn't the right place to start. Margo was as irrelevant as her new boyfriend, but Richard sure as hell wasn't. "You gave me a message for Richard," said Evan. "He called yesterday, but I didn't tell him what you said."

Her eyes and mouth opened round. *Now* she understood.

"I won't be an accessory to your throwing your life away. I want to—God, can we go inside and talk?"

Luz closed her eyes and squeezed them tight, like an infant getting ready to wail. Instead of crying—or replying—she fumbled blindly in her bag. She produced a key and opened the gate, leaving it open after she walked through. So Evan followed.

* * *

Luz staggered inside and dropped her bag on the floor. Yet another sleepless night packed with ghosts from the past. And now Evan. Evan, whose presence had become too desirable. Evan, who had ferreted out some of her secrets. Evan, whom she tried to push away by revealing her last secret.

There was only one way to deal with vulnerability—attack—but where-oh-where was she going to find the energy? Luz retreated to the kitchen and opened cabinet doors as though her cupboards held a secret stash of resolve. While she rummaged, Evan said, "You have a choice, Luz. Like I did when I decided not to give Richard your message yesterday."

Choice—that was a laugh. Her father had never given her a choice. She hadn't had a choice about leaving Guatemala. No choice about dying. Pressure built inside and provided necessary propulsion. "What the hell business is it of yours? I *made* my choice. Leave me alone."

"Richard has no business putting you up to this."

She whirled to face him "So what?"

"So you'll die," he shouted. *Die, die,* echoed. Evan looked taken aback at his vehemence.

Don't think. Attack. "No shit. And so will you, someday. Unavoidable. Like taxes and baseball season."

"Luz, you know what I'm talking about. He's using you—"

"It runs in the family, I guess."

Evan went pale. He took a step back, steadying himself with a hand on the wall. That shot hit its target, thought Luz. He'll go away. Now if she could only reassemble the tangled fragments of her convictions into a pattern that once again made sense.

But Evan didn't walk out. He said, "I messed up when we met. I should've told you about Margo. I should've done a lot of things differently. Sure—I slept with you when it was all about sex. So shoot me. It was wonderful." A rueful grin mirrored his embarrassed smile from the bus the day they met. "And when you kept saying you'd only be in town for a short time, I convinced myself it was okay—a lousy excuse, I know." He looked up and said, "But I *didn't know* what you planned, what it meant when you said you wouldn't be here very long." Evan hunched his shoulders and jammed his hands into his jacket pockets. "Maybe you only wanted a warm body to take the edge off the strain. All the times you pushed me away, said 'go home.' I finally got the message, Luz. I—I won't bother you about *that* anymore."

Evan stole a glance at her, as if to check her reaction. When Luz remained silent, he rolled his shoulders back and began to speak quickly. "I didn't come over to argue with you. I came to offer my help. I have several ideas about your job, your real job." Without any movement Luz could detect, he loomed closer. He crowded into her emotional space, still passionate, but without the touching. "I know how you can do what you really came to do. And do it without sacrificing yourself. Will you at least hear me out?"

The room began to spin as though she'd tumbled into a fast-running stream of icy water, too disoriented to know how to reach the surface. Luz grabbed hold of the counter and waited for the vertigo to subside.

Do what she came to do—he must mean the bombing. Evan wanted to help. If only she could trust him *whatever* she did. She had to have time to think.

Luz pushed past Evan and flung open her front door. "I can't do this now. You have to go."

"How about after work? I'll come back."

"Why not," said Luz, without responding to his repressed—but all-too-obvious—enthusiasm. She'd listen. Maybe by then she'd have figured out which way was up.

*   *   *

Luz wasn't noticeably clearer by late afternoon when Dominga called for her to read. It was their third session, and for the first time, Martin Benavides was on the porch when Luz arrived. The rooftop structure that housed the elevator also included several rooms, which Luz had assumed were storerooms. Martin and Raul de la Vega stood talking by an open door. Behind them was a small room with a desk and walls lined with books. When de la Vega left, Martin moved a high-backed wooden chair from his study to the edge of Luz's peripheral vision and listened. Distracted by his presence, Luz stumbled over words and lost her place so many times that Dominga finally plopped her fat hand on the side of her bed, scattering magazines and peanut hulls, and said, "Go now. Come back when you've remembered how to speak Spanish properly."

Luz returned to Cesar. Unless she could get her emotions under control, the door to Martin Benavides would slam shut as quickly as it had opened. She and Cesar had begun a game of cards when the doorknob rattled, and Bobby stuck his head into the room. He was back, as Delores had said he would be. Bobby looked different. Jazzed. Maybe even high on something. He jittered, hips thrusting, shoulders swinging. He licked his lips; sharp white teeth showed under his vacuous playboy grin.

"We're doing holiday photographs in the garden." Bobby squinted at his son. "White shirt, a nice sweater. Blue, if he has one." He snapped his fingers at Luz. "Comb his hair."

And he was gone again. Cesar, who'd jumped to his feet when he saw his father, flopped onto the couch. He buried his head in the cushion, his hands curled into fists at his side.

Gently, Luz said, "Let's get you dressed."

Asshole. How could *he disappoint Cesar like that?*

Out in the garden fifteen minutes later, they encountered a mob scene of gardeners decorating the portico with holly garlands, a dozen strangers in casual clothes, some holding big white umbrella-things, some tinkering with little black boxes. Luz found Bobby and showed off a spiffy Cesar. The man looked his son up and down as Luz would have inspected a plucked chicken at the market.

"Yes, that will do, *señorita*."

"Should I stick around?"

"Ah." Bobby edged closer, resting his fingers lightly on her arm. "Not necessary." He squeezed her arm before releasing her. "I'll bring him back when we're done."

This was it. Lethargy forgotten, Luz rushed back to Cesar's room and removed Richard's replacement drive from its hiding place inside a hollow crucifix above Cesar's bed. Tucking the flash drive into the pocket of her sweater, she jogged along the soft carpet to the seldom-used stairs where she'd have a greater chance of escaping notice than if she used the elevator. Luz pushed open the heavy stairwell door and dashed one flight down to the second floor. Bobby's suite stretched the entire length of the north side of the corridor.

Her hand rested on the doorknob. Someone could be waiting there for Bobby. She rubbed a damp hand across her forehead. Well, she was Cesar's nanny, after all; she'd brazen it out. Luz inserted her duplicate key. It turned smoothly. She opened the door and walked in, head high as though she belonged.

Luz stood near the door. The huge living room was quiet and empty. Although a muddy jacket and some unopened mail lay on one of the couches, no briefcase was visible. Luz tiptoed into the room.

The briefcase was not under the jacket or on the floor or between the couches or under the coffee table or on the counter next to his espresso machine. Taking care to stay away from the large windows at the back of the room, through which the photo shoot would be visible to her—and she to the milling participants—Luz searched the rest of the room. Not here.

She tried his bedroom next. The room was an opulent throwback in midnight-blue and gold. A closed suitcase lay on the bed, dirty socks on the floor, but no briefcase.

On to the last room. Unlike the rest of the suite, Bobby's office lay in darkness. The light from the open door to the living room revealed dark paneling and heavy wine-red curtains on two narrow windows on the far wall. Portraits of sober dark-haired men with black jackets and mustaches. Built-in bookcases and thick oriental carpets. A large mahogany desk in the center of the room was heaped topsy-turvy with books, folders, ledgers, and paper-clipped sheaves of papers. There could be tons of information Richard might like to know, but he'd been clear: Nothing else was necessary. The thumb drive contained the entire history of the drug operation—suppliers, distributors, chapter and verse of who, what, when, where, and how.

"Yeah, I skipped the *why*," Richard had added with a chuckle, rubbing thumb and fingers together. *Money*.

The briefcase sat on a small table between the two windows. Luz checked her watch. It had only been six minutes since she'd left Cesar. All the preparation, the endless rehearsals—she was in the zone. Asshole Father of the Year was going to get exactly what was coming to him.

Richard's instructions about retrieving the thumb drive indicated it would be in a zippered pouch connected to the back pocket. Luz opened Bobby's briefcase. Like the desk, it contained a messy variety of papers: travel documents, a collection of index cards held together with a rubber band, brochures for a timeshare in Rio, a pack of Post-its. Luz unzipped the little pouch and set the flash drive on the table. It glinted silver in the shadowy room.

She pulled hers from her pocket and placed it next to Bobby's. If Richard's information was out-of-date and Bobby was using a different one, Luz was supposed to abort. But they were identical. *Gotcha*.

A door opened. Someone walked into the living room. An adrenalin surge rocked her body—fight or flight. Neither was advisable: The only door led into the living room, and the intruder could easily be one of the Benavides' armed guards. Luz grabbed both drives and squeezed into the opening under the desk, pulling the chair in behind her as far as it would fit.

Someone, a soprano someone, called softly, "Bobby? Bobby, where are you? I've missed you." Footsteps receded. The voice muffled, became inaudible. Then suddenly it was right outside the office door.

"Oh, for heaven's sake, are you *working?*"

The oblong of light on the rug grew large as the door creaked all the way open. Someone stepped into the room, temporarily blocking the light. A whisper of fabric. The person paused on the other side of the desk, out of Luz's line of vision. Silence.

Then a soft shuffle of papers. The woman was looking through Bobby's correspondence. She might've hoped to find Bobby—or pretended to—but she was snooping in the office. Like Luz, an unauthorized visitor.

Rhythmic thrumming sounded overhead; long fingernails on polished wood. If *she* were doing that, Luz would be trying to decide what to do. A palm slapped lightly on the desk. Decision made. The woman was on the move, to the side of the desk, inches from Luz's cramping left leg.

High heels came into view—long, slender feet in the highest heels imaginable. Carmine toenails. Silky black pants. Gold-link ankle bracelet.

Alicia! Martin's assistant. So, Luz thought, she was either keeping an eye on his son or sleeping with him. Maybe both.

Alicia rounded the desk. If she looked down, she'd see Luz's knee. Papers swished and crackled. *Don't come closer. Don't look in the drawers.*

"Hey, baby." The voice, unmistakably Bobby at his most sultry, sounded practically in Luz's ear. If she hadn't been penned in by the chair and desk, she would have splattered on the ceiling.

Alicia sighed. A rustle of clothing. A tiny metallic click.

"Where are you?" asked Alicia.

Where are you? Luz's tremulous panting was so loud Alicia must hear it.

Silence, then Alicia again. "Nope, I don't know where she is. What is it with that drab little nanny? I simply do not get why you insisted—"

Alicia stopped as though interrupted. Luz understood then. A phone call. Alicia had Bobby's voice as a ringtone for his calls.

"Where do you *think* I am? . . . Yeah, keeping your bed warm . . . Oh, *cariño*, I don't know if I can . . . Mmmm, imagine me . . ." Alicia laughed, low and provocative. "Yeah, you, too. Bye."

A click. "Shit," Alicia said. With one last drum roll of acrylic nails, she walked away.

The office door slammed. Luz shuddered in sheer relief of being alone. Her elbow banged the chair, and it skidded away.

Alicia and Bobby. Luz tried to make sense of it: Alicia who worked for Martin spying in Bobby's office, Alicia undressing in his bedroom, Bobby—Shit, he'd told Alicia he was looking for her. That meant the photographers were done.

Luz had to get out before Bobby returned. She scrambled out from under the desk, one flash drive in each of her pockets, quickly replaying those panicked seconds before Alicia came in. Positive she'd flung Bobby's original into the left side, Luz thrust the replacement drive in the zippered pocket and closed the briefcase.

The living room, empty. The bedroom door, closed. Luz crossed the space in seconds. Down the hall to the stairs. She flung open the stair door and ran right into Bobby.

CHAPTER TWENTY-FOUR

Luz hit hard, the top of her head banging into Bobby's chest. As she bounced off, he pitched backward and began to fall. His hands grabbed at her for stability. A grunt of discomfort, then, "What the hell!"

It took a second of disorientation before Luz connected the dots—the solid flesh she'd encountered, the grunt, Bobby's voice. *Uh-oh.*

"I'm—" Luz's mind went blank. She had no business on the second floor. The tiny thumb drive in her sweater pocket felt as heavy and round as a bowling ball.

Think. She heard noises? She smelled smoke? That might do.

But Bobby had recovered enough to notice something else round and solid. His hands cupped Luz's breasts.

"No!" Luz stepped back and put out her hands to ward him off.

In a single, fluid move, Bobby captured her hands and pushed her against the wall, one hand pinning her arms above. "Yes," he said quietly as his other hand tightened on her neck. Then more decisively, "Yes."

He shoved her chin up and pressed his mouth against hers. His tongue forced her mouth open. The man must be crazy to bother with this kind of macho feel-up to assert dominance. Bobby *knew* Alicia was in his bedroom.

Bobby's mouth released hers, and his tongue and teeth traced her jawline. Luz cried out, "Stop it! Let me go!"

A searing pain—he'd bit her ear.

"Shut up," he whispered into the burning ear.

His hand left her neck and traveled south. Luz wriggled and twisted. He wrestled with the buttons on her bulky sweater—the drive! When he began to lift her shirt, Luz hunched her shoulders and swung her head, using the top of her skull as a battering ram. This wasn't a casual grope. There'd been his jittery arrogance before the photo shoot. Bobby was too keyed-up. As Luz writhed, he leaned in harder, immobilizing her with his hips, rigid and pulsing under the fabric of his pants. Dread started as a quivering cold chill in the pit of her stomach, a weakness in her legs.

Perhaps Bobby was feeling the thrill of a predator with a squirming prey. He might lose interest if she played dead like a small forest animal, so Luz went limp to avoid any contact that might further excite him.

But Bobby didn't stop, and he was strong enough to restrain her arms with one hand while wiggling his other under her shirt and pushing down her bra. He rubbed his palm roughly from one breast to the other. Then his fingers closed on her nipple, and he began to twist. "No," she yelled.

Bobby's fingers loosened. A second of blessed relief—until the back of his hand smashed her jaw. Her head struck the wall.

"Yes," Bobby said with a slow smile, "and there's not a damn thing you can do about it." His free hand moved down again.

Now she was icy with fear, and she began to thrash in earnest. There was no one in the stairwell. Only the maids used it regularly, and they were gone for the day. "Help," she screamed, although the heavy steel doors would muffle her cries.

Bobby slapped her again. This time, her tongue was caught between her teeth when her head slammed into the wall. Luz tasted blood.

In the echoing stairwell, there was only the rasp of pounding, percussive breathing, Bobby grunting while he pulled at her clothes. His underarms smothered Luz's face, damp and malodorous. She twisted her knee to the side and tried for his groin, but she couldn't get any leverage.

A quiet ringing joined Bobby's hoarse grunts. Luz's first thought was that she was losing consciousness. The sound became louder—a syncopated beee-bahh-beee—and all at once Luz recognized "Bobby." Alicia was in the hall calling for him. Bobby must've heard it, too, for the pressure eased. With a burst of strength born of desperation, Luz swung her elbow into Bobby's stomach. She ducked under his arm and darted for the door. He stuck out his leg. Luz stumbled toward the door, her momentum sapped.

"Bobby?" Alicia's voice was closer. Too close.

Bobby knocked Luz to the floor with a savage backhand. "See you later." Bobby settled his clothing, flashed a tight grin, and walked away.

Luz covered her belly with her hands, shivering, and tried to warm herself. The all-encompassing misery gradually separated into discrete injuries: bruised, battered, lacerated. Bobby had tried to rape her, and he would come after her again. She'd kill him before she'd let him touch her. *You will pay.*

CHAPTER TWENTY-FIVE

After a long while curled into a tight ball in the stairwell, Luz sat up. Hands trembling, she buttoned her sweater and squeezed the thumb drive. Bobby was going to pay.

She just needed to get through the rest of the afternoon. Cesar—thank goodness for *his* ignorance—was consumed by his own misery. Delores had been and gone. So no one noticed her tear-streaked face. The blood on her ear. Her ripped buttons.

Luz put on a DVD and locked herself in Cesar's bathroom. She drew the hottest bath she could stand and lay in it, replenishing the water as it cooled. After repeated entreaties by Cesar for her to come out and read, talk, watch TV, play checkers, finally he called out "dinner's here," and Luz knew she had to try for normal and pray Bobby would not return.

Her ear—the only mark visible to the world at large—had stopped throbbing. It was shiny-red and distended, though, so she undid her ponytail and shook her hair loose to cover it. The lump on the back of her head was tender, but her hair concealed that, too. Her jaw and neck, although sore, were not discolored. A purple bruise spread from under her ribs to her navel.

But the physical signs of damage were nothing compared to her emotional wounds. For now, Luz stifled her tears and stuffed the pain into the vault that held all her memories, a place of scars from wounds that never healed.

Before she sat down to *pollo asado* and *frijoles negros* with Cesar, Luz hid Bobby's flash drive in the hollow of the crucifix where she had once concealed the substitute. She didn't have a computer at home, but Cesar's old desktop had a USB port. Tomorrow, after her hands stopped shaking and her tears dried—tomorrow, she would read the damn thing. It was important enough that Richard planned to use it to control Bobby's ambitions. Acquiring it had cost Luz dearly.

Bobby was going to pay.

*　*　*

The night nurse, who didn't look the slightest bit sick, appeared on time and with cheery apologies for inconveniencing Luz the previous night. Luz fled for home, ignoring Cesar's pleas for a couple of her stories before bed.

Bone-weary and emotionally drained, her battered muscles protesting, Luz wanted only to crawl into bed. She'd heap on every blanket she could find. A scalding shower might help warm her, but Luz doubted she had the energy. Anyhow, the chill came from a distant scary place she was not yet prepared to probe.

Luz stepped into her bedroom and reached for the light switch. A scratchy sound from her window announced the presence of the stupid bird that liked to shelter there. Not in the mood for disturbance, she walked over to shoo him off.

She parted the curtain and rapped on the window. A bloody hand clung to one of the iron security bars. Luz dropped to her bed, trembling. Calling the police was not an option. In Guatemala, that could cause a thousand unintended complications, not a smart idea in her current situation. First, Luz needed more information. She crossed to the window, pushed aside the curtain once more, and peered into the darkness.

Now, two hands showed, as though her tapping at the glass alerted the person. In the faint light filtering in from the living room, both hands appeared to be streaked with blood. Turning on the bedroom light would let her see better, but it might also alert her neighbors. And Luz still wasn't sure how she was going to handle this.

It depended on who was out there.

The hands held on to the bottom of the bars. The man—for the rough, broad hands were those of a laborer—was hanging below the level she could see. She rapped at the glass again. Fingers tightened on the bars; blood oozed with the pressure.

Alive. Responding to her knock, not dropping away. The little window, a tiny two foot square to begin with, only slid open about six inches. She cracked it open and whispered, "Who's there?"

A hoarse moan. "Ayyydaaaaa." *Ayúdame?* Asking for help?

She had to investigate. Running a palm over dry lips, Luz turned off the porch light and opened her front door. All quiet, dark. A night bird cooed. She blinked a few times to adjust to the absence of light. Hugging her arms around her chest, she stepped onto her miniature porch. One step down to the grass. Two to the edge of her building and around the corner where a line of hibiscus bushes obscured the side wall. Four more paces to the pale square of light marking her bedroom window.

Luz flashed back to the jungle, to running in the dark away from the noise, away from the light, her mother's hand slippery with her father's blood as they raced away. Away.

More than anything, Luz wanted to run into the house and lock the door. Turn off the lights and close her eyes, find oblivion in sleep. Not tonight. Not yet.

A few more steps revealed the corrugated soles of heavy boots—and a dark lump between two bushes. The man still drooped from the lowest part of the bars. His head sunk onto his chest. Knees on the ground. He could be praying with uplifted hands. Perhaps he was.

Her arrival had been so silent that when she mouthed *"aquí estoy,"* the man writhed violently. He let out a piercing cry and loosed his grip. He slid down the wall, leaving behind a dark smear.

No longer afraid, Luz moved to his side. "Toño, what happened?"

His eyes pleaded, but his mouth couldn't form words. A hand moved to his hip and brushed a ragged hole in his pants. Toño had been shot there, and from the blood on his chest and head, possibly elsewhere as well.

First Bobby and now this. But Luz would not die tonight from the violence done to her, while Toño might. He had saved her life once. Now it was her turn. A dead cold calm replaced the earlier chill. She patted his cheek. *"Momentito.* I'll be right back." Luz grabbed a spare blanket and a pillow from her bedroom and ran back out. She knelt next to her cousin, bent close. She whispered, "I'm going to roll you onto a blanket."

He was alert enough to register understanding with a minute nod.

Bushes all around made it difficult to position the blanket. Eventually, Luz spread the blanket near Toño's legs. She lifted his legs, brought the blanket under, and pulled. Inch by inch, Luz eased the blanket under his thighs, his midsection, then his shoulders, tugging Toño out onto the lawn as she worked. Finally his head was exposed. Luz gasped at the blackened flesh. Blood crusted along his scalp and into his thick hair, matting it down. Leaves and twigs stuck to it.

Pulling a few inches at a time to minimize the shock of the uneven ground, Luz brought her cousin closer to her door. She paused at the front corner. From here, they would be more visible. A distant street-light through fluttering branches cast indistinct and wavering shadows. It wasn't perfect camouflage, but unless she or Toño made too much noise—or neighbors came inconveniently out to walk their dog—it would do.

The height from the grass to her little cement porch was only eight inches, but Toño couldn't walk, and she couldn't lift him over the rise. Luz cushioned the gap with the pillow she'd dropped there on her way back to him. The careful bump up to the door strained her arms and back, and Toño's head lolled as he let out a groan.

Inside. Door shut with a quiet snick, not the slam she earnestly desired. She locked, then bolted the door.

"Luhhh."

"You're in my apartment. You're safe." Luz tried to encourage him. "I'll take care of you." But Toño had been shot at least once and had lost an awful lot of blood. She had to do more than kneel next to the man and mouth platitudes. *Triage*—the word came out of nowhere. Then, *first things first*—a cliché that suited her situation.

Toño's head was a dark, bloody mess. A streak of red started on his temple and disappeared into his hair. She laid two fingers gently on the wound. Tacky. The blood was coagulating. Luz gently rocked his head so she could inspect the underside. It was filthy, but blood wasn't flowing. That meant the wound was superficial. Didn't it? At least it meant Luz wasn't going to disturb it immediately.

The other side of his head was merely dirty. His neck streaked with dust and blood. She lifted his right arm.

Toño's eyes opened wide and filled with tears. "Aaaaaaah," he gasped.

"Sorry." Luz lowered his arm, then ran to the kitchen for scissors and a roll of paper towels. She cut his shirt off. The injury to the right arm was a massive welt, red and pulpy. Not life-threatening. She wrapped a layer of paper towels around the injury and placed his arm back on the blanket. Toño's left arm was in good shape, except for a gash on his hand. He'd been making it worse by holding himself at the window. Now that his hand had relaxed, the blood pooled and began to thicken. She made a bandage with more towels. A red target blossomed in the center.

Luz was avoiding looking at his hip. Gunshot wounds. Toño and his men hadn't planned to decamp for another week or so, but perhaps they'd gotten an early start and run into an army patrol. Luz sank onto the floor and pressed her clenched fists to her chest. The bruise there from Bobby's assault burned under her hands. *Not now.* Once again, she pushed her fury aside. There would be time later to settle the score with Bobby. For now, she had to concentrate on Toño.

Just bringing her scissors under the fabric of his pants bloodied Luz's hand. Teeth clamped tight to keep from exclaiming in horror at the gore, Luz sliced the material until Toño's hip was exposed. Rivulets of blood—bright red, liquid—dripped like a leaky faucet.

Oh, no. Luz bowed her head and laid her hand lightly on her cousin's chest. "I need to stop the bleeding around your hip. First, I'm going to clean the area. See if I can figure out how to—oh, Toño, you picked an awful refuge—you know I don't have medical training." At her cousin's piteous hint of a smile, she said, "Yes, I know I'm family. I'll keep you safe. And I won't call a doctor unless you say so."

Toño tried to lift his hand, which Luz took and placed in her lap. He blinked his thanks, but Luz wasn't necessarily telling the truth. Although there was a price on his head, she had no intention of letting Toño die on her living room floor. If she had to call an ambulance and give him a false name, she would.

Luz warmed a pan of water and had just sat on the floor again when the telephone shattered a silence broken only by Toño's shallow breathing.

The phone. She looked at the clock over the stove. *Oh, Jesus, it was after ten.* She'd told Evan he could come by after work. He should have arrived an hour ago.

Maneuvering clumsily to her feet, Luz lunged for the phone, knocking it off the small table. *"Aló?"*

"Luz, you okay?" Evan's voice whispered from across town.

"Yeah, I—"

"I'm sorry I didn't call earlier. Listen, I've got a problem and can't make it tonight," he said, barely audible.

"Oh?" There'd been that moment in the morning when sharing her burden with Evan had felt possible—and dangerously close to comfort. Between Bobby's assault and Toño's injuries, however, Luz hadn't given a second's thought to formulating a more personal and direct plan for killing Martin. Evan's help might've given her new options but now, like sand slipping through her fingers, time had run out.

Evan's defection tonight was too much like the answer to a prayer she hadn't made. It wasn't likely his chic girlfriend had given up on him that easily. He was still whispering, probably locked in the bathroom so Margo didn't hear.

"I'll try to be at the market at the usual time," he said.

Damn him. But—the market. Juana! If Toño survived the night, she'd ask Juana for help.

"No," she said, too loud. "Don't come. I—I'm skipping it tomorrow. Call me after work, okay?"

"You sure?"

"Yeah, 'night." Luz set down the receiver. If it was Margo, she'd lost him for good, but it couldn't be helped. She turned back to Toño and dipped the washcloth in warm water.

*   *   *

Evan flushed the toilet, stuffed his cellphone into his pocket, and walked back into the studio. Luz had sounded far too relieved he couldn't come over. She could've been humoring him this morning, saying anything to make him leave peaceably. He really believed she'd been interested, but it was pretty clear now that he didn't get women. "Want another beer?" he asked in passing. "I sure do."

From the living room, a voice said, "Let's head out for dinner instead."

Evan remained in the kitchen. He tilted back his head and let the cool liquid run down his throat, then held the bottle to his overheated forehead. An hour earlier, Evan had been watching the clock as he got ready to leave for Luz's, rehearsing what he'd say, when his doorbell rang. The last person he wanted to see stood on his doorstep.

"What are you doing here?"

"I was in the neighborhood and thought I'd drop by."

The absurdity made them both chuckle, but Evan's only choice was to open the door wide and say, "Come on in."

Now a toneless whistle grew louder as footsteps approached the kitchen.

"C'mon," Richard said. "I could eat a horse—and in this country, I probably could order one grilled to perfection." He clapped Evan on the shoulder and steered him toward the front door. "We've got a lot to talk about."

CHAPTER TWENTY-SIX

Pale pearly light had begun to erase the darkness before Luz finished cleaning the gunshot wound on Toño's hip. She discovered one bit of good news: The bullet had gone clear through. At least she thought it good news that no metal fragments remained. Although she'd stanched most of the bleeding, blood still oozed. Luz suspected the bullet had done serious damage. Toño needed a doctor. When Luz told him she planned to get word to Juana, he'd nodded his approval. She would be at the market as soon as it opened to get help.

A knock on the door startled Luz out of an uneasy sleep on the couch. In her disorientation, she imagined it was Toño trying to get in, but it was daylight. People would see him covered in blood and call the police. Luz sat up and tried to shake off the remnants of sleep that prevented her from thinking clearly. A neighbor must be at the door since the buzzer at the gate had not sounded. Perhaps someone had seen Toño after all and waited until morning to confront her. Or they'd sent for the police, who now stood on her doorstep with grim expressions.

The knock again, louder.

Wake up, wake up.

Another knock.

Luz put her bare feet flat on the cold tile floor. "Who's there?" she called.

"It's Richard, honey. I came to see you."

A simple pine door, painted green, was all that stood between Luz and the ruin of her plans. She had to keep Richard out of the house.

"*Momentito.*" Luz ran into her room, snatched a loose housedress from her closet, and pulled it over her head. Toño slept on a nest of blankets. She had dragged him around the corner into her little bedroom as dawn broke, and then scrubbed her floor and counters, cleaned out her pots and the pink-tinged cloths, removing all traces of gore. His color was better now. She touched his forehead. Hot, dry.

Leaving her front door on the chain, she opened it the few inches permitted and blinked in the bright sun. "I didn't know you were in Guatemala." Luz hoped she sounded surprised and curious, but panic lurked in the undertones.

Only a few days earlier, she would've given *anything* to talk to him again. Now Richard Clement stood solid on her porch, not a figment of an overwrought imagination. Dark pants, sports shirt, a lightweight blazer, silvery hair, trim mustache—he hadn't changed a bit.

But Luz had. Aside from small social fibs, like pretending to enjoy the bizarre seafood things he'd occasionally brought as treats for her and her mother, Luz had only lied to Richard once: When he and John had first discussed the Guatemala job with her, John brought up her father's connection to the *Frente Popular de Liberación*.

"Do you have any contact with the guerrillas?" he'd asked

Luz had answered no, technically true since, at that precise moment, she did not.

"Don't you think it would be nice to connect with your cousins, old friends, people you knew when you were younger?" John asked the question, but Richard paid close attention. "*I* would," he added, as if that might make Luz more comfortable with an admission.

"I don't know who's alive or where they are," she'd replied. More or less true. "And I don't know how to contact anyone. There's no reason to bother." *Pants on fire.*

Now Richard stood less than ten feet from the top general of the FPL. Luz needed to deliver an Oscar-winning performance.

"Wha . . . what a surprise," Luz stammered. "I had no idea."

"I got the chance to come down for a long weekend, so I thought I'd get the ball rolling." Richard rested one hand on the doorframe as he looked inside, beyond her, into the dim apartment—*ay, Dios, let me have cleaned everything.* "I brought the materials you'll need. Since Evan says you haven't contacted him, you're probably not ready, but it was too good an opportunity to pass up."

I'm too exhausted to do this.

You have to safeguard Toño.

"Can I come in?" Richard flicked his fingers at the thin chain, now the only barrier between her and catastrophe.

No, I've got to get you away from here. "I'm out of coffee, Richard, and I desperately need a jolt. Want to buy me a cup? Or three?" Luz said, sidestepping a direct answer.

"That would be a pleasure."

"Won't be a minute, then."

He stepped forward as Luz closed the door in his face.

No, no. She'd screwed up. Luz squeezed her head in her hands. She'd *never* left him on the doorstep before. Plus, she had to get to Juana immediately. She couldn't spend the morning parrying Richard's questions, not telling any more lies than necessary.

Luz squared her shoulders. *He can't come in, so that's that.* She dashed to her desk and wrote a terse note to Juana. She'd have to deliver it soon. And alone. Distracting Richard would be more challenging, and way riskier than diverting Evan's attention each time she spoke to Juana.

*   *   *

"Where's a good place for coffee?" Richard asked when she joined him. He'd moved away from the door and appeared to be admiring the blooms on her scarlet hibiscus. *Oh—blood on the outside wall.* If Richard had walked around the side of the building, he might have seen it. And her bedroom curtains—surely, she'd closed them again last night after she discovered Toño. Hadn't she?

"Coffee?" Richard prompted.

"Oh." She had to get him away from the apartment. *Idea: Walk toward the market.* "This way," she said, linking her arm through his as she'd done a million times.

"Is something wrong, Luz?"

"No, just tired." So tired she couldn't remember when she'd last slept. But Luz had to pull herself together and figure out how to get rid of Richard.

The long night's work had exacerbated her cuts and bruises. The dark purple welt that stained her rib cage had spread, and her stomach throbbed. Fear and hatred, suppressed while doctoring Toño, returned with a vengeance. She simply could not return to the Benavides' today as though nothing had happened. Nor should she leave Toño alone. If the night nurse could do it, well, so could she. Luz was going to take a sick day.

"You seem more than tired. Are your health problems getting worse?"

"No, no, I'm fine." Luz laughed at the obvious exaggeration, and Richard joined in.

"Could've fooled me," he said.

"Really," she said, "most of the time I feel all right; it's just that I hardly got any sleep last night."

After that, Richard retreated to small talk while they meandered—was Luz enjoying her return to her native country? Was the apartment satisfactory?

The streets filled with pedestrians when they neared the market. Luz waved to the old melon ladies on their blanket and the Indian bird-seller who sat on the stone wall next to the entrance.

"Do you have shopping this morning?" asked Richard, looking at the bustle on the other side of the street.

"Only a couple of things. I'll head over there later."

"What's on your grocery list?"

"Fruit and eggs," she said, making it up as she spoke. She only needed Juana. Remembering her excuse, she added, "Oh, and coffee. The man I bought it from last time overcharged me, so I'm going to look around." Luz chattered to keep the conversation flowing on safe topics. "I only went to him because he'd given me such a great deal on sugar. I had to buy a new supply after the ants got into it."

Luz led Richard to a café on the corner near one entrance to the market. Whether or not it was a good place for *coffee*, she didn't know, but it was the best place for her hastily assembled ruse. She waited until they were seated at a little table under an awning and Richard had ordered *dos cafés con leche*.

"Oh, I should've used the bathroom before I left," she said. "Excuse me for a minute."

Luz dashed into the café—betting Richard wouldn't follow her to the ladies room—and ran out the side door. She sprinted across the street. Not making the slightest pretense of shopping, she went straight to Juana's stall and shook her hand. Although Juana seemed confused by Luz's formality, she reciprocated. Luz deposited her note with an extra squeeze as she released Juana's hand. "Just wanted to say hello. I'll be back in a little while to shop," called Luz over her shoulder.

And she was back in the café. Panting.

"Whew, much better," she said, sliding onto the little wrought-iron chair.

The waiter materialized at Luz's elbow and served their coffees. She dropped a sugar cube into her cup, pretending to be absorbed as she stirred to dissolve it in the warm liquid. Then another, and another. *She'd done it.* Now if only her galloping pulse would get back to normal.

When she looked up, Richard was smiling. "Still taking coffee syrup for breakfast, I see. What were you saying earlier about an infestation of ants? They got into the sugar?"

"Ugh, it was a mess. I finally dumped the whole bag and replaced it with fresh. Which I now keep in the freezer."

But Luz didn't want Richard's attention on her apartment. Better get down to business. She cleared her throat, a preliminary. Richard cleared his in unison.

They laughed.

"Yes, we're still on the same wavelength," said Richard. "So. Let's talk." Coffee in hand, he tilted his chair onto its back legs, balancing precariously against a pillar. "How's it going?"

"Smoothly. So far." Luz smiled back before taking a sip. She'd tell the truth, all that she could, and try not to lie to her oldest friend. "The work is easy. Cesar's no problem at all. But encountering *Martin* was intense—the first time he showed up in Cesar's room, it came as such a surprise. I thought I was going into shock."

"I'm sorry." Richard blew so hard on his steaming cup of coffee that choppy waves scudded across the cup. "I wish there'd been a way to cushion the blow."

"I suppose there wasn't." How she'd jumped Evan's bones as an antidote would remain her secret. Toño, a *huge* secret. Bobby's assault— yet another secret, and one she'd fight hard to keep. Years ago, she'd asked Richard what to do about a boy at school who was harassing her—nothing physical, just the sexually suggestive comments of a cocky high-school kid. Richard had totally overreacted. No avuncular advice that time; he found out where the boy lived and confronted him. And his lawyer father. Returning to Luz, Richard had promised her it would never happen again. It hadn't.

Luz couldn't imagine what Richard would do to Bobby if he knew Bobby had forced himself on her, had come so close to actually raping her. And while the thought of Richard as a knight errant riding once more to the rescue was comforting, Bobby had attacked *her*. This was *her* fight. If Richard pulled her off the job now, she'd never get her revenge.

What could *she say?* "Seeing Dominga wasn't as disturbing, but it was definitely weirder."

"Weird? How so?"

"She used to be so elegant." A nervous laugh. "To see her legs swollen and the old-fashioned black dress and little bun in a hairnet—I couldn't believe it was the same woman."

"People do get old," said Richard absently, "and they change."

I won't get old, but maybe I'm changing.

Richard's chair crashed onto all-fours, and coffee sloshed onto his cuff. That crack about aging was a gaffe she wouldn't have expected Richard to make.

Perhaps he was distracted enough for her to prod him into revealing more about the plan. Although here was a totally unexpected opportunity to find out for Toño who Richard's group was talking to in the FPL, yesterday's brutal encounter had thrust something else into first place. "Now that I know the players better," said Luz, "I'm curious."

Richard reached across the table and squeezed her hand. "That's my Luz," he said, his expression hovering at the intersection of apologetic and affectionate. "I can't remember a time when you didn't have a million questions for me. Go ahead. I'll tell you anything I can."

"It's about . . ." She chose her next words carefully. *Destroying Bobby* had superseded *killing Martin* as a priority. "About your choice of target."

Down at table level, Richard patted the air with his hand a few times and mouthed, "Watch what you say."

Luz looked around. They had the outdoor seating area to themselves, and the waiter had retreated into the café where a TV broadcast football from Madrid, but Richard was always cautious. She nodded, spoke quietly. "I understand about the father, but wouldn't it be better to take care of the son as well? He seems to be in charge."

Richard squinted and pursed his lips the way he did when organizing his thoughts. "Two parts to that answer, Luz." He raised an index finger. "First, the old man's been too slippery. His hand is all over the operation, but his actual fingerprints nowhere. The man has decades of enemies, and I've contacted every one I could. I've talked to people I shouldn't be seen with. No luck. No one can—or will—provide enough information to convict him. Our way is the only way.

"Second part." Richard lifted his other hand and extended its index finger. "The son doesn't command the fear or respect of his father. While he will, no doubt, rush in to fill the void, he's not nearly as wily. We're going to string Bobby along—with him not knowing we've infiltrated their organization—and we'll use the information you're going to retrieve to see how many others we can implicate before we bag him."

So Richard had plans for Bobby. Luz hid her disappointment. She imagined doing the job she'd set out to accomplish, killing Martin and, however the exact circumstances, not surviving. But Bobby still alive, preying on others with impunity, that was not acceptable.

"Any luck on that front?" Richard asked. "The thumb drive?"

Luz still needed to look through it before deciding how to proceed. *Bobby must pay.* "Not yet," she said, with an apologetic hunch of her shoulders.

Richard smiled. "With Bobby home for Christmas," he said, "perhaps you'll get your opportunity soon. Anything else?"

CHAPTER TWENTY-SEVEN

"I've got to get into her place." Richard slapped his palm on the kitchen table.

Evan bent to retrieve a section of newspaper that fluttered to the floor. "But you can't—"

"I explained why this is important, right? And I'm not asking you to do anything illegal." Richard began to pace. "All you have to do is follow her when she leaves for work and give me the all clear. I'll do the rest." He reversed course, back toward Evan, his hands clenching into fists and then releasing, spreading fingers wide. "She was too jumpy, keeping me outside. Nervous. Distracted."

Nervous around Richard? When Richard had left to meet Luz, Evan assumed she'd tell him she'd already passed Evan the information. He was resigned to a tongue-lashing. Then Richard had burst into the house—not pissed at him but fuming about Luz.

"I think she's seeing someone." Richard uncharacteristically ran fingers through his hair. "He may have been there this morning. She looked like she hadn't gotten a wink of sleep."

So it was *true.* Evan suddenly recalled the lemony shampoo Luz used, her soft encouraging sounds of desire. She had gotten thoroughly under his skin.

"I want to get in today." Richard pulled out his chair and straddled it, his elbows thrust out like a wide receiver protecting the football. "But we have to make sure the man's gone, too—damn!" He pinched the bridge of his nose. "Okay, here's the plan. Drive over there now. Park so you can see her gate. Keep track of who's going in and out."

"What are you going to do?" Evan hoped he sounded merely curious.

"Better you don't know. I'll tell you one thing, though—Luz lied about not gaining access to Martin's suite. I knew it would take time, and I wouldn't have suspected anything, but she's seen Dominga, Martin's wife. Dominga's an invalid. She can barely walk, and she never *ever* leaves her rooms. If Luz saw her, she's been to their side of the house. She ought to have told you."

She did tell me. And she didn't tell you she had. Was Luz really considering his offer?

"Get over there now." Richard lobbed Evan's plaid jacket onto the table. "We can't be one hundred percent certain the man is gone, but call me the second she leaves for work."

It was time to clear things up with Luz. And Richard just handed him the perfect opportunity.

* * *

Toño was awake when Luz returned. Feverish but alert. And thirsty. "Water," he whispered. Since he was too weak to sit, Luz sat cross-legged next to him and drizzled a spoonful at a time into his mouth. "What?" he began, but gave up after the one syllable.

Guessing he meant "what happened?" or "what are we going to do?" Luz explained how she had cleaned and bandaged the hole in his side. Then she told him, without mentioning Richard, about passing the note to Juana asking for help. And how, on her return to the market—solo, Richard having miraculously had other business to attend to—Juana, looking shaken and frail, had given Luz a message that someone would come for Toño in the early afternoon. Toño gave the ghost of a smile and wheezed his approval.

"I don't know how they plan to get you out," Luz said, offering another spoonful of water. "I called in sick to work, so I guess we wait."

Toño mumbled, "Don't 'member much . . . last night."

"How did you get in here?"

"Split up . . . safer . . . climbed fence . . . hiding in the dark . . ." Toño winced. He touched her arm lightly. "Your place . . . no one watching . . . trust you."

Trust.

"Don't talk any more. You can tell me later."

The buzzer to the gate sounded, shrill, an ominous note. "It's awfully soon," Luz said, "but I'll check."

She slipped out her back door and approached the gate from the side. Evan was looking up the main path. He didn't see her.

Richard must've blindsided Evan last night, much as he had her this morning. How quickly she'd lost faith. Unlike Toño, Luz didn't know who to trust. Since her mother's death, Richard had been the closest thing to family—until Toño had abducted her and she'd begun this week of upheaval. Life was so much easier when she could turn to Richard for advice and help. Instead, she was hiding things from him. And so was Evan.

Now Evan was here.

She ran down the path. Evan stood at attention, not meeting her gaze.

"Richard is staying at my place," he began.

"I thought so. When he showed up here—"

"You don't have to explain. You don't owe me anything. But Richard knows you've been in to see Martin and Dominga. He's coming here today after you leave for work. He has keys. I'm supposed to be watching to make sure"—Evan's face contorted— "the man leaves, too. Richard's in a hurry to get into your apartment."

The man leaves. The bottom fell out of Luz's stomach. He'd seen. Or guessed. Richard was no fool. She was beyond stupid to test her wits against him.

"How does he know someone's here?" she asked finally.

"So there *is* someone?"

The raw pain in Evan's voice gave Luz pause. Had Richard's version of the situation prompted Evan not to trust *her*?

"Evan, what did he tell you?"

"Richard said you wouldn't let him in this morning because you'd had company overnight," he muttered in a quick monotone, speaking to the pavement.

Light dawned. So what if Evan hadn't told her about his girlfriend; *She* hadn't told *him* she was dying. And she'd lied to him, too—about where she'd gone, about having another man. But now . . . maybe it was time for a fresh start.

Luz sighed, releasing the bolt holding the gate shut. Trust. She had to start somewhere. Luz took his arm under hers and led him up the path.

"Evan," she said, "it's time you met my cousin."

*   *   *

They whispered in the living room to keep from disturbing Toño.

"Anyhow, that's where I was last weekend," said Luz.

Only last weekend, thought Evan. "Why didn't you tell me where you'd been?"

"I wasn't supposed to be running off to guerrilla territory. Richard and his colleagues—they quizzed me about my connections to the *Frente Popular*, if I knew how to get in touch with my relatives who were still here." Luz ducked her chin. "I said no, even though my mother told me all I had to do was get to know the orange sellers, flash my mother's wedding ring—it was a family heirloom—until one of them said her name."

Luz explained about the ashes and how the abduction had gone haywire. "And when Toño told me he wasn't aware of the U.S. plans to destabilize the Benavides, I promised to wait before going ahead with the bomb."

"If you were going to wait, why'd you insist I tell Richard you were ready?"

"I thought Toño would find a simple explanation," she said. "Richard had probably cut a deal with a rival commander—something he wouldn't have bothered telling me about since I'd denied any ongoing interest in the guerillas. Just having Toño know about their agreement would remedy the situation. Also, Dominga first sent for me that day. Regular access to their living quarters was the biggest piece of the puzzle. Back then I assumed—" Luz stopped abruptly and wrapped her arms around her waist. "But now some other things have happened that we have to talk about."

We. Evan smiled for the first time all day.

CHAPTER TWENTY-EIGHT

The buzzer at the gate sounded again. Luz and Evan turned toward the closed bedroom door. It had been a blessing that Toño, who last week had insisted she get rid of Evan, had dozed off before they came back inside.

"You can't be here," she said to Evan after the buzzer finished reverberating.

"I'll hide in the bathroom." Evan got to his feet.

Luz restrained him with a hand on his arm. "But what if it's Richard?"

"He won't show up until he hears from me."

Luz nodded, but just in case, she used the back door and side path again.

Two men stood at the gate. One held a clipboard; the other spoke into a cellphone. The lettering on the panel truck behind them read "*Limpiatec Guatemala*—expert carpet cleaning." False alarm.

Luz hurried to the gate.

"*Buenas tardes, señora*," said the clipboard man. "We've come to replace your rug."

"Oh, you've rung the wrong apartment. I don't have rugs. Which number do you want?"

The man thrust the clipboard through the bars. "You'll find the work order right there," he said.

A neat computer-generated form identified Luz by name—and listed the business proprietors as Emilio and Josefina Concepcion. Her parents.

"Oh." *This was it.* "Yes, of course." Luz's hands fumbled with the gate latch. "Come in."

The men drove their truck inside. They removed a rolled-up rug from the back of the truck and trundled it into her apartment. Ten minutes later, the men were gone.

And Luz was alone with Evan. He'd crouched behind the shower curtain while the men shifted Toño onto a skinny stretcher concealed in the tube of carpeting. When she returned after seeing them off, Evan sat sprawled on the couch, head back and feet on her coffee table. Luz busied herself, gathering sheets and blankets.

"Come here," he said quietly.

Luz turned slightly, the sheet she'd been folding draped over her arms. Evan's gaze didn't waver. She stood in a spotlight, in his spotlight. Trapped.

One soft footfall at a time, she narrowed the distance between them.

He patted the couch. "Sit down. Please."

Luz eased onto the cushions, sitting straight. She bunched the rumpled sheet around her chest and hugged tight. How much Evan resembled his uncle, the man she'd been so accustomed to confiding in. He scrunched his eyes. Like Richard this morning at the café, he was lining up his thoughts before saying something serious.

"I meant what I said. If you're determined to go through with this killing, I will help you."

"Why?" Caution battled hope, caution still winning.

"Why doesn't matter. I'll help, but there's one condition." Evan held up his index finger, *just like Richard.* "It's not a suicide mission. We figure out where to place the bomb so it's certain to kill them. You'll have to get in to hide it," Evan conceded, "but I used to work summers for a paving company that did lots of excavating and demo-lition. I know how to set a remote detonator."

Ohhh. Goose bumps sparked along her arms. *Ohhh.*

"When I saw you yesterday, I hoped you would agree. I still do."

Bobby Benavides' face appeared on an imaginary bull's-eye, and a surge of energy jolted her body. Luz had not destroyed the duplicate key. Although the idea of returning to Bobby's apartment made her stomach hurt, it would be simple to get in.

"Wow," she said slowly.

"Is that a yes?"

Trust. It was growing, but slowly. Like cedar, not bamboo. "It's let's-explore-the-possibilities," said Luz, still not looking directly at Evan. "But first—what do you think Richard wants to do in here?"

"I think it might be a camera or listening device. To keep tabs on you."

Luz nodded. "The mistake I made about Dominga really pisses me off. I was so busy trying not to talk about all the secrets I knew were secret. It was a stupid slip-up."

"Luz, what if—?" Evan stood and began to pace. "We're both as-suming Richard's newly worried because you kept things from him this morning. But he set up this apartment—what if he's monitored you all along and wants to retrieve equipment to find out what's been happening here?"

Luz covered her face with the sheet. Evan in her arms, in her bed. Toño. *Ay, Dios,* not Toño. Evan was explainable; Toño was not. And the key for Bobby's suite—she'd made that here. Richard would know how far she'd strayed from the truth.

"Either way, let's get this over with," Evan was saying. "Let Richard come in, and we'll deal with the fallout. Whatever it is, Luz, we can handle it."

If Richard bugged my apartment, I might never get the chance to re-turn to the Benavides'.

"I can't walk away without knowing," she said. "I need to see what Richard's up to."

"Not inside." Evan's arms inscribed the tiny apartment. "Where could you hide—under your bed, in the closet?"

"What if I climbed the tree out back or hid behind the garbage cans? I could leave the curtains open and watch him. What do you think?"

"I think you're nuts. First of all, if you 'leave the curtains open' all he has to do is close them. Second, you're supposed to be at work—"

"I'm not going. I already called in sick. I couldn't leave Toño." *And I have to avoid Bobby.*

Evan paced, front door to back, living room to bedroom. He stopped by the back windows. "You're right—we ought to know what he does. I'll stay, though, not you. Outside, as you suggested."

Luz joined him at the window and looked out at her narrow brick patio and the trees beyond. She tugged Evan's arm. "I can do it."

"What if I'm not Richard's only watcher? You should get on the bus like you're going to work."

"No." It came out as a shout. She could not go back there today.

Evan recoiled at her vehemence. With a look in which she read pity, he said, "You don't really have to *go*, Luz. Just get on your usual bus and get away from here."

Evan was right. She had to act as though it was a normal day. "What about the curtains?"

"Can you fix it so they don't close all the way?"

"Probably," said Luz. "The damn things are off their tracks half the time anyhow. What will you say if Richard spots you?"

"If I'm careful, he won't. If I'm not, I'll say that—I'll say I followed him because I was worried. That's a lie he can't refute, unlike the one where I say you left for work."

* * *

After Luz agreed to let him spy, Evan moved two garbage cans from the corner of the patio and rearranged them to flank the gap in the drapes. He rigged a tarp over them, a ratty blue one stained with leaves and bird droppings, and weighted the tarp with rocks the way people did to keep rodents out. Evan hunkered between the cans and used his penknife to poke a hole in the tarp at eyeball level.

Perhaps he shouldn't have mentioned his suspicion about Richard. She'd reacted with such horror. Even audio, like a bug on the phone, would be damning, if not so personally embarrassing. There was also, in addition to the creepiness of his uncle catching them *in flagrante*, Luz's worry about contacting her cousin, although Evan doubted that was as big a deal as she feared. As primary anti-Benavides forces, the FPL would be on the same side of the political fence as U.S. drug agents.

As soon as they were ready, Evan drove his car several blocks away. When he returned, Luz slipped out the gate and didn't look back.

CHAPTER TWENTY-NINE

Luz had suggested meeting at the Botanical Gardens where they had their first date. In the weeks since her visit with Evan, the rainy autumn had glided into cool and breezy winter. Today, the sun shone through a patchwork of high, thin clouds. Two maintenance workers swept leaves from a path and watched, impassive, as the wind destroyed their efforts. The brisk wind swirled, then died, and the men plied their rakes again.

Aside from the workmen and a rowdy school group headed for the adjoining Natural History Museum, Luz had the gardens to herself. Although it wasn't a large park, the buffer of immense trees, shrubs, and flowers created an oasis in the middle of downtown. She strolled past the orchids and through the formal gardens until she located the massive mahogany under which they'd lain that day.

Luz sank onto a bench near a stone wall out of the wind. She sat, quivering with fatigue, quiet for the first time in days. Too tired to do anything except sit with her head bowed and feel the warmth of the sun on her back. For company, she had only a few squabbling birds. The rustle of leaves. The drone of an engine far away. Farther away, somewhere in the city, Toño was finally getting real help. Somewhere else, Bobby still swaggered. And Richard was inside her apartment.

Most of the blame for arriving at this tipping point was hers: She hadn't told Richard the whole truth; no wonder he didn't trust her. The only way to make it right was to come clean about the Benavides— Toño's presence in her apartment was a side issue that, if Richard hadn't discovered those lies, had better remain her secret. She could tell Richard about Bobby's sexual sadism, her worry for Cesar. Be explicit about her reasons for questioning his decision to annihilate Martin and spare—however temporarily—his son. But if she did, there was a good chance Richard would summarily dispense with her services. *Here's a plane ticket. Go home.* Then she'd die alone, never having been able to even the score with Bobby.

Also, much depended on what happened at her apartment. Richard poking through her things—worried or saddened at her lie—was vastly different from Richard who'd set out to spy on her beforehand. Luz sank her face into her cupped hands, and her vision filled with fireflies born of the pressure of her fingertips.

The next thing she knew, a voice called, "Luz? Luz, where are you?" Evan, in his plaid jacket, walked along the far side of the clearing.

"Here," she said, standing and waving. "I'm here."

Evan jogged over and dropped onto the bench. Panting, he said, "We have to talk."

"What happened?"

"Richard came. Right after I called. He had a gun, Luz."

"No!"

A passing couple pushing a baby stroller glanced over at them and then hurried away.

Evan shrugged. "He kept it in his hand while he did a quick walk-through of the apartment. Then he went into your kitchen. He spent maybe five minutes there—and walked out the door." Evan flung out his arms to punctuate his statement. The remaining birds scattered.

"What?" Luz shook her head. "He didn't search the apartment, go through the closet or drawers?"

"He was in your bedroom—out of sight—for maybe twenty seconds. Didn't touch a thing in the living room."

"What did he do in the kitchen?" she asked.

Evan raised his hands skyward, as though in frustration. "I couldn't see him from where I was hiding."

He'd bugged her *kitchen*, not somewhere more central—near the phone, by the sofa, in her bedroom. Luz squeezed her arms around her shoulders. "Did he have anything with him?"

"He brought a shopping bag."

"And he left with it?"

Evan closed his eyes, the way he did when he called up a visual memory. "Yes, he had the bag, and I'd say it looked about the same when he left. Something in it, not heavy."

"Five minutes?"

"Not even that, three or four."

What could he do in a few minutes in her kitchen?

As though Evan heard her question, he said, "You'll have to go see what's different."

Everything was different: her uncertainty, this tightrope of burgeoning intimacy with Evan that made her body warmer when he was near. Everything *became* different the moment she began trusting Evan with the whole truth that defined her, not the bits and pieces she thought the outside world could accept.

"Thanks for watching." Luz put her hand softly on Evan's. He laid his other hand on top and squeezed hers.

As much as she wanted him close, this hand-holding was closeness like she'd never experienced, even when her naked body lay entwined with his. This was personal and—oh, how she wanted to run away.

Evan cleared his throat, about to speak—

"While I waited for you," she said hurriedly, "I was hoping for a sign that whatever Richard did would point me in the proper direction. If only I knew what the future has in store for Cesar—" Luz broke off and laughed. "Martin Benavides said practically the same thing. Too funny, me and the man I'm supposed to kill having identical concerns."

Evan tightened his grip on her hand. "After what happened, I wondered if you'd have second thoughts about going through with it."

Of course, he didn't understand: Whatever he thought he knew came filtered through Richard and through her half-truths.

"I don't *know* what to do," she began, "although, yes, I'm still thinking about it. Martin Benavides never paid for the evil he did. On the contrary, after he murdered my father, he rose through the ranks, became president, was honored, got rich and fat and—" Luz stood abruptly, her hand slipping from his. She needed more distance to say this part.

"Last fall, it felt like Richard was giving me a present," she said. "I was alone. I was going to become progressively unable to take care of myself. Helpless." Her voice broke on the last word.

Luz turned from the bench and spoke to the trees and grass. "And for so many years, I've had this hate, a raging desire for revenge. My father's death wasn't only my father dying. My mother couldn't face life without him, so she mostly died that night, my childhood died, our whole life died. Every *thing* I knew disappeared. And every*one*. Except my mother, and overnight she turned into a bewildered old woman. And then she got sick and turned her face to the wall; she wanted to go home—to Jesus, to my father, to Guatemala. That last, of course," added Luz with a shrug, "is how I got involved with the guerrillas.

"Then Richard shows up. *Hey, Luz—*" Luz whirled around, pitching her voice to a baritone, an imitation of Richard's brusque affability. *"Want to, A, return to Guatemala and, B, kill the man who murdered your father and—while we're at it—how about C, blow yourself up in the process, eliminating that messy end-of-life stuff that's distressing you?*

"Evan, it was Christmas morning. Santa Claus had given me my heart's desire. Okay, there turned out to be some details missing, a few unmentioned strings attached. But they were *details*. Until I returned to Guatemala, and the little things became more important, and the abstractions I'd lived with for so long became people. I don't want to—" Luz twisted away again. She'd never get through this. After decades of armoring herself with hate, she didn't know how to set free the child who still cowered under the hard shell of her façade.

"Don't want to what?" Evan spoke so quietly Luz could hardly hear him over the blood pounding through her temples.

"Hurt Cesar." A jolting release, like a small crack in her armor, realigned her spine. Luz gasped in surprise, and a flood of oxygen surged through her body, spurring her to reveal more. "And even though smashing the drug network is a job worth doing, they've picked the wrong target. Bobby does all the legwork. Oh, Martin is guilty, too, but despite his political clout, he's a recluse. Assassinating *him* for propaganda value—I don't see the point."

She came to a full stop. Honesty required her to add one more thing. "As much as I hate him, his grandson loves him." Luz swallowed. "I don't know how I can live with—no, let me start over—I don't know how I can die knowing I'd annihilated the only love or stability Cesar knows. He'd grow up broken, just like me."

There, she'd said it, and the thunderbolt she imagined would strike her dead when she emerged from her shell did not materialize. Instead, a space opened inside her, warm and welcoming, where before she'd felt only the pinch. Now, there was room for something new.

Evan's old leather satchel lay on the bench beside him. He picked it up, turning it slowly in his hands. Like a string of worry beads, his long fingers rubbed the smooth leather, gently, intently.

A flash of heat, sharper than desire. A flash of wanting. Wanting Evan's hands to wander across her skin the way he caressed the leather. His fingers would feel warm—or perhaps they'd feel cool and she would shiver. Either way. She needed to know.

"Evan?"

He smiled as he looked up but kept quiet.

"I'm good at pushing people away but don't know how to let them in. Let *you* in."

Evan's mouth opened. Still he said nothing. *Damn.* She had to make him understand. Not that *she* even understood.

"Half the time I'm so angry. I'm mad at myself, furious with the people who stole my life. But it's taken a death sentence for me to understand how much that hatred diminished my life. And the other half of the time I'm scared. I'm afraid to love the way my parents did. That sort of deep and honest connection—I couldn't bear its loss any more than my mother did. Besides, I never wanted to let anyone know who I really am, how broken and dark I feel inside. It was easier to stay angry and alone than to admit to pain. But right now, here with you, I'm more afraid of being alone."

Evan sat straighter, pulled his shoulders back. The distance between them, less than three feet, became an unbridgeable chasm.

"This isn't like it was before," Luz whispered to the grass. "Before with us, I mean. I want you to know me."

He didn't move.

Luz closed her eyes. She didn't want the rush of oblivious passion. She wanted Evan, Evan of the smiling eyes and strong hands, Evan who fed her chicken soup when she was ill, who smoothed the covers over her after they made love.

A movement of air brought fleeting warmth. She didn't dare move. And then his hands settled on her shoulders. Evan's warmth seeped into her. He pressed his palms into her muscles and slowly rotated them.

Luz began to cry. He moved closer and rested his chin on her hair. He whispered, over and over, "It's okay, it's okay."

And they stood under the tree and hugged until her tears subsided.

CHAPTER THIRTY

Luz shut her apartment door behind her. She stood in the dark and inhaled, wondering if she'd get a whiff of Richard's distinctive bay rum aftershave.

Nothing.

She flipped the light switch and entered the kitchen. Richard hadn't messed with the right side of her kitchen. Evan could see that space from his hiding place outside—eliminating her stove, sink, and the tiny slice of counter between.

That left the counter and cabinets along the kitchen's back wall and the refrigerator and small utility closet on the left side, along the wall separating the kitchen from her bedroom. Primarily concerned he'd bugged her bedroom, Luz checked the utility closet first. It was deep, and her hand didn't come close to touching the back. Luz stepped in to inspect the shelves, moving everything, running her hands along surfaces.

Sponges, brushes, soap, broom, mop. The trash can was empty, the floor dusty and littered with crumbs that hadn't landed in the can. When she'd examined everything and stepped out, her foot left a clear mark on the dusty floor. Although Richard undoubtedly had access to miniature electronics, he would've had to step into the closet to touch the back wall. There wasn't another footprint. Therefore, he hadn't.

One down.

Refrigerator next. The top and sides were bare. It was wedged so tight in the tiny space that Richard couldn't have reached the back. Her refrigerator magnets? Luz sighed. It would take ages to look at minutiae like that, but they'd been here when she arrived; therefore, they were suspect. She examined each one.

Nothing again.

Inside the refrigerator. Everything she remembered being there was still there—milk, eggs, peanut butter, a few onions, a package of cheese—and nothing she hadn't bought.

Into the freezer. Ice cubes. Two pepperoni pizzas she'd bought on a whim at the *super-mercado*. Homesick for New Hampshire, which had to be the strangest phenomenon of this journey back to the place she once called home. An almost finished quart of coffee ice cream. Another homesickness remedy. Somewhere along the line, without knowing when or how she'd crossed that line, she'd turned into a New Englander. Her coffee in a big bag. The sugar in a Tupperware container. Leftovers—Luz popped the lids—black bean soup, roast chicken, cooked carrots almost obscured by freezer burn.

On to the counters—clean and bare, except for the line of empty red canisters along the back wall. Luz displayed them only for the splash of color they provided. Still she checked each one. Yesterday's mail, stacked in a pile, unread.

On to the cabinets above.

* * *

"So did you get what you wanted?" Evan asked, shrugging off his jacket and dropping his satchel onto the kitchen table.

Richard sprawled in the old green chair. He had a sheaf of papers on his lap, pen in hand, reading glasses perched atop his head. A wineglass at his elbow, argyle socks. The picture of nonchalant executive ease—not of a gun-toting prowler.

"All set," was his uncle's only reply, and Richard's attention returned to the papers.

Evan's footsteps had slowed to a crawl as he'd gotten closer to home. He'd pretended to admire the tidy paint job on the façade of his house while he looked into the windows for signs of Richard, but he wasn't visible. Finally, Evan hoisted a foot onto the bottom step, advanced to the second. Took the doorknob in his hand. Looked through the front window. His uncle sat frowning in the living room. *Get it over with.*

There'd been no explosion of outrage. No indication Richard had retrieved graphic video featuring Evan as the leading man. Or one showing Luz giving aid and comfort to an outlaw. Just that laconic reply.

Luz, back in her apartment, *might* have spotted it, whatever "it" was, but given their paranoia, they'd agreed not to contact one another until the market the next morning. Except in an emergency.

Once Luz's tears had subsided, Evan had kissed her, and she'd almost responded. Almost—but that was okay for now; her pain in struggling to acknowledge those long-denied emotions was almost like she was peeling off layers of her skin.

Evan had no idea what he would have said if Luz had asked him to talk about *his* feelings. He didn't have any more practice than she did. He was used to affairs of convenience and scorching sex, used to saying goodbye when it became inconvenient or tepid. So Evan had sat Luz down on the cold stone bench, his arm wrapped around her shoulders, and as they sat hip-to-hip, she'd opened up a little more.

He understood what she'd said about holding on to hate to avoid the torment of loss. With her experiences, he'd do the same thing. Whether he could go through with murder—that was a question without an answer.

Luz was obviously terrified about returning to work. He'd tried to talk her out of going. She didn't need the job. Her insistence focused on obtaining some information damaging to the Benavides drug operation. She seemed to be casting about for the right thing to do with it—whether Richard should still get it or if she should give it to the *Frente Popular* to use as leverage.

If he'd arrived home to a confrontation with Richard over his involvement with Luz or Luz's involvement with the guerrillas, Evan was clear he'd spill everything—even if Luz later objected. He intended to protect her. What "protecting" meant was evolving, however. Yesterday, it was helping her advance her vendetta. Today, he hoped she'd veered away from violence. Tomorrow—well, he'd deal with tomorrow when it arrived.

But he would keep her safe. From *all* quarters.

Richard had plausible answers for every single question Evan asked: He was ordered to pretend to be from the State Department to keep an eye on Josefina. *Okay.* He liked her and her lonely daughter, so he kept up the subterfuge to maintain the connection, even after he knew there was no danger. *Fine.* He met with vicious generals responsible for human rights abuses in order to find out what they were doing, with an eye toward compromising them. *Sure, why not.*

But to use Luz, no matter how sick she was, to commit murder for him—for that, Evan could not imagine any acceptable justification.

Richard stood and stuffed papers into his briefcase. With a low whistle, he stretched his arms overhead and rotated his neck. "That's enough of that." He came to stand by Evan, draping an arm casually around his shoulder. "I want to take you out to dinner." Richard added his familiar hearty squeeze to Evan's shoulder. "Let's find the best steaks in town. Some good music. Scotch. Too bad things didn't work out with you and Margo." With his free hand, Richard jabbed Evan with a couple of man-to-man right hooks. "Okay, yeah, she busted my chops a few times—that bleeding heart of hers, always on about some humanitarian crisis or another—like, why can't the United States put more effort into ending conflict than sending weapons?"

Margo was right. As usual. But without disclosing his shifting allegiance, Evan was stuck. Might as well see what he could find out. Evan moved out of his uncle's embrace. The cool air circulating around him was a constant reminder of Luz's absence. It was precisely the lacuna he'd imagined after he met her on the bus. And more.

CHAPTER THIRTY-ONE

Luz dreamed of the waterfall. She stood at the top, right on the edge, where she'd never been in real life. Water flashed by, a deep sapphire torrent, so close it splashed her feet. She was barefoot, the rocks mossy, soft, and slippery. Someone held her hand to keep her from slipping. Her dream-feet moved in tiny increments from one unsteady stone to the next, ever closer to the brink. Pressure on her hand warned she'd overreached. Still she tried another step and then another. The hand yanked her back. Luz turned to see it was Evan—so tall, a giant really, his own feet firmly planted. But the ricochet from pulling her toward him unbalanced Evan. His body swayed, his legs came out from under him. He let go of her hand and pitched into the water. She bent forward to grab him, but the pebbles underfoot wobbled. Cold water spilled through her fingers. Evan slid past and disappeared.

Luz sat up in bed. A deep pain gathered in her chest. No difficulty deciphering *that* warning from her subconscious: She'd dragged Evan into a fight that wasn't his, a struggle that would be his undoing.

Her neediness had made him vulnerable. *Ay, Dios, don't let it be too late to keep Evan safe.* He'd gone home to Richard. Evan, with his guileless face and his curiosity, might've said too much already. When she saw him at the market, she'd warn him to be careful. Look at how easily Richard had caught her lies, and she was used to being wary.

And then—get the thumb drive, of course. What had once been an afterthought now took on central importance. Even if she handed the original over to Richard, she should make her own copy. If it really incriminated Bobby . . .

Bobby.

Today she must make her feet walk through those gates. Somehow, she must separate affection for Cesar from revulsion toward his father.

Luz slid her feet into slippers and headed for the kitchen. It was early, but there'd be no more sleep tonight. She'd make coffee and try to envision that elusive best path forward. A path that would allow her to settle her scores—old and new. Do the least harm to the innocent. And leave her in peace.

Then she saw it. The slanting early morning sunlight revealed what had been invisible in the flat glare of the overhead light fixture the previous afternoon: scattered sugar crystals—perhaps no more than twenty or thirty—forming a circle about six inches in diameter on her kitchen counter.

She made that pattern every time she snapped the top onto the sugar canister. *She* had not left those grains of sugar. She'd sponged the counter after she returned the canister to the freezer yesterday morning. She always did.

Goose bumps raised on her arms. She exhaled slowly. Here was the answer: Richard had opened her sugar. Luz clapped her palm over her mouth and stared.

This was the answer, but she had no idea what the hell it meant.

* * *

"Can you talk?" Luz spoke in a breathy whisper.

Evan clutched the phone tighter. Reflexively, he half-turned. Richard stood a few paces away, buttering toast in the kitchen.

He hadn't gotten any useful information out of Richard at dinner—a lot of old stories, Richard rehashing youthful exploits with Evan's father. Without anything conclusive to share with Luz, he'd stuck to their plan of not communicating, but this morning he was sneaking glances at the wall clock. Eight fifteen, only half an hour until he could excuse himself and run to the market.

"*Sí, sí. Aquí* Evan MacManus . . . *no, señor . . . pero . . .*"

"I understand. Listen, Evan," she whispered, "I know what he did, but *why* doesn't make sense. Can you get away? I need to see you before I leave for work."

Evan was about to explode with curiosity about what Richard had done and how Luz figured it out. But he couldn't ad-lib a single innocent-sounding question. "*Me parece bien. Allá nos vemos.*"

"Please try."

"I'll come by later," said Evan as Richard ambled toward him. He bit off a hunk of toast, and sat across the table, chewing and looking quizzically at Evan.

The voice at the other end of the line dropped to a gossamer whisper. "Evan, I was having second thoughts about involving you, but I can't go on alone. Please come. Bye."

To the empty line, Evan said, "*Ciao.*" He stifled his incredulous smile of joy at Luz's admission and replaced it with a grimace of impatience.

"Problem?" asked Richard, looking up from his breakfast.

"Not exactly. A man whose wife I'd agreed to paint—do a portrait, you know—needs to make arrangements this morning before he leaves on a business trip." *Make it as natural as possible.* "I can do it after I rendezvous with the girl at the market?"

"Leave the market to me."

"Okay, I'll get dressed and be off."

When he returned from his bedroom, Richard had disappeared. Running water in the shower—and lying against a throw pillow on the floor, his uncle's briefcase. Unlocked. Unlatched even.

Turnabout is fair play. The old taunt echoed in his mind, and he crouched next to the briefcase before he had a chance to second-guess himself.

CHAPTER THIRTY-TWO

"He did what?" Evan stood in the center of Luz's tiny kitchen, hands clasped behind his neck, elbows out in twin Vs, his brow furrowed.

"He opened the sugar container," Luz said. "The top is really tight. After I spoon out what I need, I have to push it down firmly, like this, to snap it back into place." Luz lifted the Tupperware container. "See that pattern of sugar crystals? It's just like the one I found this morning."

She and Evan bent over the counter, and Luz inscribed circles in space over both patterns, a few grains of sugar expelled from a too-tight lid, almost invisible.

She had debated herself more than an hour after her discovery. Afraid to touch anything, she'd retreated to the living room and curled up on the sofa. Afraid to trust her observations, she'd replayed Evan's recital of Richard's actions and compared it obsessively to her morning discovery. She needed that second set of eyes. But she'd vacillated, afraid to abandon her new resolve to protect Evan.

Afraid to probe too deeply into what this meant. Just plain old afraid.

Fear. It licked around her, chilling her skin. It wormed into her thoughts. She couldn't move forward, nor could she go back—until she learned what this meant.

"Have you checked what's inside?" asked Evan. The furrowed brow more pronounced. He wasn't convinced.

"No, I was waiting to try the experiment with you," said Luz as she rummaged for a sieve. "I wipe those sugar crystals every day, but I wanted you to see, to confirm it." She set the sieve on a large pot, and then tipped the contents of the canister into it. A white sparkling waterfall sluiced down. All the sugar slid through fine mesh into the pot. Nothing concealed. "Oh, Evan, this doesn't make any sense."

She thumped the container onto the counter and looked over at Evan, but he seemed preoccupied.

*   *   *

Evan rested against the refrigerator, standing stork-like on one leg. Luz's demonstration had almost persuaded him. Richard *had* spent time in Luz's kitchen, and he might've opened the sugar, but Luz had been under a lot of stress. She could have forgotten to wipe the counter. Or perhaps Richard had been looking for something he thought *Luz* had hidden, although searching through everything would have taken longer than the few minutes he spent in the kitchen. There had to be something Luz hadn't discovered yet, something in that small area on the left side. Evan surveyed the space, aware of her eyes on him.

"Your mail," he said. "Was it here yesterday?"

"Yep, sitting right there where you see it."

"Richard must've seen it, too."

A doubtful "yeah, but it's just *mail*. You know, bills, flyers."

Evan lifted the pile of mail and read off the return addresses.

"*Teléfonos de Guatemala?*"

"Phone bill, duh." Luz rolled her eyes.

"*Casa Alianza?*"

"They want money for their children's shelter—I donated before and now I'm on a list." She shook her head, probably disappointed at his skepticism.

"Dr. Guzman?"

"That doctor I saw for the stomach bug. Another bill." Luz turned and drifted toward the living room.

"*Radiovision?*"

"No freaking clue," she called over her shoulder. "Isn't that one addressed to 'occupant'? They're having a sale. Whatever." She settled on the couch and hugged a pillow to her chest.

Evan flipped through the rest without further comment. She was right—bills and flyers, nothing personal.

"Could Richard have taken an envelope?"

"How the hell should I know, Evan?" She didn't bother to look at him.

Grasping at straws, that's what he was doing. Evan didn't know what to think. Aside from this lunacy involving Luz, his uncle appeared normal. Their informal arrangement meant Richard occasionally arrived unannounced, as he had this time, and Evan was expected to put him up in the bed in his messy spare room. Richard came and went, had occasional staccato phone conversations, checked his email, read the endless stacks of paper he pulled from his briefcase.

Briefcase.

"Luz, I meant to tell you—Richard was in the bathroom when I left. I, um, poked through his briefcase. I saw the gun."

Luz turned then and fixed her big brown eyes on him.

"And," continued Evan, "one other oddity. His passport was stamped on December 14—almost a week ago. So he was somewhere else in Guatemala before he came to my place."

Her mouth opened to a circle. "Ooooh, what's he been doing?"

* * *

Juana beckoned when Luz strolled toward her stall. "Here, *señorita,*" Juana said, handing over an orange section on a paper napkin. "Try one."

Luz caught a glimpse of folded paper inside the napkin. Abandoning her pretext of marketing, Luz thanked Juana and ducked across the street to the café she'd visited with Richard. She unfolded the paper: *A man you saw with your cousin will find you after work tonight. Please accompany him.* Wow. News of Toño, a chance to see him perhaps. All she had to do was get through this day first.

Luz bit her lip. A few hurdles, although not the most daunting, lay behind her. Running her theory past Evan hadn't gone as well as she'd hoped—she *knew* she'd cleaned the sugar on the counter. Too frustrating he'd gone off on a tangent about the mail. At least she'd reproduced the pattern. Evan couldn't deny that.

A waiter came over, and Luz ordered coffee. The thing with the sugar—whatever it was, whatever Evan believed—was central to the tangled knot she was trying to untie. There didn't appear to be anything in it, but there *had to be* something.

After the tenderness of the previous afternoon, she'd been awkward around Evan this morning. Perhaps it was due to the fallout from her waterfall dream or embarrassment at her emotional torrent. More likely, it was standing in the kitchen with him, the memory of standing there that first morning when he'd wound her hair into his hands, tilted her head, and pressed his lips into the hollow curve of her neck.

So conscious of the thrill of how their bodies fit together. Conscious, at the same time, of her injuries. The cut on her ear had formed a thin scab; the bruise across her abdomen had darkened to deep purple overnight. But worst were the unhealed emotional scars that meant Evan must stay at arm's length.

After he left, she'd riffled through the mail once more. The bill from Dr. Guzman caught her attention. After her follow-up appointment with him, she'd had blood drawn at a laboratory in his building. While Luz waited her turn, she'd read their posted list of services. They did chemical analysis for industry as well as medical work.

Luz had grabbed a baggie and scooped some sugar into it.

Dropping it off at the lab was her next stop. One coffee became two. Luz had plenty of time to go home and change her clothes, but she preferred anonymity on the periphery of the market bedlam. Plus, nibbling around the edges of her mind was the idea that, here, she maintained the emotional façade of being "on her way" to work. If she went home, Luz risked losing her nerve. She'd lock her doors and pull the shades. And fail. To exact justice—or retribution—required at least a few more forays into enemy territory.

So she stayed, ordered a third coffee she didn't drink, and watched the minutes tick by on the ornate clock over the main entrance to the market. She had to avoid Bobby. Every fleeting thought of him brought back his smell, his prodding fingers, the sound of his grunts, his parting threat.

In the end, her nerve almost failed her. It was curiosity about the sugar that finally got her to her feet. By the time Luz dashed into the lab and filled out the paperwork, however, she was running late.

Tension at returning to the Benavides' may have shown in her face because the guard only nodded, instead of chatting, when he unlatched the gate. The downstairs hall, where she often encountered Alicia, was silent and empty. Luz hadn't thought about Alicia much. Once she'd limped out of the stairwell, the shock and her cold hatred toward Bobby overrode her speculation about Alicia that started when Luz had been trapped under Bobby's desk: Alicia was Martin's assistant. Martin and Bobby were feuding, possibly embroiled in a power struggle. Alicia was screwing Bobby. She also foraged through Bobby's papers in his absence. Where Alicia's loyalty lay was another tangle to unravel.

Aside from its opulence, the upstairs hall was the same as downstairs, silent and oppressively empty. Until Luz opened Cesar's door. He ran to her and jumped into her arms. She winced at the collision of boy and bruise.

"I missed you," he cried. Although Cesar said no more about her absence, he latched onto her hand when she let him down. His little-boy fingers, soft and warm, curled around hers.

It was a sunny afternoon, and he begged to go play on their make-shift soccer field. That suited Luz's stratagem to stick close to Cesar and stay in public places. Initially, as she doddered after the speedy and extremely pent-up Cesar, each footfall launched a fresh ache in her ribs and stomach. Exercise soon loosened stiff muscles, however, and by afternoon's end, her soreness had subsided.

Then—too soon—sunset. Back into Cesar's room, with closed doors and lights casting elongated shadows. A quiet dinner. Cesar got out of the tub, pink and clean, wet hair plastered down. Luz re-buttoned his skewed pajama top. Five minutes until the night nurse's scheduled arrival.

The only drawback to having stayed outdoors all afternoon was losing her chance to boot up the old computer on Cesar's desk to read the information on Bobby's flash drive. While she was bathing Cesar, though, Luz remembered *Evan* had a laptop. Before she left tonight, she'd retrieve the drive from its hiding place to get it safely out of the Benavides' house. Tomorrow, she'd ask Evan to bring his computer over.

Rat-a-tat-tat—the door opened, and Bobby sauntered in. The smile stretching tightly across his face didn't hide his derision. Cesar ran toward his father, still holding tight to Luz's hand. Bobby laughed, sucking all the oxygen out of the room, and ruffled his son's hair. Luz was trapped again, this time by Cesar's pudgy fingers.

"I heard you were out sick yesterday," said Bobby. "Hope it wasn't anything serious."

The night nurse appeared in the hall behind Bobby. Luz ran out the door.

CHAPTER THIRTY-THREE

As Luz neared home, two men got out of a dark sedan and stood under the streetlight. One, a stocky man in jeans and cowboy boots, had sat with her and Toño after dinner in the mountains and recounted rambling tales of valor, stories Luz remembered from her childhood.

The men crossed the street and walked over to her.

"*Hola*, I'm Carlos," said the one she recognized.

"How is Toño? Are you taking me to him?" Luz hooked her purse over her shoulder and took a step toward their car.

"We're going into your house first." This was the other man. He was better-dressed, a city kid with a twitchy, alert gaze. "We need to get some things."

"For Toño?" Surely, they didn't require anything from her limited stock of medical supplies.

Carlos responded with a noncommittal shrug. Luz unlatched the gate. *Oh—we're going to get my mother's ashes. Of course.* Despite his injuries, Toño hadn't forgotten.

Luz motioned the men inside. The message light on her house phone blinked rhythmically. One message. Evan might've been trying to get in touch.

"Let me check this," she said.

Carlos wrenched the phone from her. "No calls."

"*Tranquilo!*" Luz took a step back, scowling. "I'm not *calling* any-one. I'm getting my message."

The men conferred. The young man who wasn't Carlos but hadn't introduced himself took the phone from Carlos, punched the appropriate buttons, and held it to Luz's ear.

"This is Dr. Hector Guzman calling for Señorita Aranda. Please phone me at your earliest convenience." He left multiple contact numbers.

"No calls," repeated Carlos.

"*Bueno, no hay problema.*" At least Evan wasn't having an emergency. And it was late. She'd phone the doctor tomorrow rather than bother him at home.

A gun appeared in not-Carlos' slender, well-manicured hand.

Cold fear coursed through Luz. She was eleven years old again, and a soldier was pointing a rifle at her. Her father lay twitching, his nerves reacting but his soul already departed. Her mother knelt on the ground beside him. Luz stood between her parents and the man with the rifle.

Shouts and gunfire came from another clearing. These men had caught Luz and her family when they emerged from their tent to join the main group. Martin Benavides had sliced twice with a machete, severing her father's arm. He motioned one soldier to remain with Luz and her mother. As he and the other men moved on, the man with the rifle planted his feet and aimed at them.

Now, tears blinded Luz. All that remained of her mother lay in the small jar on the mantel. No one would save her this time.

Carlos drew so near she smelled cigarettes and onions on his breath. He stood the same height as Luz and looked straight at her. "*Señorita,* I swear we are not here to harm you. We came at the request of your cousin; however, he means us to ensure you do exactly as we say." He held out a long black dress. "Remove all your clothes and put this on."

Luz looked mutely from the barrel of the weapon to Carlos' face. Back to the weapon. "No—please." They didn't understand. She would die before she let another man violate her.

Not-Carlos twitched the gun like a stern parent waggling his finger. "Do it."

They came from Toño. Like the night the men in the van abducted her. The guerrillas had learned not to take chances. They played by different rules. Without speaking, Carlos tossed the dress over his shoulder and crossed his arms.

From Toño. Don't be afraid. Do as they say.

Luz began with her sneakers, bending to untie the laces, easing them off her feet, pulling off her socks. She stepped away from them, and Carlos gathered them into a plastic trash bag. Then she undid the buttons on her blouse. She shrugged out of it. Luz refused to look at the men to see if they reacted to her bruises. Unzipped her pants. They fell at her ankles. She stepped out of them. Again, Carlos gathered them. Luz made her mind blank. Bra. Panties. She was ice; she was stone; she was not going to cry.

Not-Carlos with the gun stared impassively.

"Your necklace, too."

She removed it.

"And your ring. Okay, turn around."

She faced the back wall.

"Keep turning."

She slowly revolved until she again faced the men. They were checking to see she wasn't concealing anything. They suspected her of—what? She'd saved Toño's life.

"For heaven's sake," she snapped, "tell me what you want. Stop playing games."

"In a minute, *señorita.*" Carlos tossed her the dress. "Put it on and then sit over there."

He took out a comb and pulled it methodically through her hair while his companion kept the gun trained at her chest. He had her open her mouth and shined a flashlight.

"Please tell me what's going on," she burst out when he finally released her jaw. The memory of her father's death receded as the reality of her present situation intensified.

Carlos said, "Exactly what were you wearing on the night you were first taken to see our chief?"

The light of understanding dawned. "A denim skirt and my brown sweater. They're in the closet. An embroidered blouse. Folded, in the middle drawer. The same sneakers you took."

These they added to the sack.

"And your purse?"

"Yes, I had that with me."

They dumped it on the coffee table and poked through the contents.

"Did you have anything else with you that we don't have here?" Not-Carlos added her purse to the trash bag.

"No, that's everything."

When they left her apartment, Carlos took the bag of Luz's belongings and departed on foot, leaving her alone with not-Carlos, which threatened Luz's tenuous composure. He had Luz lie on the floor of the passenger seat, saying conversationally he'd prefer not to pull the trigger, but if he saw her eyes, he would. A drive of no more than ten minutes brought them to a sharp right turn. He beeped the horn twice, and Luz heard the whir of an electric gate. The car jounced over the curb, inside, and the gate clanged shut with echoing finality.

"Get up."

Luz was in the interior courtyard of a colonial house that had seen better days. Once-graceful arches had crumbled, leaving gaps that exposed rough stone. An untidy mound of damaged roofing tile lay by the main door. Cigarette butts and candy wrappers littered terra-cotta planters that once held flowering vines. Poorly lit and smelling of garbage, it could be a trap after all. *Get me out of here.*

A scrawny man leaning heavily on a crutch limped out of the house. After speaking with not-Carlos, he opened the car door. "Come with me."

Luz squeezed hard on the door handle of the little sedan; the man bent down to touch her shoulder. "It's okay," he said. "Your cousin is upstairs. He's anxious to see you. Come."

So Luz followed the man as he shuffled down a dark hallway. They came to a small room at the far end where a dim light shone. High ceilings, ornate crown moldings, and marble sills attested to its former grandeur. The room itself had a thin coating of whitewash over scabrous green paint.

Toño sat propped with pillows on a bed in the corner. He looked awful—worse, if possible, than forty-eight hours earlier, when he'd clung to life on her living room floor.

Luz was sure her face showed her dismay because Toño said, "Don't worry, Lulu. I'm healing. And it's all thanks to you."

She rushed toward him then and hugged as hard as she dared. Tears came.

"Oh, Toño," she sobbed, "you *know* I would do anything for you. Anything."

"All I ask is that you answer, honestly and completely, the questions we have." Already a line of sweat beaded on Toño's forehead. He swallowed a few times, then compressed his lips into a tight line.

"Sit down," he said, indicating a spindly rush-seated chair. "First, I will tell *you* some things. Wednesday at dawn when the attack came, I was meeting with my lieutenants. They'd just returned from making inquiries about the information you brought. We'd come to the conclusion that the other guerrilla leaders were as much in the dark as I was. No one had made a preemptive deal." Toño opened his hands, palms up. "You see what that means, Lulu? None of us are aware of any coup attempt. What that man told you is a lie."

CHAPTER THIRTY-FOUR

The spindly chair under her creaked as Luz shifted uncomfortably. A lie. The beginning was a lie. They'd tempted her with the prospect of the *Frente Popular* gaining a seat at the table but never alerted the rebels to the assassination plans. They'd enticed her with the promise of killing her greatest enemy. But *that* couldn't be a lie. She was meant to guarantee Martin Benavides' death. They'd trained her, gotten her into his house. They were providing the bomb.

Where did the lie end and the truth begin?

"Next. I didn't see the start of the attack, but we had sentries posted." Toño sipped through a straw from a tall glass and set it down, grimacing slightly. "The soldiers shot from four military helicopters. Today, I learned they motored over the mountains in a straight line, not circling to locate the camp. They formed a tight box above our position, hovered, and opened fire without hesitation. They knew exactly where we were."

The sick feeling grew in Luz's stomach. Toño was explaining what his men had done at her apartment. The only outsider brought to their camp, she had—somehow—led government troops to slaughter her friends and relatives.

For the second time that night, she recalled the melee in the forest after her father died. Her mother's screams, pelting raindrops, the salty metallic odor of blood and gunpowder. The soldier with the rifle aimed at her. His finger drifted to the trigger. His gaze focused on her chest—right where the bullet would go through her. Then he would shoot her mother where she lay next to her beloved husband. And they would all be gone.

A movement from the trees behind the soldier caught Luz's attention. The tumult of her mother's wailing and the ongoing fight deadened all other sounds. Toño emerged from the underbrush swinging a bolo. He caught the rifle in its loop, and the momentum wrenched it out of the soldier's hands. Toño yelled over the commotion, "Get out of here. Get your mother and go."

Luz hung her head. She couldn't face him now.

"I am not going to waste our time asking if you willingly helped them. I can see you did not do so—either intentionally or under duress. Since we're certain no one followed the van, only one possibility remains: Someone tracked you. These days, devices can be so small you would not notice—in a key ring, coded in a credit card, in any kind of electronics."

His equanimity was more than Luz could bear. She burst out crying.

"Stop it." Where sympathy would have reduced her to jelly, his harshness braced her. It took a few sniffles for her to wind down.

"That's better," he said. "I have a plan to determine if this is the case. For it to work, you'll have to remain out of sight tomorrow. It's still your day off, yes?"

Luz nodded. *Evan will have to cope on his own.*

"Good. You will be our guest until Monday morning."

"The idea is for no one to be sure exactly where I am?"

Toño's head bobbed in approval before she finished. "Yes, you catch on fast. My good friend Carlos has begun a circuitous journey to the mountains with your belongings. He'll spend the weekend—not too far from where you were before—in an area we will monitor from nearby. If there's a nibble on our line, we won't be trapped this time. Instead, we'll turn their certainty against them."

Toño rapped twice on the wall by his bed. Instantly, not-Carlos and a distinguished man in a dark suit came in and took seats at a table.

Toño took another sip of water. "So now, my cousin, we come to the part where you tell us everything about how you come to be here."

Everything. That was going to be tricky.

"You know about my mother," Luz began. "She died in April. Then, last summer, I started having headaches and trouble with my balance." Luz told them about her deteriorating health, the diagnosis, how she'd decided on suicide, how Richard had caught on to her plans, failed to change her mind, and then, realizing her determination to end her life, had offered her a tantalizing opportunity.

Toño's expression became grim as Luz recited the bald facts that had caused her so much pain, but no one interrupted until this point.

"Who is this Richard Clement?" asked the man in the suit.

It was a question she'd been reluctant to ask herself until now. When she'd visited Toño in the mountains, Luz had referred merely to "the U.S. government" and "a man from the State Department." Now Luz backtracked, trying to be thorough. She explained about resettlement in the U.S., how the man in charge of their welfare remained friendly with her and her mother.

Toño's men took her slowly through meeting with Richard and John—when, where, what each man said—the stay in Miami—more who, what, when, where—her arrival in Guatemala and getting information from Evan on the bus, her interview.

Not-Carlos asked, "So it was your impression the job at the Benavides' had been arranged ahead of time?"

"Yes, almost certainly."

A look passed between the two men. The suit said to not-Carlos, "I told you." And to Luz, "Then what happened?"

Luz described meeting Cesar, explained her duties. She went on to the second meeting with Evan at the market, faltering a bit when she spoke of her first upsetting encounter with Martin Benavides—and its aftermath of sex with Evan.

"That's where things stood last weekend when I visited you in the mountains," she told her cousin. "Your not knowing the plans was perplexing enough, but since I've been home, things have become really confusing."

"Like what?" asked Toño.

Reluctant to admit her wavering resolve to men who'd been at war for decades with Martin and the government he controlled, Luz started with "Like Richard sneaked into my apartment yesterday afternoon."

"Wait." The man in the suit held up a hand. "He's in Guatemala?"

"Yes," she said quietly, her body slumping. "He first came to my place yesterday morning."

The silence in the room at her revelation was so absolute Luz imagined she heard shifts and creaks as the old house settled into the ground.

"While I was there?" Toño asked finally, not voicing the obvious *while I was totally helpless.*

Luz described how she'd spirited Richard off to a café but had been too flustered to keep her story straight, leading to his suspicions. When she mentioned her worry about electronic bugging, her interrogators slowed way down. Then, since she couldn't recap *everything* without revealing Evan's role, she had to explain how she'd complied with Toño's request—command—to break things off with him, but that Evan had returned to offer his help. His report about Richard's interest in her kitchen and Luz's early-morning discovery of the sugar only confused them.

"Will this Evan become meddlesome if he can't reach you?"

"I don't think so," Luz said, praying she was right. "Because Richard is staying with him and we aren't positive my apartment is, you know, private, we agreed not to meet except at the market. I don't normally go on Sundays, but he—they— might wonder if I miss Monday."

"Assuming Carlos is prompt, you'll be home Monday morning."

In the end, she kept only two things from them: that Evan had seen Toño at her apartment—Toño had apparently been too incoherent to notice extra knocks and buzzers—and that Bobby had tried to rape her. She might've found the courage to tell them about Bobby, but the man in the suit became endlessly curious about the information on the thumb drive. He pressed her for details about what Richard had told her and what she'd seen in Bobby's room.

"And where is it now?"

"Still hidden in Cesar's room." Luz's fingers squeezed tight. Bobby's taunting laugh echoed. "I didn't have a chance to collect it this evening."

After some cross-talk, the man said, "Bring it home Monday. We'll figure out a way to get it from you. Don't—whatever you do—hand it over until we get a look."

"Anything else?" Toño asked the men.

"Think of the data she stole," said not-Carlos with a head-toss toward Luz. "Once we make that information public, the Benavides will never recover."

The man in the suit rose to leave. "And if what she says about eliminating Martin and thwarting his son's aspirations is true, it does open great possibilities for us."

Mixed in with the confusion, a tiny light of scheming avarice flickered and grew bright.

"See what else you can find out about who's behind this." Toño dismissed them with an unsteady wave. His cheeks were ashen under thick stubble. A thin line of spittle trailed from the corner of his mouth.

Jumping up, Luz asked if she should go, too.

"Not yet, Lulu." Toño's head lolled back onto the pillows after the men closed the door behind them. "I would like you to explain how you received the injuries my men noticed."

CHAPTER THIRTY-FIVE

It was after midnight when Luz was led upstairs to a bedroom. Alone, she succumbed to the tears Toño's gruffness had forestalled. He'd gone scary silent when she told him how Bobby had cornered her in the stairwell. Head back and eyes closed, moving only his fingers—*come on, more*—he'd gotten the whole story. For the first time, Luz admitted not only the facts but her shame and fury.

Toño had always been a man of action—and few words. He motioned Luz to come sit next to him and wrapped his arms around her. "I understand." Then, after a while, Toño murmured, "Hortensia Carrillo." Pause. A moment of silence passed as they remembered Luz's cousin who had been beaten beyond recognition, returned to her family in a trash bag. "Consuela Luna." Another pause for the schoolteacher wife of one of the guerrillas who had been abducted by a group of drunken soldiers and never seen again. "The Ramirez twins." Eleven years old, burned alive. Their litany of remembrance lasted a long time.

"I'm so sorry, Lulu. We won't forget."

Toño did understand.

Nevertheless, she was responsible for the deaths of more than twenty men, some of them Toño's most trusted companions. And rather than treating her like the meddler she was, like the child who thought she could play with the big boys, he'd merely enlisted her assistance in trapping their killers. It was far kinder than she deserved.

Toño's parting command to his men lingered: Find out who was behind the attack.

They obviously suspected Richard. When Luz tentatively voiced the obvious contradiction that an anti-Benavides position, like Richard's and that of his team on the drug enforcement task force, translated to a pro-guerrilla stance, Toño had replied, "But he is the one person who knows you're Emilio Concepcion's daughter, the only person who would know to use you to get to us."

And that appeared to settle it for him. Surely, though, Richard had divulged her identity to other people on his team. One of them could be double-crossing Richard, perhaps a co-conspirator in the U.S., like John-not-my-real-name from the State Department meeting, who would regard Luz only as a disposable pawn. John could easily have arranged for the tech guy in Miami to plant something on her.

Toño's men had been extra-careful, taking her shoes and clothes, but she didn't wear the same thing every day. If someone tracked her, the device was among the items in her purse—like Toño had said, credit card, cellphone. Even her photo ID for work.

Much more likely that someone here in Guatemala was responsible, someone with his—or her? —own agenda. The other agent at the Benavides', Richard's "someone on the inside," might have conflicting allegiances: Alicia, for example, who worked for Martin and screwed his estranged son. Or the mysterious greaser-of-wheels could have been Raul de la Vega himself. As head of the household staff, he'd gotten her into the house with no formal interview, *and* he'd provided her ID. Or Father Espinosa, the old priest who tutored Cesar. Both men had known Martin for years, however; it didn't make sense that either would work with U.S. forces to murder their old comrade. On the other hand, what was stopping the security-conscious

Benavides from adding a location chip to each employee ID to monitor their whereabouts?

As questions swirled like smoke, Luz inexplicably dropped into a sound sleep, waking to a knock on the door and sunlight. A boy brought in a tray with coffee, fruit, and rolls.

She'd expected to chafe at Sunday's enforced inactivity. Instead, after breakfast, having no place to sit, she curled up in bed and napped. When Luz woke again, the room was hot and stuffy. The window was nailed shut so she opened the door. A breeze wafted along the hall. She ventured into the bathroom at the end of the corridor and bathed. She reclined in the tub, slack-jawed, and let the ripples of warmth wash over her. The bruise on her belly had faded overnight, and yellow showed along the edges. She touched a hand to her ear. The scab was no longer inflamed.

With the much-needed rest, her physical injuries were healing, and possibly her mental ones as well. Doors slammed and voices called on the lower floors—Luz ignored them all. The business being conducted was not hers. Toño sent for her in the middle of the afternoon. They played cards and talked, deliberately casual and light. She figured Toño was trying not to upset her as much as she was going out of her way not to distress him further.

After dark on Sunday, she lit a candle by her bed, intending to mull over the jumbled pieces of her puzzle, but her thoughts drifted to Evan instead, and Luz fell asleep with a smile. In the morning, the candle wax lay in an opaque puddle on the saucer.

*　*　*

Richard slammed down the Sunday newspaper. "What the hell is wrong with you, boy?" His southern accent, normally held in check by the clipped syllables of his military training, resurfaced.

"What?" Evan piled aggrieved innocence into the word.

"You're as jumpy as a—shit, Evan, I don't know what. You're making me crazy with your muttering and pacing."

In fact, Evan thought *he* should be the one snapping at Richard. The interminable weekend had taken a toll on *his* patience.

Saturday afternoon: Richard went out shortly after Evan returned from Luz's sugar demonstration. Evan tried to paint, but all he managed to do was slap paints on a canvas and muddle them.

Saturday night: Richard came home with groceries from the fancy supermarket and made Thai stir-fry. He sent Evan out for beer. Both men drank too much.

Sunday morning: Evan woke with a hangover. He went for a jog—to clear his head, he'd told Richard—running past Luz's place twice and ringing her buzzer. No answer. An unusual late-season rainstorm began as loud splatters on the concrete and became a torrential downpour before he got home.

Sunday afternoon: Richard complained the weather was too bad to go out, so he parked himself in Evan's living room and read the Sunday *New York Times*. Evan, who'd been counting on having the house to himself, set his cellphone to vibrate and stuck it in his pants pocket in case Luz called. Then he took out his sketchbook, with lackluster results. Midafternoon, he gave up, popped open a beer he didn't want, and nibbled some peanuts. Apparently, he was also pacing.

What Evan really wanted to do was level with his uncle. This polite charade was driving him crazy.

"You got something to say, say it," snapped Richard.

*   *   *

Monday morning, an old woman brought Luz rolls and coffee. "After you eat, come downstairs," she said. "It's time to leave."

When Luz arrived in the central courtyard, men—Carlos among them—were loading vans with food and bedding. Guns. Toño stood off to the side, dressed in camouflage, wearing sturdy boots.

"Oh, no," said Luz. "You can't go back to the mountains. You need rest—"

"Come." Toño clapped his hand on her upper arm and led her to a small room off the courtyard. Shoulder-high stacked boxes, an old metal desk, two rickety folding chairs. Toño settled gingerly in one chair, and Luz took the other.

"I would be worse than useless to my men in this condition," he said. "I'm playing dress-up. I will send them off with a salute—and crawl upstairs to rest." His smile lit only the bottom of his face. "The rest of us *will* be leaving shortly—in case this location is compromised. As for you, based on the description you gave us, that Richard Clement did not enter your building over the weekend. Go home now. I trust you to negotiate these next few days."

Toño squeezed the sides of the chair, starting to haul himself to his feet, then winced and faltered. "Bobby Benavides, that pig," he said, as he dropped. "Word is he left the city early this morning and is not due back for three days. By then, I want you away from that house. Understood?"

Luz nodded—feigning the compliance Toño expected was easier than going toe-to-toe—although his deadline might not mesh with her plans. If the material on the flash drive wasn't unquestionably fatal for Bobby and if she hadn't gotten clearer about how to proceed with the bombing—well, she'd stick around as long as necessary to guarantee a suitable payback.

Meanwhile, Toño was sending someone to pick up the thumb drive tonight. So today was her last chance to inspect it. At the market this morning, she'd see if Evan could bring his laptop over so she could read the drive before work. Luz imagined spotting Evan in the crowd—tall and pale, wearing his lumberman's jacket. Maybe he'd be looking the other way, so she could gaze unobserved. Then he'd turn and see her, his smile would brighten, and he'd hurry over. And since Toño and his crew were relocating, she could tell him the whole story of her weekend. Tell him everything this time.

Back in the central patio, Luz retrieved her belongings from Carlos while Toño gave instructions to the young couple who'd driven Luz home from the mountains the previous week.

"*Hasta luego*, Lulu. Take care of yourself."

"You, too, Toño. I love you."

He hugged her then, hard. The barbed stubble on his cheek had grown out to soft fur. Tears pricked her eyelids. *Hasta luego*. Until later. Later, when?

CHAPTER THIRTY-SIX

Richard emerged from the bathroom in long pajama bottoms, damp hair plastered to his skull and a towel over his shoulder.

"You make coffee?" he called.

Evan gestured to the press pot on the table. "All set." He squeezed his hands tighter around his mug, lifted it to his mouth, and took another big gulp. Richard had gone quiet the evening before when Evan told him he wanted nothing more to do with the courier work. As a consequence, Evan had slept poorly, mulling the as-yet unnecessary defense he'd prepared for the angry grilling that hadn't materialized.

The older man pulled out a chair and settled heavily into it. "Ah," sighed Richard. "I'm going to miss this good Guatemalan coffee." He picked up the paper and riffled the sections apart. He selected the sports pages and slid the rest across the table to Evan.

"Miss it?" Evan asked. This was new information.

"Two more days and I'll be out of your hair." Richard shook the newspaper into a different rectangle.

"Two days?" Evan's thumb circled round and round the rim of his mug, his thoughts as unproductive as a dog chasing its tail. It was one thing to wish Richard gone. Mission accomplished. That part of his life over. Ready to get back to painting and to Luz.

Here was the frightening flip side, however: Richard wouldn't leave unless he'd completed what he set out to accomplish. What Luz was supposed to accomplish.

"Why?" Evan asked. "What's happened?"

"Not much." Richard positioned the crisply folded newspaper at right angles to edges of the table and smoothed the corners with his hands. "But things are coming to a head. I'm going to need your help to—"

The dark liquid in Evan's mug sloshed dangerously close to the rim.

"Yeah, yeah, I know. I got what you said last night, and I appreciate your misgivings." Richard chewed on his cheek before continuing. "You caught me by surprise, Evan. I didn't realize that your scruples"—Richard made it sound like an infectious disease—"would interfere with your fighting the good fight." A pause as Richard communed with the contents of his coffee cup. "However, you simply cannot bow out in the middle of an operation. I'm counting on you. You with me so far?"

With you? Not exactly. "If you mean 'do I understand,' yes," said Evan, "but—"

"Right," said Richard. "This is the last thing I'll ask of you."

Evan's breakfast of eggs and toast congealed into a lump in his stomach. After what he'd blurted to his uncle, Richard was nuts to expect him to help. His mouth opened, but no words came out.

Richard's smile was the sort that barely crinkled the eyes. Challenging, not amused. "So, about today . . ."

*   *   *

Luz trekked home from the market. Evan had not shown up. She'd made the circuit twice, just in case. Luz drummed her fingers on the little table where the phone sat and thought about risking a phone call to ask Evan about his laptop; then she thought about unintended negative consequences.

No. No call when Richard might overhear. She'd revert to Plan A, or a variation on it. She'd copy the thumb drive at work using Cesar's computer. Meanwhile, she'd stay home until it was time to leave in case Evan phoned. *Call me.*

As she stared at the telephone, it jangled. She grabbed the receiver. *"Aló?"*

A gravelly old man's voice inquired with polite Spanish circumlocution if he was indeed speaking to Señorita Luz Aranda and then announced he was Doctor Hector Guzman.

Darn. She'd forgotten to call him back. "I'm sorry I didn't return your call, Dr. Guzman."

"There is some urgency."

With the rest of her life in such an upheaval, Luz doubted anything the doctor could tell her qualified as urgent. "What is it?"

"I'd feel more comfortable discussing the matter in person."

A cone of silence descended around Luz, bringing with it a disconcerting shift of reality, so she stood in two places at once. She was here, in a bright ground-floor apartment in Guatemala City, looking through louvered windows into a backyard alive with hibiscus and bougainvillea. Holding a phone receiver, a doctor saying *Please come to the office.* At the same time, she was in her mother's brown box in New Hampshire, the third-floor apartment with uneven pine flooring covered with braided rugs, all maroon and brown. Gray outside. And on the phone a doctor whose solemnity told her everything except the dreadful details.

"As it happens, tomorrow is the earliest I can see you in my office." Dr. Guzman cleared his throat several times. "It is imperative, however, that I pass along some information immediately. You brought a substance to *Laboratorio Zetino* to be tested."

Luz rotated her hunched shoulders backward and then forward as she made the circuitous transition from her memory of that other doctor's life-changing call to the medical lab. To the sugar. To Richard.

"Because you had listed me as your physician, the lab sent the results to my office."

Ohhhh. Information. Luz jumped up so fast she bumped her knee on the table.

"Miss Aranda, the sugar tested was contaminated with cadmium."

"Cadmium?" A quick mental review of any residual chemistry knowledge came up empty. Luz asked, "What's that?"

"It's one of the heavy metals—like lead or copper or mercury. Or arsenic."

At the last word, Luz's knees buckled. She knelt on the floor, head resting on the seat of her sofa.

"Cadmium *can* make its way into the sugar supply," continued the doctor, "if the cane or beets from which the sugar is made grow in toxic soil, soil contaminated by years of fertilizer. It happens in Europe from time to time, usually causing a disease cluster—several cases, in other words, linked in proximity—but I have never heard of a case in Guatemala."

"Cadmium?" Luz couldn't get enough air into her lungs.

As though she'd asked a sensible question, Dr. Guzman said, "It's a silvery powder. There are lots of industrial uses for it—batteries, electroplating, solar panels, some paints that are particularly brilliant."

The doctor's pedantic explanation continued. "Cadmium is toxic at levels one-tenth that of lead or mercury."

"Toxic?" Only one strangled word at a time escaped her constricted throat.

"Yes, it's quite poisonous. Also, unlike other heavy metals—zinc, say, or copper, which human bodies require in small amounts—cadmium has no useful function." He cleared his throat again. "All heavy metal poisoning affects the central nervous system. Long-term exposure results in slowly progressing physical, muscular, and mental degeneration—muscular weakness, tremors, shaking, fatigue, confusion. All of which raises the question: What is it doing in such a high concentration in the sugar sample you had analyzed?"

Poison.

"It will be necessary to run two tests to be certain," said the doctor. "However, in my professional opinion, you are unlikely to be suffering from ALS."

Not ALS. Instead, I'm being poisoned.

CHAPTER THIRTY-SEVEN

The rhythmic echoing in her ears resolved into "Miss Aranda? Miss Aranda?"

"Yes?" Luz lay on the floor now, curled up like a newborn.

The doctor spoke in his soft voice. "My wife and I are visiting her cousins who live out by the lake to say goodbye before our trip to the United States. I'm calling you from Santiago Atitlan. We return to the city tomorrow morning. Shall we say ten at my office? I hadn't planned on working tomorrow, so my secretary won't be there, but these tests should be done as soon as possible—come on in when you arrive."

"I'll be there," Luz whispered. *Poison.*

"This new information about possible cadmium contamination will make testing considerably more straightforward," continued Dr. Guzman. Luz laid her cheek on the cool tile and panted. "We'll take another blood sample and one from your hair and fingernails. You do understand what I'm telling you, *señorita?*"

"Yes." *Not sick. Not dying. Poisoned.*

"Be careful," he said.

"I will." *Poison.*

"Until tomorrow, then." A click and Luz was alone.

It was all a lie. Everything. From the beginning. Luz lifted to hands and knees, unable for the moment to summon energy to sit or stand.

One hand rested on a black tile, the other on a white one. Everything she'd believed was false.

She wasn't dying. Richard had put cadmium in her sugar. In the sugar of Luz, the little girl with the sweet tooth he'd known for almost two decades. Richard had taken her out to buy school supplies, tried to teach her to drive. He'd loaned her mother money for her braces, although she wasn't supposed to know that. He sent presents at Christmas, funny cards for Valentine's Day, and always remembered her birthday. He was poisoning her.

Luz clambered to her feet and moved to the back of the apartment. She leaned her head against the glass of the window overlooking the little patio. Emerald hummingbirds flitted among the hibiscus flowers. The weekend storm had passed and towering white clouds dotted the sky. She was in Guatemala—*Richard* had returned her to Guatemala. He meant Martin Benavides to die. Since she was the instrument, that must be true. Luz had been eager to do it because Martin had murdered her father. And because she was going to die soon anyhow.

Except she wasn't.

So vast a chasm was his deceit that Luz could only scrabble around the edges searching for small pieces to examine: Richard had caused those months of headaches and dizziness, the weird numbness that began after her mother's funeral. Living alone. Richard driving up to reminisce, buy groceries, make dinner. As her symptoms worsened—blurred vision, muscle spasms—Richard consoled her, all the while knowing he was the agent of her misery, knowing her fear of inexorable decline and slow, suffocating death. Richard created that fear so she would do his bidding. So she would come to Guatemala and . . . what was she *really* doing here?

Like a newborn exploring its strange new world, Luz rotated her forehead on the glass, seeking out virgin areas where the warmth of her body had not yet raised the temperature. She was alive. She was *well*. The tests would prove it, she knew.

The first couple of weeks in Guatemala she'd been so weak and shaky. The damn ants had saved her. But now, if everything Richard said was a lie, she was free—cut loose. She could do anything. Or nothing.

As Luz stood by the back window, hummingbirds fed on hibiscus nectar, then fluttered off to taste the plumeria. Massive clouds sailed across the sky. She rocked her head to the side and considered the world from a different angle.

Of all the immediate choices, two stood out: She'd go back to the Benavides' once more. She'd retrieve the damn flash drive and give it to Toño's people; she owed him that. As soon as she handed it over, though, she was done. Finished. No more killing.

She'd call Evan then, and Luz would tell him everything. Picking and choosing what part of the truth to share—it reminded her of the old children's story about the blind men and the elephant: Each person had a piece of the truth; none saw the whole elephant and with that fragmented knowledge came disbelief and discord.

And then there was Evan. Richard was *his* family, after all. Luz pressed her fingers to the windowpane and flexed her hands slowly.

He'd either believe her or not. If he did, this time she'd listen to his plans for the future, her future. They'd go away together, or stay here together. Maybe it wouldn't work out between them. Luz recalled how Evan's hazel eyes lit up when he saw her.

Maybe it would.

CHAPTER THIRTY-EIGHT

An hour later, Luz keyed the residence floor code and entered the elevator, already preoccupied with her computer task, but Cesar pounced the second Luz walked in the door. "Let's go see my father."

"What?" An electric charge raced along her spine. Toño's informant had said Bobby was gone.

"He promised we could watch a movie with him today, and now that stupid woman with the pointy shoes is pretending he's not here. So what's *she* doing in his apartment if he's not around, huh?"

Alicia sneaking around solo was far preferable to Alicia *with Bobby* in his quarters, but Luz had to know for sure.

Cesar's bottom lip quivered. Both hands jammed deep into the pockets of his jeans. "Nobody tells me anything. I'm just *chico*, the kid who always gets in the way." When he flung his head violently to punctuate his statement, his neck vertebrae cracked with staccato bursts, like rapid-fire gunshots. "She wouldn't even take a message to *Mami* and *Papi* for me."

It took Luz an extra beat to remember that was what Cesar called his grandparents. "What do you want to tell them?"

Cesar looked at his sneakers scuffing at the tufts on the rug. "I don't know. I want to do something different. It's no use asking if I can get out of this stupid house. Maybe *Papi* will play checkers or teach me chess. He said he would when I got older."

When he got older. And now *she* was going to get older, too. If only she could stay on as Cesar's nanny. *Right*, and forget about Bobby. Ignore Richard's vile manipulation that would make her life here perilous. No, she had to get out. Today was her last day with Cesar.

Luz pulled him into a hug. She'd have to make tonight's leave-taking as normal as possible. Just another *hasta mañana*, although there would be no tomorrow. She squeezed Cesar tighter. Too briefly, his warmth flowed into her. Then the boy wriggled out of her arms and picked up the remote control for the new race car toy he'd been zooming across the floor.

"Perhaps you can come with me when I go read to your grandmother this afternoon," Luz said. "I'll get in touch with your grandfather to see if he'll be around." *And I'll find out for sure if I risk running into your father.*

Cesar ran the car at high speed into the sofa. When it ricocheted off, he sent it crashing into the wall where it flipped over and lay, wheels spinning, like a dying bug. Cesar dropped the remote and clomped into his room. The boy was right; people *did* treat him like a guest who'd overstayed his welcome or a pet—a pat on the head, good boy. No wonder he was beginning to get these eruptions of foolish, increasingly frustrated willfulness. Given time, he'd be demanding, grabbing, taking. Just like his father. Luz sucked her lower lip hard at that thought.

Now, instead of bribing Cesar with a workout on the muddy soccer field in return for privacy on the computer when they were finished, Luz had to follow through on her promise. She had no direct line to Martin and Dominga's suite—everything went through Raul de la Vega or Alicia. Since Cesar's description of the "stupid woman" could be none other than Alicia, Luz called Raul. And quickly had answers to her questions.

It would only have taken a minute to fill Cesar in. He wasn't a baby or a miniature adult. He was a lonely, unhappy child—a boy who needed *someone* to love and console him, someone with the patience to help him negotiate the world around him. Otherwise he'd grow up knowing nothing except the dry bones of book learning.

Luz's nose ached from the pressure of unshed tears. This was too close to home. Her mother had no understanding of the new world in which they found themselves. Luz had grown up in libraries, in classrooms, copying the sounds and behaviors she learned there. Cesar should have *someone* looking out for him.

Luz sniffed once more and opened Cesar's door a crack. "*Bueno, mijo,* here's what's happening." Cesar lay facedown on his bed, his face buried in the pillows. "The storm over the weekend made it impossible for your father to fly out yesterday, so he postponed his trip for a couple of days. Then the sky cleared sooner than expected, so he rescheduled for today. It's a shorter trip now, so he'll be back tomorrow morning."

He really was gone all day. That was the information Luz needed.

"Señor de la Vega checked with your grandparents," she continued. That got a wiggle from Cesar, and he stretched his neck turtle-like. "They'll send Joaquín for us as soon as your grandmother finishes physical therapy."

Time was growing short, but reading Bobby's purloined drive would have to wait until later.

* * *

Although he greeted Cesar with affection, Martin's hands trembled, his skin was gray, and his pants hung in folds. The belt had an irregular gash where he'd added a tighter notch. And after his initial warmth, he seemed weary and disoriented, like he wasn't sleeping.

Cesar commandeered the game board and requested checkers, leaving Luz to read to Dominga. She lay with her swollen legs elevated on the rolling daybed, not in her wheelchair. Her lips pinched tight, as though warding off pain.

Luz began *Men of Maize* where she'd left off. "*Los mozos le entreban al huatal...*"

After several games, Martin said he needed to check on something and left the garden for his study. Cesar came over to listen to Luz but quickly became bored.

"Can I read you one of my books, *Mami*?" he asked.

"Of course," she said. "Pick one on the shelf." To Luz, she added, "Wait under the pergola. There's lemonade on a tray."

Luz sat in a wicker armchair sipping the tart-sweet lemonade as the breeze on the rooftop ruffled her hair. In the magical world of the book she was reading to Dominga, life and death were fluid concepts, and humans could assume animal form. In Luz's world, dead was dead, and protectors shouldn't be able to shape-shift into predators at will. In the book-world, perpetrators of violence were condemned by sorcerers and punished. There was no counterbalancing force to mete out justice in Luz's universe.

Luz had imagined *she* could be that sorcerer, with the power—and the duty—to destroy the wicked. Knowing Richard had betrayed her, however, she was released of any obligation to him. Still, her hunger for justice remained—retribution for Martin's murdering her father and a chance to even the score in Toño's decades-long struggle for legitimacy, thwarted by the Benavides at every turn. She couldn't walk away from that.

Martin emerged from his study and shuffled across the rooftop patio, sagging into a chair near Luz. He kept his gaze on Cesar, apparently uninterested in talking. The silence between them was peaceable.

Eventually, Martin turned to her with a meandering glance and made a sound— "ehhh?"—that might've invited conversation.

Luz experienced a sudden, insane desire to tell the whole story to this man, her oldest enemy. She'd never get out of the house alive, though, if she did. *Think about something else.*

"It's hard on Cesar, not being around other kids," Luz blurted.

Martin looked swiftly over to Cesar on the far side of the patio, the boy's dark hair bent over his book, his outstretched finger keeping place. Then he nodded. "It was an imperfect solution," he said. "I thought we'd try it for a while. My old friend Father Espinosa was willing to come in every day so Cesar's schoolwork didn't suffer, but . . ." Martin lifted his hands fractionally above his lap and then let them drop as though the effort to elevate them required too much energy.

"No," he said in reply to a question that existed only in his mind, "I'm afraid we'll have to send him away, like his sister. Like Paulina."

"I hear she's in Spain?"

Another nod, another hungry stare at Cesar.

Luz had assumed nothing more was forthcoming when Martin suddenly began to speak. "They ambushed Paulina's car on her way to school." His words picked up steam like an accelerating locomotive as Martin explained how the tactical driver they'd hired for Paulina varied the timing and the route to her school, but one day men with guns had been lying in wait. They killed Marco, her driver, but the security guard fought them off, killing two, wounding another. Then he pushed Marco onto the street, got behind the wheel, and raced home.

"Paulina saw everything." Martin swallowed hard after the last word.

Luz had lived through her father's murder at the same age; she still remembered *everything*. "Someone tried to kidnap her?" Luz leaned forward and came within a hair's-breadth of patting his liver-spotted hand before she remembered who he was. "How awful."

Martin shook his head in time to an internal rhythm. "Not kid-napping. The attackers were rebels affiliated with the FPL."

Luz let out an involuntary gasp. "I don't understand," she said. "Why would they—?"

But Martin wasn't listening; the story had taken over. "We made the wounded one talk. Eventually. They had orders to kill her. And that was their second attempt. Paulina had to leave." His eyes narrowed. "I am telling this much to explain the precautions we take with my grand-son, but you notice I do not reveal precisely where Paulina is."

That morning in the forest, Toño had told her how he deplored the necessity for violence—deplored it, but employed it. He'd said some-thing about power not being what you did, but what people believed you were capable of doing, so you pushed for *any* angle to increase it.

Oddly, she didn't suspect Martin of lying. Evan—courtesy, no doubt, of his gorgeous do-gooder girlfriend—had told similar stories about the guerrillas' cruelty, not that Luz believed them at the time.

Now she did; it was even *easy* to believe. Dr. Guzman's revelations had obliterated her trust in Richard, a trust she'd believed as im-mutable as the earth revolving around the sun. Its loss was disorient-ing, like the sudden absence of gravity. Richard—and now Toño. Neither was who Luz thought. Sure, Toño killed people; he was a sol-dier. He'd killed, as a teenager, to save her life. But as an adult, he'd ordered the cold-blooded murder of a child.

The killing had to stop. The line of dead men, women, and children from both sides would stretch clear across the country. If the dead joined hands, they would connect every village and town. Everyone in Guatemala had lost someone to the war.

"It will be the same with Cesar," Martin said. "We've become pris-oners. Only my son Roberto, with the army clearing a secure path, is free to come and go. He takes off in the helicopter, lands on another roof, somewhere else guarded."

Martin sagged against the cushions and closed his eyes. For a minute, Cesar's halting voice as he read was the only sound.

"But you know," Martin said, sitting straight again, "that talk of helicopters gives me an idea." As though by a trick of lighting, Martin's color improved. He said to Luz, "The Lions are playing a home game tomorrow afternoon. My son—and thus our helicopter—will be back by then. What do you think Cesar would say to an excursion to the football game with his father?"

"He'd *love* it," said Luz immediately, "but what about security?"

"A onetime event is reasonably safe. Using the helicopter makes it even safer," said Martin. "They take off from the roof here. They land inside the stadium." Martin began to speak rapidly; his leg swung back and forth. "I'll call the chief of police. He can arrange everything. There's always lots of security at the stadium. No one will notice a little extra. Cesar will have a wonderful time."

Martin clapped his hands, apparently a signal. The guard at the elevator entrance approached. "Please escort my grandson home," he said.

CHAPTER THIRTY-NINE

As Luz and Cesar waited for the elevator door to close, Martin leaned in and whispered in his grandson's ear, "Be ready at noon tomorrow. I've got a surprise for you."

Cesar skipped all the way back, pestering Luz with questions, his good humor restored in the flash of his grandfather's simple gesture. He asked to play cards, but it was after four already—*a day like any other*. Luz resisted the urge to fold Cesar into an uncharacteristic hug.

"Let's get you organized." Luz tugged him toward his desk. "With your big day tomorrow, you'd better make a head start on your multiplication worksheets."

"Luz, what's *Papi* planning? Is it a good treat?"

Luz permitted herself a quick squeeze around Cesar's bony shoulders. *A day like any other.* "It's such a good treat you'll be glad you finished all your math problems."

Cesar beamed at Luz and scooted into his chair.

After she settled him down, Luz extricated the thumb drive from its hiding place inside the hollow crucifix in Cesar's room. Back to the computer to insert the drive into the USB port. The old computer booted; it whirred and announced it had detected a new device and offered to display its contents. There were three folders: Bookkeeping, Insurance, and Inventory.

Inventory sounded like drug shipments. Opening the folder revealed a list of documents, titled by month and year, going back about five years. She picked the most recent one. The hourglass cycled monotonously. Finally, the document appeared. It was in calendar format, a detailed record of ships, notations for where they loaded and unloaded. Dollar amounts. Cryptic listings that might be names, other stuff she couldn't decipher. A gold mine.

U.S. law enforcement should see this. She'd make *two* copies—one for Toño and one for her future. There were writeable CDs in the desk drawer. Thank goodness for old-fashioned technology, thought Luz, who hadn't remembered to buy additional thumb drives. Keeping Bobby's drive in its port, she slipped first one disk and then another into the CD bay and copied all the material. Then she tucked the CDs into the cardboard front pocket of her day planner, behind some receipts.

Essential business accomplished, Luz went back to the menu. Insurance and Bookkeeping. Curious about the idea of insurance on a drug business, Luz tried that next. The top-level folder contained several files, with names in all-caps initials like "LD" and "MCK." Picking "SPG" at random, Luz double-clicked. That folder contained dozens of jpegs, but the contents were displayed as alphanumeric file names. Rather than opening each file to see the image—which could take all afternoon on this old computer—Luz selected "large icons" from the view menu. The jpegs were groups of men. She switched to "extra-large icons"—and gasped. Men, yes. Armed, bloody. A grisly form on the ground.

Cesar called out, "Luz, what's nine times seven?"

"Sixty-three," Luz shot back, her attention riveted to the screen. The photos in the file appeared to be a series, some taken before the captive had been stripped and mutilated. When he'd been alive.

And after.

Insurance. Insurance of the sort designed to keep someone in line. Luz waited for a wave of nausea to pass. She closed the folder.

Her index finger hovered over the remaining file folder, Bookkeeping. Queasy or not, she was here to evaluate the damn thing. No retreat; she double-clicked, then opened the only file, a spreadsheet containing a grid of banks, account numbers, deposits and withdrawals—another bonanza of information for law enforcement. The column at the far right, with a header reading *acct.holders*, caught her attention. Luz's elbows crashed to the desk and her chin collided with her balled fists as the last prop supporting her collapsed.

Along with several anonymous-sounding corporations and a few names she didn't recognize, Roberto Benavides and Evan McManus controlled accounts in six banks in Colombia, Belize, and the Cayman Islands. *Evan* working with Bobby Benavides?

She blinked twice. The information was still there, still damning.

People did horrible things for money—but Evan? Evan, who drove a car so old it was practically an antique and shopped at the Guatemalan market? Evan, who haggled over the price of a pair of sneakers? It wasn't possible that he was sitting on a pile of money so vast she couldn't begin to imagine it. Was it?

Another devastating thought exploded on top of that one: It wasn't only Evan's name on the bank accounts—it was cadmium, the poison. *Used in paints*, the doctor said.

No, wait. She was getting confused: Evan couldn't have been involved in poisoning her last summer in New Hampshire. *He* was in Guatemala; *Richard* was there. There had to be some mistake. She was missing something... Her head hurt too much to think.

"Luz," called Cesar. "I'm all finished." His chair scraped back; his feet hit the floor with a plop.

She ejected the drive and laid her forehead on the desk.

*   *   *

One last goodbye in a day of endings. She checked Cesar's math, and they played two hands of Go Fish, Cesar winning both so easily he whined that Luz was babying him. Pasta for dinner. A monosyllabic Luz brushed off Cesar's cheerfully manic wheedling for information about his grandfather's surprise.

Luz's thoughts returned to New Hampshire, to a time before she got sick—*not sick*, before Richard started to poison her. She had a job; she enjoyed Portsmouth, a small city with art galleries and coffee shops, parks along the river, the ocean nearby. She'd considered finding a new apartment after her mother passed away, her own place, a fresh-start kind of place. Then she got sick—*no*, then Richard began killing her.

The notion that Evan was in business with Bobby Benavides ached like acid in her gut. If he was, Luz would start over. Pick a city, any city. Stick a pin in a map. Turn it into an adventure. She could still do that. Soon, she would be done here.

She'd be on her own. Again. A stranger in a strange land. Again. Guatemala, which she'd endowed with magical properties as her homeland, was no more her country than the windswept shore of the Atlantic Ocean in New Hampshire. From her experiences in New Hampshire, however, Luz knew precisely how to disconnect when loss and loneliness threatened. She was just out of practice.

She hugged Cesar goodbye when the night nurse arrived and walked away.

CHAPTER FORTY

Evan stacked the breakfast dishes and cleared the table in one trip. He dumped everything into the sink, squirted soap, and blasted a jet of hot water over them. It was Tuesday already, three tense days of rubbing elbows with his increasingly irritable uncle, three endless days since Luz's Saturday morning discovery of the sugar circle. He hadn't heard a word from her since then. Come hell or high water—his father's old battle cry—Evan was going to see her today.

"Off to the market," he announced as he hung the dish towel to dry.

Not even a grunt of reply from the living room where Richard was busy with email.

"I said, I'm off now." Evan picked up his satchel and keys.

Richard stood near the front window, pointing at a rectangle on the floor. "What the hell is this?"

* * *

Luz got off the bus at her usual stop across the street from Dr. Guzman's office and waited with the crowd of pedestrians for the light to change. A bus going to the airport stopped while she waited. Luz imagined stepping on board. Ready to run. Run from Richard and his unfathomable betrayal. Run from Toño and the guerrillas' warped idealism. Run without bothering to assuage her doubts about Evan. Run until nothing remained of her memories. Far, far away to a place where, finally, her wounds—another word for the memories she'd held so dear—would heal.

Once upon a time—yesterday—she believed living long enough to exact revenge was a worthwhile mission. Now, that seemed pathetic. Revenge and hatred were like the revolving door across the street in Dr. Guzman's building, following each other in a circular parade.

It wasn't quite time to leave yet, though. This morning she'd see Dr. Guzman for the tests that would confirm Richard's treachery. This afternoon she'd take her mother's ashes to Juana.

A copy of Bobby's thumb drive was already in Toño's hands. Luz hoped she'd done the right thing by giving it to him. The more people who knew about the crimes of the Benavides, the better. And the guerrillas' contacts were eager to publicize the information. Plus, she owed Toño the last seventeen years of her life; she owed him reparation for the damage her visit to his camp had caused. So when Luz had seen the dark sedan parked near her apartment on her final return home from the Benavides', she removed one of the CDs from her purse. The man cranked down the driver's window as she neared and held out his hand. Luz dropped the disk into it without breaking stride.

* * *

As Luz neared the revolving door of Dr. Guzman's building, a tall man exited the circuit. The shape of the head and the close-cut sandy hair reminded her of Evan, although she was probably overreacting to her uncertainty about confronting him about the drug money. Maybe she'd listen to his explanation, hoping he was innocent, praying her bullshit detector was up to the task of sorting lies from truth. But it was far simpler to disappear without a word. Those words, once spoken, would cement a layer of bitterness over their brief encounter.

The door still spun gently when Luz reached it, and Evan's familiar plaid jacket was receding into the crowd. It really was him, but she hadn't decided whether or not to challenge him, and she was late for her appointment anyhow. She pushed on the door, it accelerated, and Luz found herself once more in the cool, hushed lobby. She drifted up the stairs, her legs strong, all the twitching and tingling gone.

Dr. Guzman's anteroom was vacant, so Luz walked toward the office. She smelled it before she saw anything. Sweet and sickly, like watermelon left too long in the sun. It was the smell of blood, the smell of death. Panic started cold in her belly and spread through her chest. The room closed in on her, becoming a dark forest set with traps for the unwary. No one was left to hold her hand this time.

The ringing in her ears warned her she was in danger of passing out. She put her hands in front of her face in a vain attempt to avoid the smell. Luz trudged toward the desk, the most difficult steps of her life. File drawers yawned open; papers on the big desk askew. A delicate red spray decorated the window.

An outstretched hand held a pen. She moved a pace to the left. Dr. Guzman lay on the floor. On his back. A gaping hole near his heart accounted for the blood.

Her head swam again. And now she ran—out the door, along the corridor, down the stairs, through the lobby. Through the revolving door. Once outside, she halted, obstructing the flow of pedestrians. As people swerved to avoid bumping into her, a stout woman dropped her large shopping bag and, with little success, attempted to bend to collect the small packages rolling along the sidewalk. A little girl, separated from her mother, began to cry. Luz drifted away.

Was *Evan* at the center of the maze of contradictions that refused to make sense?

Everything she'd learned since her arrival in Guatemala had been funneled through him. Everything except that conversation with Richard the morning he showed up unannounced on her doorstep. Other than that, she only had Evan's word about Richard's movements. *Evan* told her Richard planned to sneak in. *He* spied. *He* said Richard stayed in the kitchen. Richard might not have been there at all. Evan could have done everything she suspected Richard of doing.

The light at the intersection turned red. Luz already had one foot in the street when cars began whizzing past. Flinching, she pulled back onto the curb and conducted a silent war, arguing both sides in turn.

Evan was a painter, with access to cadmium, but he hadn't been in New Hampshire last summer. In her apartment here, of course, he could've quietly doctored the sugar almost any time. So inventing that story about Richard sneaking in didn't make sense unless—a crowd of pedestrians, set free by the green light, surged across the street, pushing Luz forward—unless it was a ruse to make Luz suspicious of Richard.

How could anyone except Richard be responsible for the beginning? Step by step, Richard had maneuvered her to Guatemala, gotten her into the Benavides' house.

But Evan had tried to steer Luz away from considering the sugar circle significant. He'd focused on the mail instead—he'd seen the envelope with the bill from Dr. Guzman.

That shouldn't matter, though. She'd *told* Evan about seeing Guzman the night of her first consultation when she was sick from the stomach bug. Plus, Evan had known Toño was hiding at Luz's. No government soldiers had barged in. Evan had known for days, too, about Juana being the go-between, and Juana had been very much alive, cheerful even, an hour earlier at the market.

But she'd *seen* his name linked with Bobby Benavides. She'd *seen* the hole in Dr. Guzman's chest. She'd *seen Evan* leaving the doctor's building.

Not his office, though, just the building.

Back and forth until Luz reached Evan's street. Without conscious plan, Luz had been walking toward his house. She'd been kidding herself about running away. Oh, she'd go, but on her own terms. Time—past time—to get things straight. Trees lining the center of the avenue cast dappled shade that blurred outlines. She leaned against a tree trunk. The street was empty, quiet except for the rattle of cicadas like static zapping her brain. Then a curtain fluttered at Evan's house, too deliberate to be a draft. Time to take those last few steps; time for answers.

Her footsteps clattered on the rough cobbles.

Evan cracked open the door before she finished crossing the street, frowning and shaking his head. "I wish you hadn't come," he said as he took a step back, now almost behind the door.

He began to close the door in her face. Luz rushed to the top step and smacked the door hard with her fist. "I saw what you did. That poor old man never did you any harm. How could you?"

"What are you talking about? Go—" He lurched backward, and the door swung open revealing an interior as disordered as Dr. Guzman's office. Paintings tossed on the floor, Evan's big easel on its side, a bowl of flowers lying cracked in a puddle of water.

As she edged toward the threshold, Evan arched his back and bucked his head. He threw out a hand, pushing Luz away. "Run!" he yelled. "Get out of here!"

The heavy wooden door in her peripheral vision zeroed in on her as it closed. She dodged away from it. Too late. The door connected with her shoulder, and a blow to the side of her head made everything go dark. A strong hand closed on her wrist.

CHAPTER FORTY-ONE

When her head cleared, Luz was lying on Evan's living room floor. He looked down at her, so pale his freckles stood out like golden sequins on a ball gown. "Don't move," he said. But *Evan* wasn't speaking. The figure behind him, a man wearing Evan's plaid jacket and holding a gun, straightened.

Richard Clement said, "If you take one step toward her, son, I will shoot your foot." He squinted at Luz. "You have royally fucked this up, kids. But we are not backing out of this one." He poked Luz with his loafer. "No, sir—we are going forward."

"You killed Dr. Guzman." *It wasn't Evan after all.*

Richard failed to hide a smile.

"For heaven's sake—why?" *Not Evan.* That house of cards she'd designed and then sent crashing reassembled itself like a high-speed video running in reverse. Richard had manipulated both of them.

"It's all your fault." Richard pinched the bridge of his nose—a beleaguered man with an incipient headache. "You should never have gotten the old man involved. I told him I was your guardian come to pay what you owed him, but he was suspicious from the start. He figured out too much." Evan had grasped part of the truth, then: Richard had seen the doctor's bill on her kitchen counter. "And now you are going to help me exactly the way you said."

"I won't," Luz shouted, rising on one elbow. Richard kicked her supporting arm, and Luz's head crashed down.

"You will if you ever want to see your boyfriend again." Richard's hand brushed from the scrapes on Evan's cheek, along the front of his ripped shirt, and down to bulges where Evan's belly was taut. A web of wire and lumpy tan rectangles circled his waist.

The puzzle pieces had been shaken and rearranged too many times over the last twenty-four hours. Toño had tried to kill Cesar's sister. Richard was cold-bloodedly arranging her suicide. He killed the doctor who discovered his secret, and now he'd turned on his own nephew. From what Luz had learned in Miami, Evan was probably wired with C4.

"You're right, Richard," said Luz. "I'll go through with it." With Evan as hostage and a gun pointed at her, there was nothing else to say.

"An excellent decision, Luz." Again, that ever-so-slightly harassed smile. "So now it's time you get suited up, too. I have Evan rigged on remote—see?" Richard rummaged in his jacket pocket and retrieved a small gray box. He lifted the lid and turned it so Luz and Evan could see two red buttons on the face. "In case you're wondering, it doesn't matter which one I push. Unlike maneuvering a toy car, forward or reverse amounts to the same thing with explosives."

Richard, his mask intact and manner eminently reasonable, nudged Evan with the barrel of his gun. "Have a seat," he said. "Make yourself comfortable while Luz and I take care of business."

Evan shuffled his feet, ping-ponging his gaze from Richard to Luz on the floor, back to Richard.

"Move." Richard aimed the gun at Luz's upper arm. "I won't kill your girlfriend, but I can make her bleed all over your rug. Can't miss from this distance, and it'll hurt like bloody hell but—as long as I bandage her—she'll be fine for the next few hours."

Her last few hours. Her life and Evan's depended on her ability to think. She had to get herself under control.

Evan sank into the chair, and Richard turned his attention once more to Luz. "Where's the thumb drive from Bobby Benavides' briefcase?"

"You tell me why you want it, and I'll tell you where it is." Luz flung out the retort without thinking.

Richard burst out laughing. "You are too funny for your own good. Okay—in a word—insurance. I need it to control Bobby's ambitions. He's done a shitload of things he'd rather not have the folks in his native country know about."

"And *you* haven't?"

Richard's laugh morphed into a tight-lipped grimace. "I've been a tad more careful to keep my name out of it."

Your *name*, thought Luz, with sudden recall of the tall pale man who stood, face partially eclipsed by a camouflaged bush hat, on the periphery of those bloody jpeg images forever etched in her memory. Yes, Richard might've substituted his innocent nephew's name for his own, but she'd bet her life that if anyone had been keeping an insurance policy on the other, it was Bobby who'd been documenting Richard's corruption. He'd had her steal *Bobby's* insurance policy on *him*.

Luz nodded as though accepting his explanation. "It's under my mattress." One lie deserved another. If he insisted on going to get the flash drive, she had bought herself and Evan valuable time.

Richard squinted, assessing. "Let me give you a chance to reconsider your answer. I'll kill Evan if it's not there."

Evan flew from the chair and wrapped his uncle in a bear hug. For one wonderful second, Luz thought Evan could bring him down. She rolled to her side, ready to pounce on Richard when he fell. Somehow, the man got his elbows up and, with a powerful upstroke, broke Evan's hold. The next second his fists jabbed outward, hitting Evan's jaw so hard he crashed back into the chair, bleeding from a cut on his cheek.

Richard didn't even appear winded. "Strike one." His stony glare turned from Evan to Luz. "The drive?"

Evan had tried to keep her outside, tried to overcome Richard. She'd tried, too. Without success. Of course not—Richard played by different rules. She and Evan couldn't win playing his way; they had to find a different advantage.

"It's in my purse." No matter if Richard got the original. Toño had a copy, and she had another hidden in her day planner. She'd prefer Richard not find that copy—it would only ratchet up his anger—but it didn't matter.

"Get up. Slowly." Richard took a few paces back and leveled his gun at her as she rose.

Luz eased the shoulder strap of her purse over her head, handed it to him. "Center pocket."

Richard set the bag on a small table and rummaged through it while splitting his attention between Evan and Luz. He removed the tiny thumb drive and threw a packet of tissues to his bleeding nephew. "All this drama is taking a lot longer than I anticipated. You have to get to work on time, girl. So, same chance to reconsider. I'll be checking this after I send you on your way. Will you guarantee this is what you took from Bobby's briefcase? With Evan's life?"

"Yes."

A long stare, a nod. "Okay, now for the grand finale. You, unfortunately, can't be set up like Evan. You must ensure Martin and Dominga are together when the bomb goes off, and that Bobby and Cesar have left for the game."

Luz gasped. "How do you know about the game?"

Richard bit the side of his cheek, as though preventing the eruption of another grin. "That's not important," he said. "The problem is the timing. So, as we planned, you get to detonate your own little device. I've got yours right here." He lifted a white vest, like a life jacket with slots for destruction instead of flotation. "It goes under your shirt."

It was the devil of a choice: Stand up to Richard here. Delay, fight, kick and scream, trying to goad Richard into a big enough mistake that she and Evan—two amateurs whose tolerance for violence was perhaps a three compared to Richard's perfect ten—could somehow overcome him. Or let Richard wrap around her belly enough explosives to flatten a house and get away where she might be able to wiggle out of the vest and safely detonate it. Then return for Evan.

It had to be the vest. She turned away from Evan and pulled off her shirt. If Richard noticed her yellowing bruises, he didn't react.

"Arms out," he said and slipped the vest on. Then he pulled out duct tape. When he finished, Richard shot his cuff and squinted at the gold watch on his arm. "You've got until three o'clock to blow the place up. If we don't hear a loud explosion by that time, lover-boy here is going to die in your place—one more death you'd rather not have on your conscience."

"I promise I'll do it," Luz tried, "but let Evan go. This is between you and me."

"Nope, I'm not leaving this to chance. After you do *everything* you promised, I'll release Evan. He won't tell anyone."

Richard would never let him go. If Luz—an unknown Guatemalan—was a danger, how much more credible Evan would be. If only she could get Evan far enough away, she'd push her detonator—or threaten to—but to do it now would be mutually assured destruction.

Once she left Evan's, though, even if she managed to get free of the vest, Luz didn't know how to rig the explosion. "I want to say goodbye to Evan," she said.

Richard's head began a sideways swivel.

"Please, Richard. *Please!*"

He paused mid-swivel.

"I promise you I will detonate the bomb. I will kill Martin and Dominga. I'll do everything exactly the way I'm supposed to. I *promise.*"

Part of Luz believed what she was saying. If that was the only way to save Evan, she'd go through with it. But it wasn't. Not even close. Once Luz was dead, Evan might as well be, too. She had to make him understand that.

"Please," she said again.

"Okay," said Richard, with an upward slant to his lips that suggested amused affection, "you have two minutes." He stood. "Oh," he added, as if an afterthought. "You can't have imagined I'd leave you *alone.* I'll watch"—he smiled— "from over here."

He settled at the kitchen table and set the remote detonator in the center.

CHAPTER FORTY-TWO

"Hurry up," Richard said. "Two minutes are all you got and time's a-wasting."

Two minutes are all that remain.

Two *hours* ago, Evan's life had begun its slide into this topsy-turvy rabbit hole. That's when Richard found his half-finished portrait of Luz. "What the hell is this?" he'd shouted. Seeing that image in Richard's hands—Luz with her I-have-a-secret smile—was Evan's moment of reckoning.

His admission Sunday night that he no longer wanted any part of Richard's intelligence work had been satisfying, but his relief at coming clean about his involvement with Luz was profound. He was a guilty man dying to confess; words tumbled out.

Although Richard listened without interruption, Evan knew his uncle well enough to know he was pissed as Evan explained how he persuaded Luz to model, how one thing led to another, how he learned about her illness, about the bomb. Careful—Evan had been *so* careful—not to blame Luz. He took full responsibility.

When he finished explaining, Richard, tight-lipped, had told Evan to forget about the market, that he was going out instead. Evan assumed Richard was going to meet Luz at the market in his place to confront her about their affair.

He'd called Luz the second Richard left. No answer, so Evan couldn't warn her about a potential Richard ambush. On the other hand, that meant she'd already left for the market. Evan assumed Richard would stick to guilt-tripping, coaxing and cajoling her into performing her role as directed. But even if his anger got the better of him, Luz would be safe from coercion in a public place.

When Richard returned an hour later, however, he was sweating and swearing. With a sweeping backhand, he toppled the table with the vase by the door, knocking over stacks of paintings. He muttered something about Luz arriving soon.

Although at odds with Richard's obvious rage, for a brief moment, Evan allowed himself to believe his uncle meant Luz was coming so they could talk things over.

Then Richard reached into his briefcase, took out his gun, and trained it on Evan.

*　　*　　*

That gun now pointed at Luz, who walked unsteadily across the room to him. She knelt at his side. Her hands were icicles gripping his thigh; Luz sneaked a quick look toward the table where Richard sat watching them, then dug her fingers into Evan's leg and shook it. "After I leave, keep Richard here if possible." Luz spoke so quietly Evan could scarcely hear her. "So I can find you later."

"You can't—" It came out as a ragged squawk.

"Shhh!" Luz squeezed his hand. "Shhh, we'll talk about everything later."

Her eyes had the unfocused stare that occasionally came over her, as though she was peering into the dim past. Or fifteen minutes into an uncertain future. Like a long camera shot panning across a crowded room to a narrow focus, Luz finally homed in on him. "Later," she repeated, while attempting an encouraging smile, but Richard's violence had shredded their masks of social convention. Her fear glittered like Fourth of July fireworks.

"There might be an explosion," Luz was saying. "Don't—don't assume anything. I'm going to get out of this thing and bring help. You understand, don't you? I've got to make it look realistic."

But Luz's vest tied in back. Richard had yanked the straps tight around her and knotted each one securely. Then he used half a roll of duct tape—around and around her body, concealing the labyrinthine coil of wires that connected the sticks of explosive to the detonator.

How could she get free from *that*?

"Evan. Focus." Luz tapped his leg. "We never talked about wiring. How do I set this up to detonate from a distance?"

He'd bragged, oversimplified. He wasn't sure he could explain so Luz would not make a fatal mistake. "You've got to be careful removing the vest," Evan began.

"I know that." Luz wiggled her fingers and tapped his leg again. "The remote part. Hurry."

His brain blanked with the pressure of getting it right. The weight of seconds piled up like snowdrifts in a blizzard. Evan began to speak quickly. "The important thing is to avoid *any* stress on the wires, and for God's sake don't cut into one. There'll be some "give" to make sure the connections don't get strained and part prematurely, but you'll need help—"

"Evan!"

"One more thing." Couldn't she see *everything else* depended on her first getting free without blowing herself to bits? "The box where the switch is? Don't open it until the area is clear. You might trip a tilt switch, a hidden wire that will interrupt the current. To rewire, you'll need..." While Evan broke down the process, his hands, hidden from Richard's view, mimed the actions she'd make. Luz's mouth worked, forming the shapes of his words, memorizing.

"Time's up." Richard pushed his chair away from the table and stood.

Evan swallowed. No more words came out.

Luz's head bobbed, imploring him to finish.

"So after you anchor the vest and run the extra line—"

Richard's shadow fell on them. "Say goodbye." He took Luz's hand from Evan's leg.

"A gentle tug, no more," whispered Evan.

* * *

Richard steered Luz to the door. "Three o'clock," he repeated. "Evan and I will be waiting."

He nudged her across the threshold, the door closed quietly behind her, and Luz was on the street again as church bells chimed the half-hour. Twelve thirty.

Luz trudged through the shady streets of Evan's neighborhood, her extra five pounds of bulk disguised with an oversized windbreaker. The military man who'd taught her bomb-making stressed that C4 was remarkably stable. You could drop it from a third-floor window onto the street, run it over with a bus—nothing. In the abstract, sure, but with it embracing her like a lover, Luz measured every step as though it were her last.

As she'd told Evan, Luz had to make the blast realistic, and that meant only one destination was possible. A shiver traveled from head to toe. No time for a bus today. When Luz reached the broad avenue leading downtown, she hailed a cab. The cabbie didn't give her a second look, only a curious glance when she told him where to take her. He merely said, "Have to go by way of Arroyo Seco. There's streets blocked off for the football match this afternoon."

The game. Cesar, at least, would be out of the house. That surely was for the best, less chance of him getting involved and possibly getting hurt.

"What time does the game start?" she asked.

"Supposed to be one thirty. Just took a fare there, though. Long lines of people looping around the barricades, waiting to get through security. Probably closer to two."

Luz sat carefully on the sprung vinyl seat and watched the Virgin Mary on the dash bobble as the driver snaked through back roads toward the Benavides' house. She'd get to work on time, but since Dominga called for Luz at *her* convenience, Luz had to invent a reason to get in to see them immediately.

The guard at the gatehouse didn't notice anything wrong either. Luz stuck her ID into the reader, and he waved her in. So many times during the first weeks of her employment, she had fantasized about this moment. Wired and ready to sacrifice her life. All the planning done and goodbyes said. Not like today when her brain was ticking overtime to adapt to the changes.

The office area downstairs was hushed. Luz didn't see a soul as she padded down the hall. She rapped twice and stuck her head into de la Vega's office. "Has Cesar left for the football match yet?" she asked.

The old man did a double-take of surprise at her abrupt entry. "No, the helicopter is refueling."

"Whew—I was afraid I'd be too late. *La Señora* asked me to read early this afternoon, so I'd be there to wave goodbye to him," said Luz, lying blithely. "Can you arrange for me to scoot up to the roof?"

As though it was a done deal.

But the old man bit his lower lip and drummed his pen on the immaculate stack of folders on his desk instead of replying. If de la Vega balked, merely getting in was going to get messy. To begin by making a hostage of Raul de la Vega—so protective of Martin and Dominga—would complicate an already fraught situation.

His phone rang, a jangling sound that made Luz jump. "De la Vega," he barked into the receiver. "What? Just a minute."

He covered the receiver with one hand and, waving Luz away with his other, said, "Okay, go on now. I'll get Joaquín to meet you at security on the third floor."

She fled.

Joaquín met her at the bulletproof door. Bulletproof but not Luz-proof. She clutched the front of her windbreaker, nodded to Joaquín, and she was in.

CHAPTER FORTY-THREE

Cesar, flushed and smiling, dashed from one side of the balcony to the other as he followed the descent of a big red and silver helicopter. When he spotted Luz, however, he ran over. Luz crouched, knees protecting the lumpy circle around her chest, and Cesar hugged her.

"Luz! Luz! *Papá*'s taking me to the Lions game. In the helicopter. Isn't that awesome? And he said he'd let me—"

The roar of the rotors drowned him out, and turbulence blew dust every which way. Luz's jacket billowed and flapped, exposing the duct tape around her waist, just as Bobby emerged from his father's study. He looked her over, frown-lines etching gullies in his forehead. Luz hurriedly smoothed her jacket. Bobby altered his trajectory, walked toward her. All at once, like an awkward dancer, there seemed to be no natural place to rest her hands.

The helicopter settled on a concrete pad about fifty feet away. The sound of the engine died, and in the sudden silence, Luz and Bobby stared at one another over Cesar's head. Lines of stress tugged at the corners of his eyes. Broken veins disfigured his aquiline nose. She'd only seen Bobby once since he attacked her—when he came to Cesar's room and she fled, too distraught to remove the original pilfered thumb drive. Luz pressed her palm to her chest where he'd punched her. The bruise still ached, but she was healing.

"*Señorita*," he said, clicking his heels in a parody of courtliness, "to what do we owe the honor of your presence?"

Not exposure; just Bobby being an asshole. Tempted to tell the truth, an ephemeral fantasy that nonetheless curled the corners of her mouth and crinkled her eyes, she said only, "Saying goodbye to Cesar before the big game."

Cesar pulled Luz toward the helicopter, and Bobby was out of sight. Out of her thoughts. She clutched Cesar's warm hand. *If only last night had really been goodbye. He'd be leaving for the game, and I'd be leaving town. Instead, Cesar was leaving behind a walking bomb. What would he find on his return?* The boy shook off her hand and ran toward the helicopter.

The sleek silver chopper had a wraparound windscreen of smoked glass. A uniformed man jumped down onto the helipad. Bobby herded Cesar into one of the dark leather seats in back. He slid in next to the pilot, who revved the engine. The rotors kicked up bits of gravel and blew around loose leaves from the roof-garden. Luz protected her eyes with one hand and waved slowly back at Cesar's animated goodbyes. He was gone. Safe.

Martin retreated to his study as soon as the helicopter had gained twenty feet or so, and Luz was reluctant to call him back with the guards around. The copter turned northward and grew small. Joaquín wheeled Dominga toward her usual spot under the pergola. The remaining guards shuffled off to their stations downstairs. Luz tagged along with Dominga, her mind working furiously.

After Joaquín settled her, Dominga dismissed him.

Luz picked up the book she'd been reading. "Since I'm here, perhaps you'd like me to read for a while." Joaquín stepped into the elevator. The doors glided shut.

They were alone. *Now.*

Luz stepped in front of the old woman, opened her windbreaker, and pulled up her shirt.

The sound deep in Dominga's throat was halfway between a sob and a howl. "What do you want?" she whispered.

"Get your husband out here." Luz removed the roll of duct tape from her pocket.

"You can't make me."

Luz pushed Dominga against the back of her chair. She took a sharp pull at the tape and began wrapping it around the woman's torso.

"You're right," Luz said. "In a sense, I can't *make* you do anything."

Dominga visibly deflated at Luz's matter-of-fact agreement.

"I won't argue," Luz said. "But if you call him, there's a way out of this. If you don't, we'll all die."

"A way out?" Dominga's fingers twined and untwined about one another. "What do you mean?"

"I mean I don't want to die any more than you do, but first I need to speak to Martin."

"To Señor Benavides."

"To the man who's been betrayed by those closest to him," Luz fired back.

"I still won't do it."

She didn't have time to argue with this silly old woman. "Have it your own way." She ripped off a rectangle of duct tape and, while the woman jerked back and forth, covered Dominga's mouth. Luz picked up the walkie-talkie. Keying it as she'd seen Dominga do, she said, "I need help out here."

Martin replied immediately. "Who's this? What's going on?"

"It's the nanny. Luz. Your wife is feeling faint. She asked me to call for you."

"I'll be right there." The connection closed. Luz kicked the leg of Dominga's chair around so she faced away from the door.

"I'm coming, *mi amor*." Martin ran out of his study and hurried toward them. To Luz, he added, "Lean her head down. It will—"

He stopped. He registered the silver tape circling the back of the chair, the bucking form of his wife. His eyes came to rest on Luz.

She unsnapped the windbreaker again.

Martin drew himself up tall and straight. "So, it is time for me to pay." He sat heavily in the chair next to Dominga, pale, with sweat beading his forehead. He nodded twice. "I have wondered when you were coming."

"My real name is Maria Luz Concepcion. Emilio Concepcion was my father."

"Emilio," whispered Martin. "Emilio." A sound full of despair.

"I watched you murder my father," said Luz. "I've hated you for seventeen years. I came to Guatemala to kill you. To avenge the death of my father and his men whom you slaughtered in the forest that night."

Martin's chin fell to his chest. "I understand. I won't ask for mercy." His voice was scarcely audible. "It was the biggest mistake I ever made, and I have been paying for it ever since."

Luz had expected arrogance, bluster, pride, anger. Not total capitulation.

After a moment of silence, he half-rose from his chair, and his voice boomed. "I made a deal with the devil."

"Sit down," Luz yelled. *It couldn't be the bomb. Not yet.* She needed time to explain.

Martin sagged back and continued more quietly. "All through my years fighting the corruption and brutality of the *junta*, when I spoke about duty and sacrifice, people listened. There were others whose vision was different than ours, but the Benavides have always thought of the country first. I dreamed of big things—roads and factories, schools, hospitals. But we needed money to make my dreams come true. Lots of money. So I agreed to provide protection for the men who were moving drugs through Guatemala." Martin sighed and patted Dominga's shoulder. "Once we made the deal, their agent told me where to attack the other guerrillas. When. How. They made our victory easy."

"Who was this agent?" Exquisite calm, like a silk shawl, floated down on Luz. She knew what Martin was going to say.

"A gringo. I knew him as *El Pelirrojo*."

The Redhead. *Yes, his hair, now silver, was once coppery like Evan's.*

Martin continued, "But I occasionally heard his confederates call him Rich."

Richard. *So, it* was *true. The bastard.*

"Others would have jumped in if we hadn't." Martin squeezed the arms of the chair as he leaned forward. "Yes, a justification, but one as true today as it was then. If I had declined, they would have found another pawn, and I would have lost my chance to shape the future. Now," he said, tears welling, "now I understand the price was too great."

A wave of pain washed across his face. "I remember you and your mother that night. I wondered what happened to you." Martin bowed his head. "The boy I left guarding you—the boy you killed to escape—was my son. Like your father, called Emilio. Seventeen years old." The old man looked away, and Luz knew he was seeing the same awful scene in the jungle that haunted her. "I left Emilio with you because I didn't want him in the thick of the fight. When we came back—triumphant—he lay on the leaves with his neck broken, and you were gone."

The boy pointed the rifle at her. Her mother was wailing; her father's blood rhythmically spurting onto the leaves. This time she remembered how the boy—Martin's son, Cesar's uncle—looked anywhere except at the blood, how the end of his rifle wavered. Toño peeping out of the thicket.

"For years, I kept my end of the bargain," Martin was saying. "The drug people paid handsomely for our blind eye to their activity. I built schools, factories with the drug money. Clinics. Malnutrition became rare. People could buy shoes and cars with their wages. For many years, I accepted the trade-off, the loss of my Emilio and the loss of my good name, for involvement with the drugs. But lately, I've fallen into despair over the crime, the lure of easy money, the loss of our country's youth to taking the drugs. I wonder what sort of life Cesar can look forward to. So I told the man *no more*." Martin tugged at his collar.

"He was persuasive; he offered more money, but I held firm. Finally, he agreed I had done enough. I learned later he struck a deal with my enemies; the insurgent forces who control much of the countryside took over the business. Drugs again flooded the city. More dangerous drugs now—and the police cannot keep control."

Luz had to add one more nail to the coffin of this demoralized old man, sick and ashamed of the legacy he would leave. "The guerrillas don't control the drug supply routes. Your son Roberto does."

The lion Martin once was appeared in the jutting chin, the flare of his nostrils, the thinning of his lips. "You have proof?" But even asking that question was tacit acceptance he might have been lied to again.

"Yes, in my day planner there is a CD with files I copied from a flash drive that was in your son's briefcase. It documents money and shipments going back five years."

"Five years?" he snapped.

What was significant about that? Light dawned a second after the question occurred—it was when Martin walked away from the business.

"That's right," Luz said. "I stole the files—supposedly for information to discredit Bobby, but I've found it implicates the man who sent me here to kill you as well."

Martin telegraphed his question with a brusque up-tick of his jaw.

"Your *Pelirrojo.*"

He didn't move, but immediately he seemed to shrink. Then his head bowed with the slow finality of last hopes annihilated.

Luz knelt in front of Martin. "In the beginning, I came to kill you, but I see now I must beg your forgiveness. I'm truly sorry about your son Emilio. There's been too much killing, too much bad blood between men who could be brothers." She raised her palms in supplication. "If you will help me, we can all get out of this alive."

Martin's gaze dropped to the tape around her. "How?"

"Richard no longer trusts me—with good reason—so he's taped over the wires connecting each packet of explosives. In order to get this contraption off, we'll need to cut carefully through the tape, without pulling or cutting any wires." Luz licked her lips and pointed to the small box near her hip. "The detonator's inside here. It works like a plunger. You unlatch this clip on the bottom of the box and push a pin down. Once we get this thing off, I'll run a line so we can explode it from a distance." Luz ought to have qualified her assertion to "I think I can," but she couldn't afford to show any lack of confidence.

"We don't have much time," she said. "Richard's taken a hostage, a man very dear to me. If this thing doesn't destroy part of your house by three, he'll kill him."

Dominga, whose taped mouth had forced her to remain silent during the exchange, began to writhe. Martin jumped out of his seat, then he stiffened and faced Luz. "With your permission, *señorita,*" he said, "my wife has trouble breathing, and this is too great a strain on her. She won't call out. Isn't that right, *mi amor?*"

Dominga nodded. Martin deftly tore off the strip of tape.

"Joaquín! Help!"

Martin plastered his hand over Dominga's mouth and bent close. "We have no choice, *mi amor.* Or rather, our choice was made long ago."

He cradled her plump hands in his trembling ones. Their arms vibrated as though a current ran between them, and Dominga sat up straighter.

When Martin stepped away, she remained silent.

"You ask us to extricate you," he said, "and trust your handling of this bomb, let you destroy our home." Martin paced, tossing the accusations over his shoulder like bullets. "First, I want to see proof my son is behind all this. If you're telling the truth, I'll need to call in Joaquín, at least. Perhaps others."

"Don't alert anyone yet." Luz could imagine Joaquín's trigger-finger reaction. "Cut the vest off first."

Martin's index finger shot out like a gun. "Proof."

"We'll all be safer with this contraption at a distance." Perhaps it was the cool rooftop air, the contrast between the chill on her cheeks and the dribbles of sweat that oozed from her pores and stuck the vest to her body, bringing with it the maddeningly impossible need to scratch—like a broken arm in a cast. More likely it was a delayed reaction, now that she had survived the initial drama of confrontation.

"No." Martin folded his arms across his chest.

The clock was ticking. She'd make some idiotic—and deadly— mistake or the elevator door would whoosh open, and a guard would react instinctively to the unmistakable tableau. There wasn't time for this argument. "Is there a computer up here?"

"In my office."

Luz folded her own arms and nodded. "Okay, ten minutes. The three of us in that little room." She patted the vest to remind them what else would be sharing the space. "And then we get this thing off before anyone with a gun shows up."

Martin licked his lips. "Deal."

Yes. For the first time in an hour, Luz allowed herself to hope.

Slowly, she laid her purse on the wicker table next to Dominga. She lifted out her day planner and removed the last CD. With equal slow-motion gravity, Martin received it. Then he took the handles of the wheelchair, and they processed funereally into the office.

Martin pulled a pair of half glasses from his pocket and inserted the CD. His insistence on verification was reasonable, but Luz's stomach said *hurry, hurry, por el amor de Dios, hurry.*

The clock on his desk read 2:07. Only fifty-odd minutes left, but surely Richard wouldn't *execute* his nephew too hastily. It should be enough time. *Think about what came next. And next.*

It was 2:15, and Luz was still mentally reviewing Evan's wiring instructions when Martin pushed back his chair. "Okay," he said, his face pinched. "I believe you." Then he held out his palsied hands. "However, we have a problem."

No. No way out. The evanescent bubble popped. Luz couldn't cut herself loose, and neither could he.

"We'll have to call in the guards," he said.

They would shoot the second they saw her. "No."

Martin had outmaneuvered her after all. He'd tricked her into revealing the evidence against his son, and now—by dragging his feet, waiting for the inevitable appearance of a guard—he'd eliminate her as he'd done so often to those who opposed him.

But Dominga snapped her fingers. "Martin, for heaven's sake, let me. I'm much surer with my hands than you."

The old lady sounded like she really meant to cut Luz loose. For her to wield the scissors, however, Luz would have to release the tape binding Dominga's arms. The Benavides hadn't had a chance to concoct a plan, but surely an unspoken understanding had grown up between them over time. Luz didn't trust her, but then she didn't have much of a choice.

Both women looked at Martin. He nodded.

Luz pulled a pair of sharp scissors from Dominga's sewing basket and sliced the duct tape binding her arms. A pause—dead air louder than any explosion—as the three people in the rooftop garden took stock of the balance of power. Luz handed over the scissors and put one hand over the detonator box. One questionable move on Dominga's part and this would end the way Richard had ordained after all.

Dominga held up the scissors, opening and closing them dexterously. "Stand here," she ordered.

Luz walked in front of her.

"Clasp your hands behind your head."

"What?"

Dominga brandished the scissors perilously close to Luz's chest. "It's important that you remain motionless and your arms and hands stay out of my way while I'm cutting."

The old bitch was right. Luz lifted her arms and laced her fingers together. She'd have to move fast if Dominga double-crossed her.

"Martin, go get me some lemonade."

"He stays," said Luz quickly. So it was a trick after all—Dominga was going to stall while Martin alerted the guards. Or get her husband out of range and blow them both to kingdom come.

Dominga shot Martin a look of regret, love and regret. She took a tiny snip with the scissors.

CHAPTER FORTY-FOUR

In the little house on *Calle Ocho*, the bang at 2:52 p.m. sounded at first like a truck backfiring on a nearby street. Then echoes started bouncing off multiple buildings. Evan jumped up, but Richard waved him back. In the hours since his uncle closed the door behind Luz, Evan had remained in the green armchair, not confined by ropes but by his own fevered imagination. And by the detonator on the kitchen table in front of his uncle, his uncle who was wearing the blue-patterned sweater Evan had given him for Christmas two years earlier.

After repeated entreaties, Richard had finally let Evan have a sketch pad, but he'd only allowed him a single soft charcoal stick. Still, Evan took it as a small victory. Under the guise of sketching the all-too-familiar scene out his back window, he made surreptitious notes on the page underneath. He stuck to the facts, too shaken to try reconciling them with the person he'd loved his entire life, the stranger who sat coolly at Evan's kitchen table having sent Luz to her death.

"My uncle has tied ten sticks of explosive around me," Evan wrote, remembering the Christmas Richard had spent with him and his mother. The three of them had gone ice skating on the pond near his mother's place. Richard forgoing a winter jacket, he said, to show off the handsome blue sweater his nephew had given him.

Evan looked over to his uncle, then to the distant volcanoes. He wrote, "He'd just come back from killing the doctor who treated Luz." Sentence by awkward, damning sentence, Evan chronicled the events of the past days.

The charcoal skittered from Evan's fingers when the first blast sounded. As Richard warned him to sit, the reverberations continued. Nearby car alarms shrilled.

Like a wild animal picking up a scent, his uncle shot across the room and turned on the television. Since it was a weekday afternoon, the program was a *telenovela*, the elaborate Latin-style soap opera. In a plush boudoir, a woman clad in infinitesimal patches of lacy white caressed a chisel-jawed man wearing low-slung jeans as he stared out the window, arms crossed and impassive.

After several minutes, an announcer interrupted the show to report that a large explosion had demolished a home in an exclusive neighborhood in *Zona* 10. Reporters rushing to the scene. Details to follow as soon as they were available. Back to the soap opera—the man was buttoning his shirt; plump glycerin teardrops streamed down the actress's face.

Richard muted the audio and stretched his arms over his head, cracking his knuckles. When he turned to Evan, he, too, had tears in his eyes. Tears and a small smile that wouldn't go away no matter how he tried to shape his lips into a straight line. "Really, son, I'm sorry it had to end this way. This is hard—and you're too sensitive to understand how these decisions get made." Richard strolled to the chair where he'd installed Evan and laid a well-manicured hand on his shoulder.

Evan shrank from his touch and turned his head away, light-headed from a toxic mixture of hope and despair. Luz must've gone to the Benavides'. But after that—the unknowns his meticulous note-taking had kept at bay during the silent hours since Richard closed the door on Luz rose up to torment him. Luz was walking a tightrope of pitfalls and traps that would sway perilously with her every decision: enlisting Martin Benavides' cooperation—or had there been a standoff, followed by gunfire, ending in a massacre? Switching the wiring—or had the explosion been premature, an accident? He wished he could *feel* whether she had stayed alive, but he couldn't feel anything.

An abrupt change of lighting appeared on the TV screen—fat black words scrolled along the bottom. Richard turned on the sound. Blaring sirens filled the air. Fire trucks. Ambulances. A swirling cloud of dark smoke served as a backdrop for the TV reporter who licked her lips repeatedly, her professionalism strained. A huge crowd on the street drowned out her words. She began again, pitching her voice louder to be heard over the tumult.

"Fifteen minutes ago, an explosion rocked the residence of Martin Benavides, former president of Guatemala and one of our most respected leaders." Her voice quavered. "Although there has been no official word, a member of the staff reported both Señor Benavides and his wife were home." Visibly losing composure, she cried out, "How could anyone survive that?"

The camera panned, zoomed. The focus adjusted on a black hole with smoke billowing out. Roof gone. Red and gold flames flickering out windows. The side wall had ruptured. Unidentifiable charred objects littered the lawn and gardens.

"Time to move," said Richard. "We have one more stop before the promise of this day is fulfilled."

"Where?" The picture of absolute destruction shredded what little optimism Evan retained. As the TV reporter said, *how could anyone survive that?*

Evan decided he didn't even care whether he lived or died now. Nothing Richard could do to him would be worse than knowing he'd sent Luz to her death. Evan would do everything in his power to thwart Richard. No matter what.

The picture on the television changed. Three solemn men sat at a news desk while Guatemala City's well-known evening anchorman gave a concise summary of what was known. Then he asked the man to his left, "Is it possible, Enrique, that this attack is linked to a raid on the *Frente Popular* in the jungle around Las Margaritas, rumored to have occurred last week, in which the rebels sustained a direct hit by government forces?"

"Highly likely, in my judgment. The rebels have long operated under the principle of an eye for an eye."

An earnest young man in a three-piece suit added, "Our sources tell us one of their leaders was severely injured, possibly killed. That would certainly account for this escalation of their struggle against the government, this assassination of a former head of state, and as Claudia said, a beloved statesman."

More pontificating in support of this point of view. With perfect teeth and somber mien, the evening newscaster announced they would be returning to the scene at the Benavides residence where Claudia Ramos was standing by.

So that was the underlying idea: The FPL was being set up as responsible. Once Luz was identified as the bomber, Evan was sure her connections to the guerrillas would be leaked.

On the TV, there was no audio at first, just a camera sweeping— this time from a different angle, higher and farther away, so you could see into the crater that had once been the west side of the house.

When the reporter began to speak, Richard clicked off the TV. "Let's go to the football stadium. We have transport arranged."

Keep him at the house, Luz had said. *Luz*. Evan pressed his mouth into a tight line and clenched his muscles. He'd go mad unless he could sustain the belief that she'd survived. He stared at the wreckage of his living room. He pictured her at the door, smiling as she dropped her handbag and loosened her heavy knot of hair.

Luz was alive. *She had to be.* He'd see her soon.

When Evan didn't instantly respond, Richard jiggled his arm. "I said nothing was going to happen to you as long as the girl did her part, and I meant it. She probably tried to convince you otherwise, but I am your ticket home, son."

"I don't want to go *home*—this is home." *Keep Richard there so Luz could find them.* Besides, he thought, the Lions were playing a home game this afternoon. Downtown would be a zoo.

Jesus. Scores of people jammed into a small area. Detonating another bomb in the crowded stands would compound the terror of the earlier explosion. The belt cinched around his waist grew hot. Evan tugged at it, then yanked away his hand. Richard wouldn't do that to him. This . . . this contraption was only a threat to coerce Luz into cooperation. Richard had contorted his values into sacrificing her, but Evan was *family*, his sister's only child. He would never do that.

Even if it's only a threat, I don't want to walk out the door.

"Time for us to leave," said Richard.

"Why do we have to go anywhere?" Still leery of his uncle's intentions, Evan would continue to question and frustrate, rather than defy.

But Richard kept moving, packing his briefcase, didn't engage. Finally, he snapped at Evan. "Get your butt out of that chair. Now." He shook the jacket pocket that held the remote control. "You have no idea how much is riding on this."

Evan stood and tugged at the white canvas snugged tight around his waist. "Can't I take this off now?" *Delay, obstruct. Test the limits.*

"Better not touch," said Richard, brushing his hand away. "I need your complete compliance for a little longer. Until we're on the helicopter."

A helicopter. That sounded like he was wrong about being wired as a second bomb, but if Richard got him in the air, he would be miles away so fast that he and Luz would never find one another.

Evan moved slowly, clumsily—and only part of that was on purpose. His legs were stiff and cramping after so much inactivity. Finally, his stonewalling came to an end. Richard had Evan cover the explosive-filled belt with a sweater and marched him out to the car. Smiling and nodding, genial as always, but with an unsettling glazed brightness to his demeanor.

When Richard didn't bother to lock the door behind them, Evan knew he was not supposed to be coming back. Ever.

CHAPTER FORTY-FIVE

Dominga's fingers never wavered as her tiny sewing scissors inched through the tape. Luz had been afraid to breathe, afraid to have the tape move even a fraction of an inch. Martin sat, mesmerized.

Once the tape was separated and the knotted straps slashed, Luz walked to the far end of the rooftop terrace, where she inched the works from her shoulders and laid the vest at the edge of the open space. Then she and Martin wheeled Dominga to Cesar's bedroom, which was on the opposite side of the house, about as far from ground zero as possible. There, Martin assembled his staff. Swearing them to secrecy, he began to make plans.

At 2:40, Luz was led to the roof by a soldier who was there to help her lay the line—and probably to make sure she proceeded as promised. Luz set a heavy oak chair on a cloth section of the vest to keep it in place. Then she gingerly opened the detonator box and began to attach a length of cable the way Evan had said.

Even on the far side of the house, the explosion sent them tumbling, except for Dominga who remained upright in her wheelchair, although the chair itself skidded against the wall. The row of windows above Cesar's bookcase burst into a hard rain of shards. The roaring in her ears diminished in waves and then died. It was over.

Immediately after the shock wave dissipated, Martin dispatched Joaquín along with a detachment of household guards to take Bobby into custody. They were instructed to tell him they were escorting him to a safe location where a general had important news for him. The night nurse, wide-eyed at the drama, accompanied them. Her job was to finish watching the game with Cesar, keep him amused and away from news broadcasts, and, under no circumstances, return with him until called.

*   *   *

Luz sat behind the wheel of a brand-new black Cadillac, her foot pressed hard on the gas pedal. A bandage covered her left hand where a piece of flying glass had ricocheted, but that was her only injury.

"I could give you an escort," Martin had suggested.

"Not a good idea. If Richard spots soldiers, he'll know I betrayed him. He's berserk enough to kill Evan at that point, rather than surrender."

So Martin himself had walked Luz to the garage and had chosen a Cadillac for her. "Big and solid," he said, "in case you need it." And he gave his security team instructions to smooth her path past the police barricades so she would not be delayed.

He embraced Luz then. The hands that had murdered her father hugged her close, and he said, "*Vaya con Dios*. Once you have freed your friend, do with *El Pelirrojo* as you wish. His soul is forfeit. We both have many reasons to wish him dead."

Luz sped through the quiet streets toward *Calle Ocho*, Evan's street. It had been months since she'd driven, though, and that was a very small car in a small town on another continent. The quickest way to Evan's house didn't follow the bus route, but those were the only streets Luz knew well. Even so, idly gazing out bus windows was inadequate preparation for the free-for-all of urban congestion. Cars and buses streamed around her. Luz unerringly chose the wrong lanes. A hesitation and she was instantly cut off. A detour and she was lost. Sweat-slick palms and a pounding in her skull. Flashbacks to the blast when the house shuddered and the windows shattered.

Perhaps she should've accepted Martin's offer of an escort, but she couldn't trust his men's restraint. More than anything, she wanted Richard to see her face and know—instinctively, as Martin had—that she had returned to exact retribution.

Finally, Luz reached the intersection where she could make a left onto *Calle Ocho*. While she waited for a rumbling dump truck approaching from the opposite direction, a pale blue sedan came up *Calle Ocho*, paused at the stop sign to let the truck pass, and accelerated behind it onto the avenue. Richard, intent on driving, didn't notice her, but Luz and Evan made eye contact.

Instant change of plans. With a quick glance in her rearview mirror to make sure there was no one behind her waiting to turn, Luz let two oncoming cars pass before executing a tight U-turn. She pulled into traffic, returning the way she had come.

Richard tailgated the big slow-moving truck, repeatedly steering to the left to see around it, honking at it to pull over so he could pass.

Evan had seen her. He knew she was following. Luz had intended to cut through the yard of Evan's Guatemalan neighbors, the ones who ran the bike shop, and creep into his house from the back, where the garden door was left unlocked during the day. Not that she had a firm plan beyond that. Sneak up on Richard and grab the detonator— something like that. Yell to Evan to strip the device and toss it away.

They weren't at Evan's house now, but the same element of surprise might work when Richard parked the car. Evan should be on the alert, knowing she was close behind. So much depended on where they were going.

The street became more congested. They passed the turn leading to the Benavides' and continued into the central city. More cars, more people, and a sense of panic. The pantomime of rushing people with horrified faces told her that news of Martin Benavides' demise was spreading.

Martin had been adamant that the confusion not continue for too long. Although resigned to the truth of Bobby's perfidy and to the work ahead to repair his legacy, Martin still wielded considerable power in Guatemala, and he intended to hold on to it. At least, he told Luz, until he personally had seen to the destruction of the drug network and to his son's part in it.

He'd agreed to let the misinformation spread until he confronted Bobby. Then he and Dominga would be discovered to have been—by a miracle—safely out of the building, enjoying an impromptu drive into the country. Martin planned to have the police chief announce the blast had been caused by a leak in the gas line. He would appear live on television in front of the burned-out shell of his home.

Luz had to subdue Richard before that happened.

* * *

Richard led Luz on a zigzag course through increasingly clogged streets. They reached the neighborhood of the football stadium. Groups of people gathered at street corners. Vendors laden with all manner of cheap souvenirs kept up a raucous patter as they rambled haphazardly along street and sidewalk.

Traffic came to a standstill. Horns blared. Richard's head and shoulders appeared. He lifted himself onto the kick plate on the car door for a better view. How natural it had been to mistake him for Evan outside Dr. Guzman's office—same rangy build, same close-cropped hair, same jawline.

Whatever Richard saw persuaded him to open the car's back door. Evan emerged. The men walked away from the car. Luz bumped the big Cadillac onto the sidewalk, jumped out, and followed on foot. Although she was more mobile and more confident now that she wasn't driving, so was Richard. He darted through the crowds, keeping a tight hold on Evan. And Evan looked back too much, trying to spot her, which meant he kept stumbling. Richard jerked him upright each time. Evan was going to give the game away if Richard turned to see what kept attracting his attention.

Richard's usual languid body language had been replaced by intense focus. He buttonholed a city policeman attempting to direct traffic and apparently asked directions. The policeman flapped his arm to the right and air-tapped his index finger at an angle—over there. They hurried off.

Luz slid around the corner after them. In the center of a cordoned-off rectangle sat the silver and red helicopter she'd last seen carrying Bobby and Cesar to the stadium. It was guarded at ten-foot intervals by soldiers, their black carbines at the ready.

If her quarry passed through that line of defense, she was out of luck. Cursing herself for not having made a move before this, Luz considered her options. There were too many innocent people around. And too many soldiers. They would hardly stand idly by while a little native girl pummeled a well-dressed Anglo. Luz was fresh out of ideas. She couldn't imagine any scenario where Evan could strip off the bomb belt and escape. Richard was going to get away with it.

She peeked from behind a ramshackle newsstand. Richard proffered an envelope. A soldier on the perimeter opened it, took out a folded paper, which he read and then called over another. They conferred. Evan used this time to look around. Luz stepped out into the open. He waved her back and shook his head—no—then raised the hand away from Richard. He pointed to the helicopter and slit his throat with an imaginary knife. He mouthed *Help*.

As other soldiers joined the huddle, Luz stepped into view again. She gestured frantically to Evan, praying he would understand.

CHAPTER FORTY-SIX

The argument churned around Evan. Because of the destruction of the Benavides' rooftop helipad, the captain had received orders to ground the helicopter. It was to be kept in reserve in case of further emergency. Richard's letter giving him authority to use the helicopter, on official stationery and signed by Roberto Benavides, swayed the officer but did not catapult him into acceptance.

"Listen, Richard," said Evan, tugging at his uncle's arm. "Let's not push this now. We can return when things have settled down." He hoped he'd gotten the correct gist from Luz's inventive charade. Now that Richard wasn't going to send him into the stadium as Act Two of today's destruction, he'd stay by his uncle's side sounding pleasant and reasonable. And encourage the soldiers to continue denying them access.

Richard ignored him, but one of the soldiers picked up on the idea.

"That's right, *señor*. In another hour or so, when the situation has stabilized, they will no doubt lift the travel ban."

Evan recognized the beginning of the Latin *mañana*—do it later. "And we can go have coffee while we're waiting," he said, in his role as conciliatory, helpful nephew.

Richard glared. With eyes narrowed, he said matter-of-factly, "You can shut the fuck up right now. I see what you're after."

But Evan had given the soldiers the mantra they needed. Not *no*, but *come back later*. The captain was reiterating his polite denial for the third time when Roberto Benavides, walking inside a phalanx of security, rounded the corner. The helicopter guards stood to attention at his approach. Richard hailed him. Bobby detoured. He spoke first. "Apparently, there's bad news. I've been summoned." A tic worked at the side of his face.

Richard murmured some public platitudes before walking Bobby away from the guards. Keeping his hand glued to Evan's bicep, he spoke in an undertone. "She did it, Bobby. I told you."

"Fucking-A, man." Bobby became momentarily unsuccessful in hiding his elation. "The hot little nanny came through."

They were talking about Luz. Richard was working with *Martin's son*. Richard—Evan's mind rebelled against making sense of this new revelation—his uncle and Roberto Benavides were *on the same side*. Martin's son was part of the plot to murder his parents. The cry that escaped Evan's lips was the loss of his last illusion.

As he compiled his note, Evan fit his uncle's actions into the framework of an overzealous agent who'd become determined to take the law into his own hands to get a job done. Now his assumptions tilted and came crashing down. Richard was not advancing the interests of the United States government; he was *partnering* with a drug dealer, murdering for profit.

"So now we move on to the endgame, Bobby," Richard said. "One last task and it's all yours. Everything. But we gotta hit the remnants of the rebel group today, while tempers are frayed. Tell these men to let me go. We've only got ninety minutes of daylight."

Bobby turned to the captain. In rapid-fire Spanish, he instructed the man to have his friends taken wherever they wanted to go.

"But my orders," protested the captain.

"These are *my* orders," said Bobby. He shoved the letter at the man's chest. The captain took two steps backward and saluted.

The next thing Evan knew, they were ushered inside the perimeter. Time was running out. He couldn't get on that helicopter. Evan looked around for Luz but didn't see her. He saw only the back of his uncle's head, a man he'd loved all his life, who'd helped him out of more scrapes than Evan could count. Today Richard was a stranger who'd dragged him from his front door deep into a world of evil.

Bobby shouted something about the pilot that Evan didn't catch. The captain saluted again and spoke hurriedly to a minion.

"What's that all about?" asked Evan.

"Damn pilot sneaked in to see the match," said Richard. "They're going to get him." He loosened his hold on Evan as he checked his watch.

Evan ducked and spun toward the edge of the enclosure.

The next thing Evan knew he was falling, hitting facedown on the hard ground. Richard had tripped him. Bending to help Evan to his feet with ostensible solicitude, he leaned close. "Strike two," he said.

* * *

Luz made her move when Evan ran. While Richard's attention and that of the soldiers fastened on him, she dashed to the far side of the enclosure. It was momentarily unattended, and a web of metal struts descending from the wasp-like silver body gave Luz cover as she crouched and rolled under the copter.

Evan, with his foot-dragging, had come so close to success, but the second Bobby intervened, their path to victory narrowed. The guards were taking Bobby to an army base in central Guatemala City. It would appear to Bobby a safe location for his debriefing, but the base also housed Matamoros Prison. No one except Joaquín knew Bobby's real destination, however, and Joaquín couldn't countermand Bobby's orders without tipping his hand. For an instant, she'd considered showing herself. She'd shout to Joaquín that the strangers hoping to board the helicopter were the men she was after.

Of course, then Richard would know she'd double-crossed him. Bobby would run. Too many guns. Too great a chance Evan would get caught in the crossfire. While Luz hesitated, Bobby and the armed guard marched off, and his orders stood.

She hunkered, panting, near the rear of the helicopter, where intersecting shadows camouflaged her. The arc of metal above her, the fumes, the mere presence of the machine brought her back to the clearing in the jungle, fifteen minutes after her life had changed forever. Luz, her mother, and the other terrified survivors, after running a shadowy gauntlet of roots and vines, had emerged on a hillside pasture in the center of which was a snorting, fire-breathing bull. Strange men shouting strange words herded them to a gaping hole in the beast.

Bright lights from within created grotesque shapes that danced on the trees. Luz had gone rigid with fright as her mother surged ahead, and she fell a few yards from the monster, bringing her mother down with her. The others trampled them in their panicky rush to escape.

And then they were alone on the ground. Her mother rose to her hands and knees, screaming for Luz to get up, yanking her arm. Shouts from inside—some encouraging, some in terror—and then with a blast of hot air, the machine elevated and rocked. Relief that the scary apparition was leaving washed over her. Then Luz turned to her mother. Josefina was looking back into the woods. While the roar of the beast muted all other sounds, Luz saw the near future playing out in her mother's mind; the death they'd temporarily escaped was going to overtake them. The soldiers were coming. Still, her muscles wouldn't cooperate. They were going to bleed out into the rich volcanic soil like her father and, like him, remain forever part of the forest.

As the helicopter swayed a few feet from the ground, a man jumped out and scooped Luz into his arms. Hands pulled them in. The beast rose higher, over the treetops. Lying like stacks of kindling in the yawning hole, Luz and her mother watched their life shrink to nothing and disappear.

On the Benavides' rooftop, with explosives strapped around her chest, with Cesar dancing around and Bobby suspicious, she'd been able to keep this particular anxiety at bay. There'd be no helping hand this time. Luz shivered in the shadows.

* * *

A slight gray-haired man strolled across the parking lot, just enough alacrity in his stride to skirt insolence. He stopped in front of Richard with an exaggerated middle-finger-extended salute.

"Hey, Angel," Richard said. "Long time, no see, ol' buddy." He slapped the pilot on the back, and they exchanged a complicated series of fist bumps. Dark glasses concealed the pilot's eyes, but his smile was wide enough to display a gold molar.

Evan held a grimy cloth to the abrasions on his cheek. *Damn*. He couldn't expect any help from Richard's *old buddy*. Another dead end.

"Bobby give you instructions?" asked Richard.

"Señor Roberto, he tell me we going to hit the commies again."

"Yeah, that's the plan. Get us in the air, and then get on the horn and raise the forward base. Tell 'em we'll be over their position in twenty minutes."

Then Richard pushed Evan toward the helicopter. "Get in the back," he said. Gun in one hand and the other ostentatiously in the pocket where he'd stashed the detonator, he watched Evan struggle up the steps. The helicopter was luxurious, red and silver on the outside, black leather and chrome on the inside. Two seats in front, separated by a console, and two in back. A cargo area in the rear where a third row of seats had been folded out of the way contained a few boxes wedged in one corner, with a tangle of tarps on the other side. Evan dropped into the closer seat.

Richard squinted into the cabin and bit his lower lip. Then he whirled and called, "Time to scramble." Angel hurried over and climbed behind the controls.

The rotors whipped up a whirlwind and muffled sound. Richard attached Evan's seatbelt.

"I've got the coordinates," Richard called to the pilot as he bound Evan's wrists together with a length of strapping tape. "The other choppers follow us. Tell 'em when we dip twice, hold their position until we clear the area, then spray three hundred and sixty degrees. Don't hold back. This time we knock them out for good."

Richard clambered into the front to strap himself in. The doors slammed closed. Within minutes, they were hundreds of feet up. The men ignored Evan as the helicopter turned north toward the mountains. The running lights flashed in the early evening sun. One side of the helicopter in bright daylight, the other in shadow.

Angel spoke into the mic a few times, but although it was quiet for a helicopter—he and Richard didn't even need headsets to communicate—a monotonous thrumming of white noise smothered his words.

Richard ignored him. Around Evan, the soft black leather seats were empty. The cabin enclosure was pebbled silver, all curves, no sharp edges to slice the tape on his wrists. Nothing that would serve as a weapon. The boxes behind him *might* contain something useful, but Evan couldn't reach them unless he got his seat belt off, which wouldn't happen until *after* he'd freed his hands.

Even if he released his seat belt, he could hardly escape while in the air. His best shot might be to distract Richard and grab the remote. The tape was loose enough to permit him to wiggle his wrists. Evan could gradually stretch it out, but he didn't know how much time he had.

It sounded like Richard intended to lead others to an air strike on the guerrillas, then leave. If Richard meant to return to the U.S. like he'd said, they'd trade the helicopter at some point for a longer-range aircraft. With all Evan knew, Richard couldn't possibly imagine it was safe to let him return. And Evan remembered his unlocked door.

Trying to escape on the ground would get him a bullet in the back. It was now, up in the air, that killing him was problematic—a bullet ricocheting, someone squeezing the remote by mistake. There must be *something* he could do now. *Think!*

But all he could think about was Luz. When he saw her face as they passed in the car, he'd gasped, too full of stunned delight to control the outburst. *She'd done it!* Richard glanced suspiciously—but at *him*, not at the other car.

That she survived the firestorm at the Benavides' suggested she was able to enlist their help. If only he'd kept Richard at his house, together they could have overcome him. Or if he'd gotten Richard away from the helicopter before Bobby Benavides showed up and ordered the pilot to take them. Together—Evan fought against a wave of loss that squeezed his gut into an aching fist.

Luz must've seen him forced onto the copter. But however resilient she'd been, Evan doubted she could mobilize help for him now. His survival depended on turning the slight advantage of Richard's being trapped with him on the helicopter into a plan. He had to do something soon.

A burst of static. Angel grabbed the mic and barked into it.

Angel. Perhaps Evan had been too hasty in discounting him. Richard's buddy would be understandably jumpy if Evan managed to reveal the explosive belt. Angel might insist they land the chopper and get Evan off. The problems with that surfaced instantly: Evan wanted to stay in the air where Richard would think twice before pulling the trigger—or pushing that button.

Off to the north, four huge helicopters rose above the trees, not fancy executive models like the Benavides', but solid no-nonsense equipment with splotchy camouflage, twin rotors, and enough room for a dozen armed men.

Something sticking out from under the seat scraped Evan's ankle. He reached awkwardly, two-fisted, to push it out of the way. A hand grabbed him—small, warm, squeezing hard—and before he could react, yanked him farther down. Evan looked under the seat. Luz was tucked between two panels of gunmetal-gray equipment in the rear cargo area, her body hidden under sacks, her head on the floor between his seat and the door. She pushed her head close to his.

"How did you get on?" This wasn't a mirage. He smelled the lemony shampoo in her hair.

Luz lifted her finger and mimed *shhh*. "When you distracted everyone." She wriggled her hand forward and touched his cheek, sending a current of electricity through him. "That was brilliant."

It was the miracle he needed. Together—

"Listen," said Luz, "we have a bigger problem than you think."

Evan shook his head. Now that she was here, alive and beside him, his options had skyrocketed.

"No, really. We have to get this thing turned around before we get where Richard is going. Are you still wired?"

Evan nodded. Getting the bomb belt off was the first order of business. Luz squeezed her eyes shut as she mouthed a choice expletive.

"Can you undo it yourself? Maybe while you're doubled over like that?"

"No." Evan's knuckles had been on the floor, bracing him. He squirmed in an attempt to show Luz his bound wrists. *He* couldn't do it, but now he had Luz. Together—

"What the hell are you doing?" Richard yelled. He'd turned almost a full one-eighty, his fingers gripping the seat back for leverage, glaring at him.

Evan popped up. Blood drained from his face. "I—I don't feel so good," he said.

"Well, you look like shit, but don't you fucking dare puke in this helicopter. Angel would slit my throat. Right, Angel?"

The pilot eyeballed Evan in the rearview mirror. He said something low to Richard, who laughed and then raised his voice. "Angel says to suck it up until we're on the ground again."

"How long is that going to be?"

When Richard didn't immediately reply, Evan said, "I don't think I can hold it much longer. I feel horrible, Uncle Richard."

"Another half an hour should do it." They didn't have long, then.

"I have to lie down." That would make it easier to talk to Luz.

"Go ahead—but no puking."

"Thanks." Evan made a show of gagging as Richard released his seat belt. He staggered to his feet and, without the use of his hands, dropped gracelessly to the cabin floor and lay on his back. His uncle surveyed the back-seat area through narrowed eyes before turning around.

Evan glanced to the left. Luz had disappeared. "That's better," he said quietly.

The edge of the tarp lifted. Only Luz's eyes and a bit of nose were visible. The tarp inched forward. Luz eventually pushed so close to Evan her lips were almost touching his. It was by the pressure of her breath as much as by sound that he heard her say, "We have to get off the helicopter. They're heading into a trap. We'll all be killed if we get there."

CHAPTER FORTY-SEVEN

For Luz, a chain reaction of facts snapped into place with Richard's words to the pilot as they took off: They were flying to a place Richard knew about by GPS coordinates, where he planned an aerial assault. Richard *had* tracked her to the mountains, then. And Evan had said Richard's passport stamp indicated he arrived in Guatemala the same day she returned to the city—he probably led that first attack on Toño's camp, too.

But Toño's suspicions had led him to take the bag with her stuff to a place where ambush was easy. Without a doubt, *this* was the maneuver for which Toño had appropriated her belongings.

When the choppers came this time, the guerrillas would blow them out of the air. Toño wouldn't know she was in one—even if he did, he'd still give the order to fire. He was family, a loyal man, and he'd once saved her life, but Toño had been fighting too long, and this time, while he'd mourn, he'd accept her loss. She'd never even had a chance to tell him she wasn't dying.

What Richard said also began to make sense of Luz's earlier confusion when he greeted Bobby so warmly by the helicopter. Richard wasn't working to destroy the Benavides drug network. He was working to destroy *Martin* Benavides and devastate the guerrilla opposition in order to give Bobby free rein—politically and financially.

Bobby was Richard's *someone else* inside the Benavides'. He'd known Luz's real mission all along, and he'd guarantee she—and her insurgent comrades—got the blame for killing his parents. Luz was on her way to thwarting their plan, but she'd heard Richard say thirty minutes, too. They didn't have much time.

"That was quick thinking, getting him to let you out of your seat belt," she whispered, "but now we have to get this thing off you. How is it attached?"

"It's like a belt, looped around my waist, fastened in back."

"Taped?"

"No, only tied."

Good. Luz hadn't seen how Richard had bound the explosives to Evan. She ought to be able to free him. "Roll so you face the front. That should make them feel confident you aren't trying anything. I'll untie you."

"Then what?"

A tentative edge to Evan's question worried her. Trauma or not, she needed him sharp. "Let's both think about it while I undo you."

Luz wormed her hands up under the back of Evan's shirt. The heat of his body startled her. His panicky, erratic breathing matched hers. With one hand on Evan's feverish skin and the other above the layers of cloth, her fingers moved slowly along his back. A strip of canvas about six inches wide was cinched between Evan's ribs and his hips. Stiff cord, knotted at the bottom and top, wound through big metal grommets. She felt the shape of the knots and began to work the cords, loosening them, straightening the kinks, so she could begin untying.

* * *

Evan lay on his right side. Luz's fingers, like small birds feathering a nest, plucked at the knots holding the explosive belt around his waist.

Freeing his wrists was the first step in helping her, so Evan stretched his hands beneath Richard's seat, probing the underside. Lots of round bars, but nothing useful until his fingertips found the smooth curved end to a bar under the seat. It wasn't sharp, so he couldn't abrade the tape, but if he slipped his bound wrists around it, he could use the rod as a lever to loosen the binding.

Better than nothing.

Evan strained his chest and shoulders forward and slid his bound wrists over the bar. Now his arms were hanging from the fitting. While Luz fiddled with the knots, Evan threw all the strength he could leverage into the ends of his arms.

Bits of conversation from the front seat floated back. Angel, with his nasal delivery, was easier to hear than Richard. He was talking about another *excursion* they'd taken, making it sound like a jaunt in the country. The story had the ring of familiarity, as though he'd heard it before. Of course, he hadn't, but Evan quickly registered the emotional similarity, lying in the dark, eavesdropping on his father's friends as they drained beer after beer and regaled one another with tall tales of machismo.

"He never saw it coming," said Angel.

Richard's reply was lost in static.

"What an idiot. I mean, you take the asshole under your wing, train him, finance his pathetic revolution, and he thinks he can walk away?"

Richard laughed, a sharp staccato bark. Into a momentary gap in the blanket of white noise, Richard said clearly, "I hated to lose Emilio, but he never should have threatened me. Huge fucking drain of time and money, getting Benavides up to speed afterward—" and then the mic buzzed, static filled the cabin, and the rest of the conversation was lost.

Evan was left with the dangling phrase. But he knew that story. Richard had told it, when Evan was a kid hiding in the dark. Richard

had bragged to his buddies about taking out the double-crossing guerrillas and making an alliance with an up-and-coming group who
knew better than to stab him in the back. It was Luz's story.

*   *   *

Once the knots were untied, Luz unlaced the stiff cord one inch at a
time and peeled the canvas aside. Finally, with a small but satisfying
thunk, it slid to the floor. "Got it."

Evan flopped onto his back. He looked years older, weary and griev-
ing, like her father and his companions. Resolve, however, had replaced struggle and doubt. "Look." He rotated his arms to show Luz
the abraded tape.

"That's great." The loosened loop of tape, Evan's steelier body language, the way he flexed his arms, gave Luz an idea.

"Time to get the bastards," said Evan.

"Right." A shiver of disquiet at Evan's implacable tone made the
tiny hairs on her forearms prickle. "Does Richard still have the gun?"

Evan nodded infinitesimally.

Damn. They'd better get it first. "Where is it?"

"Not sure," Evan whispered.

"Last time you saw it?" Luz nudged.

"In his hand when we first got on board." Evan squinted, thinking.
"Yeah, and then he stuck it in his jacket pocket to attach my seat belt."

"Which side?"

Evan closed his eyes. "Right. The remote's in the left pocket."

"Evan, we have to do it now. We have to get the pilot to turn
around."

"I'm going to kill Richard."

Evan violent was an unexpected, but welcome, metamorphosis. She
needed him ruthless for this. "Okay, how's this? Get to your feet,

slowly, non-threateningly. You've created enough play to slide your arms around Richard's neck, and the tape around your wrists will keep your grip secure. While he's arguing with you, I'll grab the gun."

Evan's smile didn't reach his eyes. He lumbered to his feet and cleared his throat, a thick deep noise. Then, loud, above the whine of the engines, he said, "Whew, that's better." One foot staggered forward, like someone off-balance on a moving aircraft, but his other foot stayed planted to give him a wider stance. Then his arms were over Richard's head, around his neck, and Evan pulled up sharply. Richard's head snapped back.

"What the fuck are you doing, you stupid shit?" Richard slapped at Evan's arms.

The pilot's attention was split between flying the helicopter and the scene playing out at his elbow. On hands and knees, Luz squeezed along the right side of the helicopter.

Richard struggled and bellowed. "You idiot. You're asking for trouble."

Luz reached into his pocket. She wrapped her hands around the cold steel barrel and lifted it out. Time slowed to freeze-frames: The whump of each blade of the propeller. Drops of spittle, lit by the instrument panel, flying from Richard's mouth. The cold sheet of metal vibrating between her and hundreds of feet of cold air. The equally cold piece of metal heavy in her hand.

Richard's hands were up, pushing Evan's arms out, away from his throat. Richard shouted for Angel to do something.

Luz stood, gun in hand. "Freeze," she yelled. Just like in the movies.

And they all did. Her unexpected appearance gave Luz a second of total surprise.

Richard recovered first. "Sneaky little bitch."

CHAPTER FORTY-EIGHT

While Luz lay on the scratchy gray floor covering, the sensation of motion hadn't been much different from a car on a bumpy road. Standing, the expanse of open sky was disorienting—gray and purple clouds all around, looking solid as islands but giving way to cotton-wool as they flew into them, glimpses of green-black treetops hundreds of feet below. A smear of orange atop the western mountains told where the sun was setting. There was no road, only the blinking lights of the dozen or so gauges on the control panel to indicate their location.

For stability, Luz wedged herself into the narrow space between the back seats and the exterior wall. Luz pointed the gun at Angel. "You're flying into a trap. We have to turn around."

He looked from her to Richard, back again, assessing. "I won't abort the mission unless he says so." Angel jerked his head in Richard's direction.

"And I say don't listen to her, Angel." Richard swatted at the gun, but Luz had stayed out of his reach. "She won't shoot you. Not only is she chicken, she knows you're the only one who can fly this baby. Without you, she's as good as dead."

"And so are you," Luz retorted. They *had to* persuade Angel; he was the key.

"Mexican stand-off then." Richard held out his hand. "Give it back, Luz." He was smiling, but his hand trembled.

Luz squeezed the gun tighter and, for the first time, it became an extension of her hand. Richard's contempt had removed the final obstacle. With her free hand, she yanked his jacket back and removed the remote detonator from his left pocket. Luz cranked open the small passenger-side window.

"No," Evan shouted. "Get rid of the explosives, not the remote."

She glanced at the fat cylinders now lying on the back seat. "Won't fit. Have to open the door."

Angel whipped around, taking in the lumpy pockets protruding from the canvas. "Not the door," he yelled. "We're too high." His hands tightened, then flexed on the controls. "Wait 'til we're down."

Luz eyed Angel as she pocketed the remote. He'd gone all squirrelly when he saw the explosives, but she didn't know if it would be sufficient to sway him to their side. "I've almost died several times today," Luz said. "I'd be lying if I said it doesn't matter—I absolutely do want to survive this. And I'm telling you, you're flying into an ambush. I know because I set it up."

As Angel jerked his attention to Richard, Richard turned to face Luz.

"You used me," she said, looking at him directly for the first time. "You got me here to do your dirty work. You lied. You lied about so many things—for so many years—that I don't know where to find the truth."

"Luz, put the damn gun down and tell me how you pulled it off." Richard, genial, patient Richard of the State Department. Richard of the chuckle that proclaimed his solidarity with whatever stupid thing Luz had once done or said. Her friend.

Her friend no more.

"You tricked me into believing I was dying."

At Evan's gasp of surprise, Luz called out, "Yes, that was a lie, Evan. I'm as healthy as you are. Richard made me believe I had nothing to live for, so he could manipulate me."

She turned back to Richard, but like the magical beings in the book she'd read to Dominga, Luz was also with Dr. Guzman—alive and showing her a photo of his grandchildren in Iowa, dead on a carpet discolored by his blood, covered with flies struggling to extract wings stuck in the viscous puddle. "He's a liar and a murderer." Luz was with Bobby in the stairwell, too, smiling as he promised to finish the assault he started. With Bobby and Richard laughing beside the helicopter.

Luz slapped the side of Richard's head with his gun. "He's a coward who sends others to do his dirty work."

"Luz, you've got it all wrong."

Fury and overwhelming sadness met in her veins, then mingled, like a vicious cocktail of explosives. "No, you knew I'd been raised with hatred for Martin, knew that with my mother gone, all I needed was a push. How could I resist when I thought I had one last chance to right that wrong?"

"Let me explain."

"I'm not listening to your lies. You brought me here because Martin Benavides stood in your way—yours and your partner in crime. You never meant to compromise Bobby. You're working together. Although I'd say your relationship is somewhat lacking in trust." Luz thunked him with the gun again. "Somehow you and Bobby persuaded Martin the guerrillas had taken over the drug network. And those questions about my reconnecting with Toño. Did you intend to put the idea into my head?"

"Luz, no—"

She talked over his protest. "But I intended to find my cousin from the start. Did you know my mother had begged me to bury her in the mountains? I expect you did." Luz answered her own question. "She told me how to contact her aunt who kept in touch with the guerrillas. I bet you knew about that, too. After your first attack, they figured out someone had tracked me there, so they turned the tables on you."

Luz looked over to the pilot again. "The guerrillas aren't camped where you're going. It's an ambush. I don't know how long they'll wait to open fire after they spot you in the area. Turn the helicopter around now."

Angel lifted his hands from the controls and rubbed his cheeks and chest. For a second, he appeared to capitulate. Then—abracadabra—a gun appeared in his hand.

"Careful, lady. If you fire at me, I will shoot him." He leveled the gun at Evan. "Señor Clement?" Angel didn't sound so buddy-buddy now. "What do you think about her assertions?"

"With the old man dead, these rebels are the only people standing in Bobby's way," said Richard.

"Martin Benavides is alive," said Luz. *Come on*. She had to convince him pronto. Every second counted now.

"She's lying. You saw the destruction."

"Don't take my word for it." *Dios mío, let me be right*. "See for yourself." Luz gestured to the control panel, a heart-shaped console with dozens of switches and round dials. "Can that thing receive commercial radio stations?"

"Yes." Wary.

"How?"

"You flip a lever to change the band."

"Show me where but don't touch it."

Angel stretched his right hand to the instrument panel and pointed to a long slider near the center bottom.

"Which way does it go?"

"Push it two notches to the left for AM. It's set to 820, *Emisoras Unidas.*" *A news station, good.* Angel was, if not exactly friendly, at least cooperative. Although the gun still pointed right at Evan.

Luz clicked the switch. Once, twice. *Dios, por favor.*

"... and it was clearly a result of a gas leak in the kitchen which, fortunately, occurred when the majority of the palace staff was home with their families. To recap, a Christmas miracle that there was no loss of life from the tremendous explosion that rocked the residence of former president Martin Benavides."

A male voice chimed in. "That was Angela Gonzalez's exclusive interview with the fire marshal, live from Guatemala City." The announcer continued, "In an emotional statement thirty minutes ago, Señor Benavides thanked God for his deliverance, crediting the quick thinking of a young staffer, one of the few remaining, who smelled gas and alerted security."

The pilot had already brought the copter into a tight turn that increased pressure in Luz's ears. *They were going to get down.*

"Too many questions," said Angel. "I'm not letting go of my gun, but I won't shoot unless provoked. We'll head back until I get a few answers." Indicating the control panel, he said, "I need to alert the others."

"Sure," said Luz, "but for heaven's sake, hurry." Her hands gripping the weapon were slick with sweat. The dashboard clock now read 5:22, and it was almost fully dark.

Richard reached out to yank Angel's arm, but Evan took a step back and jerked Richard's neck. Richard was still objecting when the cabin illuminated. A split-second later, a huge concussive force sideswiped the helicopter. They spun in half a circle and tilted almost ninety degrees. As Angel tried to regain control, another helicopter burst into flames, the canopy of the jungle lit up from beneath. More shooting erupted. Angel took them low at a steep angle.

Richard was shouting, pointing out the side.

"Sit down," yelled Angel. "I'm trying to evade their fire."

Luz fell into a back seat when Angel swung the nose of the chopper, while Evan, still restraining Richard, struggled to remain upright. They zigzagged at tree level, now separated from the other copters. At least one of them had crashed. One must've still been operational because a blue-white beam above them probed the forest canopy. The trees whipped dizzyingly beneath them.

All at once, the rear of their helicopter bucked. The back end pivoted straight up, throwing Luz from her seat. They swung to the right. Luz boomeranged across the cabin and crashed into the side wall. Evan lost his balance, his bound wrists came loose from Richard's neck, and he collapsed on top of her. The thrum of the rotors stopped, and they began to fall.

Luz threw her arms around Evan and held on tight. Their newborn life together would perish before it drew its first deep breath. "I love you," she said, not knowing if Evan could hear her over the scream of wind.

Orange and gold flames engulfed the tail section. It became a weight dragging them down, down. The harsh light illuminated the sweat on Angel's face. Richard sat immobile.

A violent twist marked an end to their precipitous descending spiral. They'd hit the forest canopy. But as the flimsy upper branches gave way beneath them, their inexorable plunge continued, one bump at a time.

Then the helicopter hit something solid, flipped onto its side. Vibrated. As Luz and Evan tumbled to the low side, the windshield shattered into a million tiny shards. Angel's chest and neck disappeared as a large tree limb impaled him.

Luz lay under Evan in a heap on the floor behind the pilot's seat. Blood everywhere. The smell of hot metal with a bitter undercurrent of gasoline. Had they come down far enough to climb out to one of the trees supporting them? The helicopter lurched again, like a cranky elevator. The discarded circle of explosives rolled onto Evan's legs.

C4 was stable, yes, detonating only in a combination of extreme heat and a shock wave. So ... a helicopter crash, now a fire. They had to jettison the belt *now*—but with his wrists taped together, Evan couldn't reach it. Luz, trapped under him, couldn't get to it either. She pointed to a sharp fragment of metal near Evan's head. He twisted around, pretzeled his arms above him, and sawed through the tape. Then, using one hand to raise himself, he hurled the explosive belt out the smashed windshield.

As he tossed it, they dropped once more and banged hard. The pilot's side door crumpled. Broken palmetto fronds and scrub grass invaded the cabin. They'd crashed all the way to the forest floor, coming to rest with the pilot's side down. What remained of Angel lay crushed in the wreckage mingled with the broken tops of vegetation. The fire had spread from the tail section into the cabin and was licking at the packing materials behind the back seats.

"Out! Out!" yelled Evan. "Before it explodes."

CHAPTER FORTY-NINE

Jagged glass and a wall of tangled shrubbery blocked their exit through the nose of the helicopter. The pilot's side lay smashed and twisted, half-buried in the ground. The fire in the rear burned hot. Their only way out was up, through the passenger door.

Evan was tall enough to grasp and twist the door handle, but each time he flung the door out, it crashed back into place. He had to get closer, so he wedged one foot into the frame of Richard's empty seat.

Evan hoped Richard had been thrown from the wreckage, crumpled like a broken and discarded toy, but then he saw him, lying near Angel, dead or stunned. A fiery death wouldn't be as satisfying as wrapping his hands around Richard's throat again and throttling him until his last gasping breath, but he had to get Luz away before they were incinerated.

Praying the fuel tanks were well forward, away from the fire, Evan braced himself between the edge of the seat and the center console. This time he was able to flip the door open. He lowered a hand to Luz, whose attention had been split between his balancing act and the encroaching fire.

Richard rose at the same time Luz did.

"Watch out!" she shouted.

Richard held Angel's long-barreled gun. Instantly, Evan grabbed the door's rim with both hands. He kicked out with his feet and bashed Richard's jaw. As Richard absorbed the blow, the gun flew toward the shattered windshield. For a second, it caught on a jagged spur. Richard extended his arm. He touched the glass, which fractured, spilling the weapon into the inky void.

"Fuck." Richard lunged toward the broken window but recovered in time to avoid impaling himself. The gun was gone.

He glared at Evan, still swaying overhead. Richard's fury and desperation in the flickering orange light gave him the pasty, inhuman look of a subterranean creature. He caught Evan's leg and yanked.

Evan kicked at him, but his left hand slipped. He dangled, trying to recover his grip. Richard got his arms around Evan's knees and hung on.

"Get away from him," said Luz, pointing Richard's own gun at his belly.

Evan could barely hear her over the crackle of flames, which had now reached the back of the seat. Smoke filled the cabin. "Luz," he called, "I can't hold on. Shoot him."

The barrel of the gun wavered, pointed at the sky. A shot. Richard's grip on Evan loosened. She'd only startled him, but that was enough. The pressure dragging him down abated. Evan got both hands back on the door. Once secure, he looked down. Richard crouched near the missing windscreen. The fire had jumped to the back seats; there was no time to waste. Since his upper body strength wasn't sufficient to hoist both of them, Evan pushed himself up and out instead. His head cleared the edge of the chopper. A gulp of fresh air. Then he pivoted onto his stomach and reached his arms to Luz, who remained in a silent face-off with Richard.

"Come on, Luz."

Luz's eyes flicked to him, back to Richard, gauging distances, reaction times.

"I'll cover him," Evan called.

Luz nodded. She raised her hand. Evan swept the gun from her and trained it on Richard.

"Let's go," Evan shouted. He gripped Luz with one hand, held the gun in the other. The fire now engulfed the back seats. As Evan hauled her up, Richard angled so Luz's body was between him and the gun. He grabbed her legs, much as he had Evan's, and used her body like a tree trunk. Hands to her thighs, knees clasped around her legs, reaching with a free hand, shimmying up.

Evan's shoulder failed to absorb the extra weight, and he dropped lower, almost toppling back into the cabin. He tried to get off a shot, but Richard and Luz were entwined.

Sweating and weakened, Luz slipped from Evan's grip—as Richard's hands grabbed the rim of the open door.

Evan stomped on his fingers. Hard. Richard dropped.

"Hurry, Luz. Let's get out of here."

Before Richard could recover, Luz leveraged her weight onto the seat again and, with added momentum from Evan's pull, vaulted up and out the door. Another second and they scrambled to the edge of the chopper. Ten feet to the ground. They jumped.

Without any sense of purpose beyond gaining distance from the blaze, they sprinted away from the burning hunk of metal. When the explosion came, it filled the air with light and concussion and debris.

They'd ducked behind a large fallen log that formed a natural barrier a hundred feet from the now furiously burning helicopter. The air cleared. Fire crackled. The metal skeleton writhed.

A dark shadow emerged from behind a tree to their left. Richard.

Evan stood, and Richard immediately raised an arm in greeting. The asshole had escaped.

Richard ambled closer. "Whew," he said, a whistle of relief. "That was close."

Richard couldn't possibly think Evan would disregard his violent frenzy in the wreckage. Besides, now Evan knew Richard's part in the rest of Luz's story. There was no turning back. "Tell Luz about you and her father," said Evan.

Richard's head inscribed an erratic whiplash arc, and he whirled a half-circle, like he was going to charge off into the jungle. Instead, he clenched his hands into tight fists and spoke directly to Luz. "You should be grateful to me for getting you to the States, you know, instead of turning against me. What kind of life was that, always on the move—"

"It was *my* life," Luz screamed.

At her outburst, Evan hiked the gun level with Richard's chest. "I'm going to kill you, you murdering son of a bitch."

"Don't, Evan," said Luz.

Without taking his eyes off Richard, Evan called back to her. "He's responsible for decades of corruption and violence. He cheated you out of your childhood. And he would've killed both of us today."

"Don't listen to him." Richard swept away the accusations with a flick of his wrists.

"What you don't know is that he is directly responsible for your father's murder."

Luz's footfalls popped in the underbrush like rifle shots as she walked toward Richard. Evan followed. He would pull her away before she got close enough for Richard to grab her and use her as a shield, but she stopped outside his reach.

"How?" Luz asked.

"Tell her," said Evan again.

"I loved him like a brother," said Richard. "I gave him everything. And then I asked him for a favor—something he'd done for me already, only on a larger scale."

"What did you want him to do?" Luz asked with dangerous calm.

"He'd been keeping my supply lines open." Richard shrugged. "For a price, Luz. A hefty price that had bought the FPL lots of weapons, lots of ammo. The fighting in the mountains was screwing up everything for me. All I wanted was for him to put armed guards on our deliveries, and the asshole gets religion—'Oh, no, *Pelirrojo.*'" Richard fluttered a hand at his chest and went soprano. "'Oh, no, I'm not going to get more involved.' So I had to find someone who would."

"You killed my father."

CHAPTER FIFTY

You killed my father. That lament had poisoned her life for decades. Now, like finding the last clue in a crossword puzzle that makes sense of a whole row of words, Luz filled in the blanks she'd never questioned.

Why her father had periodically disappeared, returning to the camp, grim, but with much-needed supplies. Why Richard had so patiently, so steadfastly maintained a relationship with her mother. But mainly, why the big helicopter was idling in the clearing that night. *Pelirrojo*—or his accomplices—airlifted Martin Benavides and his men to the mountains and let them slaughter their rivals.

If only she'd put all the pieces together sooner.

Luz came to Guatemala to kill, to right the wrong done to her and restore order to her universe. She found instead a lonely boy, a broken old man with one dead son and another who'd wrecked his life. She found Evan, who loved her, and together they unraveled the sordid double-cross that had ruined so many lives.

Heroes and villains? They were just men, some of whom had chosen badly. The heroes tried to atone for their mistakes. The villains tried to make others pay.

She ran to Evan, but he elbowed her away, keeping the gun pointed at Richard.

"No, you can't!" Luz cried, tugging at Evan. "It's not about him—
it's about you, Evan. Can't you see what's happened to Richard? I saw
it in Martin, too. Living with the aftermath of cold-blooded murder
ruined their lives. You *can't* shoot him, Evan. Having that on your
conscience will destroy you, like it destroyed them."

Evan swung around; his face radiated hatred.

"That's why I didn't shoot him in the helicopter," said Luz.

Evan shook his head.

Luz tried again. "Let him go. Martin Benavides is on the lookout
for him. So are Toño's people. Or the jungle will get him. He'll kill
himself one way or the other. Don't *you* be the one to fire the shot."

For what seemed like a long time, the only sound was the crackle of
the fire fanned by faintly stirring leaves. Evan didn't move. Behind
him, rivulets of burning grass crept closer.

Richard kept a half-smile on his face. Behind the smile, his jaw
worked restlessly as though he was working out whether to continue
his deceit or beg for mercy. Or perhaps try to goad Evan into making
a mistake.

Evan was staring at betrayal on a scale he'd never envisioned—with
a gun in his hand and too little time to reconcile the uncle he knew
with this cruel doppelganger. Luz stared at Richard, too, but she was
thinking about how Martin justified accepting drug money to fund
his struggle until he grasped the world Cesar would inherit from him.
His actions could never be undone, any more than Richard's could.
Their words, their lies, could not be unsaid. The dead would not live.

Rather than making amends, however, Richard had drawn Evan,
his future, into his unscrupulous dealings. He'd exploited Evan. Then
he wrapped him in a cocoon of explosives and threatened him. She
didn't know if Evan would be strong enough to resist the allure of
retribution. If their situations were reversed—if, say, she'd wrestled

Martin's machete from him the night he betrayed her father—she might very well have plunged it into him.

Wind sighed high overhead. Sparks danced in Luz's peripheral vision.

Finally, Evan nodded. "Find your own way," he said. "Don't follow us."

Gracias a Dios. Luz exhaled gently, so as not to break the spell.

Richard looked from the barrel of the gun to his nephew's grim face. Back to the gun, which didn't waver. "Goodbye, Evan," he said. "Goodbye, Luz."

They remained silent. After a pause, Richard turned and walked away. He skirted the portion of the jungle floor still burning. He slowed and appeared to consider the lay of the land. Then he strode into the darkness and disappeared without looking back.

The fire in the helicopter hadn't spread far outside the radius of the initial explosion. It died to snapping embers in the damp undergrowth. The light flickered, dimmed.

Evan lowered the gun. "Thanks," he said.

Luz wrapped her arms around his waist and buried her head in his chest. She thought he was crying, as she was.

"I'll feel safer when we get away from here," he said after a while. "I saw some clearings when we were coming down, so there must be a settlement nearby. Plus, getting away from the crash makes it less likely we'll run into men who'll shoot first and ask questions later."

Luz took Evan's hand and, as one, they turned in the opposite direction from Richard. The light from the burning helicopter faded to a ghostly glow. They kept it behind them until it became too faint to register. No light from stars or moon penetrated the forest canopy. Although it would have been easier to walk single-file, Evan kept hold of Luz's hand. She didn't feel like talking. For now, that connection was enough.

They stumbled over rotting logs, fell into a shallow pool. Vines attacked their faces, legs. Twice, they heard distant gunshots. The adrenalin wore off, but they staggered on. Then, after countless steps through immeasurable time, one minute they were in the dense thicket, the next they stood at the edge of a narrow mountain track.

"Stars," Luz whispered, looking up. And after eons of trudging blindly, she could see Evan, not just feel his warmth beside her.

"Look over there," said Evan. He pointed downhill, where a faint glow flickered above the treetops.

Luz caught the barest hint of a tinny melody and a whiff of charcoal. "A town," Luz breathed. "People."

Joining hands once more, they stepped onto the path and walked side by side toward the light.

*   *   *

The waterfall at last. Evan's hand in hers. And this time it wasn't a dream. Slick rock made the footing treacherous, but Evan's grip was strong as he steadied her. Luz had forgotten the secret beauty of this glade in the forest. Blazing sun overhead; icy water below. In between, warm breeze, flowers, birdsong, space to heal—if not forget.

"Are you ready to go?" Evan asked. Only that simple question; he'd posed it several times. Never pressing harder. Not "Are you ready now?" or "Are you finally ready?"

A week had passed since the night they stumbled through the jungle and found the small town at the end of a dirt path. The inhabitants had seen the firefight overhead, heard the helicopter crash, the gunfire. At first, they were suspicious, but they allowed Luz to use the telephone in the mayor's office.

"You are safe?" Martin had asked.

"For now."

"I'll send a car. Cesar is miserable; he misses you."

"No." That was too shrill. "No," Luz repeated, as evenly as she could. "I need to stay here for a while."

Perhaps he heard her panicked emptiness. Certainly he, too, was healing from the raw pain of love betrayed. "What can I do?"

"My mother died." And Luz explained about the jar on her mantel.

"It will take a few days to arrange it. Let me speak to the mayor."

Here in the remote mountains, the villagers may have been supporters of the regime in power. Possibly, they were rebel sympathizers who feared Martin's security service. Most likely, they were an uneasy mix of both, but with Martin Benavides vouching for her, all doors opened.

The mayor's cousin offered them the use of an empty cottage he owned on the outskirts of town. Luz slept around the clock, without dreams, suspended in time, and woke to *Noche Buena*, Christmas Eve.

The mayor came at dusk and escorted them to the church. Luz and Evan sat in the front row with local dignitaries while the village children performed the familiar tale of the infant born to save the world. After the priest ended the Mass by exhorting them all to go in peace, there was a Christmas feast at one of the fancier houses in the village—cinder block with a tin roof and a gate guarded by ten-inch-tall rampant lions.

The adults sat around a heavy oak table while children milled around on a floor strewn with pine needles. But the traditional Christmas tamales in this region were stuffed with pork and a red sauce, instead of the simpler turkey and potato filling Luz remembered. And the fruit *ponche* was too sweet—even for Luz.

A full moon overhead bathed the ground in white light that looked like snow—snow with palm trees, their swaying fronds silhouetted against the starry sky. The radio played Bing Crosby and the Harry Simeone Chorale. The unreality of the preceding days caught up to her: the food, so close, but not quite right; the music that, after decades in New Hampshire, evoked ice-skating and hot cider. Luz tugged on Evan's arm and motioned to the door.

The firecrackers, when they began at midnight, startled Luz out of another sound sleep.

* * *

Luz spent the next days wandering the village and the nights sleeping beside Evan. They cooked simple meals and ate them at the tiny table by the front window with a view of cornfields. While Evan sketched charcoal portraits of the local children, Luz tried to imagine her path forward.

Answers came slowly.

Martin checked in daily. True to his word, he turned over the records Luz had stolen—in fact, news of his providing incriminating information leaked even before Toño's contacts were able to publish the material. Bobby had been arraigned on drug trafficking charges. Martin swore he would not use his influence to sway the outcome.

Luz correctly guessed the allegiance of the village schoolteacher and, through him, sent Toño a message conveying Martin's offer of a truce.

A black SUV arrived, trailing plumes of dust, Joaquín bringing her mother's ashes. The entire population of the village came out to stare. The mayor made a speech about the future.

Joaquín also brought news that Richard's body had been found, not far from the site of the helicopter crash. When he began describing the wounds to Richard's body, Luz screamed at him to stop and bolted for the forest. Evan found her, hours later, sitting on a mossy log.

"I was thinking about the time Richard brought lobsters for Christmas dinner," Luz said when Evan sat beside her. "My mother set the bag on the kitchen counter—not knowing they were alive—and we went off into the living room. The next thing we know, these gigantic orange and black *bugs* are scuttling across the floor. My mother's swatting them with the broom, and the lobsters are banging into the furniture and each other like bumper cars, and I'm standing on the sofa screaming..."

They told stories from simpler days until the light failed.

Before Joaquín returned to the city, Luz gave him the reply she'd received from Toño, a guarded, qualified yes. So the two men—or their lieutenants—might sit down one day and put an end to the bloodshed.

Her part was finished.

One task remained.

Instead of enlisting Toño's help, she hired a boy from the village to lead them into the mountains to the waterfall. The makeshift cemetery was overgrown with vines. On a gentle slope in the shade of a towering cedar, Luz found where her father lay, his name on the makeshift wooden cross faded to ghostly squiggles. Evan and Luz spent hours digging into the warm earth together to clear a space next to the cross.

Luz placed the urn with her mother's ashes deep in the dark, rich soil. One handful at a time, she sprinkled dirt into the hole. "You're home now, Mama." She smoothed the soil, patted it as she might caress a sleeping child. "Sleep well."

Luz stood and walked to the cool running water, knelt to wash her hands. Evan joined her. They slipped off their shoes and waded into the stream. Luz thought about Evan's question as her gaze wandered from the waterfall, to the valley, to the surrounding mountain peaks, back to the profusion of bright flowers in the glade where her parents lay in peace, together once more. To Evan at her side.

"I'm ready," she said to Evan. "Let's go home."